THE LIBERTY OF THE WHOLE EARTH

KEEPING DEMOCRACY, YOUNG AMERICA, BOOK 3

GORDON SAUNDERS

Published by mediaropa press.

The Liberty of the Whole Earth

Copyright © 2023 by Gordon Saunders

Ebook ISBN: 978-1-956228-18-2

Paperback ISBN: 978-1-956228-19-9

Hardback ISBN: 978-1-956228-20-5

Audiobook ISBN: 978-1-956228-31-1

This is a work of fiction. Names, characters, places, and incidents are either the product of the author's imagination or are used fictitiously and any resemblance to actual persons, living or dead, business establishments, events or locales is entirely coincidental.

Cover Image Credit: 'The Taking of the Palace of the Tuileries, 10 August 1792', by Jean Duplessis-Bertaux, from the National Museum of the Chateau de Versailles. Public Domain. *via Wikimedia Commons*.

Cover design by Gordon Saunders

*For my kids who also grew up:
Kim, Jason, and Jeremy and their families
whose kids are also almost all grown up*

1

————

MAIDEN VOYAGE, APRIL 1790

Lewis never expected to be standing on the quarter deck. As Second Mate, he was supposed to be on the main deck with the rest of his watch. In fact, he would have preferred to be 'forerd' in the fo'c'sle with the 'idlers,' including his friends Gilly and Crispin. But JJ Green, the First Mate with whom he and Gilly had sailed to China, was below with the Captain. Someone had to be on the quarter.

The tug dragged them out of their berth at Hunts Shipyard near the southern tip of Manhattan, turned them east to avoid the Copsey Rocks, and soon turned southwest to round Nullen Island toward Staten Island. As they passed Nullen, chosen crew members raised the topsail yards from the caps, loosed the reef tackles, spilling-lines and buntlines, and let out the topsails. When they were underway on their own power, the tug left them. The pilot manned the helm until just after they passed the dock of the Staten Island-Long Island ferry, where a crew member replaced him and he was discharged to the pilot ship. The watches had not yet been set, so all hands were up.

With a few shouted commands they made all sail and then mostly stayed on deck, confining themselves to the fo'c'sle.

Lewis leaned against the starboard rail and returned to his musings. He loved the sound of the bow slicing through the water, the scent of salt air and tar and wet canvas, the sight of land sliding by the ship as she raced along, faster than anything but the fastest horse. Wouldn't it be amazing to be a seagull, maybe the one flying ahead of them, to see the barque with wind behind her, sails sheeted down and jibs up, springing forward like a flushed grouse.

Then the Captain and JJ came up.

JJ told Lewis to have the crew assemble. Lewis had developed an acceptable sea voice, with which he shouted them toward the mainmast.

Captain James stepped up onto the spar deck. "Gentlemen," he said. He waited while the crew quieted down.

"I'm a patient man," he continued. "And as long as every man pulls his weight, obeys orders, and does his duty, we shall get along famously. To him who does not choose this course of action, however, this will be a rather miserable voyage. I should prefer that we all enjoy it."

There was the usual murmuring. Most of this crew had not sailed with Captain James before, but this initial presentation was promising. Lewis, Crispin, and Gilly had been working with him for months and knew him to be fair and firm. The weather, the apparent experience of the crew, and the character of the Captain all boded well for a smooth voyage.

"One more thing," he said. "Theoretically, we're not at war."

That brought about sudden, intense listening. "But we've, ah, 'carefully'—"

Lewis and Crispin exchanged glances. That meant 'secretly,' as they knew.

"We've carefully, as I said, made a few provisions, just in case. Mr. Green will fill in the details."

He nodded and walked away toward the stern, leaving everyone else in a state of agitated expectation. JJ moved to the spot the Captain had vacated. He waited for quiet.

"And theoretically," he said, "we have no cannon on board." He looked over the eager, anxious faces slightly below him. "But if we did, they'd be in the hold masquerading as apples in a barrel. The cannonballs, should we have any, would be in the carpenter's storeroom, and the magazine would be pretending to be the bo'sun's storeroom."

The crew gave a great cheer. Though they would be in serious trouble because of the cannon if taken by a warship, they could hold their own against other vessels. No one wanted to be taken by a privateer.

"Now if some of you in the first watch would like to follow the Second Mate into the hold, he'll show you where those special barrels of apples are to be found and what to do with them." He looked over the crew again. "And if some of you second watch fellows would follow 'Chips' down to his storeroom, he'll show you where to find some large round metal 'apples,' and where to put them in case they're needed."

Instant chaos began as Lewis headed down the main hatch, followed by nearly the whole first watch.

Lewis stood on the quarterdeck again, even though it wasn't his watch. He hoped to chat with Crispin, Gilly, or even JJ, but none of them had appeared from belowdecks yet. He could guess what Crispin and Gilly were doing, but what were JJ and the Captain talking about that was taking so long?

Well, he supposed, it gave him a moment of peace—a rare

thing on a ship. He took a deep breath of salt air, and surveyed the ship with satisfaction, lastly looking up at the masts and sails. At first, all that rigging up there had looked like the web of a large, careless, spider. It was called the shroud. And now that Lewis understood it, he realized that was more appropriate—since a shroud was designed and woven, like all those lines and sheets and stays.

They were fifty or more nautical miles east of Sandy Hook, close-reached on a larboard tack, making a steady five or six knots. Lewis appreciated the relative quiet following the placement of the eight cannon—two 18 pounders in the Captain's cabin, two 12 pounders larboard and starboard, close on the fore and mizzen masts, and two 8 pounders in the bow that could swivel through 90 degrees. *Enterprise* could do real damage to any ship that might care to chase her, could hold her own in a broadside exchange with a privateer, and could annoy any vessel approaching her belligerently from the front.

Provision had been made to hide the cannon since *Enterprise* was not officially authorized to carry weapons. Besides, no one wanted to destroy the beauty of her lines. *Enterprise* was 126 feet long from billet head to taffrail, with a beam of 26 feet and a draft of about 15 feet; a sleek vessel, though looking slightly older than her six-months after being battered by a hurricane on her first trial run. Oh, everything had been repaired so one wouldn't know the mizzen had splintered and dozens of lines and sheets had been shredded by the combination of wind and little packets of ice like musket balls. No, they'd all been replaced. But they helped Lewis understand the fragility of the ship—of any ship that boasted against the wild seas.

He'd not seen much of wild seas on his trip to Canton, China, in '84 and '85. Lots of rain, but not so many huge waves. He hoped this trip would be similar. With respect to storms, the Atlantic was reputed to be worse than the South China Sea, though if they had timed their departure well, they would avoid both nor'easters from the north and hurricanes from the south. *If.* It had been a late hurricane that delayed their departure for Marseilles until mid-March of '90. Lewis didn't want to experience another.

He'd used the time well, though. As a 'boy' on the *Empress of China,* he'd learned a few things about decks and rigging and sails and storage and the plain hard work of keeping a ship fit for sea. More recently, between October of last year and March of this year he'd been on *Enterprise* through every bit of her refitting. He knew each element of the shroud, every cringle, earring, sheet and line — buntline, clue-line, bowline, deep-sea line, hauling-line, knave-line, life-line, and spilling-line, whether white or tarred (and some of them even chains). He didn't know how many miles of rope was needed for all this, but it was a lot.

He knew all about decks—the poop, quarter, forecastle (popularly called the 'fo'c'sle'), main, orlop, spar, berth, hold — some of which didn't apply to the flush-decked *Enterprise.* But he had learned it all. And the sails... the beautiful sails of which they had more than thirty if you counted the studding-sails — about which no one was supposed to know except the crew that would furl them — in all, totaling nearly 20,000 square yards of canvas.

"WELL, you're certainly lost in thought, Mr. Elliot," said a voice close beside Lewis. He turned on his heel to see not JJ, but Captain James.

"Yes, Sir," he hastened to respond. "Looking out at the great expanse of wavy greyness from our fragile little refuge does that to me."

"Not so fragile as it looks," said the Captain, "and I assume it will get us where we want to be well enough, as far as sailing goes. But you know we're headed into pirate-infested waters."

"Yes, Sir. The South China sea was similarly populated. But, I suppose, the two French warships we were with dampened their enthusiasm for examining our cargo."

"They could have that effect." He looked out at the calm sea. "Would that we could be similarly escorted."

He turned back to Lewis with a serious look. "But since we won't be, the First Mate and I have made contingency plans for leadership."

"Yes, Sir?"

"Should anything happen to me, Mr. Green will take over as Captain and you shall become First Mate. Mr. Williams..." — he looked over toward the helm and nodded toward the sailor handling the wheel — "will become Second Mate."

"How likely is that, Sir?"

"Not at all likely," said Captain James. "But should we be captured, the Captain is often separated from the crew and you'll have to carry on without me."

Lewis turned toward him with a frown and a quizzical eye. "Why would that be, Sir?"

"Because the pirates want to get their ransom, and the Captain's usually the best channel."

"Then why are we going to Marseilles when there are ports on France's Atlantic coast?"

"Because that's where we can get the best price."

"For apples?"

"You didn't guess it's not apples we're carrying?"

"I suspected, Sir." Lewis raised the right side of his mouth slightly in what resembled a grin. "Gunpowder, right?"

"Even more valuable than that."

"What's more valuable than gunpowder in a revolution?"

"Flour."

Lewis opened his mouth to say something, closed it, pursed his lips as though he was about to blow a trumpet, and said, "Oh."

The Captain nodded. "Ordinary people are starving in France. The price of bread has become unbearable to working people — when there is bread — but it's easier to get up north than down south. So, we're going south."

Lewis wondered if what he thought of saying would get him in trouble but said it anyway. "We're not taking advantage of the situation, are we?"

The Captain gave him a sideways look. "We're not gouging them, if that's what you mean. But the price we'll get will provide a reasonable profit."

The Captain said no more and Lewis waited a moment before speaking. "My choice would be to not be captured," he said.

"Good choice, lad." The Captain turned toward the helm and started off toward seaman Williams. "We'll endeavor to give you that choice."

He hadn't taken two more steps when he turned and said, "Oh. And get the sextant. Take a reading while we have the sun."

"Yes, Sir," said Lewis, thrilled to be asked. It wasn't normally his job and he wanted to demonstrate how capably he could do it — realizing that this was precisely the opportunity the Captain was offering him.

He headed to the aft hatch to retrieve the sextant from the Captain's quarters.

~

NEXT MORNING, as the Captain had predicted, *Enterprise* found the Gulfstream. It was like someone coming up behind you as you were running and suddenly pushing you from a jog to a sprint. *Enterprise* skimmed the northern edge which would take it northeast past New England and Nova Scotia, and then due east past Sable Island, off east southeast to the southern verge of the Great Fishing Bank, and finally more southerly until it freed itself from the current and proceeded toward the Azores and the Straits of Gibraltar.

Seven bells had rung and most of the men were still at breakfast as Lewis surveyed the deck. The spun-yarn winch was humming nicely as crew from second watch pursued the never-ending yarn process of making new rope from the strands that came off the old. It was sunny and warm enough so the deck had mostly dried from its swabbing at six bells. Yet, though it was a pleasant and hopeful morning, Lewis reflected that things at sea could change rapidly.

"Sail, ho!" cried the watch from the foregallant top.

"What flag?" shouted Lewis.

There was a moment of silence during which Lewis watched the sailor gaze larboard through his spyglass. "Looks like the Union Jack," he said.

"Warship or merchant?"

"No white border," said the sailor. "Square sails and head sails."

A crew member called Garrett emerged from the hatch.

"Garrett," cried Lewis in his sea voice, "Get the Captain. Now!"

Garrett scurried toward the aft hatch, lifted it and immediately disappeared. In what seemed seconds, the Captain was on deck.

"What is worthy of disturbing my breakfast, Mr. Elliot?" he asked, wiping his mouth with a large napkin.

"British warship."

"Adding stunsails," yelled the foregallant watch.

"We're directly athwart his hawse," said Lewis, "and now he's seen us."

Captain James showed no sign of indecision. "Call all hands," he said. He walked toward the helm, shouting. "Williams!"

Lewis strode to the aft hatch and shouted, "A-a-ll Ha-a-n-n-ds!"

He backed away from the scuttle barely quickly enough to avoid being trampled.

"Mr. Elliot," shouted the Captain. "Get those stuns'ls hove!"

"Stuns'l crew," yelled Lewis. "Get your booms and sheets up there. The rest of you, up and at 'em. Haul all sail! Smart! If you don't want to enlist in the British navy!"

A flurry of activity followed; sailors clambering up the ratlines, climbing around the tops toward the gallants. With a great flapping, all sails not already in use were unfurled. *Enterprise* slowly picked up speed.

"Stuns'ls, Mr. Elliot?"

"Coming, Sir!"

More crew ascended the ratlines now, carrying spars, sheets, and the smaller triangular studding sails that, by law, no merchantman was supposed to be sporting, but which might be their only means of salvation.

"Broad reach to starboard," yelled the Captain. "Williams! Hard-a-starboard."

Enterprise sheared to the right and suddenly caught the full-on northerlies, shuddering and jumping ahead like a startled rabbit.

In a moment, the coordinated furling of the stuns'ls on the

foremast and mainmast laid out their last bit of canvas and *Enterprise* made more speed.

"Can we outrun her, Sir?" asked Lewis.

The foremast and mainmast gallants of the warship were now just visible from *Enterprise's* deck.

"Depends," said Captain James.

JJ came up behind the two of them and handed a spyglass to the Captain.

"What should we do about the cannon, Sir?" he asked.

"Nothing, yet." Captain James surveyed the visible cannon one by one. He shook his head. "I don't think we'd get them overboard without being seen. So we run and hope we can keep them." Then he raised the spyglass and examined the pursuing ship.

Now they were directly in front of it, at least two nautical miles.

"Ship of the line?" asked Captain James. He handed the spyglass to Lewis. "What do you make of it?"

Lewis knew Captain James had learned everything about the ship he needed to know during his short examination and that this was a test. He lifted the spyglass to his eye, maneuvering it so he could see over the taffrail and around the sheet of the mizzen course.

He handed the spyglass back to the Captain. "Third rate, Sir. Seventy-four gun. Probably *Ajax* class."

"Old and slow, then," said JJ. "We should be able to outrun her."

But just then they saw a spark of light from the ship behind them, followed quickly by the sound of a cannon. In a moment, they could see a tiny splash a half a mile behind them.

"Haul your wind on the starboard tack," said the Captain to Lewis.

"Haul wind," Lewis yelled up into the shroud. In a few

moments the sails were adjusted accordingly, and *Enterprise* gained a knot or two of speed.

Captain James watched the ship behind them for a moment before lifting the spyglass to his eye again.

"They're not gaining on us," he said.

But they weren't losing any ground either, it seemed.

Crispin and Gilly came up on deck and joined the three officers.

"Can we get any more speed?" asked Crispin.

"Possibly," said JJ. "If we were to run on the larboard tack and catch a little more of the Gulfstream current."

"But we'd lose speed for a time while the change was made," said Lewis.

"I'll decide that, gentlemen," said the Captain. He headed toward the aft hatch. "Let me know if anything changes.

NOTHING CHANGED throughout the rest of that day. *Enterprise* ran before the wind, as close to due south as she could manage on the Gulfstream. *Ajax*, or *Terrible*, or whatever British ship it was, dogged their tail but made no headway against them.

After dinner and clean-up, Crispin and Gilly (known as the Doctor), the Steward and Cook respectively, walked the weather gangway to the taffrail and found Lewis looking at a book of charts and numbers.

"What's that?" asked Crispin.

"*Ephemeris*, or *Nautical Almanac*," said Lewis. "I'm figuring how we'll alter our course following this little, ah, side-trip, to get to the Straits."

"Of Gibraltar?" asked Gilly.

"That's where the pirates are," said Crispin. "Couldn't we go somewhere else?"

"That's where the Captain says we're going, so that's where we'll go."

"And what are you figuring?" asked Crispin.

"If we can get this guy to give up the chase by tomorrow, we should be able to stay on the Gulfstream and turn northeast toward the Azores. From there, it's almost due east to Gibraltar."

"Ees that good?" asked Gilly.

JJ walked up as they spoke. "Doesn't matter," he said. "Good or bad, that's what the Captain says we must do."

Gilly looked over the taffrail to the rapidly dimming horizon. He could still see the topgallants of their pursuer.

"'Ee no geeve up, yet," he said.

"No," said Lewis, "but hopefully, he'll be gone in the morning."

"We'll put out all the onboard lights and alter our course three points north," said JJ. "And we'll be quiet! He shouldn't be able to follow us."

HE WASN'T GONE in the morning. He was south of their course, but they were still visible to him. And, to make matters worse, first watch had discovered a tear in the main topsail. Because the sail was too large to replace, it would have to be taken down and repaired before it got worse. That would mean losing speed. JJ passed the bad news on to Lewis because second watch would have to do it.

Lewis called his best menders and Crispin — because he'd discovered that Crispin had learned to mend in the British army, — had the sail furled and brought down to the main deck, and commenced mending.

After half an hour, JJ came over from the quarterdeck. "We

have lost speed," he said, "and old *Ajax*, there, is gaining on us. Any chance you could hurry this up?"

Lewis glanced up and snapped, "Can't you see we're doing the best we can?"

JJ seemed to take no offense. "So is he," he said.

In the half-hour it took to finish the repair, all of *Ajax*'s sails could be seen. The British were closing in.

"Get it back up there!" shouted Lewis. "Sanders, Shumann, give them a hand."

Six of them lugged the sail up the ratlines and over the main top. Lewis watched them until JJ called.

"Look at this," he said, pointing aft.

"What?" said Lewis.

"They're shortening sail."

And in that instant, as Lewis watched, their pursuer luffed round to larboard, saying adieu with a parting broadside that fell well short.

"They gave up!" cried Lewis, elated. Until he heard the sails filling out and backing against the mast with a sound like cannon.

He and JJ turned and looked forward. A great bank of dark clouds was directly before them. Waves were whipping up, and winds began to gust from every direction.

"They didn't give up," said JJ. "They saw what we didn't because we were looking back, and they were looking ahead."

Lewis didn't wait for instructions. "All hands ahoy!" he cried. "Tumble up! Take in sail!"

Before they completed reducing to storm-staysails and close-reefed main-topsail, they were in it.

Everyone was soaked through, so instant had been their entry into the storm. It wasn't cold like a blizzard, no sleet or hail came with the rain. But 'rain' could hardly describe the amount of water coming down. Sheets, waterfalls, mountain torrents—water in quantities they had never experienced from the skies—hit *Enterprise*'s crew, scattered them, threatened to wash them overboard. But they had to hold on, had to trim the few sails still unfurled.

Lewis had climbed the mainmast ratlines to lead in reeving the main topsail. He hadn't much of a reputation with the sailors yet, since they hadn't been long together and little had happened. But in one of their many conversations in New York before leaving, JJ had told him what he must do as Second Mate. Thus, he made certain he was the first one up, that he was first to the main topsail weather earring, secured that, then got into the slings to be one of the four crew to make up the bunt. These were the trickiest parts of reeving, and the ones that took the most strength. If the Second Mate didn't do them, he lost respect in the eyes of the crew.

He had done them. He would be able to look the men of his watch in the face and see that he was accepted. Now, he climbed up still further to adjust the boom of the main trysail. From what he could see through driving rain, the crew had managed to set the three lower non-square sails so they'd reduce strain on the masts but leave enough sail for steerage.

With raw, wet hands he scrambled down the larboard ratlines his boots kept slipping off. He spied Schumann on the starboard ratlines, opposite, and shouted at the top of his lungs, "See to getting the hawserbags secured. Find Sanders and tell him to be sure all hatches are battened."

He jumped the final two feet to the deck—almost losing his footing as a foot-high wave swept along toward the quarterdeck —ran forward and was slashed by a snapping line he managed to grab. He eyed it up to its origin, discovered it was the halliard for the staysail, and was almost knocked over by the sailor who was trying to catch it.

"Sorry, Sir," the sailor yelled as Lewis handed him the line. The sailor ran back to the ratlines, rolled the end of the halliard around his right arm twice, and scooted, squirrel-like, up to the fore-top-sail braces.

Lewis left him to his task and ran forward by fits and starts, grabbing whatever he could hold on to, with the goal of setting up a lifeline. He pounded on the bottom of the cutter as he passed it to be certain it was secure. Then, as some crew came down off the foremast ratlines, Lewis pointed at three and shouted for them to help him. The rest he sent below.

Captain James and Williams held the wheel, keeping *Enterprise* on the same westward heading as the gale.

THE MAIN WORK WAS DONE. The ship was secure—though pumping was necessary for some hours because of the sea that had gotten in before she was fully secured—and the watch not on duty had fallen into their hammocks, soaking clothes and all. By dinnertime, the yawing and pitching was more regular, and life could resume its normal course.

Nothing much changed for a couple of days and nights. But on the third day, the gale freshened still more, and Captain James called for a conference in his cabin.

Lewis was surprised to see all four of the so-called 'idlers' there, as well as himself and JJ.

"Because each of you will play a role in what I intend to do," he said, "I've invited you here to explain it."

He looked around the room. "This is not a discussion. I'm not looking for your opinions," he said. "But I am looking for your complete cooperation and the fullest effort you can muster."

He glanced at the charts on his desk, barely visible in the small light provided by the two storm lanterns, one of which swung overhead.

"Hurricanes are not supposed to happen in March," he said. "But the falling barometer and the southwest direction the compass tells me we are being taken, lead me to believe that this is, in fact, a hurricane."

He pointed at his chart. "Calculating from our known position three mornings ago when the British gave up their chase, and estimating our velocity from the log line, I can tell you it is unsupportable for us to continue on our current trajectory." He looked at each of them again.

"The storm is pulling us in toward its center. We must get out." He turned from them for a moment and looked out the windows of his cabin, then back.

"You are young and inexperienced. Only a few in the crew, like Williams, have seen it all and know what to do. The maneuver we are about to make would be difficult for even the most experienced crew. Therefore, I will rely on all of you to do what I ask, and we must rely on the skill and willingness of the crew to do what they are asked. They will not be told ahead of time what we are doing but will just follow orders. Make certain you give them clear and specific orders."

"Now, for the idlers, here are my orders."

He looked over at the ship's master carpenter, a man named Bloom. "Chips, secure lumber of various sorts on deck. We'll also need blocks and sheaves and material for seizing."

He looked at Greaves, the bo'sun. "Bring up lines and sheets from the bilge and stow them in the sleeping quarters. Have everything in readiness."

Next, he turned toward Gilly. "Doctor, make whatever

flummery or lobscouse you can, as hot as you can, and get it to the crew for dinner. Also, get out the large barrel of rum so the Steward"—he looked over at Crispin—"can bring grog up to the watch on deck, or to all hands if necessary, at about mid-watch. We may be days at this, and I don't want them to freeze." He looked back at Gilly. "Dinner will be at six bells, afternoon watch."

Lewis had just struck two bells, forenoon watch. He pulled his chronometer from his pocket. It was nine-fifteen. Gilly had less than six hours to make something from nothing for nearly four-dozen men, and he had to keep it hot with only the galley's small fire.

"Right," said the Captain, gazing at Lewis's chronometer. "Get out of here, Doctor, and get busy."

Gilly scurried out as well as the heaving deck allowed and shut the door behind him.

"Chips and Greaves, you'd better get to business as well."

The two nodded and headed out.

The Captain looked back at JJ and Lewis. The storm lantern swung over him, alternately lighting his face and placing it in shadow. But even the shadow could not conceal its lines of anxiety.

"There will be no dog watches until further notice. Only one watch at a time is to be on deck unless I call all hands. We want the manpower we need, but we don't want people swept overboard."

He looked to Lewis. "Lifelines larboard and starboard, no free halliards."

"Yes, Sir."

"We'll be luffing nearly 75 degrees to be close-hauled on a starboard tack," said the Captain, studying the faces of Lewis and JJ alternately. "With gallants, jibs, and stays. Can you handle that?"

"Yes, Sir," they said in unison.

"Once we can steer our course it shouldn't be too bad. It's the maneuver itself that's tricky. You gentlemen talk over how you'd like to do it and bring me your plan by two bells in the afternoon watch."

He nodded dismissively as he removed his glasses and rubbed his forehead. "In the meantime, I have to decide how to get back on course to France once we're out of this."

He looked at the map before him and then up. "You're still here?"

Lewis and JJ made haste to depart.

ENTERPRISE WALLOWED in the lee of an enormous wave for a few seconds, yawing crazily, masts describing an arc of nearly 90 degrees. Sailors who had just set the yardarms to close-hauled now worked out on the yards, unreefing the sails, holding on to whatever they could, trying desperately not to lose their footing on the horse.

Enterprise rose with the wave, responding with agonized slowness to the rudder and sails that were just starting to fill. As a gust took them, however, she listed suddenly to starboard, bow plunging into the wave, sea surging over the knight-heads, all along the deck, and out the aft scuppers, carrying with it anything the sailors had failed to tie down.

Several sailors emerged from the wave, coughing and gasping, but still onboard thanks to the lifelines. The yawing continued. From the helm, Captain James gave Lewis the order to change tack to beam-reach so the ship would be closer to perpendicular to the waves.

Getting the order was one thing. Relaying it to the crew was another. Lewis found they could not hear him unless he climbed the ratlines at least to the head of the top mast. He did that for the mainmast, returned to deck, and made his way to the foremast.

He was only half-way up the larboard ratlines when the bow pitched into the wave again. A great crashing and rending shocked him into almost releasing his hold as something careening down the top of the wave crashed into *Enterprise.*

As it plowed through the shroud on the starboard side at about his height, moving diagonally across the deck, Lewis caught a brief glance of what he thought was a foremast from some unlucky ship. The end ploughing forward was splintered, various blocks, eyes, and stays hung from it, and it was smoother and straighter than nature could have made it.

Lewis watched it bounce off the larboard cutter with a hollow boom, continue aft with a few more significant detonations like artillery firing, and grind over the taffrail, finally disappearing into the sea. After which, everything was eerily quiet for a few seconds—even the wind seeming to hold its breath while the damage was ascertained.

"The Captain!" yelled JJ. "We've lost the Captain!"

The wind picked up its volume again. "What do you mean you've lost the Captain?" shouted Lewis.

"He's overboard," screamed JJ. "Overboard! He didn't have time to attach to the lifeline."

"We've lost steering!" shouted Williams. "That...thing took out the binnacle and the steering post. The wheel's gone!"

Which became all too obvious with alarming swiftness as *Enterprise* turned back to port and began to founder in the trough.

Another crash made it impossible to hear whatever was next said as the spanker boom let loose of the mizzenmast and swung into JJ and what was left of the steering post.

"JJ?" shouted Lewis, now scrambling down the ratline to the deck. "JJ? Are you hurt?"

No one responded. Lewis sloshed aft as quickly as possible, aware that the next wave might sweep him out to sea as well. JJ was on the deck by the collapsed steering post, bleeding from his neck, holding his arm. Lewis rushed to him.

"Never mind me," said JJ through clenched teeth. "The ship!"

"Chips!" shouted Lewis, "Go below and stabilize the tiller!" He looked around but saw only Williams. "Chips?" he shouted at the top of his lungs.

"On it, Sir," said the welcome voice of Bloom.

"Ahoy! All hands," yelled Lewis, turning to look up and choking on rain falling with renewed vehemence. "Reeve all sail but the stay sails! Full stop!" He hoped they had heard him. "Man overboard!" he shouted with all the strength he had. "Man overboard!"

He looked at the nearby larboard cutter and shook his head. "First Watch cutter team," he yelled, "get the starboard cutter off. Look for the Captain!"

He knew this would be no easy task amidst the swells and sheets of rain.

"Tie a line to the boat so we don't get separated."

A dozen sailors rushed to the cutter, unloosed it from its stays, flipped it upright, set it out over the skid beams, and held it while another half-dozen darted into it. Additional sailors manned the winches and began turning them as still others threw rope heads into the boat whose bottom end was secured to the main bitts. In seconds, the cutter was lowered along the boat slide. Sailors yelled at one another as they endeavored to keep the boat from being smashed against *Enterprise*'s side. Finally it was loosed and lost to Lewis's sight. He didn't have much hope of finding the Captain, but they had to try.

Williams helped JJ sit up and lean against the back of the nearly-destroyed wheel post as Lewis slid across the deck almost into him. *Enterprise* pitched and yawed in the rolling waves.

"What are we going to do?" yelled Williams.

"First," said Lewis' "Look for the Captain. Second, secure the vessel."

JJ groaned and said through clenched teeth, "Did you see that thing that hit us? Where it went?"

"It's aft," said Lewis, "but lost to sight in the rain. Hopefully the cutter will pick it up and find the Captain clinging to it."

JJ shuddered. "I don't think so," he said. He groaned again and held his left arm against his chest with his right hand. He pushed out words with great effort. "That thing hit him square in the head and shoulder after it took out the binnacle and wheel." He shuddered. "I don't think he even knew he'd been hit before he was gone abaft."

Lewis looked at JJ for a moment and then over to Williams. "You're Second Mate, at least for the moment," he said. "Make certain the sails are set properly so we maintain enough headway for steerage but no more. The cutter will go as far as the ropes allow and make a sweep. We don't want to move too far forward of where the accident happened."

"Aye, Sir," said Williams, standing quickly and heading amidships.

"What can I do for you?" Lewis said to JJ.

JJ grimaced and leaned forward, holding both arms together over his chest. "Check the binnacle and see what the damage is."

Lewis stood and looked forward at the spot where the binnacle—that had contained their compass and other navigation instruments—had stood.

He stooped so his mouth was at the height of JJ's ear.

"It's gone," he whispered, "or at least it might as well be. All that's left is the wreckage of the cabinet that you're leaning against."

"All the instruments?"

Lewis nodded, his mouth a grim line.

Then the rain turned to mist. The swells abated. The cutter went back and forth, back and forth, a hundred yards aft. They were out of the storm. Lewis shook his head. If only this could have happened thirty minutes ago they wouldn't be looking for the Captain.

A couple of hours later Lewis waved them in. Half-an-hour after that, the soggy cutter crew quietly clambered up the rope ladder from the cutter. The team leader shook his head at Lewis.

He nodded. "Thank you, sailor," he said. A chair had been brought from the Captain's cabin for JJ, who sat on the larboard companionway.

"Please assemble the entire crew," JJ said to Lewis.

When they were all there, except those still manning the yards, Lewis helped JJ stand. With an amazing effort of will JJ spoke.

"Is anyone else missing?"

"No, Sir," said Williams. "All's accounted for."

JJ nodded. "Thank you, Mr. Williams."

He looked back over the crew.

"Does anyone think we could have done more to save the Captain?"

No one spoke.

"Anyone?" he repeated.

"Ye done all ye could," said a voice from among them. Nods of assent and a few affirmative noises followed.

"Then I'm the Captain now," said JJ. "Mr. Elliot is First Mate, and Mr. Williams is Second Mate."

More affirmative noises.

"Mr. Bloom has made the tiller fast," said JJ. "But we do not have helm control. You've all seen the rest of the damage, including the loss of the spanker boom and the stove-in larboard cutter."

He was quiet for a few more moments except for a suppressed groan.

"As you can see," he continued, "I'm not in the best of shape, either. Mr. Elliot will be my stand-in most of the time—"

He leaned to his left, away from the crew, and retched. Lewis saw that the sputum was bright red.

JJ looked up again. "We'll all have to work together if we want to survive. I'll inform you at seven bells tomorrow where we'll be headed next. For now..."

Just then, a cloud cleared away and the setting sun emerged, its ruddy light settling on JJ's face and the shattered larboard cutter. With a collective intake of breath, the crew turned involuntarily to see the sun.

"For now," said JJ, "we'll continue on this course to the north."

2

FRANCE

"A Yankee ship comes down the river," Lewis sang out in his loudest baritone.

"Blow, boys, blow," sang the dozen sailors rowing the surviving cutter as it towed *Enterprise* through the small opening to the bay at Angra, Tercera, in the Azore Islands.

"A Yankee ship with a Yankee Skipper," Lewis bawled.

The ends of twelve oars leapt out of the water as the men returned, "Blow, my bully boys, blow."

"How do you know she's a Yankee liner?"

"Blow, boys, blow."

Ten oars dipped suddenly into the water and ten sweaty men put their backs into plying them with every ounce of strength to move their recalcitrant six-hundred ton wooden refuge the last few hundred yards to safety.

"The Stars and Stripes float out behind her."

"Blow, my bully boys, blow."

The ship seemed to sigh and give in, catching a small bit of tide to float past the ominous Sao Joao Baptista Fort on the larboard side, which welcomed them with an ear-bursting thirteen-gun salute as the Portuguese longboat tugs accepted lines thrown from the deck.

"Who do you think is the captain of her?" shouted Lewis, no longer bothering with the tune.

Enterprise responded to the fort with a salute from the four cannon that remained to her.

"Belay, men," Lewis said, more softly. "Let's get back to the ship."

"Blow, boys, blow," sang a lone sailor as they performed the awkward turnabout and headed to midship, starboard. A couple of sailors stood to catch the lines tossed them from above, securing the cutter. Within seconds, Lewis and the ten sailors had scaled the rope ladder to the deck. Williams supervised the recovery of the cutter as Lewis reported to JJ.

"We did it," said JJ, wincing with pain.

Lewis glanced at him, trying not to show his concern. "Yes, Sir, we did."

Then he looked JJ in the eyes. "And the first thing we do when we're ashore is get that arm looked at."

The Capitao do *porto* shook his head as he surveyed the ship while the *Medico* checked crew members for signs of disease.

"How long you plan be here?" he asked. JJ looked to Lewis for an answer.

Lewis shrugged. "It depends on what we find. But at the least we have to replace the steering mechanism and the binnacle. Oh, and the spanker boom."

The Capitao pointed at the nearby mizzen mast. "And I theenk, theeze too."

Lewis twisted to see what he was referring to. Then it was Lewis's turn to shake his head. A thin crack, through which the westering sun shone, had appeared in the mast. "Must have just happened."

"Eef you have wood, we can do. Eef not..." he trailed off.

Did they have wood enough to replace a mast? Lewis didn't think so.

"We'll have to bind it until we can get to a larger port," said Lewis. "JJ? What do you think?"

But it was clear that JJ couldn't follow the conversation.

Lewis tilted his head toward JJ while saying to the Capitao, "Can he go ashore with the Medico?"

The Capitao nodded. "We do what we can," he said, then shrugged.

SOME DAYS later Lewis was walking up the wharf from the dry dock toward the city. A distinguished looking man dressed in a civilian suit— but standing in a military posture— paused at the street end, apparently waiting for him.

"I was going to try to come aboard," said the man as Lewis reached him, "but then I saw your uniform and decided to wait here." He held out his hand for Lewis to shake. "I'm Colonel David Humphreys, and if I find you've told anyone I'm here," he continued with a laugh, "I'll deny it!"

"I'm..." Lewis began.

"I know who you are," said Humphreys. "Lieutenant Elliot."

"Ah," said Lewis, "that was a long time ago. Newburgh?"

Humphreys nodded. "But you made an impression," he said.

"That's surprising," said Lewis. He pointed inland. "Is there a café nearby? I'm dying for a coffee."

Humphreys nodded and headed directly away from the harbor with Lewis having to trot to keep up with the unexpected speed of his stride.

"Your Captain is doing better," said Humphreys as Lewis caught up and they wended through a tiny alley and up a hill toward what Lewis thought must be the main street.

"Thank you for visiting him," said Lewis. "And, um, this is a little surprising—both finding you here and having your attention like this."

"It's an important moment," said Humphreys, turning right on the larger street and heading toward a sign that read 'Angra Café.' "Yours is the first American vessel to dock in Angra, and the Portuguese gave you the honor of a salute—which is a propitious indication that my mission here will be successful."

"Your mission?"

They entered a café that was dim despite it being an hour or so before sundown.

The proprietor obviously knew Humphreys, because he came over immediately with two of the tiniest cups Lewis had ever seen.

"Every country does coffee differently," said Humphreys, grinning. "It's small and not very hot so you can take it in a single swallow." He showed Lewis how it was done and then nodded for him to try it.

Lewis did and almost choked.

"Whew!" he said, when he was recovered. "That's the strongest coffee I've ever had!"

Humphreys laughed. "And there's plenty more of it." He turned and looked around the nearly empty café. Then he said quietly. "I think you wouldn't get back to Philadelphia in time to tell anyone, in any case, but what I'm doing is secret. President Washington asked me to set up a diplomatic mission with Portugal."

"Why secret?"

"Because we don't know how the English, French, or Spanish will react to such a venture." He looked around again. "Right now, there is relative calm in Europe. No one is fighting anyone else. But historically, that doesn't last. We don't want to become someone's enemy unwittingly because of the alliances we've chosen to make."

Lewis made a grimace. "Diplomacy is complicated," he said.

"But you must have learned something about it since you worked for Hamilton."

"What do you mean?"

"Hamilton had enemies back during those Newburgh days, and he has more now — though the president is fond of him."

"So-o-o?"

"Didn't you know that when you worked with Jay you were working with a man who became one of Hamilton's enemies?"

"Huh," said Lewis. "Maybe that's why he dropped me so suddenly."

"Did he?"

Lewis nodded. "One day I was his clerk and the next he told me I needed to find employment."

"He's like that," said Humphreys. "You're his friend or his enemy. There's nothing in between. He's even had a rift with Madison."

"With Madison?" said Lewis incredulously.

Humphreys nodded. "Madison can't support his excise tax, for moral reasons I'm told, so that's the end of their friendship."

"What happened with Jay?"

"I guess he was not oriented enough toward the English for

Hamilton's liking. And, of course, Hamilton thinks he's incompetent."

"I worked with him," said Lewis. "He's definitely not incompetent. But perhaps he's more patient and accommodating than some people would like. He certainly didn't make the slightest dent in the resolve of Don Diego de Gardoqui."

"No," said Humphreys with a little sidewards nod of his head, "but we're also not at war with Spain."

The proprietor arrived with tiny custard pies and more coffee.

"*Pastel de nata,*" said Humphreys, nodding toward the diminutive pastries. "You'll want to eat them while they're warm."

Conversation was overtaken by Portuguese cuisine for a few moments. Lewis watched Humphreys between bites, thinking he looked like a man who'd just made a decision.

Humphreys threw his head back to take his swallow of coffee and gently replaced the cup in its saucer.

Lewis had already finished his and looked at Humphreys in anticipation.

"Would you like to work for me?" Humphreys said.

Lewis paused for only an instant. "I would," he said. "But I can't. With Captain Green injured, I have to get *Enterprise* to France."

"Where are you headed?"

"We *were* headed to Marseille. But now, I'm afraid, we're going to have to go to some port on the west coast in order to have a mast replaced."

"Can't they do it here?"

Lewis shook his head. "They don't have the wood. And neither do we have enough with us for that."

"Pity," said Humphreys. "But I may not be in Portugal for a while, in any case. Once this is set up, it could be months before

I get to Lisbon. If you come find me there, I'll have a job for you."

"As?"

"As my aide," said Humphreys. "Second in command."

"That is very tempting," said Lewis. He remembered that Humphreys had a reputation for being congenial and decided it was well deserved. "I should very much enjoy working for you, Sir. Perhaps after I see to the disposition of *Enterprise*..."

"How can I reach you?"

"I don't know," said Lewis. "I guess I'll just have to come to Lisbon."

"Do that," said Humphreys, standing. He took out his pocket watch and glanced at it. "In a few minutes I have an appointment with the Captain-general who will inform me of the king's decision. I think we already know the result."

He extended his hand to Lewis. "I hope I will see you soon."

Lewis shook his hand and nodded, not knowing quite what to say. "Thank you for the coffee," he finally said. "And I also hope to see you soon."

WITHIN A FEW DAYS of his meeting with Col. Humphreys, Lewis received a note saying that Humphreys was departing for Philadelphia. He asked Lewis to meet at the coffee shop on the morning of his departure. There, he confirmed his desire for Lewis to work with him, and also gave him a gift.

"You'll be sailing through both French and British waters," he said. "There's no telling what treaty agreements will be in place on any given day, nor whether the captains will honor them. An American ship is simply at their whim. Therefore, his Most Faithful Majesty has graciously allowed me to offer you a Portuguese flag to use on your journey. Since Britain and

France are at peace with Portugal and actually comply with treaty obligations, you should be safe."

He pulled a canvas sack from his baggage and handed it to Lewis.

"I don't want you to be impressed into the British navy before you can get to Lisbon!"

IT WAS six boring and frustrating weeks before *Enterprise* left dry dock, and a couple more before everything could be tested and found seaworthy. So it was late June when a fair wind took her north around the western shore of Tercera sporting the Portuguese flag.

Though JJ was onboard, he was still suffering greatly, so Lewis was effectively captain for this part of the voyage. At Gilly's insistence, they were headed for Le Havre rather than Brest, which was closer but had a much greater French naval presence. Gilly was afraid the French navy's impressment teams would kidnap *Enterprise's* crew, including its cook, and that would be then end of his dreams.

They replaced a few of the cannon thrown overboard during their desperate trip to Angra. But though they might be able to hold off pirates for long enough to make an escape, they placed most of their hope for a safe arrival in France in the Portuguese flag flying astern. The Captain-general of Angra had also provided a few masthead banners indicating that the ship was of Portuguese registration, so ships viewing them from a distance wouldn't bother to move in for a closer inspection and discover that no one on board spoke Portuguese.

As it turned out, not being in the main shipping lines, they saw scarcely another ship on their northeasterly trip until they approached the British Channel. They skirted the Ile d'Ouessant, west of Brest, headed more easterly than north, and gave *Enterprise* her head as they passed east of the channel islands where there was reason to expect more British shipping.

They saw a few sail in the distance, but nothing approached them, so they were able to circuit Cap de la Hague unmolested, and then make slightly south of east toward Le Havre. When they had passed Cherbourg they felt it safe to replace the Portuguese insignia with the stars and stripes. They were still a few miles away from the mouth of the Seine when they were met by a pilot ship.

"*Bonjour, mes amis!*" shouted the friendly pilot as his launch pulled alongside. The ladder was thrown down to him and he whistled as his head topped the break by the poop deck.

"You 'ave 'ad some trouble, no?" he said, climbing the rest of the way onto the ship.

"*C'est si èvident?*" (Is it so obvious?) said Lewis.

"To zee ordinary man, no," said the pilot. "*Mais, moi...*" (But, me...)

"*Oui, oui,*" said Lewis. "*Bienvenue!*" (Yes, yes. Welcome!)

THE PILOT quickly took control of the helm and gave Williams some commands for arranging the sails. As they negotiated the tricky currents, he and Lewis spoke in French.

"I ask only for your safety," said the pilot. "What is your cargo?"

"Mostly flour," Lewis replied. "It was supposed to go to Marseille, but..." he indicated the damaged mizzenmast and some of the shroud that was still not right.

"Then I recommend that you not come to the dock. If you do that, the mobs, they will storm your ship and take the flour. We will anchor you by the Jete Sud-est, just below where they build the Retenue de la Floride. We will bring in your cargo by boat at night."

"I heard there was famine in Paris," said Lewis, "and in the south. But not out here."

"Puh!" said the pilot, back in English, "There is no bread. And where is bread, is so dear one cannot pay. So, *oui*, they know you have flour, they overwhelm or kill you. They take it all."

"But we have an injured man who must go immediately to hospital, and we must make extensive repairs. We must certainly go into the harbor."

"Leave it to me, then. I speak with *Maître de la port* and we work something out for you, yes? Maybe *docteur* find sickness onboard?"

Lewis was prepared for something like this. "*Ah, oui*," he said. "You know I had a little gift for le Maître and yourself."

He felt in his pockets and pulled a few things out, ostensibly emptying those things he didn't need on to the top of the helm.

"Now where did I put it?" He took the few steps to the binnacle and opened the doors, glancing inside. "Can't seem to find it," he said, head in the cabinet. He pulled his head out and shrugged, not looking at the helm.

Just outside the harbor mouth the pilot instructed them to furl all sail as four longboats appeared to tug them in. The pilot instructed the lead officer in one boat where they were to go, and they were hauled past the Tour François Premiere to Ecluse de Bas de la Barre – a gated passageway to the most heavy-duty shipyard. The tugs kept them a good two hundred feet from the dock until it was clear that *le docteur* had arrived. He was ferried over to the ship in a small boat.

After the pilot departed, Lewis noted with a grin, that the

materials he had placed on the helm, including a significant number of French livres, were gone.

In due course, the quarantine flag was raised to the top of the mainmast and *Enterprise* was anchored slightly shoreward out of the main channel, but not close enough to the dock for a gang-board to reach. The doctor took JJ away with him in the boat.

Lewis called the crew together on the waist and addressed them.

"Gentlemen," he said, "in a few days you will be able to take shore leave. Our cargo, it seems, is more valuable than we thought — valuable enough to kill for. Therefore, it's going to be off-loaded at night, quietly, over the next two or three days."

The sound of low grumbles made its way forward.

"I know," said Lewis, "it's been a tough voyage. And we don't know how long we'll need to stay here for repairs. But once cargo is off-loaded and we've been paid, the quarantine flag will come down, we'll pay you off, and you'll be free to go. You can wait to ship with *Enterprise* when she's ready, or you can find another ship."

"If you have money, food can always be found. And there are other things you can enjoy," said Lewis, shrugging. "If you want, you could book a ship to England. Those of you who were British navy might be able to find a job..."

Lewis stopped for the tittering.

"You can stay onboard until they lay us over to scrape the hull. When that happens, we'll all have to be ashore. By tomorrow afternoon I should be able to give you more information. Until then, I've instructed the Doctor to double your rum ration."

That brought up a mild cheer and the men dispersed as Lewis turned to go back to the Captain's cabin. He went inside, shut the door, sat in the Captain's chair, leaned his head on his two hands, and heaved a huge sigh. He sat that way for a moment, then allowed his head to rest on the table. His hands were stone cold and his whole body was tense.

I put on a pretty good show, he said to himself. *But I really have no idea what I'm doing. Do I want to be a sea captain?* He thought of Humphrey's offer. *Do I want to be a diplomat? Do I want...* But he fell asleep before he could finish the thought.

THE CREWS that came at night to unload *Enterprise's* cargo were, from what Lewis could make out, dark-skinned, fine featured, short and stocky. They whispered among themselves in a language Lewis did not recognize. Almost silently, they loaded the barrels of flour on to flat-bottomed boats that had an upright tiller, no sail, and very few oarsmen. Additionally, the oars were swathed in rags so they made less noise coming in and out of the water. The workers unloaded the Enterprise on the side away from the nearest docks, presumably so as not to be seen from shore.

That's smart, thought Lewis, appreciating the quiet, and hoping their appearance of not speaking French was actual fact rather than ruse. Because if they didn't speak French, they couldn't tell starving French peasants what they were unloading. Which they would otherwise, since some of the barrels had been breached by rats and flour was sprinkled liberally from the hold to the main hatch, across the deck, and over the larboard side, amidships. Lewis wondered how much of their cargo would prove to be useless.

Before dawn he had Williams get the first watch not only to swab the decks, but also to scour the larboard side of *Enterprise* so no white powder showed.

Two mornings later, with relief, he saw the last barrel

loaded on one of the punts. At the same time, the *Maître de la port* arrived.

"*Nous sommes vraiment désolé,*" he began, as soon as he had been handed on board. (We are truly sorry.)

Not a good sign, thought Lewis.

Then he switched into English. "...zat so many of your cargo, zey be *ruiné*...by zee rat. Wee cannot pay zee so much," he said.

He showed Lewis a paper that had an amount in livres.

Lewis looked up from the paper to the man's face and spoke quietly, distinctly in French. "You know that's not half what it's worth."

The little man in the fancy uniform shrugged, seemed taken aback by Lewis's French. But without losing a beat, he said, "Take it or leave it." He paused. "You may be aware that we already have the flour."

Lewis felt himself seething, but remembered they were just at the beginning of the *négociation*.

"*Ah, oui,*" he said. "But being a man of honor, as you are, I know you would like to help us in another way. Perhaps you have a disused mast someone has left, *malheureusement* (unfortunately), that we could use to replace..." Here, he sighed and nodded toward the mizzen mast.

"*Peut-être,*" the Maître said, noncommittally. "But perhaps I have a better offer."

"I'm listening," said Lewis.

"We buy all ship," he said.

Lewis stood silent for a moment, stunned. That's an interesting development, he thought. But maybe a good one.

"It's not my decision," he said. "But I can speak with the Captain about it."

"Speak quick," said the Maître, "before he die." His eyes followed the final punt as it wound its way among the ships, northward, toward the main docks. Then he turned back toward Lewis, handing him the paper. "The offer be there on the paper. I be back tonight for answer."

LEWIS WAS NEEDED to supervise the unloading of the cargo, preparations for the larger repairs they would do here, and oversight of the crew impatiently waiting to disembark. He should not take the time to visit JJ to get his opinion about the offer. Of course, to maintain the illusion of quarantine, he should stay onboard anyway. But this was France. In France, he was learning, there was always a way.

A little after noon he found himself aboard a tiny local fishing vessel that dropped him off just East of the Basin du Commerce, a few blocks from the naval hospital. With a bit of searching, he found the hospital and, finally, JJ — who was not looking at all well.

They greeted one another and then Lewis nodded toward JJ's left arm that was firmly bandaged to his chest.

"It is not my arm that's the problem," said JJ. "They repaired that well enough in Angra. It's my left lung." JJ looked toward the solitary, small window that gave a view of the yard and the backs of buildings beyond, almost in a daze.

"I wish you had been here," he said, "as my French is poor. But I think he said a broken rib punctured my lung and I've been bleeding inside ever since."

Lewis gimaced. "I'm so sorry," he said.

"They made an incision and bled it out, and maybe tried to stitch up the wound. I don't know. It's not as if it's an arm they can take off if it's causing trouble."

"What was the prognosis?"

"That I'll live, but I may not enjoy it." JJ laughed a little, which precipitated a coughing spell that caused little pink droplets to spew from his mouth. He saw Lewis's reaction when he had recovered. "Really," he said, "it's much better than it was."

"I'll have to take your word for it," said Lewis. "And I hope you're well enough to discuss an offer the Maître made this morning."

"Oh, I know about it," said JJ. "He broached the subject just after my surgery, but I wasn't clear enough in my head to understand it. What did they offer?"

"A lot," said Lewis. "And in gold. They must really want this ship."

"Are there not others around?"

"That's the thing. There are almost no ships in the harbor. And the sail-worthy ones are mostly schooners. They want a larger ship."

"My father gave me and Captain James discretion over this."

"Why Captain James?"

"He was part-owner of the ship. But now there are only two owners, my father and me. So the decision is mine."

"And?"

"What do you think?"

"There is one proviso we should talk about. I don't want to leave you here alone. If you want to go back to America, I want to accompany you. If you want to stay here, I will stay with you."

"They want you to stay on as First Mate," said JJ.

"Yes. I know the ship, and they'd like to keep as much of the crew as possible."

"Do you want to do it?"

"I have mixed feelings."

"Do it," said JJ. "I want to sell the ship, go back to America, become an accountant, a farmer, a cobbler. Anything but a sea captain!"

"But how will you get back? And how will you get the money back?"

JJ grinned. "Not in gold, I assure you. There is money to be made in French furniture, French fabric, French tableware, silverware, glassware; French wine. *Enterprise* will return to America in the form of very profitable French goods."

"Shall I tell the Maître *Yes* tonight, then?"

JJ nodded. "Could you oversee repairs until the purchase is finalized?"

"I'll be glad to stay onboard as much as possible, but I think we're going to have to trust the French with the repairs. I know so little!"

"And please thank the crew for me. I won't be able to be there when they're released."

"Of course."

Lewis saw that JJ's energy was flagging. "Rest," he said. "Get better." Whether JJ heard, Lewis couldn't tell. He tip-toed out.

"THE SHIP WILL BE under repair for at least a month," Lewis told the gathered crew. "The bursar will settle up with each of you now, and you may decide what you'd like to do." Lewis understood the grumbling that followed this. What would they do in a country with no food?

"There's another thing, though," he said. "If you sign on to go with us when *Enterprise* leaves the dock as the French ship, *Avance*, we'll continue to pay you while she's under repair, and give you a bonus once we're underway."

A few cheers.

"Captain Green sends his regards and his thanks," Lewis

continued. He nodded to the bursar who stepped up onto the quarterdeck and opened the ledger he carried. Beside him were two burly seamen, each holding a thick canvas bag.

"Gentlemen," said Lewis, nodding, then retiring to his cabin.

LEWIS ANSWERED the knock on his door to see Gilly and Crispin hovering there.

"Does the exalted Captain have time for a word?" asked Crispin.

"Of course," said Lewis. He invited them into the Captain's quarters. "Captain in function only," he said. "Not in pay and not in expeerience. And still me. Still your friend."

"Wee know," said Gilly. "But, even so, wee must part. Crispin and I go to Paris."

"He feels he must go," said Crispin, "and I can't let him go alone."

"We find Lafayette," said Gilly. "Maybe Gouverneur."

"Maybe some rich countess?" asked Lewis.

Gilly glared at him. "No funny," he said. "Ees new country, like yours. All just citizens now. I want be part."

"And what will you do, Crispin?" asked Lewis.

"I'll keep him out of trouble, at least for the first few weeks, and then I may go back to England. I'm American now, but that was my first home." He grinned. "Maybe I'll get some back pay."

Lewis grinned back. "Not likely," he said. He turned and walked to the Captain's table and picked up two cloth satchels. He came back and handed one to each. "I thought you'd want to be moving on. It's not much, but it's my back pay. I'll be getting paid and getting a living allowance here. Maybe that will keep you from starving."

"Merci," said Gilly. "Oowhen wee see you?"

Lewis shook his head. "Only God knows," he said, reaching out his hand first to Gilly and then to Crispin. "Godspeed!"

The door shut with a soft snap.

And now, who will care what I do, thought Lewis. Who that I care about will even hear what I'm doing? Captain? Diplomat? Something else? I wish I knew.

3

____

TWO DEPARTURES

Enterprise was laid over on her larboard side, practically all the way. Lewis stood on the dock with arms crossed over his chest, watching, as two French workmen carefully applied her new name over the recently painted hull. They had chalked an outline of the letters, *Avance*, and were applying gold-leaf. They had completed the A and the v when Lewis was hailed by a man in a uniform he had not seen before. The man held out his hand to Lewis.

"Hans Axel, Count von Fersen," he said. "I understand you are Lieutenant Elliot."

Lewis shook his hand. "I was, briefly," he said. "Who told you that?"

"Word gets around," the Count answered with a grin. "I was aide-de-camp to General Rochambeau. I heard the story of your father."

Lewis tried to determine the nature of Fersen's accent. His English was excellent. He had been with the French army. But the accent was not French.

"Swedish?" he asked.

"How could you tell?"

"Just a guess, but it had to be either Swedish or Danish. The Danes were very kind to us in China, so I heard that accent. But yours was not quite the same."

"Very astute."

"But to what do I owe the honor?"

"Ah," said Fersen. "I'm here to tell you that the purchase is officially complete. We have not yet chosen a captain, but as you are to be First Mate, I've been appointed to inform you that your mission is diplomatic. You'll be exchanging diplomats in Lisbon, Madrid, Algiers, and Tripoli. It's not particularly secret, but there may be those who wish your mission not to be a success. Hence, French marines have been assigned to guard *Avance* during reconstruction and will accompany you on your mission."

He took a valise he'd been holding under his left arm and opened it, producing a thick envelope and handing it to Lewis.

"These documents authorize the procurement of supplies you will need both for the diplomats and for the marines. My card is also in there. If you find you need anything else, you may contact me at the Swedish consulate in Paris."

"I'm curious," said Lewis. "How is it that *you* are conducting this business?"

Fersen smiled. "I'm a friend of the king and queen. In these uncertain days, they occasionally desire a disinterested party to, shall we say, facilitate some of the affairs of France."

"And the uniform?"

"Yes, well you see, I am still the *colonel propriétaire* of the French Royal-Suédois regiment. Sometimes the uniform enables me to accomplish my tasks more easily."

Lewis nodded. "I understand that."

"And, as well, it has also proved useful to two of your colleagues."

"How is that?"

"A Mister Graves and a Monsieur Y'vant were visiting your Captain Green in hospital as I arrived to complete the disposition of payment for *Avance*. After a short conversation, I discovered that they desire to go to Paris. I invited them to accompany me in my carriage."

"That is very kind of you!"

"Not at all. They will make the journey so much more interesting. Besides which, I will need to show them into Mr. Morris's rooms."

"What?" said Lewis.

"During the course of our conversation it was uncovered that you, your colleagues, and I have at least two friends in common."

"That would be..."

"The Marquis de Lafayette, and Mr. Gouverneur Morris."

Lewis shook his head. "I'm afraid I didn't know the Marquis well enough to call him friend. But he certainly was our benefactor."

"He is generous to many," said Fersen.

"Gouverneur is another matter."

"Indeed he is," said Fersen with a grin and a twinkle in his eyes. "But he has asked me to look after his rooms. Having your colleagues stay there will release me from that burden."

"It has been a pleasure meeting you," said Lewis as they shook hands once more. "I hope we shall meet again."

"I am certain of it," said Fersen. He turned to go, but then turned back and motioned Lewis to come closer. "I was at liberty to tell you less or more of what will become of *Enterprise*. I've decided to tell you more. *Avance* is actually being refitted as a warship. It will fly the French flag. The First Lieutenant will come aboard soon and take over all responsibility for refitting. Rather than being First Mate, you will be

Second Lieutenant in the French navy, if that is acceptable to you."

Lewis's jaw dropped. "Ah," he said after a moment. "*Pourquois pas?*" (Why not?)

"After our short conversation, I thought you would say that," said Fersen, holding out his hand again for Lewis to shake. "Your responsibilities will begin when Mr. Short and Mr. O'Brien arrive, some few days before you sail. You will keep them comfortable and occupied - as well as keeping Mr. O'Brien's, shall we say, 'companions' in their place. In the meantime, you are free to come and go as you please."

He nodded at the valise Lewis was holding. "Your first month's pay and money for personal expenses are in there."

Lewis nodded. "Merci!"

Fersen smiled. "Now, I really must be going. *Au revoir!*"

WITH FOUR HORSES, the Count's berlinette was a good deal faster than any carriage Gilly or Crispin had ridden in before. Which was a good thing, as it helped them mostly stay ahead of dust and flies. Even so, there were times they needed to shut the window flaps against midges and biting horseflies. This occurred particularly after they crossed the Seine on Pont de Tancarville and began skirting the Verier swamp, only about ten miles out of Le Havre. But the dim light and regular clomp-clomping of the horses set the three of them to sleep, so by the time they reached Tocqueville to change horses, they were refreshed and more eager to hear what Fersen was telling them about everywhere they went.

He was remarkably knowledgeable concerning the names of villages through which they passed, crops being farmed along the way, recent and historical events in those parts, and even local politicians and their revolutionary or royalist tendencies.

"You see, there," he said, pointing to the charred stumps of a building next to the Seine. "That was a mill that tried to charge exorbitant prices for flour. The peasants, and, to be truthful, the rabble, didn't like it. You would think they might have chased the miller away and put the mill 'under new management,' as it were. But no. They had to burn it. And now they have to walk three extra miles to La Bouille to get their flour."

"We were told there was a famine," said Crispin. "That there was no flour."

"Ah," said Fersen. "It wasn't so much that flour was not available, as that no one could pay the price wanted for it."

"Why was that?"

"No money."

"*Pas d'espéces? Pas d'argent?*"

"No notes, no coins, no money at all."

"*Pourquoi?*"

Fersen, sitting across from Gilly gave him a strange look. "You don't know?"

"*I* can guess," said Crispin. "The treasury was empty; a great deal of it having gone to pay for the American Revolution."

"*Exact!*" responded Fersen. "Very good. How did you know?"

"I worked for newspapers in Philadelphia, New York, and Boston after the war. One learns things."

"So, your revolution led, inadvertently, to the one here."

WHEN THEY ARRIVED in La Bouille, Fersen told them they'd be staying the night. "It's about a third of the way to Paris, but tomorrow we'll make better time and have fewer vermin. We leave before dawn. Much of the way is through the Forêt de la Londe. We change horses at Caudebec. More forest. We cross the River Eure at Louviers, change horses at Gaillon, and hopefully make Vernon before dark."

"That sounds like a very long day," said Crispin.

"Our longest," said Fersen. But then we make Paris by midday on the 13th, in time for the fête on the 14th."

"*Ah, oui,*" said Gilly. "*Nous célébrons la prise de la Bastille!*" (We celebrate the liberation of the Bastille!)

Crispin frowned and turned to Gilly. "Why are you speaking only French, now?"

"And why you speak only Eenglish in America?" said Gilly, raising his voice.

"I *speak* English," said Crispin.

"*Et alors! Je parle français!*" (So then! I speak French!)

"Gentlemen," said Fersen. "What's this all about?"

They both immediately began speaking in their own language, trying to make their case.

"Please! *S'il vous plaît!*" said Fersen, over the two of them. "*Un à la fois!* One at a time."

Gilly and Crispin looked at one another and settled back into their seats. "*D'accord,*" said Gilly. "You first."

For much of the rest of the evening and into the next day, Crispin in English and Gilly in mixed English and French, told the story of their meeting, of Lewis and Gilly's escape from Chesapeake Bay, the adventure of the plums, getting back across the York River, the surrender at Yorktown...

"Where I was the drummer who beat for parley," said Crispin.

"And wee never knew until *beaucoup plus tard,* (much later)" said Gilly.

They told him about Robert Morris and their interaction

with Gouverneur Morris. Then Gilly told about his time in the boarding house in New York City and Crispin of his travels and travails in New England, his flight to Halifax and then back to New York via Ireland. By the time they reached Vernon, the next day, they understood one another much better.

"I try to speak more Eenglish weeth you," said Gilly.

"And I'll try to learn more French," said Crispin.

"But perhaps you should hold on to your English," said Fersen, grinning. "I have friends at a newspaper that longs for news from England. Would you like to have me speak to them about an employment for you?"

" 'ee also do *merveilleux* portrait *et gravure*," said Gilly.

"All the better," said Fersen.

"I would like that," said Crispin. "We can't live for long on the small amount of cash we have with us."

"Probably for many fewer days than you think," said Fersen. "Wait until you see the prices in Paris!"

But day two did not prove to be the longest day of their travels. On day three, the trip from Vernon to Paris took far longer than expected because the road was overrun with men, women, children, dogs, pigs, chickens, a few horsemen, and a small number of carriages like their own. Peasants ambled, beggars sauntered, children cavorted, thieves slithered, and soldiers – the *fédérés*, bearing banners of a few of the eighty-three *départements* into which the Assembly had recently divided France – marched. Above the prodigious uproar of the crowd the occasional flute or drum could be heard. Bottles were handed round as the mass moved forward.

"This is quite a party," said Crispin when, for a moment,

they got to a place on the road relatively free of traffic. "Is France always like this?"

"One year since the storming of the Bastille, tomorrow," said the Count. "They come for the *Fête de la Fédération!*" (Celebration of the Federation!)

Finally, just before dark, they crossed the Seine at the edge of the Boulogne Forest, on the northwest, and neared Paris.

The Count knocked on the roof of the carriage to get the coachman to stop.

"Out," he said, opening the door and by-passing the step to jump directly to the ground. Crispin and Gilly followed. He pointed ahead.

THE SQUALOR of broken down tenements, refuse running riot, filthy people, and rotting carcasses pervaded their immediate vicinity. But the slight elevation on this side of the river presented a panorama of the reddening sunlight reflecting off palaces, government buildings, church spires, and the blackened hulk of an immense stone building just beyond the mansions of Île St. Louis, straight ahead of them.

"The Bastille," he said. "What's left of it."

"*Incroyable!*" said Gilly, squinting into the distance.

More immediately obvious, however, was the profile of a burro pulling a two-wheeled wagon on top of a mountain of freshly dug dirt the height of the tallest tower of the École Militaire, just beyond it. It was followed by more burros and more wagons, depositing their loads of dirt and disappearing from sight as they turned and trotted off the top of the pile.

"*Mais,* oowhat ees that?"

"Ah, *oui,*" said the Count. "The *amphithéâtre du peuple.*"

"The what?" asked Crispin.

The Count looked over at Crispin and smiled. "At least, that's what I call it. The Convention planned a great *fête* to celebrate our new status as a republic. It is to occur right there in front of the military school, on what they're thinking of renaming the *Champ de la Réunion*. They decided to make an amphitheater for 70,000 people, but they started too late and realized the twelve-thousand or so men they hired to move the dirt couldn't do it on time. So they made a public announcement, *et voilá*! The people came. Come. I will show you a wonder."

The Count spoke to the driver and they re-entered the coach. In a short while, they left the main road, turning right on a side road that led up a hill. When they got to the top, the stage pulled up and they got out again.

Directly below them, the river slid along like a flat orange snake, carrying reflections of the fiery torches that came to life as the sun set to their right. Once they could see it more clearly, the enormous mound across the river took on a more rational shape; something like a horseshoe with the rounded end toward them.

"It's like an ant hill that a tree has fallen on," said Crispin.

Gilly laughed. "*Et* thee ants, they run *furieuxment partout!*" He looked over at Crispin. "*Pardon*, I no know thee Eenglish."

"They run furiously, everywhere," said the Count. "That is a good description. But wait until you see the crowds tomorrow!"

The Count took them to his mansion on Boulevard Cerutti where they were met at the entrance by a bevy of servants. Before going in, the Count said, "The day after tomorrow we will go to Monsieur Morris's rooms on Rue de Richelieu," he pointed east on his street, "just over there. The Bourse is near-by—and that one has everything you need." He handed his gloves to a valet and his hat to another. "I will be engaged tomorrow, but you will have no trouble finding your way to the ceremony. Be sure to arrive early if you want to see anything."

He tilted his head toward one of his servants. "Jean-Pierre will show you to your rooms."

He went his way and Crispin turned to Gilly. "The Bourse?"

"'Ees beeg market," said Gilly. "Maybee beegist in world."

EVEN INSIDE A CONSIDERABLE EDIFICE, with heavy curtains drawn, noise from gathering crowds woke Crispin much earlier than he would have liked. He poked the inert form of Gilly.

"*Touchez pas!*" came the mumbled reply. "*Endormi...*" (Don't touch! I'm sleepi...")

"Sleeping people don't say they're sleeping," said Crispin. "Can't you hear that noise?"

"*Quel bruit?*" (What noise?)

"I thought you were going to speak more English."

Gilly turned to face Crispin and sat up. "That was not Eenglish?"

Crispin rolled his eyes, shaking his head. "And we'd better get up if I am to get a good spot from which to draw."

Gilly flopped back onto the bed as Crispin opened the nearby wardrobe and began emptying the contents of his valise onto the floor.

"Ah," he said. "Here it is." He turned and held up his easel for Gilly to see. "I haven't unpacked this since New York. Today I will use it so I will have something to show the publisher when I apply for the newspaper job."

Gilly turned onto his stomach, pulled the covers over his head, and made snoring sounds.

"Hey! It's your revolution. Don't you want to celebrate?"

A great sigh was emitted from beneath the covers. "*J'n' peux pas...*" (I don't care.)

"I can't understand you," said Crispin in a sing-song voice.

"Not at thees hour in thee morning," came the grumpy reply. Nevertheless, Gilly sat up in bed and stretched.

"If you hurry," said Crispin, "you may join me for *petit-déjeuner.*"

THEY WALKED west on Boulevard Cerutti toward Le Madeleine, glancing casually into the shops. Increasingly people of every age, size, clothing style, apparent profession, and pace, joined them. The glowering clouds and constant drizzle didn't slow the pace or quiet the noise. Though the mass of people had to slow occasionally as a shopkeeper dashed out the door of his shop to hand a ham or a length of sausages or a bottle to the leader of a troop of *fédérés* marching down the street, there were no eddies or slow spots in this human river.

At Rue Royale, more noisy celebrants joined the march toward the overflowing Place de la Revolution, at whose southern end hundreds of people at once tried to squeeze onto the narrow Pont de la Révolution. Then it was turn right, past the Maison de la Révolution onto the Esplanade des Invalides, where the crowd split into a thousand directions – each person trying to find the shortest route to a seat on the muddy tiers of the new amphitheater.

Crispin held his easel close sand Gilly, walking behind him, held the large, canvas-covered, drawing pad. With the crowds shoving in every direction, it was impossible to stay on the graveled walkway. So Crispin turned, nodded at Gilly, and took off perpendicular to the main flow of the crowd. Soon they reached the southern tip of the amphitheater where Crispin clambered upward, as close to the edge as possible. When he was happy with his location, near the top on the northwest side, he set up his easel.

Almost immediately, trumpets could be heard, and drums, and the coordinated singing of troops marching from the Bastille, now along the quays of the left bank, soon into the Esplanade des Invalides, and toward the amphitheater. In front of them, making their way as a group through thousands of people jammed together on the muddy dirt floor of the amphitheater, were the hundreds of members of the National Assembly, France's current legislative body.

The overwhelming cacophony, incessant activity, and vast numbers of people had a numbing effect on Crispin until he suddenly shook himself and pointed toward the front end of the Hôtel des Invalides. "Look," he said. "There, on the white horse. That's Lafayette! And not far behind him on a chestnut is the Count."

Gilly turned in that direction, shading his forehead to keep the rain out of his eyes. Behind Lafayette and Fersen and the two-dozen or so horsemen with them, was an enormous, covered carriage drawn by six horses. "And that must be the king!"

As Gilly said that, the rain stopped. Under skies from which the clouds were quickly scudding away, hundreds of men and women in dark suits and dresses, carrying instruments from violins and cellos to flutes and bassoons to giant horns, made their way to the center of the amphitheater floor. The crowd made way and Crispin saw that chairs had been set up for them. A couple of women dressed in the king's livery were busily wiping chairs off so the orchestra could be seated.

"Oh lá, lá!" Gilly shouted to Crispin over the din. "Thees took some planning!"

But their attention was drawn from the orchestra immediately as another large group, dressed in white robes and scarves of red, white and blue, followed them into the middle of the amphitheater where it became clear, as the crowd separated, that an altar had been set up.

Crispin took his pad out of the canvas bag, set it on his easel, and began drawing furiously.

WHILE HE COULDN'T CATCH the enormity of hundreds of thousands of people singing the *Te Deum*, accompanied by the more than one-thousand instruments of the orchestra, he did manage to sketch Charles-Maurice de Tallyrand Périgord with hands raised exuberantly over his head, conducting them.

Then the Parisian National Guard, led by Lafayette—the banners of the eighty-three departments of the new France surrounding them—and the National Assembly, swore to be faithful to the nation, the law, and the king. And finally, even the king joined them at the altar along with Queen Marie Antoinette and her firstborn son, the Dauphine, who joined in affirming their intent to maintain the new constitution decreed by the National Assembly. Cries of *"Vive le Roi! Vive la Reine! Vive le Dauphine!"* arose from all over the amphitheater and the fields beyond.

And then it was over. That part, at least. Fireworks threatened their eardrums that night, and Crispin and Gilly joined the throngs in feasting and dancing and all manner of things that happen in the midst of a colossal celebration.

~

EARLY ON THE morning of July 15, despite the informal celebrations still taking place all around them, Crispin and Count von Fersen entered the make-shift office of *Amis du*

Peuple near the Place de la Victoire Nationale. This new news sheet, *Friends of the People*, benefitted greatly from the reduction of censorship brought on by the National Assembly having put a rein on the king. It could now almost tell the truth, most of the truth, and mostly the truth.

"But we are cautious," said the publisher, Monsieur Montreuse, after Crispin asked him about their status. "For example, we do not publish information such as the fact that the constitution to which the king falsely swore allegiance yesterday does not yet exist. But we do what we can."

"I leave you two together," said the Count, waving briskly and heading out the door.

"Merci, Monsieur," said the publisher, waving back.

Crispin took that moment to remove his sketch pad from its bag. "I don't know whether you do illustrations, but if you are interested, I have these."

He turned the pad toward Monsieur Montreuse, whose eyes seemed to bulge as they took in the first sheet.

"So you did this?" he asked, looking up at Crispin.

"Yes," said Crispin. He took out the few leaves of paper from the sketchpad bag on which he had written up the stories behind each sketch and held them out. "And also, this."

Monsieur Montreuse took the papers and glanced at the first page. He focused on it for a moment and then looked back at Crispin. As his gaze rose from the papers to Crispin's face it paused momentarily on Crispin's left hand.

Being used to this, Crispin grinned and said, "It was rather cool on one of my assignments and I seem to have left a couple of fingers behind."

"It doesn't hinder your drawing?"

"Well, I'm not left-handed. But look at the drawings and decide for yourself."

Montreuse stood, taking the sketchpad from Crispin and

setting it on an easel off to one side. He flipped the sheets over one after another.

"And you speak English."

"Yes, but very little French, unfortunately."

"Nevertheless," said Montreuse, looking from the sketches to Crispin and back, "I would like you to work for me. Can you do that?"

Crispin nodded. "I would like that, Sir."

"No need for 'Sir,'" said Montreuse. "We abolished all that. And, just a few days ago, the clergy as well."

Crispin raised his eyebrows, puzzled.

"*Tiens*, enough of that. I have an urgent assignment. Two, actually. Come to my office."

They walked the few feet to the only door in the room and Montreuse ushered Crispin into his office. They had scarcely crossed the threshold before Montreuse began.

"As it happens, the National Assembly, aware of the jaundiced interest being taken in our revolution by the royalty of multiple other countries, is exceedingly eager to determine what the people of other nations are thinking – particularly the ordinary people of nations in a position to oppose us. *Amis du Peuple* publishes just that sort of information – when we can get it. Can you get it?"

"I believe I can, Sir" said Crispin. "Where would you like me to start?"

"CAN your new job wait for a few days so you can accompany me back to LeHavre?" Crispin asked Gilly as he organized his clothing and art supplies on the bed.

"*Oui, je pense.*"

Crispin looked at Gilly, annoyed. "You think so?"

"Now you must learn French," Gilly said, "since you work for a *Journal Française.*"

"I'm certain you're right," said Crispin. "But I'm not going to do so between now and the 25th when I'm supposed to be in Liverpool to board a packet for Dublin."

"How you get to Liverpool that soon?"

"Not by standing here talking," said Crispin. "Want to collapse my easel for me?"

THE COMMERCIAL CARRIAGE ride to LeHavre was nowhere near as quick or pleasant as the ride to Paris had been. When they finally got there four-and-a-half days later, they went to the dockyard and saw that *Avance* was in the water. Crispin found a man just about to go fishing and Gilly found that two livres was an adequate enticement for the man to take them out to the ship.

"Ahoy, *Avance*," shouted Crispin when they arrived amidships. No response. Then they shouted it together. "Ahoy, *Avance!*" Still no response.

They had just about given up when a head popped over the railing and, with much clearing of the throat, a voice said, "Allo?"

"Lewis!" shouted Crispin. "It's me. And Gilly."

Lewis stood, buttoning his jacket. Then he ran his hand through very messy hair.

"Aren't you supposed to be in Paris?"

"Wee were in Paris," said Gilly. "I go back tomorrow. *Peut-être.* Ah, Maybee."

"And I have an assignment in Ireland," said Crispin.

Lewis appeared to look around the deck. "Guess I'll have to do this myself," he said, heaving the rope ladder over the side.

He looked down at the two friends in the boat. "If you want to get back anytime soon, you'd better have your boat stay."

Crispin nodded. He handed another livre to Gilly. "Can you ask him to stay?"

The man complained bitterly, gesticulating and whining. Crispin pulled out another livre. The man reached for it, but Gilly pulled it back.

"*Plus tard*," he said. (Later.)

The man grumbled, but tied the boat to the ladder and pulled out his rod.

"Ireland?" said Lewis as he held out his arm and pulled Crispin aboard.

Now it was Crispin's turn to look around. "No one here?"

Lewis shook his head.

"There are some groups in Ireland that want to revolt against the British. The French want to know who they are and how they can help them. They want to see revolutions everywhere!"

Lewis turned back to the rail and held out his arm to Gilly.

After Lewis had pulled Gilly aboard, Crispin looked at Lewis and said, "See what you started?"

"*I* started?"

"Joking," said Crispin. "Maybe it's just the right time. I hear there is even talk of revolution in England."

"Really?"

"I'm supposed to find out."

They decided not to say farewell. Instead, they made a plan to meet at Le Havre with the first ships in from America in the Spring of '92. So at low tide the next morning, Lewis and Gilly waved to their friend without saying 'the word.'

"See you soon," finally escaped Lewis's mouth when the packet was so far out that Crispin could not have heard him.

~

CRISPIN STOOD on the starboard side, aft, and watched France fade over the horizon. He stood on what would have been the poop deck on a naval or merchant vessel, to distance himself from the landlubbers from whom the rolling waves were stealing breakfast – amidships, below him. The crossing was notoriously unreliable, particularly from Calais to Dover. But this larger packet didn't do badly going northeast past Ramsgate and then due west into the Thames estuary. Besides which, nothing would have phased Crispin after their Atlantic crossing.

The packet stopped at Gravesend, where, with most of the other passengers, Crispin transferred to the flat-bottomed punt whose mast could be laid over in order to clear the few bridges between there and the Horse Ferry wharf near Westminster. From there Crispin took a carriage up Mill Bank and Abingdon Streets, past parliament and Whitehall, to Charing Cross. As Count Fersen had suggested, he then walked west, towards town rather to the less savory streets by the river, and found the small hotel on Cockspur Street the Count had recommended. He glanced south, over the low stables of the Carleton Guard, at just the moment when the last of the setting sun hit the steeples of Westminster Abbey.

A short, ruddy woman in an apron as large as herself, opened the door.

"Um," said Crispin, "Count Fersen..."

"Come in! Come in!" she said cheerily. "Anyone who knows the Count is a friend of mine."

He stepped in and set down his valise, sketchpad bag, and easel.

"Yee'll be wantin' your supper, then, won't ya lad," the woman said. She turned around and yelled in a surprisingly robust voice. "George! Take this here gen'man's bags up to room six. And be quick about it!"

A harried, thin young man, appeared from around a corner and rushed toward them. The woman brushed past him, gesturing to Crispin.

"I don't suppose you're off steak and kidney pie, are ye?"

"No, m'am," said Crispin, his mouth watering in advance at the thought of one of his favorite dishes that he hadn't had for ten years. Probably with his parents at home. He decided he'd rather not remember.

He followed her down the hall into the brightly lit dining room. A few of the several men sitting there nodded at him as he pulled up a chair, but most of them continued to dig into their pie. The woman bustled out of the room and returned almost immediately with a large bowl she set before him.

Ah, he thought. *Home in England. And what, do I suppose, is next? Will what I think is next really be? Or will there be more surprises like the hurricane, or going to Paris, or..."*

He gave up thinking about it and dug into his stew.

NEXT WAS the carriage to Liverpool; not that it was one carriage that would take him all the way to Liverpool. In fact, as he studied the schedule, Crispin realized he'd have to choose his towns along the way and make use of routes that would get him there most quickly, though not most comfortably.

So it was that he was assaulted with the stench of the paper factories along the Wye before he ever got to his first day's stop,

High Wycombe. The prospect approaching Oxford, the next day, was more appealing—its towers being visible a few miles before his coach entered the city, the road being lined with deep green hedges, and the occasional distant village he could see through breaks in the foliage. Besides which, since the coach was full, Crispin accepted the invitation to sit up with the driver. So he had an excellent view of parts of his homeland he'd never seen.

Early next morning, Crispin managed to catch the market wagon headed for Banbury that took them along the Cherwell. This enabled him to catch the late coach to Stratford-upon-Avon, saving an entire day. But after spending all day traveling on July 24 and getting into Birmingham after dark, Crispin realized he'd never make the packet to Dublin on the twenty-fifth that was his goal. He'd have to take another.

Thus, he decided to stay an extra day in Birmingham, testing the famous hospitality of Freeth's Coffee House in order to see what he could learn. He unexpectedly aroused some curiosity that night, as it was the meeting place and time for the Birmingham Book Club, called the Jacobin Club by its opponents, after the club in Paris where revolutionary politicians met. Locals on the other side of the political spectrum stayed away on these nights.

Club members arrived in twos and threes and eventually filled most of the seats, including those near the table where Crispin was taking his late dinner.

"So what brings you here on this night?" asked one.

"I'm traveling back home to Liverpool," said Crispin.

"From where?" asked another. It wasn't exactly an unfriendly crowd, but it seemed as though everyone in the room had hushed their own conversations and turned to stare at him.

Crispin wondered which recent location he should tell

them about, if any. Finally he opted for farther back. "From the war," he said.

"Which war?" said another.

True, he thought. England is always at war with somebody. He knew the answer to that question could determine the attitude these men would take toward him and, perhaps, even his fate. He thought about the best way to indicate the war he referred to and finally came up with, "The American War of Independence."

That silenced the room. Now he was under even greater scrutiny.

After a few moments, another said, "You're a powerful long time in coming home."

"I got my parole after Yorktown," he replied. "And then stayed on for a few years to study."

Another stood, then came up to his table, bent, and studied him.

"That's a great lie, lad," he said, "You're way too young for that."

"I was the drummer."

Mumbles and whispers filled the room.

"He was just a kid, Jake," said another, finally. "Maybe his story is true."

"So you come from America, then. Philadelphia? Boston?"

The mood was softening. "From New York, actually," he said, "via Tercera and Paris."

"Paris?" one shouted. "Why ever would you go there?"

"One of my colleagues is French. He wanted to see what their revolution was doing to his country."

Several moved chairs toward his table. Some men even got up and moved their tables and chairs closer.

"And what was it doing to his country?"

Someone stood and made a cup of his hand around his

mouth. "Johnny," he yelled. "Get some ale for this lad. Here's a tale we've got to hear!"

John Freeth, the proprieter, along with several serving girls, appeared shortly with multiple flagons of ale that instantly disappeared from the serving trays. One was set in front of Crispin.

"Now. Tell us!" Several concurring voices spoke up at the same time. Crispin took a major swallow of ale and proceeded to tell them about the amazing *Fête de la fédération*.

They were there for several hours. At last, after several had dozed and one had fallen out of his chair, the men stood to leave.

"You come in on the late coach?" asked one. "In the dark?"

Crispin nodded.

"You get you out tomorrow and look at our town. You might see a few reminders around town that others have different viewpoints."

Crispin sat until the last one had gone, and Mr. Freeth was re-arranging the chairs and tables as the girls picked up empty flagons.

Crispin asked him, "Did you hear that?"

He nodded.

"What did he mean?"

"Had ourselves a regular riot, we did, near a fortnight ago, on account'a a fella name of Priestly."

"About what?"

"You read the graffiti out there. You'll see."

"Like what?"

"Oh, like, 'destruction to the Presbyterians,' 'Church and King forever,' 'Get out, Priestly.'"

"So it wasn't these fellows that were rioting?"

"Heck, no. It was these fellows the riots were about. Seems we got those who want to keep the King and the Church just as they are—which would be most of us—and those dissenters who want any old rabble to come in here and preach whatever they like and then get rid of the king, like they did in America."

"If you disagree with them, why do you let them meet here?"

Freeth stopped what he was doing, raised up his head and laughed. "First, they drink a lot of ale." He leant down and wiped off a table. "And second, they don't do no harm. It's just talk."

"But evidently, there was more than talk a couple of weeks ago."

Freeth seemed to clam up. He didn't speak for a moment. "Can't talk about that. Crown says we have to prosecute, but that ain't going to happen. We may disagree with that lot, but we ain't puttin' them in jail."

Crispin stood up, found his coin purse, and offered a number of coins to Freeth—who looked at them appreciatively, took them, and stuffed them in a pocket.

"You have a good night, now, hear," said Freeth.

CRISPIN SLEPT UNTIL HE WOKE, not having any reason to get himself up earlier. After a full English breakfast, he grabbed his easel and paper and set out to survey the city. He got a couple of sketches of people scrubbing graffiti off their buildings, but they couldn't scrub away the remnants of the little Methodist meeting house that had been burned down.

As he passed the courthouse a trickle of men leaving became a flood until some dozens had exited. At the bottom of the courthouse steps they laughed, patted one another on the back, and began to go their separate ways. Crispin set himself discreetly among foliage in the park across the street and did a quick sketch of the scene. Then he packed up and was gone.

He got back to Freeth's in time for dinner, but it was a much calmer affair than it had been the night before. As he rose to leave, Freeth, himself, appeared.

"My thanks to you for staying with me and for, uh, entertaining the club last night."

Crispin nodded. "Glad to help, though it hadn't been my intention."

Freeth pulled out a package he'd had behind his back and handed it to Crispin. "They left this package for you while you were out, today."

"Oh?" said Crispin. "Do you know what it is?"

"They said something about Burke and Paine and you should read these. That's all I know."

Crispin glanced at the package but did not unwrap it. He reached for the sachel at his side to find coins for Freeth, but Freeth raised his left hand, palm out.

"You don't owe me anything. What you gave me yesterday—and all the ale they drank," he said, grinning, "was more than enough."

Crispin returned to his room and realized he was too exhausted to do anything but sleep tonight. He tossed the package into his bag and allowed himself to fall into the bed.

The next morning Crispin took the coach to Stoke-on-Trent. The slight bouncing of the coach as it trundled along muddy roads amidst gently undulating green countryside, nearly bereft of trees, lulled Crispin to sleep. When bedtime came he was wide awake—giving him more time than he really desired to think about what might lay ahead. Eventually, despite his dream-like re-creations of the carriage accident in which his parents had died, of his cousin throwing stones at him and his Uncle taking him to the army post, he fell asleep.

The following morning, he took the coach toward Liverpool. He was annoyed at their late start, which indeed led to a problem later as their tardiness caused them to miss the ferry over the Mersey at Runcorn. At least his final day was short. After the crossing next morning, the coach made the last fifteen miles, all the way to the Salthouse Dock in central Liverpool, by early afternoon.

He got out and stretched, then gathered his things. Not home, he thought. I won't go there. They wouldn't be glad to see me. So he picked up valise, bag, and easel, and headed west toward George's Dock and less expensive lodgings than those closer to the center of town. When he was settled, he went outside again. The odor wasn't as immense as usual, since few of the usual slave ships were in port. But the smell of fish and sweaty men and mussels boiling was just as he remembered. And the sounds of pounding in the shipyards, fishermen yelling their wares, horses clomping in front of heavy freight wagons; they were also the same.

He decided to head toward his uncle's house, after all, to see if that was still the same. He wouldn't knock or attempt to go in, but he would look at it. He walked up the west side of Kay Square, past the old dock, to Pool Lane, where he turned left. His heart beat more quickly as he turned right on King Street and approached his uncle's house—anger and fear battling for priority. The odors of baking meat and sugary puddings from the grand houses here, from one of which he had been expelled by greedy relatives, reminded him of opposite odors down by the river; the odors of the enslaved men and women from whom this wealth had come.

But, in fact, the house turned out to be different. It was falling apart. Shutters sat at angles away from windows, many of the panes he could see were broken, paint was peeling, bricks were crumbling here and there, and it looked as though someone had tried and failed to break through the great padlock keeping the door shut. Then he spied what looked like

an envelope at the top of the door, nailed just under the doorframe. He strode up the walk and the few steps to the porch.
Even reaching as far as possible, he couldn't touch the envelope
with his fingers. So he retrieved the small knife he always kept
in his sock, unsheathed the blade, and attempted to remove the
envelope.

He saw immediately that it was fragile, as it came to pieces
at the point of his knife and the pieces fluttered to the porch.
He picked them up and reconstructed the front of the envelope. His name was on it.

4

———

DIPLOMATIC MISSION

Longboats full of French sailors plied Le Havre's interior channel as Gilly and Lewis walked past the Perrei Lock and Tour François 1er back into the city. Sailors were clambering up the slippery rocks of the breakwater just as they arrived.

"Ah, thee memories," said Gilly as the two stopped to let the sailors rush by them into town.

They turned from watching them, continuing their conversation, just as a shout rang out. "Gilly! *Est-ce tu?*" (Is it you?)

Gilly stopped suddenly and turned his head around. "Luc?" He swiveled all the way around in time to collide into a bear hug with the person who had called his name. In a moment they separated.

"*Que fais-tu ici?*" (What are you doing here?)

"Que fais-*tu* ici?" said Gilly.

Luc turned and pointed at a forest of masts on the other side of the jetty. "We just got in," he said gleefully in French. "We have shore leave for two whole days!"

"Have you been to Brest?" asked Gilly.

Luc became suddenly serious. "Ah," he said, "Have *you* been to Brest?"

"I've been practically all over the world," said Gilly, "but not to Brest."

"Walk with me," said Luc.

"Oh, sorry," said Gilly. "Let me first introduce my friend, Lewis; an American."

"*Enchanté*," said Luc, extending his hand.

"Luc is one of my oldest friends from Brest," said Gilly. "We were picked up together by the impressment gang."

Luc nodded at Lewis but then he turned back to Gilly. "We must talk. Can we take a walk by ourselves?"

"That sounds ominous," said Gilly. "But Lewis may hear anything you want to tell me. He speaks French, so he will understand."

They walked east to the corner of the jetty and turned north, toward the King's Lock.

"I don't know how to tell you this," said Luc, his hands fidgeting in and out of his pockets.

"Just say it out, I guess," said Gilly.

"I'm afraid your mother died."

"Ma*man?*" cried Gilly. "But she was so strong! I thought she would live to be one-hundred!"

"*La fièvre jaune*," (yellow fever) said Luc. "It doesn't notice how strong she is."

"And Renée?"

"She lives," said Luc. "But she is not well, and her money runs out. If she does not pay the rent, she told me, she will be put out of your house. That was weeks ago."

Gilly looked to Lewis. "*Je dois y aller!*" (I must go!) Will you come with me?"

"Renée is your sister?" asked Lewis.

Gilly nodded.

"Of course!"

Gilly turned to Luc. "Only Providence could have brought us together. Thank you so much for telling me!"

Luc still fiddled with his hands.

"I would love to spend time with you during these days," said Gilly, "but you understand I must leave at once."

Luc nodded. "A packet leaves from the fleet to go to Brest this evening. Perhaps they will let you on it?"

"*Avance* has a captain now," said Lewis. "Let me see if he will ask on our behalf – and also if he will let me go."

Gilly quickly shook hands with Luc, then jogged with Lewis along the *chaussée* to the King's Lock. Within twenty minutes they were at the head of the Bas de la Barre Lock, where Lewis used his whistle to call the ship's boat. Captain Belmont was willing to let Lewis go. That evening they sailed into the sunset to try to rescue Gilly's sister.

The Rade de Brest, outside of Brest harbor, was filled with French men-of-war, as was the Port de Guerre and the Port Militaire. The city streets were filled with sailors on leave. Evidently there had not been much of an epidemic, or the city would have been in quarantine. Just a few people had died. The wrong ones, thought Gilly.

With Lewis following, he ran from the Dock Consulaire where the packet had berthed, up Rue Monge toward the Cours Dajot, on the edge of a ridge on the south of Brest, and then to the building where his family had a few rooms.

He knocked on the door to no avail. "Allô! Allô!" he cried, running down the few steps by the door and looking toward the windows on the top two stories. "*Quelqu'un là? Allô?*" (Anyone there?)

Finally a grizzled head shot out a third story window. "Quoi?" (What?)

"*C'est Gilly! Est-ce que Renée est là?*" (Is Renée there?)

"Gilly? Gilly Y'vant?"

"*Oui! Ou est Renée?*" (Where is Renée?")

"*Elle est à l'hôpital.*" (She's in hospital.)

"*Laquelle?*" (Which one?)

"*Je ne sais pas.*" (I don't know.)

Gilly headed back down the street at a run.

Lewis shouted, "*Merci!*" and ran after him.

Days later they arrived back in Le Havre. They'd scoured one hospital after another until they finally found her—not in a bed, but in an overcrowded waiting room, huddled against a wall, shivering. Gilly scrounged a blanket from one of the more sympathetic attendants, covered her, picked her up, and carried her back to the packet.

Now Lewis and a French sailor, who had met the packet with the news that *Avance* was ready to sail, watched from the east side of the *Bassin de Roi* lock as Gilly, on the west side, walked beside the palette on which two sailors were carrying her from the ship to the same hospital where JJ was recuperating. Gilly turned for a moment and waved to them. Lewis waved back, turned, and literally sprinted with the sailor down the cross-street that led to the lock of the *Bassin de la Barre* and the longboat waiting for them.

Lewis was amazed at the change in *Avance*. She now looked like a warship, not a merchant ship. The painted portholes intended to fool pirates and enemies from a distance had been made into real portholes. Toward the bow, cannon were being rolled back in and covers being shut as their boat made for the ship. They had to wait after pulling around the bow to their usual amidships entry, since other boats were arriving as well, shore boats bringing passengers. Additional passengers were already being handed up.

Lewis boarded as soon as he was able and made straight for Captain Belmont's cabin. He knocked, heard the Captain's '*Entré!*' and walked in. The Captain looked up briefly from the map he was studying, nodded once, and looked back at the map.

Not looking up again, he said in French, "As soon as the lock chamber is full, they will open the gate for us. We will be taken outside the harbor. We leave at low tide." He looked up at Lewis. "...which is at 6:07 in the morning. Check with your charges now, before the gates are opened, to be certain they have everything they need." The Captain looked up briefly. "And get into your uniform! You will have a couple of, ah, interesting charges coming on board momentarily. See to it that they are kept on the Poop, well out of the way of everyone, and that they are not allowed to examine the ship."

"Yes, Sir," said Lewis. He saluted even though he wasn't yet in uniform. He didn't know the degree of personal interaction typical of a French Captain, but since he was now an officer on a military vessel, he would assume he should interact as he would have interacted with a superior officer in the army.

"Oh," said the Captain just as Lewis opened the door. "Be certain that O'Brien's companions are disarmed. Make clear to them that if they do not surrender their weapons, they will be confined to their cabins for the entire voyage."

Lewis said "Yes, Sir," once more, closed the door quietly, and went to find the quarters for passengers – nearly bumping into a wandering passenger as he turned.

He apologized profusely in French.

"Oh, it was my fault...ah, I mean, *pardonnez moi, s'il vous plait*," the man said with a decided drawl.

"Ah. I see," said Lewis. "No need to speak French. I'm Lewis Elliot, actually, Lieutenant Elliot, but I haven't had a chance to uniform properly. How can I help you?"

The man extended his hand. "William Short, United States Chargé d'Affairs for France."

Lewis shook his hand.

"I'm afraid it's my fault you have to stop in Lisbon," said Short. "I'm to confer with our new consul there, Col. David Humphreys."

"The Humphreys who worked with General Washington?" asked Lewis.

"Do you know him?"

"He offered me a job. But since I didn't know how he could reach me or what I'd be doing, we agreed that I'd come to Lisbon to get it."

"You're American?" asked Short. "But your French is so good!"

Lewis nodded. "Comes of trying to teach Frenchmen, one in particular, to speak English."

"So are you going to take the job when we get there?"

Lewis sighed, then said, "No, I'm committed to this post until we finish our voyage. Then we'll see. But I'd very much enjoy seeing him."

"Then you certainly shall."

"In the meantime, are you looking for your cabin?"

"Yes. I'm afraid I'm deplorable with directions."

"The number?"

"I'm not good with that either. I think he told me number seven."

"Let's get you settled, then," he said. Walking aft he saw that in his short absence several tiny cabins had been erected where the crew was supposed to sleep. He shook his head. They'd have even less room than before.

"Here it is, Mr. Short," he said. "Have a pleasant voyage."

LEWIS DRESSED QUICKLY in his new uniform, not certain that he really needed the sword at his side – particularly since he didn't know how to use it. But he decided he must wear it to play his part. He hurried up on deck, motioned to a couple of French marines standing near the mainmast, and arrived at the rail just in time to see a grizzled man in a merchant captain's uniform surmounting it, followed immediately by two characters Lewis never expected to see on a French ship.

What he saw first were the turbans. Then the massive beards on dark faces, linen robes decorated with bright vertical sashes which were criss-crossed by harnesses for a massive sword and a musket, three thick leather braces on their lower right arms, and wide leather belts around their waists, beneath which were at least one curved dagger sporting an ornate hilt, and a couple of powder horns.

"Greetings, Captain O'Brien," said Lewis. "Your companions must be disarmed."

The merchant captain turned to face the two men and said something to them in a language Lewis did not understand. Their hands went immediately to their swords, and Lewis backed slightly to stand between the marines whose rifles were trained on them. They lowered their hands.

"Their weapons will be returned when they leave the ship," said Lewis. "If they will not give them up peaceably, they will be confined to their cabins."

O'Brien turned to Lewis and said in English, "I believe that if you leave them their *jambiyas*, they will comply. But if you try to take those, it may be the beginning of an international incident."

Lewis tilted his head at O'Brien, who said, "Their daggers."

"Fine," said Lewis. "But the two of them will be separated from one another and accompanied by a marine at all times when not in their quarters—which will be guarded."

O'Brien nodded and turned back to them. He spoke in a language at once guttural and smooth. The one with a larger, more colorful, turban nodded once. Then both removed their musket and large sword and handed them to the marines.

"Thank you," said Lewis to O'Brien. "How do you say 'thank you' in the language you're using?"

"You don't," said O'Brien. "The corsairs would see it as a sign of weakness. But I will welcome them to the ship on your behalf."

"Excellent. Please do so."

O'Brien turned and said something else and the senior one, looking straight ahead and not at Lewis, again nodded once.

"I'll show you to your quarters," said Lewis. He turned, followed by O'Brien, the two corsairs, and the two marines. He was now glad of the sword at his side. The fact that he had his and the corsairs did not have theirs was some comfort. And, he realized, it was an important part of the game they played to see who was superior to whom.

"YES," said Short, as he, O'Brien, and Lewis chatted by the taffrail. "I have heard the sorry tale of the *Dauphine* and its crew. My superior, Mr. Thomas Jefferson, is most concerned about you and them."

"But there has been nothing you could do," said O'Brien, not hiding the bitterness in his voice.

"Not having a navy, nor even the protection of someone else's navy, anymore," said Short.

"Which," said Lewis, "is why we are all on a French naval vessel."

They were greeted by gulls once more as they came closer to land at the south extent of the Bay of Biscay. The silhouette of Cape Finisterre loomed in the distance, all black and rugged, as the southerly sun made its way westward.

Lewis had been trying to lessen the tension between Short and O'Brien since they had begun conversing, just past Ushant Island, as the British called it. With this new shore coming into view and the birds screeching, Short said his good-byes and left for his cabin.

"I haven't heard the story," said Lewis, though he had heard something about it.

Rather than telling him the story, O'Brien only nodded and looked out at the western horizon. "It's never anyone's fault," he said, "but no one is able to help."

Lewis nodded but could think of nothing to say. He turned and glanced inland, chancing to see the corsairs on the poop deck, about fifteen feet apart, each with his marine. He wondered how long it would take for one of them to slit the throat of an unsuspecting marine with his *jambiya*, which Lewis had no doubt they could do and *would* do if the circumstances were right. And how many American vessels would have to be taken, and how many American sailors would have to endure slavery, before someone did something? He came to a sudden realization. He might be someone who could do something. But how would he go about it? An idea crept into his mind.

He turned back to O'Brien. "You seem to know their language well. Do you suppose you could teach me?"

O'Brien turned from surveying the horizon. "Do you know any languages other than English?"

"French and Spanish," said Lewis.

O'Brien sized him up. Then nodded. "Arabic is very different. Do you think you can do it?"

"I'm certain of it, Sir."

"Then I will teach you. But I will not be easy on you. We do not have much time."

Lewis nodded. "I learn quickly," he said.

LEWIS AND O'BRIEN commandeered a spot at the starboard taffrail, and by the time they had passed Grande Berlengas and neared the outlet of the Tagus River, where Lisbon was situated, Lewis had learned the basic structure of verbs, of word order, and of polite speech. When he could be alone in his cabin with a little time to spare, he began practicing how to write Arabic.

When O'Brien was below deck, Lewis interacted with William Short. "The *Dauphine* was captured in 1785," said Short.

"That long ago?"

"Yes, and with little prospect of freeing the twenty or so sailors now being used as slaves for maybe another five – and not even then if we don't get a navy."

"Why isn't O'Brien a slave?"

"Oh, he is," said Short, nodding towards the corsairs on the other side of the ship. "But they let him go out, under guard, to try and raise money for the ransom. I hear he's had some success with the Habsburgs and the Dutch."

"Not the French?"

"They have no money. So now he will talk to Humphreys and then to the Portuguese to see if they will help."

That evening *Avance* traded salutes with *Forte de São Julião de Barra* some miles south of Lisbon. She moored several hundred feet out from it, waiting for high tide to carry them in against the current of the Tagus River. By about 9AM they picked up the pilot and were able to begin cruising east. As the river mouth narrowed, the hills of Lisbon, with their white-washed, coral-roofed buildings, became visible. In addition, evidence of the 1755 earthquake was still abundant, naked columns and piles of rubble filling wide gaps between newer construction. Even from the waterfront, the new city structure was evident in the wide boulevards and straight commercial avenues stretching inward from the *Praça do Commercio* where they would berth.

The 1788 smallpox epidemic had made the city cautious of visitors, and *Avance* had to wait a few hundred feet from her berth while the *médico* came onboard, ostensibly to examine the crew. Proof of being disease-free proved to be fairly expensive, and the médico's departure saw Captain Belmont shaking his head and frowning. At length, *Avance* was towed in to her berth and disembarking commenced.

She was met by the exuberant Col. Humphreys who embraced Mr. Short and shook Captain O'Brien's hand enthusiastically. Lewis saw his glance pass by him superficially, and then suddenly return. "Mr. Lewis?" said Humphreys.

"In the flesh," said Lewis, smiling.

"And in a French uniform! I'm certain there's a story there."

Lewis nodded.

Captain O'Brien's corsair companions strode down the gangway at that point, and everyone at the end got out of their way. Humphreys ignored them and turned to walk inland with Short and O'Brien, corsairs following. After a moment, he turned back.

"Mr. Elliot, are you not coming?"

Lewis turned to Captain Belmont who nodded his head.

"Yes, Sir," he said, walking as fast as possible while maintaining some semblance of dignity. He soon caught up with them, and the six of them disappeared into the Rua Augusta.

~

THE NEARBY PALACE Square hosted a café, *Martinho de Arcada*, run by an Italia—which meant it would have the best coffee in the city, or so the garrulous proprietor was loudly proclaiming to a customer in broken English.

"We'd better rescue him," said Humphreys, hastening to the table and greeting the proprietor in Italian as though he was his best friend. The proprietor, who obviously knew Humphreys, raised the volume of his new dissertation, threw up his hands in greeting, and might have succeeded in hugging Humphreys had he not sat, suddenly, beside the man first accosted.

"Barlow!" he said, reaching over to shake the man's hand. "So glad you could get here!"

"Gentlemen," he said, turning to Lewis, Short, and O'Brien—who had just escaped custody by leaving his corsairs outside the door—"one or two of you, at least, may know my friend Joel Barlow."

Barlow stood and reached over Humphreys to shake Short's hand. "William Short!" he said. "I'd not expected to see *you* here!"

"Nor I, you," said Short. "But it's a pleasant surprise."

Then he reached out to O'Brien. "Now, Humphreys did tell me that you'd be here. It's a pleasure to see you after hearing so much about you."

He looked to Lewis.

"I'm Lewis Elliot, who somehow managed to be part of this unusual entourage."

"And, as I said," said Humphreys, "there must be a story there—as the last time I saw Mr. Elliot, he was First Mate on an American merchant ship run up to Tercera for repairs."

"Well, I'm sure you're not here to talk about me," said Lewis, following the other two in sitting on the bench opposite Humphreys and Barlow.

"Well, no, actually," said Humphreys. "But later!" He turned back to the others. "I wanted to get you all together because, Barlow, here, as you know, Short, is a friend both of Jefferson and of the National Assembly there in France. Besides, he's a businessman who does quite well and..." at this point he looked to O'Brien, "he might be able to connect you to a source of funds."

O'Brien nodded.

"If you don't mind, I'm going to send him with you to Madrid to see my friend, Carmichael, and see if he's placed to get some help from the Spanish crown."

O'Brien tipped his head at Humphreys as if to ask a question, which Humphreys intercepted. "Oh, I know what you're thinking. What about the Portuguese crown? Well, they don't even have funds to repair the damage from an earthquake and tsunami that took place thirty-five years ago. In addition, they have their own current arrangements with the Barbarys, and are not likely to include us in future negotiations, much less help us out of the trouble we're already in."

Coffee came, along with a tray of *Pastel de nata*. Humphreys looked at the tray and then toward Lewis. "I would have ordered more had I known you were coming!"

"How I long for a bowl of *café au lait*!" said Barlow, before taking a sip from the diminutive cup. He then sipped. "But this is not bad!" Which, evidently, was the signal that everyone should imbibe. So it was silent for a few moments.

Lewis surveyed the group. Sitting across from him in the dim light is David Humphreys, Washington's trusted assistant and now consul to Portugal—certainly the most senior person here, with the most authority. On his right is William Short, Jefferson's trusted assistant and now *Chargé d'Affaires* of the U.S. Mission to France—no doubt awaiting appointment as the actual Consul. On the other side of Short is Richard O'Brien, Captain of the *Maria* and negotiator for the sake of American sailors enslaved by the Algerian pirates while still a slave himself. Then, beside Humphreys, is Joel Barlow. Lewis hadn't actually figured him out yet. Evidently a businessman whom William seemed to know from France—which assumption was buttressed by Barlow's yearning for *café au lait*. But what his role would be, Lewis didn't know—unless he had a lot of cash he could use to help ransom the sailors.

And then there was himself. He felt like an imposter. Because, for the second time, he was wearing a Lieutenant's uniform he hadn't earned. In both cases he'd been given the uniform—along with the rank, he supposed—because it was necessary for the mission. The rank would last as long as he wore the uniform. No longer. And certainly he was the youngest one there, with the possible exception of Barlow.

What am I doing here? he asked himself. He was comfortable, though, the others seemed to accept him, and he liked what he was doing. He liked being part of this discussion.

Which, he realized suddenly, as Humphreys rose from his seat, was ending. Lewis stood as well, and the others, as Humphreys called the proprietor over and paid him. When they were outside, Humphreys spoke.

"Gentlemen, Mr. Barlow will lead you to my office over on

Rua das Pedras Negras. I'd like to spend some moments with Lieutenant Elliot."

Lewis's eyebrows raised involuntarily, but he fell in step with Humphreys as they headed in a different direction from that taken by Barlow and the others. They walked for a few blocks in silence until Humphreys led Lewis through a door in an overly high wall that ended at the side of a building which seemed to be a church.

"Church of the Convent of San Francisco," said Humphreys, "a quiet place to talk."

Lewis turned his face toward Humphreys, head tilted.

"It looks peaceful here in Lisbon," said Humphreys. "But you'd be surprised at the number of foreign agents around, all attempting to find ways to promote their agendas at the expense of yours. And I have a proposition for you I'd just as soon none of them heard."

Lewis's innards jumped at that. *Maybe this is the answer to what I should do with my life,* he thought.

They entered the massive church, dim and cool inside, feeling somehow infused with an aura of holiness, and Humphreys led them to a pew. Before going in and sitting, Humphreys circumflexed and bowed his head toward the altar. He nodded at Lewis to do the same. After he had done so, Humphreys moved into the pew with Lewis following.

"You're not Roman Catholic, are you?" asked Lewis.

"No, but even in this murky light, there are eyes watching. It calls attention to ourselves if we do not do that. Besides, I worship God," he turned to face Lewis, "and there's only one God, and I have no problem with that gesture of respect."

"Is religion a big issue here?" Lewis asked.

Humphreys nodded. "And more-so now, with the French having secularized the clergy and confiscated church property and lands."

Humphreys looked up toward the altar. Lewis followed his gaze, and saw a priest followed by acolytes or nuns, he couldn't tell which, going about their business there.

Then Humphreys looked back at Lewis. "I'd like to appoint you as my assistant *now*," he said.

"But..."

"I know. You must finish this mission. You can work for me at the same time you work for the French, though. And you'll need credentials for the task I have in mind for you."

"Yes, Sir?" said Lewis.

"I need you as a courier. A courier no one is likely to suspect. When we get to my office, I'll let you look over and sign the contract. Then I'll give you the special clothing and devices used to hide messages. I had this in mind for you when..."

"You were behind this voyage and my role in it?"

Humphreys said nothing, but the expression on his face was answer enough.

"You'll get to Tripoli with my friend, James Cathcart, whom you'll pick up in Madrid. And then, when he's assessed the situation there, you'll have to get back to New York with a dispatch for Jefferson—who's now Secretary of State, as you may know—so he can make a report to the congress. This mission is of the utmost importance. Can you do it?"

Lewis had no idea how he would do it, but he simply determined he would.

"Yes, Sir. I will do it."

There. Decision made, Lewis thought. *I'm going into diplomacy.*

"Good. I thought I could rely on you."

Humphreys stood. "Now let's get to my office. You're leaving on the tide very early tomorrow morning."

AT DAWN, two days later, *Avance* passed Tarifa at the southernmost point of Spain, where the Castle of St. Catalina sat on a hillock, its silhouette showing against the rising sun. They entered the Straits of Magellan having seen few Barbary vessels, and the ones they had seen gave them a wide berth. By afternoon, the forest of masts at the battered British port of Gibraltar could be seen on their larboard side, dwarfed by the 'rock' itself, rising like the sharp head of a hatchet out of the sea.

They rounded Gibraltar without stopping, heading mostly east into that part of the Mediterranean called the Alboran Sea, and then northeast to the Balearic Sea and Valencia. The sea part of their journey proved to be uneventful. This meant that Lewis had more time to study Arabic with Captain O'Brien, but not much time to enjoy the scenery.

That changed after they landed at Valencia. They now had more than two-hundred miles to travel to Madrid, rising nearly three-thousand feet through mountainous terrain. Lewis, Barlow, O'Brien, and his two corsair guards left *Avance* in the harbor on August 20, and began the dusty, sweltering, stinging-fly-infested ride. O'Brien and Lewis agreed that continuing to study Arabic in the tiny confines of the coach would, at the least, be annoying to the other passengers—even if they were only members of their party. So Lewis did watch the scenery here, which soon proved to be unrewarding as it was mostly sparsely-vegetated rocky hills, only seldom interspersed with Roman ruins and stopping places. With the sun beating down on their already hot carriage, the only solution was to remove their coats, close the flaps on the sunny side, and attempt to rest.

It was so hot that the horses had both to stop and to be changed more often than Lewis was used to, though he didn't mind getting out of the stuffy coach. O'Brien's corsairs, on horseback, kept their distance—one in front of the carriage and one after it—only approaching it more closely when stopping to change horses or for the night. Lewis had no idea where they went at night, but he was pretty sure there was no point in O'Brien trying to escape—which he didn't want to do, anyway, out of fear for his men.

Coming into Madrid from slightly north of west, they had only to cross the ford at the little Rio Jarama, and not the broader Rio Manzanares to the northeast. Sunlight glinted off spires and turrets deep within the city, as well as off the Guadarrama Mountains behind them.

Lewis was reminded of his introduction to the study of Spanish with Señor Rendón. He grinned as he remembered his embarrassment on discovering that while the Spanish language did not have the single-volume dictionary he had arrogantly thought unlikely, it did have a seven-volume dictionary. Why he had assumed the Spanish would be backward or uncivilized, he could not fathom. He sighed. It was just a prejudice he had, undoubtedly along with many others he would have to discover and dispose of. But this city, rising up before them, was to Philadelphia—America's largest city—what the Spanish dictionary was to Samuel Johnson's single volume. It was immense, overwhelming. Lewis hoped someone in their party knew how to find William Carmichael's house, which he assumed was where they were going – or, better still, that Carmichael might be there to meet them.

They came into Madrid from the *Calle de Valencia y Cartegna*, then down the *Calle do Atocha* to *Plaza Mayor*, weaving through a maze of horses and carriages, vendors with handcarts, and market stalls, with little boys and beggars following hot after them, until they stopped at a large hotel. Opening the carriage door, Lewis felt a re-doubling of the assault to his nose of offal, cooking, unwashed people, and other unnameable calamities, as well as an immensely increased barrage of noise from all directions.

As it happened, they were met by the two Josés, Don Diego's aides with whom Lewis and another of John Jay's clerks had wrestled their way to an impasse rather than a treaty a few years before. Lewis saw them as soon as he stepped down from the carriage and strode over to one, José Ignacio, holding out his hand. José Ignacio shuffled back slightly until a broad smile filled his face.

"Lewis?" he shouted, in English. "In a French officer's uniform?" He took the proffered hand, shook it vigorously, and then let it go in time for José de Jaudenes to take it.

"You know these people?" yelled Barlow over the surrounding noise.

"We spent many a day and night working together," cried Lewis, "uselessly attempting to draft something that would please both sides. The sides were not reconciled, but we became friends."

"Both *sides*?"

"John Jay for the Americans, Don Diego de Gardoqui y Arriquibar for the Spanish."

"You know Jay?" asked Barlow.

Lewis nodded. "Yes, but right now let me introduce you to my friends so we can get away from this place."

"Please get into our carriage," shouted José Ignacio, pointing to a massive conveyance with four proportionately monumental horses, standing some yards away. "We can make introductions there."

THEY TRAVELLED, then, in a luxurious coach accommodating four to a seat with liveried coachmen on top, front and back.

The coach drove them not to Carmichael's house, but north-west to Don Diego's Madrid residence, stopping all traffic on the *Calle de Guadalajara* to get across—corsairs following on their horses. His house fronted on the *Plaza Saõ Diego*, encompassing an entire side of the trapezoidal plaza. They passed in front of the house, turned left immediately, then drove a hundred feet forward before turning left again and entering a great courtyard through an equally great door that was shut as soon as they were through.

Servants opened the carriage doors almost before it stopped.

"You will pardon, I hope," said José de Jaudenes, "our coming in the back way instead of the front. Don Diego instructed us to be careful."

"What will become of my corsairs?" asked Captain O'Brien.

"They will stay out here with the servants," said José Ignacio.

Several groomsmen were trying to get the corsairs to dismount so the horses could be cared for, but both had drawn their swords and were backed up to the door, waving the grooms away.

"You should send a higher servant to talk with them," said O'Brien, "or they will be offended."

Captain O'Brien walked to a spot between the horses, speaking to his corsairs in a language Lewis was beginning to grasp. He said something like, "They are not enemies. They will care for your horses and for you. I give my word that I will not attempt to escape."

With that, the corsairs reluctantly sheathed their swords and dismounted. Lewis turned his attention to the house.

"*Pero Señora...*" (But Mistress...) squealed a loud woman's voice just inside the largest door at the back of the house.

It was thrown open. "*¡Disparates!*" came the startlingly bright reply. "*¡Soy la señora aquí y los saludaré!*" (Nonsense! I am Mistress here and I will greet them!)

The horses were led swiftly away as the owner of the second voice came through the doorway, and Lewis's glance lit upon the most beautiful woman he had ever seen. With both hands, she held her lavish gown above the courtyard dirt as she rushed toward them with an alacrity both surprising and graceful.

"*Por favor,*" she said in a clear voice as smooth and unflustered as pure Madiera, "*Ven comigo.*" (Please, come with me.)

She then spied Lewis in his French officer's uniform and said, "*Oh, pardonez moi, Monsieur. S'il vous plait, venir avec moi.*" (Oh, pardon me, Sir. Please, come with me.)

His mouth fell open. His feet were paralyzed. He was overcome by her perfect, glowing profile, her sable hair, the blazing eyes she turned on him, eyes in a stunning face wearing an expression just short of laughter.

"Don't mind Isabella, Lewis," said a male voice in English from behind the young woman. All heads in Lewis's party turned to the source of the voice, where an elegantly attired, middle-aged Spanish gentleman appeared.

Lewis recovered himself enough to bow slightly. "Don Diego," he said.

Don Diego tipped his head minutely. "Her mother died some years ago, so my lovely daughter serves as the hostess of our little *refugio de la ciudad.*" (refuge in the city.)

Don Diego looked at her fondly, though her hands were on her hips and she had turned to glare at him.

"I believe your Mr. Jefferson had somewhat the same arrangement in Paris," he said.

Lewis glanced back at Isabella, who looked as though she might have quite a few words to say to her father later about

Jefferson and his daughter and their arrangement in Paris. But instead, she turned toward the house. "*Caballeros, Monsieur?*" she said.

Don Diego said softly, in Spanish, "You needn't speak French to Lewis, *Tesoro* (Treasure). He speaks Spanish. And English as well, as you have seen."

She flounced slightly, ignoring her father, and led them toward the house.

Lewis watched, transfixed, as everyone else followed her. Until her father, with a grin, said, "Lewis?"

Lewis started. "*Sí!*" he said, and he walked toward the door after Don Diego and several servants.

5

THE MEDITERRANEAN

After entering the back door, they marched along a grand hallway to the front of the house where they turned right into a far more opulent hallway. The front windows illuminated the far wall, on which hung multiple life-sized portraits of people Lewis thought must be Don Diego's ancestors. They turned right again, where the gallery ended, and entered a smaller hallway with doors on both sides. Isabella led them to the second door on the right, knocked softly, and it was opened from the inside by a servant. She turned toward the party, stood by the door, curtsied ever-so-slightly, pointing inside, and said, "*Caballeros, Monsieur.*"

Lewis entered, last in the group, attempting unsuccessfully to gaze at Isabella without her noticing. That is, he gazed at her and didn't want her to notice. When he realized she was looking straight at him, he turned quickly away. His face felt hot and his hands sweaty, but he was pretty confident she hadn't noticed that, at least. *Who am I fooling?* he thought. *She must be having herself a good laugh.*

He tried to keep from grinning at her slight affront to Don

Diego, continuing to call him Monsieur. But all levity drained away as he entered the... what? Audience chamber? It was as massive and cool as a cave, only slightly illuminated by the little light allowed in by the mostly-closed velvet curtains. The outside light was helped slightly by two enormous candelabras – with only a few of their multitude of candles burning – hanging over a wooden table that would not have fit in John Jay's conference room in New York even had all the other furniture been removed.

"If you will be so kind as to wait just a few moments," said José Ignacio in perfect English, "refreshments will be coming. Don Diego hopes you will accept his poor hospitality and remain with us for the duration of your stay. He will be in momentarily. You may be seated at the table or on the couches-" which Lewis now noticed, lined the wall opposite the windows, "whichever better suits your comfort."

Lewis took a seat at the table, from which he could survey the entire room. He felt as though Don Diego's 'haven in the city' had the solidity of a mountain, its walls being of stone, its windows held together with lead, the gravitas of its monstrous furniture further keeping it from sliding. It was settled for all time on that spot. He, on the other hand, felt as fragile and evanescent a dandelion puff. How could one short encounter with a young woman so radically undo him?

He shook his head, as if that would clear it, and dragged his thoughts to the meeting which lay ahead. Clearly this was planned in advance, but what were they trying to accomplish? What difference would what they did here make to anything? With a rueful smile, he recalled the months of 'negotiations' Don Diego and John Jay had endured in New York, with him, Benjamin (Jay's clerk), and the two Josés, writing up mountains of documents. No wonder they had gotten nowhere. These people knew what they wanted. They'd been warring for centuries—maybe millennia—to get it. And they knew *how* to get what they wanted. America, on the other hand...

He didn't bother to finish the thought, but the word 'upstart' came to mind unbidden. Still, if we Americans are upstarts, we're upstarts who have accomplished something. And now it seems as though some of the world is following. Though, as Lewis thought about it, it occurred to him that *this* country and *this* household would not wish themselves to follow America.

THE DOOR WAS OPENED ALMOST SILENTLY and two servants entered, standing one on each side. Don Diego entered then, followed immediately by two men dressed as American gentlemen, followed in turn by numerous servants bearing trays of food, coffee and tea service, bottles of wine, and too many other things for Lewis to identify.

"Gentlemen," said Don Diego. "May I present Captain James Cathcart, formerly of the *Maria*, and Mr. William Carmichael, newly in Spain to promote the cause of the United States—unofficially, of course, until his credentials arrive."

Don Diego gestured toward the room, facing the newcomers. "Gentlemen," he said, "I hope you will enjoy the acquaintance of Captain Richard O'Brien, formerly of the *Dauphine*, Mr. Joel Barlow, businessman and friend extraordinaire of Mr. Thomas Jefferson, and Lieutenant Lewis Elliot, onetime clerk to Mr. John Jay, and currently in the employ of Mr. David Humphreys, United States Consul to Portugal.

Everyone stood. Handshakes and polite greetings were exchanged.

Lewis wondered how Don Diego knew so much. He shook his head slightly. Is this what it is to be a diplomat? Somehow to gather news about what's happening everywhere, who's doing what, and where everything in the world is heading, so one can use it to one's advantage? If so, Don Diego was certainly gracious about it. But he was deadly serious about achieving his desired outcomes.

They were soon seated, making small talk over the refreshments. When that was completed, Don Diego called them to order.

"It is most fortuitous that you are all here," he said. "I believe we can help one another in such a way as each to achieve our goals."

He began to share an overview about the situation with the Barbary pirates, their depredations to shipping, but also their raids on the continent to capture men and women—women especially—for their slave markets. He shared his distaste for the treaties made with them by the 'powers,' England, France, Spain, Denmark, the Netherlands, and now, perhaps, the United States.

"What they need is a show of force!" he said. He looked at Lewis, "As your wise Mr. Jefferson has suggested. Though, sadly, you haven't the wherewithal to carry it off."

He was just warming to his subject when interrupted by a servant who merely came and stood by his side. Don Diego turned to the servant who spoke softly to him in a language unlike anything Lewis had heard before.

Lewis thought back to his study of Spanish in Señor Rendón's library, where he had also learned something about Spain's geography and history. He realized with a start that the language must be of the Basque people, though he didn't know what it was called. Don Diego was from Bilboa, a city in the Basque region. He nodded to himself. Yes, Don Diego would not want his Basque servants thinking about independence, nor would the king of Spain wish to see Catalans, or other groups now subsumed into the Kingdom of Spain, thinking about independence. That had to be at least one of the undercurrents of this meeting. No diplomatic meeting would be without undercurrents as well as a number of unspoken agendas.

"Gentlemen," Don Diego cut into Lewis's thinking. "My daughter reminds me that some of you have had a long journey and may wish to rest before dinner. We dress for dinner here and begin promptly at half-past ten o'clock. I think we can complete a small amount of business now and then let you depart to rest or freshen up, or whatever you wish. Evening wear has been provided for you in each of your rooms, and you are free to ask the servants for anything else you may require."

Don Diego again summarized the situation in the Mediterranean, suggested the topics of their discussions over the next few days, and dismissed them. They were led by servants, each to a room of his own on the second floor.

Lewis turned his head this way and that, trying surreptitiously to catch a glimpse of Isabella, should she be near. She never was, but he consoled himself that she would, most likely, be the hostess at dinner. But ten thirty? He hoped he'd be able to stay awake.

Lewis would not have known how to put the fussy clothes on, nor would he have been happy to be seen in them by his Virginia relatives—who would certainly have thought them pretentious. And a wig? But, after the servant had assisted him in dressing and he was able to view himself in the largest mirror he had ever seen, he felt somewhat satisfied with the outcome. This might be a better visage to present to the wondrous Isabella, should, of course, she have any interest in having his visage presented to herself, or acknowledging his existence by anything more than calling him by the language of his assumed country of origin.

He shook his head. "What am I thinking?" he said aloud, in English. The servant looked at him. "Señor?"

"*Nada*," said Lewis. "*¡Lo siento!*" (Nothing. Sorry!)

He headed out his bedroom door and toward the stairs, the servant following.

DINNER WAS a lovely affair on handsome French dinnerware with gold Spanish cutlery, replete with the Spanish cuisine Lewis had tasted at Señor Rendón's home as well as other dishes he had not seen before. His attention, however, was not on the setting or the food. The lovely Isabella presided in glory, tossing conversational tidbits in English to each and every man at the table (with the exception of her father, of course). So the conversation moved smoothly enough until Lewis received one of her openings.

She had just listened to Barlow present a light and, from Lewis's perspective, largely imaginary, recitation concerning the events in France, and now she asked Lewis what he thought.

"I can't rightly say much about what may be happening all over France," he said. "I can share only what I have observed."

"And what, precisely, is that, Lieutenant?" she asked in a tone he suddenly realized was mocking him. Lewis found himself annoyed by that tone, despite the beauty of the speaker. He decided to give an answer that might, somehow, equalize the social superiority she seemed to think her status as the daughter of a Don allowed her.

"The peasants are starving," he said. A stunned silence filled the room, but Lewis continued on, doggedly. "They would have boarded our ship and stolen our cargo of flour had we not already unloaded it at a very poor price to the authorities—so they could sell it to those same peasants at an impossible price." Then he then realized what he had done in his moment of ire and looked to Don Diego with a stricken face.

Don Diego wiped his mouth with a large *serviette*. Lewis waited in desperate suspense to see the outcome of his gaffe, but slowly perceived that Don Diego was laughing behind the napkin.

Don Diego pulled it down and let everyone see his smirk as he eyed his daughter. The tension in the room diminished remarkably as he said, "I like someone who tells the truth."

Isabella stood abruptly. "As there are no other ladies present," she said in a flat, dangerous voice, "I shall retire. You *caballeros*"— and here she glared at Lewis with those flashing, deep brown, eyes—"are invited to the library where port and cigars are served." Then she turned, lifted her chin, and made her deliberate way out.

No more 'Monsieur,' thought Lewis. Well, any chance I may have stupidly thought I might have with her is certainly gone now.

To BEGIN WITH, the meetings were mostly about pirates. Of course, that meant they were about the slavery O'Brien's and Cathcart's crews were enduring—to the extent that they were actually enduring it, because several men from each crew had already died. O'Brien shared what he knew about the Dey of Algiers and the British Consulate there where he had been allowed to work. Cathcart discussed the Bashaw of Tripoli, his treacherous and murderous dealings with his family—particularly his brother, the rightful heir—and the prospects for peace with him.

Don Diego gave an overview of the Spanish dealings with the Barbary states. Barlow piped in now and then about how grand the French Revolution was. Lewis had no report to make, but he became a careful observer. He noticed the tension developing between Barlow and Don Diego, of which Barlow seemed blissfully unaware. For some reason, inexplicable to Lewis, Cathcart seemed to have taken a dislike to O'Brien. At least he was abrupt in his speech and dismissive of what O'Brien said. It was not a happy table.

And Lewis wasn't particularly happy, either, although he relished being a part of these discussions. But he kept thinking about what he'd said at dinner the first night. Isabella had not deigned to reappear after that, and he wondered if he could really have offended her that much.

He was heading back to his room for a rest after an acrimonious meeting, thinking about Isabella and what he had said, when he said, "But it was true!" He hadn't meant to say it aloud, but apparently he had because a response came from behind him.

"But one needn't *say* everything that is true!" It was Isabella's voice.

Lewis spun around to see Isabella and two of her maids in the hallway behind him, not twenty feet away. She stood straight as a pole, though a pole leaning forward, hands on hips.

"Why did you 'umiliate me?"

What is the correct answer to that, Lewis wondered. He hadn't meant to humiliate her, but she had provoked him by her way of making him feel like a little boy who amused his mother. He thought of asking, Why did you mock me?

But when he looked carefully at her, he decided against it. Yes, the deep brown pools of her eyes that he could have fallen into were all aswirl with lava. And her chin was pointed belligerently at him. But he sensed a fragility in her, nevertheless; a keeping up of appearances rather than an inherent shrewishness.

He looked her in the eyes, and then lowered his eyes, bowing his head slightly. "I'm sorry."

He raised his head, then, and looking back up at her, was startled to see a tear at the corner of one eye. It was as if she had been leaning into the wind and the wind had stopped abruptly. Evidently, that was not the response she had expected.

Lewis stood there awkwardly for a moment, wondering what to say next. It occurred to him what Don Diego had said when he and the others had just gotten out of the coach. It was a gamble. Maybe she wouldn't want to talk about it, but he said it anyway, very quietly.

"I heard that your mother died."

Lewis feared that he had misstepped again when she didn't respond for a few seconds.

"It was a long time ago," she said, finally, equally softly. "I hardly remember her now." She turned to her maids, shooing them backwards with a gesture, then turned back and took a few steps toward Lewis. She looked at him differently now, and though she still leaned forward, it was in an enquiring way, her eyes soft and looking into his.

"But you were sad?" asked Lewis.

"*Muy triste*," she said, (very sad) seeming distracted.

Lewis realized she must have transitioned back to Spanish out of deep feeling, and a lump formed in his throat.

"And you?" she asked.

Lewis exhaled through his nose, looked back into those eyes, and said, "Yes, mine, too."

"And *you* were sad?"

"I was *furious!*" said Lewis, hands clenching into fists. "It was because she had been hurt horribly by a British soldier slamming the end of his musket into her back. Later, when we were taking her body to the cemetery, I tackled a British officer who walked past the wagon. I almost got myself and my cousin killed."

Isabella stepped even closer and slowly raised an outreached hand, almost as if she would touch his face. But then she seemed to think better of it. She did examine him intensely, though. "Do you think we could talk?"

"I would love that," said Lewis, looking at her lovely face, wondering how this state of affairs had come about.

She stepped back and straightened. "I can't go out alone, and no one ever comes here," she said. "I mean, no young people ever come. It is only father's friends and colleagues. I never have anyone to talk with."

"But do you really want to talk with me?"

"Why would I not?"

"I'm a *man*. Wouldn't you rather talk with a woman?"

She got that pert look on her face she had worn when coming to greet the coach. She turned her head quickly this way and that, then turned her body right and left, arms extended. Coming back to face him she said, "Do you see any?"

Lewis looked past her shoulder, straight ahead, nodding slightly, eying the maids behind her.

She took his meaning. "Sometimes men are not very smart," she said, the corners of her lips raising only enough to create dimples Lewis had not noticed before. "How could I really talk with them? They are in terror of losing their position—not that they ever would. And, they have no education. No experience. What would we talk about?"

"Will your father not object?"

"Never fear," she said, a twinkle coming into those eyes, along with a grin on her lips. "My maids will be present. I will not be allowed to bewitch you."

"That's a relief," said Lewis, at which she laughed out loud, a musical sound. She turned and gestured for the maids to come back. She pointed at the taller one. "Sophia will call for you at your room in one-half hour. You will not mind meeting me for tea and perhaps a few *pastelo* in my waiting room?"

"Um, no. That sounds wonderful."

Isabella nodded slightly, twirled, and strode away.

Lewis watched her until she turned left at the end of the hallway, and feeling as though he had just fallen off a whirlwind, he turned and headed to his room. He mused that maybe she had already bewitched him.

LEWIS WAS IN A STEW. It was August 31. *Avance* was due to leave Valencia on September 6 in order to reach all its scheduled destinations, before weather in the Mediterranean became too difficult for sailing. To get to Valencia from Madrid, the coach would have to leave on September 1. Lewis didn't want to leave Isabella, but staying wasn't an option.

Don Diego ended their morning meeting with suggestions to both O'Brien and Cathcart about dealing with their respective Barbary leaders. Barlow had still made no commitment to fund the release of the sailor-slaves. Lewis thought maybe he had just come on a lark and wouldn't do anything. Carmichael had left them some days ago, saying the pirates weren't his affair. Lewis would summarize all this and more in his notes for Humphreys. Altogether, he thought, a lot of talk and little accomplished. Don Diego interrupted his reveries.

"I must leave for Bilboa and then go up to Paris to see — actually, I don't know who is in charge of foreign affairs in France these days — but whoever it is, I must see him. Our relationship with France is not going well at the moment. But I have a problem."

Lewis looked up to find Don Diego looking directly at Cathcart and then at him. But before telling them the problem, he said, "Captain O'Brien, would you mind leaving us for a few moments? I don't wish to burden you with this since you must return to Algiers."

O'Brien nodded, stood, and exited silently.

Don Diego began without preamble. "Captain Cathcart, what is the situation in Tripoli?"

"It is settled, Sir. They are not seizing American shipping at the moment, and relations with all the major powers have become secondary to their internal issues. But those, also, are nearly settled. Yusuf Karamanli is sufficiently in control that the situation should remain stable there for several more years. His brother, Hamet, the rightful Pasha, is not a strong man. He does not have the followers or the stomach to challenge Yusuf now. In my opinion, not ever. But we have discussed this. Why do you ask again now?"

Don Diego sat with his chin resting on his fist, looking down at the table. In a moment he looked up and said, "Because my daughter wishes to go there."

"Tripoli?" said Cathcart and Lewis in unison.

"Whatever for?" asked Cathcart.

"She will not stay here without me. She does not wish to stay with either of her grandmothers in Bilboa. She has finished her education." He shrugged. "She wants something to do."

"You would allow her to go?" asked Cathcart.

Don Diego looked at Cathcart for a moment before speaking. "*Is* there anything for her to do there? Could she be of help to you?"

Cathcart breathed heavily, looking down at his fingers that had started drumming on the table, then looking up.

"Truthfully, Sir, could she help me? Probably. She might make it much easier for me to entertain their leaders and even to go into the court. But it would be deuces awkward." He returned his eyes to his diddling fingers. "And she would have to dress like they do, every bit of their costume, or she would be thought a whore."

Don Diego nodded. "Anything to do?"

"Besides that? I suppose she could learn Arabic, go with my staff to the market, learn the ways of the people. But would she want to?"

Don Diego sighed. "I don't know, but she's the one who wants to go."

"They would have to think we were married, or she was a relative," said Cathcart.

"I have an idea about that," said Don Diego. "But would you be willing to have her there?"

"If she could remain happy, she would be a light that is sadly missing now."

"Thank you. Now would you mind giving me a moment alone with Lewis?"

Cathcart, like O'Brien, nodded and left silently.

Don Diego and Lewis watched him go. And before Lewis had even turned his head back, Don Diego said, "I know you've been talking with my daughter."

Oh, no, thought Lewis. Now I'm in trouble. He turned back to Don Diego with the same feeling he'd had when he made the gaffe at their first dinner. Diego must have read it on his face. He chuckled.

"You're not in trouble, Lewis," he said, smiling. "In fact, I'm rather glad. She has so few people near her age to talk with. Do you like her?"

Lewis blushed and mumbled. "Very much, Sir."

"Do you know, in our society she's considered unmarriageable?"

Lewis's eyebrows rose involuntarily. "How could that

possibly be? She's beautiful, she's your daughter, she's winsome..."

"Well, not everyone finds her winsome," said Don Diego, looking out the window and then back. "But that's not the reason."

Lewis turned his hands outward in a gesture of 'why?'

"First," said Don Diego, holding up his thumb, "she's educated. While I was in the United States she went to a young woman's finishing school in England—where I suspect she was taught a lot more than how to speak English, how to knit and dance and how to play the piano." He then held up his thumb and forefinger. "Second, she's not Catholic."

"Not Catholic?" said Lewis, incredulity bleeding through his tone.

"She converted to Anglicanism while in England. I've asked her to tell no one, but she warned me that she would tell anyone bold enough to be her suitor. And she did. And the word went out. There will be no more suitors."

"And you think Cathcart is suitable?"

"What?" said Don Diego, pushing himself back in his seat. "Certainly *not*. But I think *you* are suitable."

Lewis couldn't speak for a moment he was so surprised. Don Diego filled in the vacuum. "For example, during our first dinner together you rather put her in her place."

"But..."

"No. It was good. She needed that. And she needs someone who can do that."

"But..."

"And she likes you."

"But..."

"And I will be travelling most of the time. She needs someone who will..." He stopped and examined Lewis.

"You have no interest?"

"Oh, I have *great* interest. But I am becoming a diplomat, also. I may be travelling as well."

Don Diego nodded. "Yes, David sent me a letter about you. So I know. But she cannot come with me. I'm not like Jefferson. I won't be getting a house and staying somewhere for a period of years. And I could not deal with the ...ah...entanglements her being with me might entail. But she could go with her husband."

"You do know I have no family," said Lewis, "except for an aunt and uncle and a couple of cousins in Virginia."

"We would be your family."

"I have no money," said Lewis.

Don Diego just looked at him and shook his head a little. "Look around you," he said. "Do you think I need her husband to have money?"

"Perhaps not," said Lewis. "But her husband would want to support her in her accustomed manner."

"You might be surprised at how little she really desires to be accustomed to this manner," said Don Diego with a smile. And then, tilting his head, "As well as she carries it off."

Lewis sat back in his own chair and looked up at the ceiling, quiet for a moment. "I've known her only six days," he said. "But in that short time, she has become indispensable to me." He looked over at Don Diego. "She would have to choose me, however. It would have to be as though we never had this conversation."

"And you will have to choose her, as well," said Don Diego. "But know that if you do, and if she does, I will support it."

Lewis remained silent for a moment, then gathered his nerve. "Do you mind if I ask you something, Sir?"

Diego's thin face and fine lips took on an expression Lewis could not read. But he said, "What is it?"

"In Philadelphia," said Lewis, "and I hope you don't mind

me saying this," he looked at Don Diego to see if his expression had changed. It was becoming more like a grin than a frown. "Well, you ...ah...dressed quite differently. And you were more stern. I don't believe I ever saw you smile."

Don Diego smiled then, though, and began to chuckle. "And you want to know why that is?"

"Yes, Sir," said Lewis.

"Two reasons," he said, still smiling. "One, I was on a mission. I needed to get something, and I needed to prevent Jay from getting something." He glanced at Lewis. "Oh, I see. Yes, that doesn't account for the clothes—those amazingly silly and pompous rags I wore there?"

Lewis nodded.

"Perhaps not one of my best ideas. But designed to keep Jay—and everyone around him—guessing as to what I was truly like. Was I crazy? Was I a fop? Was I a simpleton? It wasn't effective and I didn't like the clothes. So, no, you don't see them here."

Lewis looked at him expectantly. Now there was no smile.

"Number two, this is my daughter we're talking about."

Lewis nodded.

"Should you marry her, I believe you would be faithful to her. And I believe you might even have the ability to enable her to be faithful to you. Such a thing is unlikely in Europe."

"If she will have me, Sir," Lewis looked Don Diego in the eyes, "I will certainly be faithful to her."

"Good," said Diego. "That is all I ask."

ISABELLA AND LEWIS had gotten used to speaking to one another in English because it seemed to be the best way to keep the conversation private in the presence of her maids. At first, they had talked about everything in the world that was not themselves, and then they'd shared a few things about themselves, and then many more things apart from their present circumstances: their childhoods, their studies, funny things that had happened. But there had still been a reticence. On the coach ride to Valencia, Lewis wanted to say so much more. He even wanted to tell her what her father had said, but he feared it would be the fastest way to chase her away.

Isabella had decided to bring only Sophia with her, whom she had further decided to treat as a companion rather than a maid. She, therefore, asked that their conversations be in Spanish so as not to leave her out. That reduced conversation to the weather, the ride, what Tripoli might be like, and then, often, to falling asleep.

Their travel arrangements in the two coaches to Valencia usually saw Captain Cathcart on a seat with Isabella, Sophia between them, with Lewis on the other side. Barlow had elected to stay in Madrid for the winter, so O'Brien had the second coach to himself most of the time, his Corsairs riding shotgun alongside the driver or on the back. Occasionally, however, Cathcart would ride in the second coach to chat with O'Brien.

Finally, on September 5, the day before they would arrive in Valencia, Cathcart went to O'Brien's coach during a change of horses, and Isabella and Lewis were alone in the coach with Sophia. Isabella asked her if she'd mind them speaking in English for a while. Sophia smiled, turned toward the window, and closed her eyes.

Isabella turned to Lewis. "My father thinks if I go to Tripoli maybe I'll become a Musulmana. 'Then,' he said, 'I could cover you up completely and no one would need to see you.'"

"Why in the world would he say such a thing?" asked Lewis. "You are so very pleasant to look at."

She laughed lightly. "I went to England to study how to become a lady but somehow became an Anglican instead. So he thinks if I go to Tripoli, I may become a Musulmana."

"Will you?"

She laughed again, but became suddenly serious. "No," she said. "I've found the right way to worship God, and I don't plan to change."

"What does the rest of your family think?"

"Neither of my grandmothers will speak to me."

"But I know your father dotes on you. I've seen the way he looks at you."

She smiled. "Yes, but it is difficult for him. *I* am difficult. He does not know what to do with me."

Lewis almost said, I have a suggestion. You could marry *me*.

She continued softly, seriously, "No one will court me, you know. No one wants the stigma of having a Protestant in the family. But I won't allow any suitor who won't take me because of my faith. I told father I would have to tell anyone he wanted to court me, and I did. Now no one will court me. I'm afraid I shall become *soltero*." (an old maid).

Lewis suddenly couldn't help himself. "*I* would court you, if you would let me."

She looked at him, eyes suddenly moist. "It is so sweet of you to say that. But I have told you so much that I never tell anyone. I could not let you do it out of pity."

"Believe me," said Lewis, "it is not out of pity. It was only because I felt I could never be accepted by your father because of my religion, my lack of family, and my lack of money, that I did not ask him."

"He likes you, you know."

"I know. But that is not enough reason for him to allow me to marry his beloved daughter. I didn't think it would be possible for us."

They were quiet for a while, looking out the windows, thinking their thoughts, until Isabella gently placed her gloved hand on his knee.

He turned to look at her.

Very softly she said, "I would let you."

THEY WERE at the docks in Valencia watching the coachmen unloading baggage from the stage, passing it to the sailors on the longboats that would take it out to *Avance,* when Lewis rushed over to Isabella.

"Would you mind if I wrote a letter to your father and sent it back with the coaches?"

She nodded at Sophia who understood that was her cue to move a discreet distance away. She looked intently at Lewis. "Are you certain you want me?"

Lewis opened his mouth to speak, but she put a gloved finger on his lips.

"I am difficult to please, moody, unpredictable, arrogant, and often late."

Lewis nodded. "True," he said. "But I want you anyway."

She glared at him, expressing mock outrage with lowered eyebrows, furrowed brow, and hands on hips. But then she turned her head right and left, evidently checking to see if anyone was watching, quickly stood on tiptoes, kissed Lewis on the cheek, and was instantly back to her former posture as if nothing had happened. She examined him again.

"If, under those conditions, you still want me," she said, "who am I to refuse you? Write away!" She glanced at the driver, just stepping up to his box. "But you'll have to hurry. They're ready to leave."

Lewis knocked hard on the coach to get the driver's attention. "*Un momento por favor. Tengo algo que darte.*" (A moment, please. I have something to give you.) He reached into his right inside suit pocket, pulling out a diary and pencil, tore a page out, and wrote hastily. Then he folded the paper, reached into a pocket on the left side from which he produced an envelope. He stuffed the note into the envelope, wrote on the outside, and handed it to the driver.

"Please be certain Don Diego gets this," he said in Spanish. "If he has already left when you arrive back in Madrid, please be certain it follows him and he gets it, wherever he may be."

The driver nodded, took the envelope, and placed it in the side pocket of his livery jacket. Lewis turned back to the others, who were preparing to board the longboat.

There, he thought. *Now Don Diego will know, and Isabella need never find out about our conversation.*

AVANCE MANAGED the trip to Algiers in just over four days. For most of the waking hours, Lewis continued his lessons in Arabic with Captain O'Brien, Isabella and Sophia joining in. Having the women present changed the nature of O'Brien's training from the intricacy of diplomacy to the simplicity of daily life. Lewis thought it was probably more useful that way. The difficulty, he had thought, would be assisting Sophia since she spoke only Spanish.

Which didn't actually turn out to be the case.

"She's my only confidante," said Isabella, "and she's been with me since Mother died. Of course she speaks English."

"But..."

"I never said she just spoke Spanish, did I? You should have known."

Lewis realized that was probably true. Though Isabella had consented softly that he could court her, and in English, Sophia had shuddered as if startled. He had thought at the time, if truthfully he could say he'd thought about it at all, it must have been something in a dream she was having. Lewis realized he had a way to go before he really knew Isabella.

"Uh, no," he said. "You didn't." He decided to swallow the rest of what came to mind to say. She was from a different world – Spain, nobility, wealth, servants, every advantage and privilege. He would have to uncover this world and learn to live in it. Or at least with it.

But the Barbary nations were a whole new world to all three of them. The first thing they had seen when approaching north Africa was the mountainous coast, surmounted by castles and forts of peculiar shapes, flying flags and banners they had not seen before. And minarets. Lots of minarets. As they approached more closely, they heard mournful wails.

"The muezzin," said O'Brien. "Call to prayer. Five times a day."

Lewis reflected that this little arm of land jutting out into the Mediterranean before him, while heavily walled and forti-fied, could scarcely have contained a harbor on either side of the Atlantic. It was filled with busy little vessels with one or two sails, most of which had ten or twelve oars on each side, and which were sailing hither and yon with no apparent order. A few larger vessels stood out from the peninsula, with these little vessels apparently carrying goods from them back into the city. The city, Algiers, sat behind the harbor, winding like a narrowing triangle up the incline toward the top of a mountain, which was only slightly smaller than the one where the largest fort stood.

From the highest points of its three masts, *Avance* unfurled triangular tri-colors; the largest, longest banners Lewis had ever seen. When it had done so, it fired its salute: seven resounding canons firing one after another in quick succession. The round fort at their end of the peninsula responded in kind, and shortly one of the little boats could be seen coming their way.

The corsairs were first to disembark. After they were in the boat below, Captain O'Brien shook hands with Lewis, Cathcart, and Captain Belmont. He bowed to Isabella, who curtsied slightly in return.

"I hope I will see you all again, sooner than later, with a reprieve for my suffering sailors."

Lewis nodded. "We hope so, too, Captain." But he rather doubted 'soon' would be part of the picture.

THEY ARRIVED IN TRIPOLI MID-MORNING, two days later. The harbor there had more of a natural basis, being tucked into a ninety-degree curve of the land, with a short peninsula extending several hundred yards to make a sort of enclosure. Perhaps because the land rose less steeply there than in Algiers, the city spread over a larger area, though primarily behind the harbor.

Cathcart interacted with men on the first boat that came out to them and asked for a few supplies. Later, upon its return in the afternoon, and the lifting of various strangely-shaped parcels onto the ship, Cathcart provided Isabella and Sophia with clothing befitting their stations, but more importantly, conforming to the local expectations of women's dress. He told Lewis to remain in his uniform, as that would afford an additional modicum of respect.

After they landed, Cathcart engaged a couple of open carriages just off the dock, and their baggage was loaded on to one of them. Lewis helped Isabella and Sophia, newly attired, into the other.

"Do you have a pistol?" Cathcart asked Lewis.

"Yes, but it's in my chest," said Lewis.

"Get it out and let it show prominently. You will sit in the carriage with the women, and I will sit in the other. Now watch what I do."

Cathcart pulled a musket out of his mammoth sailor's bag on the back of the carriage, got up on the seat, and held it prominently across his lap. In a moment, he made an exaggerated show of cleaning it, filling it with powder, and ramming a ball down the muzzle.

Lewis half-watched as he retrieved the pistol from his chest on the carriage.

"Now you do the same," said Cathcart.

"Won't it make us seem belligerent?"

"It will make us seem strong. That is all that is needed."

"How will anyone know who has not seen us here?"

"Everyone will know, my friend. News travels faster than lightning here."

Lewis followed suit as they moved away from the dock. Then he could look around. The first impression he had was of dust. Except for the palm fronds, everything was covered with fine sand. Nothing at all was green. His next impression was of the crush of heavily swathed bodies, human babble, and the squawking of animals. The odors, laying in heaps on the superheated air, were so numerous and coming from so many directions, that they could not be identified. It was worse than Madrid.

On the journey from Algiers, Lewis had studied the only available map of Tripoli, which was in Italian. When they left the docks, he placed it on his lap. He determined that they travelled along the Lungo Mari dei Bastion, then down a diagonal to the Plaza Italia. It seemed that the slave market was just re-opening after the mid-day *qylula*, as Cathcart had taught him 'siesta' was called in Arabic. Lines of barely dressed white and black men and women, chained together, were being dragged toward elevated boxes along the edges of the square, whips snarling in the background. Bile came to Lewis's throat and he turned quickly away.

They were soon on the old Roman Via Piemonte—heading directly south, up into the hills—and finally, took a right onto the Via Puglia where they entered a courtyard at the base of a steeper hill. Men who appeared to be servants rushed out from the *balda* (villa) and immediately began collecting the baggage from the carriage. Cathcart spoke softly to one of the men, who nodded and rushed back into the balda. In a few moments he returned leading two women.

Isabella and Sophia had been watching the unpacking operation, and they were made to understand that it was now their turn to be unpacked. The women helped them down from the carriage and led them into the balda. Lewis stood between the balda and the carriages, and at the completion of the unpacking operation, watched the carriages as they trundled back through the open courtyard door. Servants closed the wide wooden doors with a snap and then locked them. Then Lewis turned to look at what was behind him.

He couldn't believe what he saw. Colors! Greens on greens, every shade of green. And a profusion of flowers. Some were on the ground and some were on trees. Lewis glanced back at Cathcart who came over to him.

"Beautiful, aren't they?"

Lewis nodded. "What's the bright red flower on the trees?"

"That's pomegranate. You'll come to love the fruit."

"And what is that vine climbing on the trees and the wall at the back?"

"The one with the little red and black seeds poking out of open pods?"

Lewis nodded. "And rows of pink petals."

"That's called rosary pea or jequirity bean. It's not native. I don't know who brought it here, or why. I'd like to see it gone."

"It's kind of attractive. Why would you want to get rid of it?"

Cathcart looked directly at Lewis. "Two chews on that berry and you're dead."

Lewis snapped his head back to look at it.

"It's like this place," said Cathcart, looking toward the courtyard door and waving his arm that way. "Like Tripoli and the whole Barbary Coast. Beautiful in places. But deadly." He looked back at Lewis. "If you don't know what you're doing."

6

DEVELOPING REVOLUTIONS

Inside the crumbling envelope, Crispin found another envelope in much better shape. It had his name on the front and the address of his uncle's solicitor on the back. He tore it open.

"I'm sorry to have to inform you that both your uncle and your cousin have succumbed to consumption. That leaves you as sole heir of their estate. Upon receipt of this notice, please repair to our offices at your earliest convenience to settle estate matters. Bring proof of identity, such as your Army enlistment papers or a copy of your receipt from the paymaster.

Your humble servant & etc..."

Crispin crumpled to the top step and sat, elbows going to knees and fists supporting his chin. He couldn't really weep for his lost uncle and cousin, since they had never been the slightest bit kind to him, nor would they have given him a single pence had they been alive. In fact, he couldn't weep at all.

But he did feel a sensation overcoming him that he had often kept at bay; deep pit in the middle of his being, making itself known like gnawing hunger or debilitating thirst. He was alone in the world. Not a single relative remained to care if he lived or died. He might have some money, now, even without collecting the minuscule back-pay he would receive from being a drummer. But money did not replace people. He had done well enough with very little money from the time he was trundled off to the army until today. But he had known, at least, that somewhere in the wide world was someone who knew his name.

He grimaced. And there still are people who know my name, he thought, who have been better to me than family. He nodded and stood. Lewis cares. And Gilly cares. And they would do anything for me, as I would for them. So, when I've done my assignments, I'll go back to Le Havre and find them. They will have to be my family.

Crispin stood, turned around, and examined the house more carefully. He hadn't been allowed into most of it, so he didn't know what treasures it might contain, if any. He didn't even know how many rooms it had. It was a fairly common type of house; mostly red brick, two stories with a couple of gables for the attic. One of these, at least, he knew well, since it had housed his bedroom for the few weeks he'd lived there. Two large windows stood on either side of the door on each of the two stories and a single large window, curved at the top, was over the door. Now that he looked carefully, he saw that the bottom sets of windows were boarded up from the inside and the upper were partially boarded.

Bushes by the stairs could hardly have grown any larger without blocking the stairs. Their branches protruded through the rusting rails. The stairs were chipped in places, and some enterprising individual seems to have carried off the granite tops that had graced each stair earlier. Crispin wondered whether anyone had gotten inside to similarly ravish the interior.

He strode down the rest of the stairs and along the street to the side of the property, also overgrown, but providing little space between his—yes, it was now his—house and the next house to the north. Seeing that he was likely to be severely scratched by the undergrowth on that side, he walked back the thirty yards or so to the left and discovered that someone had made a path between his house and the one on the south. Wondering if it was wise, he headed down the path and around to the back. Almost past the house he encountered a hedgerow overgrown with stinging nettle.

Do I really want to go through this? he wondered. Curiosity got the better of him, however, so he took off his shirt and used it to gingerly part the bush and its nasty stowaway.

Suddenly, someone yelled, "Ho! Away!"

Several negroes who had been sitting and eating around a cooking fire between his house and the alley behind it bolted toward the alley as if scalded.

"No!" Crispin yelled. "Don't run! I mean you no harm!"

He didn't seem to have convinced any of them to return, so he shook out his shirt, pulled it back on, and resumed his examination of the house. The back windows had been boarded up from the outside and none of the boards pulled off. It didn't seem to have been entered. He wouldn't have minded much if they had broken in, since he knew a little about their plight. But they hadn't.

"What you say, 'You mean us no harm?'" came a voice from nearby, behind him. "How you know we here?"

Crispin didn't turn around. "I didn't know you were here," he said. "And I won't tell anyone that you are. You may stay."

"How I know you ain't lyin'?"

"You don't," said Crispin. "I can only tell you that I'm not.

Also, I can tell you that I own this house and you may stay where you are."

He looked back at the cooking fire whose smoke would certainly be visible from inside the house. "Don't let anyone else see you, though. I'll be back in a day or so with my solicitor, so it might be better not to have a fire going. Don't let him or me see you then unless I call out to you." He started to turn around but thought better of it. "Can you read?"

"No, but I got a fren' who can."

Crispin pointed to the back door. "After I come back and find out what will be done with the house, I'll leave a note tacked to that door. When I'm gone, you come and get it. It will tell you what you need to do."

Runaway slaves in England? Crispin shook his head as he walked back toward his lodgings. It was well past mid-day so people would have finished their dinner and returned to work. Given that it would provide the identity information required, Crispin decided to get that minuscule back-pay. He returned to Pool Street and went west to the Town Hall and Exchange to see if the army still had a paymaster there.

They didn't. The notice on the door said it was now down by George's Dock on Goree Plazzar.

Whoops! Not there either. They'd moved over by Salthouse Dock.

Well, the walk was not without profit. It seemed that Graves Shipyard, owned by his family, was over in front of Salthouse Dock. Crispin discovered this by means of a small sign in the middle of the plaza between Dry Dock and Salthouse Dock. He wandered down toward the Mersey to see this source of wealth that had enriched his family for decades.

Apparently, the absence of family oversight had not diminished its business. Three ships were under construction, and a massive amount of timber lay on the quay behind the dry docks. Half the rest of the space on the quay was taken up by the enormous steam boxes used to curve the timbers into appropriate shapes for the stem, the hull planking, the framing, and whatever else was needed that required the reforming of recalcitrant wood. Smoke from the fires under them barely rose to head height in the languid air.

It looked as though these ships would have three masts. From the one closest to completion, Crispin gathered it would have quite a bit of open space on the deck. It also had what appeared to be small black stakes protruding from the deck at regular intervals.

Further along the quay, smithies pounded metal braces that would fortify rudders and hinges. Another group of metalworkers pounded on something else. But it was small enough so Crispin couldn't see it. He walked toward their work benches. Yes, this was where those black stakes were being produced. But what were those other things?

He stopped dead in his tracks as a notion of what they might be occurred to him. Even before someone loudly snarled, "Hey! What's you doing, there?"

"Just looking," he said.

"You get your ass outten there and look somewheres else," shouted the voice, accompanied by its rapidly approaching belligerent owner.

Crispin turned toward him. He'd faced bullets and cannonballs and soldiers searching for him and storms on the high seas and he wasn't cowed by this man—who, evidently had expected a different response. Crispin didn't glare or grimace or make a threatening move. He just stood and looked at the man.

"I mean, yer 'onor, Sir," said the man, stopping a few yards away, "If y'd be so good as to be on yer way..."

Crispin turned slowly and walked back toward the city. He'd seen enough. He'd seen too much. The other things the smithies were making were shackles; shackles that would be chained to the iron stakes on the decks. These were slave ships. His family fortune came from making slave ships.

He was glad he hadn't had his own dinner yet, thinking he probably would have lost it. *What will I do?* he thought. *I'm now the owner of this? My family's wealth came from this?*

He finally found the paymaster's office and after an hour or so of dithering came away with enough money for dinner. Well, he would be able to have many a dinner on this Army payout, but only for a couple of months.

This is all we're worth to the king? he thought. *We risk all, it's for the king's gain or at his whim, and we can't even live on the wage.*

That only diverted his thoughts for a short time, however. He pulled the solicitor's letter from his pocket and looked at the address. Back over on Goree Plazzar. He started that way, paying minimal attention to people and storefronts he passed. Until one caught his attention.

'Gore's Liverpool General Advertiser,' said the letters over the front window. And the window itself was covered from the inside with the newspaper. True, it was mostly ads, but not entirely. And it was mostly about Liverpool, but again, not entirely. Beside what seemed to be all of Gore's Liverpool General Advertiser were front pages of multiple other papers. Crispin read 'Nottingham Journal,' 'Sheffield General Advertiser,' 'Newark, Gainsborough, Chesterfield...Retford...'

That was enough. He entered the shop.

A man with blackened hands and apron looked up from

his station beside a small manual press. A larger press, behind it did not seem to be in use. "Do you want something, young man," he said. "I'm short-handed today and kind of busy."

"Well," said Crispin, "I was going to ask you something. But it can wait. If you're short-handed, I think I could help."

The man looked at him skeptically. "This work takes years to learn and years to practice."

"Yes it does," said Crispin. "I can do engraving in several styles, compose type, and..."

"All right," said the man. "I'm Gore. You're..."

"Crispin."

"That's all?"

"For now," said Crispin. "Would you like to see what I can do? I see your in-basket over there, filled with requests. Would you like me to typeset them?"

"You don't even know my style," said Gore.

"I read your paper in the window," said Crispin.

"The forms and sorts are by the table over to the left of the window, there," Gore said, pointing.

Crispin wandered over to the massive table and and examined the sorts set in slots in the shelves behind it. "Bell's take-off on Baskerville," he said. "That's what I thought. Doesn't it take up a lot of space?"

Gore looked up sharply. "I'd get the Bodoni if I could afford it. But I can't. Make it as tight as you can."

"If you like what you see, may I ask you something tomorrow?"

"Why tomorrow?" said Gore, looking back at his press and turning the crank.

"I'll have something to show you that I don't have with me now."

"Believe me," said Gore, "if you can compose even one

page, I'll be open to anything you want to ask." He placed paper in the letterpress and cranked out another page.

Crispin took out a form, set several type cases in different point sizes on the worktable with the in-basket beside them, picked up a composing stick, and got started.

He managed to compose two pages. Though it took him longer than usual because it was such picky stuff—trade names, numbers, symbols for weights and measures—Gore was effusive in his thanks after looking it over.

"I couldn't have done it better myself," he said. "And with these eyes of mine, it would have taken me much longer. Would you like to work for me?"

Crispin smiled. "Tomorrow," he said. "Let's talk tomorrow."

Which, it turned out, would also have to be when he spoke with his uncle's solicitor, since their office was closed by the time he got there.

BACK AT HIS LODGINGS, Crispin took out the sketches he had done before leaving Paris and those made along the way. The 'Priestly Riots' in Birmingham, as he had decided to call them, were old news to him. But they might not be old news here. He decided to bring the sketches he had done in Birmingham to Gore, along with some of the others, to see if he was interested.

He was reaching into his larger bag, hoping to find something smaller than his valise to carry them in, when his fingers bumped the mysterious package from Birmingham—which he'd entirely forgotten. He pulled it out, untied the twine holding the coarse paper together, and revealed two books: *Reflections on the Revolution in France*, by Edmund Burke, and *Rights of Man*, by Thomas Paine. Crispin pulled a small note from the top of the Burke book. It said, "Read this first. You need to know what it says. But we subscribe to the philosophy of the Paine book. The Lunar Society."

When he opened *Rights of Man,* a handbill fell out. Crispin collected it from the floor and examined it. "Reasons for Revolution," seemed to be the title, though it had gotten wet and become smudged so he couldn't be certain. No author was indicated. Crispin unfolded it carefully, trying not to tear it. As he did, another small note fluttered to the floor. "This was not us," it said, "though we agree with most of it. TLS."

Burke was tedious, made worse by the fact that Crispin disagreed with most of what he said. Crispin wasn't convinced that the French Revolution was entirely benign, but he espoused its stated principles. Burke was just trying to preserve his elite status and, especially, his property and the money he earned on the back of his, what did they call them? Well, they were like serfs, even if they weren't called that. And, of course, he was attempting to flatter the king and his sycophants to his own benefit.

Tired eyes and smoke from the lamp caused Crispin to give up some time after midnight. He'd read Paine tomorrow, he thought. But as he set *Rights of Man* on the nightstand beside his bed, he inadvertently flipped the cover open.

"Dedicated to George Washington and the Marquis de Lafayette," caught his eye. From personal experience he knew the marquis to be a good man. He assumed Washington was. Not that the king was necessarily a bad man. He didn't know. It was a clash of ideas. But Burke's and the king's ideas were based on their desire to maintain their supremacy, not on any overarching philosophy or creed—though they trotted out various philosophers and religious ideologies to support them. He would read Paine and see what he had to say, but not tonight.

As he slipped into sleep, he reaffirmed his commitment to go to Ireland to see what the Irish thought of the French Revolution and what they might want to do about it. He had no idea what Gore's political leanings were, but he would offer to be a reporter for him as he was for *Amis du Peuple*, anyway. He was building his friend list. It might be useful one day.

IN THE MORNING, Crispin took his sketchbook with him to Gore's shop.

"Young man," Gore said, a smile lighting his face, "I'd like you to know that I got an extra hour of sleep this morning because of the work you did yesterday. I'd like to pay you something."

"No need," said Crispin. "I just collected my back pay from the army, so I have plenty of funds at the moment." Not to mention that he was probably about to come into some kind of fortune. "I'd like to show you some of my other work and see if you're interested."

He opened his sketchbook to a page spread that had two pencil drawings of the events and aftermath he'd witnessed in Birmingham and set it on the worktable. Gore would have to leave his press and come over to see them. He did.

After examining the open pages and turning a few more, he stood back from the table and looked at Crispin.

"Where did you get these?"

"Get them? I *made* those sketches. They're from Birmingham, London, a few towns in-between, and Paris."

"I thought that was the case—at least the part about you drawing them. Except for Birmingham, I didn't know where they were from. They're wonderful. They truly are. But don't you know you could be in trouble for some of these, especially the Birmingham ones? Do you think the king wants anyone to know the rioters were not punished?"

"Probably not," said Crispin. "The King and I have an ambiguous relationship."

Gore laughed. "As do probably more than half of his subjects." He turned serious. "But he has a whole army to clarify such ambiguity."

"Didn't work so well in America," said Crispin. "I was there."

"Listen," said Gore. "I'm guessing you were going to ask me if I wanted any of your sketches. Well, first, that would only work if you did the gravure work—"

"Which I can do," said Crispin.

Gore looked keenly into his face. "After what you did yesterday, I don't doubt that," he said. "But second, I'd have to have the equipment. Third, I'd have to be presenting news, which I'm not."

Crispin started to raise his hand, but Gore cut him off. "And fourth, I'd have to be crazy."

"Is it that...um, is there that little freedom of speech, here?"

"It's not just the king," said Gore. "It's the people, too. After all, it was the dissenters against the rest of the people in Birmingham, according to my sources. The army only intervened when they were asked to do so by the local constabulary."

"So you know the news, but you can't print it."

"Let's just say I *won't* print it. This business is precarious enough as it is."

Crispin went to the table, closed his sketchbook, and gathered it to himself. "Yes, I was going to ask if you—or some of these other publishers around you—would like me to send news to you. I did that for a New York paper a few years ago. And, as it happens, I'm on assignment for *Amis du Peuple*. I'm supposed to find out what the Irish think of the French Revolution and whether there's any support, even if just moral support, to be had from that quarter. I'm on my way to Dublin to see what I can discover."

Gore went back to his manual press and inked a form before responding. "If you want that sort of information, you'd be better off going to Belfast. That's where things start in Ireland these days."

"Isn't Dublin bigger?"

"Yes, and more in line with the king. If there's sympathy for the French Revolution, it's more apt to be found in Belfast." Gore set paper into the press and turned the handle. "I have a friend in Belfast who's wanting to start a paper which, I fear, the King will not like at all. You might want to speak with him."

Crispin frowned. "It seems..."

Gore raised a palm to stop him, again. "Look. I live in England. I will always live in England. I've never been out of England, and I never will. I go by the rules of England, spoken and unspoken. You may do as you wish and because I like you, I will help as I can. But, except to my friend in Belfast, please never mention my name. I have to live here, and I'd like my life to go as smoothly as possible. Do you understand?"

Crispin nodded. "I can't disagree with you," he said. "Could you tell me the name?"

"Give me your sketchbook," he said. "I'll write it."

Crispin nodded again, took a pencil from a pocket, and handed both to Gore. Gore took them, set the sketchbook against his leg, and wrote on the inside cover.

Gore looked up at Crispin after he'd written. "He's a draper and a haberdasher. He knows nothing about producing or running a newspaper. But he wants to try it anyway. Perhaps you can help him." He handed the book and pencil to Crispin.

Crispin nodded once more. "Thank you for this," he said.

"For what?" said Gore, turning back to his press. "I wish

you well, young man, but it might be best if you didn't visit me again."

Crispin left the shop without another word or nod, amazed at what the thought of freedom—and the cost of freedom—did to some people. He opened his sketchbook and viewed what Gore had written.

"Samuel Neilson, 14 Princes Street."

"Well then," said Crispin aloud, to the concerned stares of passers-by, "that's where I'm going next."

NOT QUITE NEXT, as it turned out. He decided he'd better check with the solicitor before he left in order to establish his claim. He entered the office and was met, primarily, with skepticism. Perhaps I shouldn't have come in my travelling clothes, he thought. But then, that was all he had. A man, dressed as a gentleman, finally emerged from a door behind the gate-keeping receptionist. His manner, facial expression, and tone of voice would not have convinced Crispin that he was a gentleman, however.

"Who are you and what do you want?"

Rather than answer, Crispin passed him the letter that had been on the door of his uncle's house.

"Hmph," said the man. "Anyone could have taken this down and pretended to be the rightful recipient."

Then Crispin handed him the certificate he'd received from the paymaster yesterday, indicating that he was honorably discharged from the army.

He took it, looked over at Crispin and then down to the certificate.

Crispin wondered how difficult he was going to make this,

suddenly realizing that since the estate had an heir, this solicitor was likely to lose a good deal of money.

He looked at Crispin, then at the paper once more, and relented.

"Mr. Graves," he said, not particularly graciously, "it looks as though everything is in order. Please follow me into my office."

Though the receptionist glared at him as he walked by, he couldn't help but smirk.

"Mr. Wright, at your service," the solicitor said, gesturing toward an elegant armchair done in crimson leather.

Crispin sat, placed his arms on the arms of the chair, and leaned back as if to become really comfortable. But then he suddenly sat up. "I've been back and forth across the Atlantic multiple times. I fought with the British at Yorktown. I reported on troubles in the new America. I met with disaffected freed slaves in Quebec. I hobnobbed with a Danish Count and the Marquis de Lafayette in Paris. I know I'm young. But I am not stupid or inexperienced. Do we understand one another?"

"I...um, we..."

"You didn't expect me to come back."

"No, we didn't."

"I don't plan to stay, either," said Crispin. "But if you do right by me, I'll keep you on to run the estate."

"Oh, well—"

Crispin stood, turned away from Mr. Wright, and walked to the window that looked out on Dry Dock. Then he turned back. "Now. Tell me about the estate."

Crispin didn't show his grin to those standing at the rail near him. The little bit of turbulent weather caused many of them to regret they'd eaten even the small mid-day repast that came with their ticket to Belfast. They had no idea about rough weather. He didn't wish it on them, but he couldn't help feeling a little smug.

In any case, the packet pulled into the wharf on High Street at the scheduled time—which he knew because bells in a church tower to the north chimed nine times as he stepped onto the gangplank. It smelled like every other city on the sea that he'd been to; fish, horses, smoke, excrement, salt, sweat, disease, wet wool. In the dim light, longshoremen unloaded barrel after barrel from a vessel on the other side of the wharf, placing them on drays that ferried them the short distance to warehouses on the quay.

Though Crispin had Mr. Neilson's address, he didn't know a soul in Belfast. That wasn't so unusual, not to know anyone in a new city. He knew how to meet people and he knew how to establish himself—but it was getting a little old. He had no idea how long he'd be in Ireland this time, or where he'd go from here. He recalled the promise he'd made to meet Gilly and Lewis at Le Havre next spring. To his chagrin, it was almost an anchor to him. He wanted to think of himself as independent. But despite the fact that his own family had failed him spectac-ularly, he wanted family. He wanted friends. He wasn't designed to be a loner.

Holding his bag in the left hand, his valise—containing his large drawings—in the right hand, and his easel under his left arm, he walked west and then south around the end of the wharf, then east slightly, toward Princes Street. He wished he had asked someone where he might find lodging, but he supposed there had to be somewhere he could tolerate once he got past the bars and dives that catered to sailors and dock workers.

Though the crossing had been cool, with wind from the

south requiring them to tack back and forth, Crispin found the land cooler. The mist turned suddenly to rain. He pulled up the collar of his new coat just in time to keep the rain from going down his back.

He reflected. *I'm alive. I'm here. I'm on an adventure, no matter that it's a bit stressful.* He looked up, allowing a trickle to flow from the rim of his hat down his left cheek. He immediately ducked back down.

"I'm grateful to You, anyway," he whispered, "even though I can't look up to thank You."

"*Dia gwitch!*"

Crispin was startled out of his revery.

"What's that?" he said, lifting his face toward the young man he'd almost bumped into.

"It's 'God be with you,' to you English. It's how we greet one another around here."

"Well, God be with you, too," said Crispin. "I was just talking to Him, in fact."

"Do you often do that?"

"Not as often as I should, to be sure," said Crispin. "And who might you be and why are you offering me good wishes?"

"Because I believe you're Mr. Graves and I've been sent to find and fetch you. I'm a bit tardy, I fear."

"Well, you did find me. And I'm at a disadvantage. Who are you?"

The young man chuckled. "Sorry! I'm a clerk for Mr. Neilson, whom I think you know."

"I don't, yet," said Crispin, "but his is the only address I have in Belfast."

"He knows you, though."

"How may that be?"

"He got a letter from Mr. Gore of Liverpool on yesterday's packet."

Crispin stood stock still. "Wow! That was quick!"

"I'm Seamus, by the way. Seamus O'Connor. And may I carry something for you?"

"I'm Crispin. I don't know this 'Mr. Graves' fellow." Crispin set his valise down and held out his hand. Seamus shook it, nodded toward the valise, and picked it up.

"Shall we be great friends?"

"That would be nice," said Crispin. "I seem to have left mine on several continents." He nodded toward the valise. "Be careful with that," he said. "My life is in there."

Seamus nodded. "Right," he said. Then he shook his head. "And to think I never asked if you had a mouth on you."

They walked past one of the sparkling gas lights, so Crispin could see Seamus as he looked his way, shaking his head. "You heard me speak. Where did you think it was coming from?"

Seamus gave a hearty guffaw. "Oh, we shall have great fun!"

"Really," said Crispin. "What was that 'mouth' comment about?"

"It means, 'Are you hungry?'"

Crispin pursed his lips and shook his head again. "I knew I didn't know French," he said. "I hadn't realized I didn't know English."

"Oh, that's not English," said Seamus. "It's Irish or Ulster or Hibernian stuck into English words. You'll run into a lot of that."

"And you'll help me with it?"

"Of course, and the first and most important phrase is *'Slawn-cha!'*"

"Which means what?"

"Cheers!" he said, pulling Crispin into a pub.

. . .

Seamus headed to the back of the pub and set the valise down against the wall beside the last booth—which was occupied by two men. He glanced at Crispin's bag and nodded toward the wall. Crispin set the easel and his bag down beside the valise. As he did so, the two men stood and moved out of the booth. He turned toward them and the closest one stuck out his hand.

"I'm Samuel Neilson," he said. "My friend, Gore, in Liverpool, told me all about you. I've been looking forward to meeting you."

Crispin shook his hand, but before he could say anything the other man said, "And I'm Henry McCracken. Sam does wool and I do linen after my mother's family which also does the best local paper anywhere, 'The Belfast News Letter.' My father's family owns ships. We're all Presbyterian."

Crispin shook his outstretched hand, as well.

"That may be a lot to take in at once," said Sam.

"Well, he needs to know right away what he's getting in to," said Henry. He turned to Crispin. "What do you think of Paine's *The Rights of Man?*"

A pause ensued as both Seamus and Sam drew in a breath and looked to Crispin. He glanced at Henry's face, then at the other two, perceiving that his answer here was the fulcrum on which his success in Ireland would depend.

"I can't say, yet," he said. "I read Burke and found him... shall we say, not the slightest bit compelling. On the contrary—"

"Dull, stilted, antiquated, offensive?" filled in Henry.

"You could say that. I have Paine's book right here in my bag and planned to begin reading it tonight."

Henry stared at Crispin for a moment, then nodded.

"Good," he said. "That's a good beginning. Read that tonight then."

"But in the meantime," said Sam, "we have a proposition for you." He looked around as if he'd just realized they were still standing. "Please! Have a seat. What would you like to eat?"

"Their shepherd's pie is outstanding," said Seamus. The other two nodded.

"That will be fine," said Crispin.

"A pie and a pint for the lad," shouted Sam, waving to a nearby serving girl.

Crispin managed not to smirk as he watched both Sam and Henry. They were not much older than himself, if they were any older. Yet they seemed to be upstanding and productive citizens here, devoted to a cause. He wondered if Lewis had had attitudes like theirs at the beginning of the American Revolution.

Seamus ordered a pie and pint as well, and the others tucked into the remains of their dinner as Crispin and Seamus waited for theirs to arrive.

The girl brought the two pints, smiled, and went back for the tray on which the pies were waiting. She set them on the table and smiled again, just standing there.

Sam fished in his coin purse, found what he wanted, and held it out for her. She took it from his hand and gave a little curtsy, but remained there, ogling.

Sam shook his head. "Not tonight, miss. Now be off with ya." She frowned and flounced off. Sam looked over at Crispin. "We're both married," he said, "but she tries every time we come in. Seamus has a fiancée, but maybe you'd be interested."

Crispin shook his head. He could think of a hundred reasons why it would be a bad idea, but he didn't choose to say any of them. "What was *your* proposition," he said.

"We want to start a newspaper," said Henry.

"Didn't you say your mother's family had a newspaper?" said Crispin.

"Well, yes," said Henry, "but that's mostly British news. We want local news, commentary, essays, rhetoric…"

"He wants to start a revolution," said Seamus, just a bit too loudly.

Sam gave Seamus a hard glare as a couple of nearby patrons turned their way.

Seamus whispered, "Sorry!"

Henry surveyed the room and, seeing that no one was looking their way any longer, said, "'The Northern Star' is going to be the mouthpiece of *Cumann na nÉireannach Aontaithe*, The Society of United Irishmen."

"They want me to be called the editor," said Sam, "but I know absolutely nothing about producing or running a paper. That's where you come in."

"Does this Society of United Irishmen exist yet?" asked Crispin.

"No," said Sam.

"We plan to establish it in October and want to have the first edition of the paper out by January 1 so we can tell the world who we are and what we want to do," said Henry.

"Seamus, here, will help you," said Sam.

"Funding is not a problem. And you can get some of the rest of what you need from my mother," said Henry.

"Wait! Wait! Wait!" said Crispin. "Aren't you getting ahead of yourselves?"

"I told you it was too much, too soon," said Sam, glaring at Henry.

Henry looked at Sam and then back at Crispin. "Well, what do you say? Do you want to do it?"

Crispin hesitated for only a second before saying, "Yes. It's something I'd like to do. But aren't you trusting me a bit too soon?" He lowered his voice. "Do you know what happens in revolutions?" He looked around at the three of them. "People get killed! Limbs get blown off. Homes and businesses and whole cities get destroyed. I know. I've been there. Are you ready for that? And do you trust me so soon, without really getting to know me?"

"Oh, we don't want a revolution," said Sam, "despite what Seamus said. We only want a little more freedom. A little more self-determination."

"That's what the American colonists said and look what they got. Seven years of war!"

"Can't happen here," said Sam.

"Why not?" asked Crispin, growing agitated. "Same king. Same parliament. Same army."

"But look at what's happening in France," said Henry. "Their king has given in to their wishes. They have more freedom now than they ever dreamed of."

"I've been there, too," said Crispin, "and I'm suspicious of it. The peasants have the freedom to pay more taxes, to be drafted into the army, to starve—since the cost of food is almost unbearable—to work hard and get almost nothing for it, to...".

"Well, if war ever happened here, would they help us?" asked Henry.

Crispin looked his way, and then at Seamus and Sam, sitting across from him. Hope sat on their faces, in their eyes, yearning for him not to crush it.

He sighed. "I think they might," he said. "If things continue as they are now." He looked down at his barely tasted pie. "But I don't know if they will. The French are so...so...volatile. So changeable. Not like the Americans. They're both passionate, true. But the American passion is... is like the passion for a wife and family, for a life. The French passion is more like for a mistress. Strong. Imminent. But not lasting."

"Wow!" said Seamus. "Who are you?"

"I'm someone who has seen too much," said Crispin. "I applaud your desire, but I doubt your wisdom."

"So you'll do the paper?" said Henry.

"I'll do the paper," said Crispin. "But I won't be the editor. I'll get you up and running—"

"You mean like masthead and statement of purpose—"

"Perhaps," said Crispin. "I'll help with those things. But chiefly I mean all the fiddly things. Like type and press and paper and format and the daily grind."

"Probably weekly," said Sam. "Not daily."

"There'll still be a daily grind," said Crispin.

"Right," said Henry. "That will be your purview."

THEY BEGAN ARRIVING IN OCTOBER, having crowded aboard any ship that would take them, regardless of destination.. The first ship filled with refugees from Saint-Domingue happened to be captained by Henry's father, John McCracken. It arrived from Port-de-Paix with the *grand blancs*, the "great whites" or white French plantation owners, from the northern sugar plantations. These were the few who had survived Yellow Fever epidemics and not fled back to France immediately, like most of their minor nobility compatriots. These were the ones who realized that their slaves would rise up against them and kill them as had happened at a number of inland plantations.

The ship had brought in so many more people than it should have carried that it looked and smelled, at first, like a slave ship—except that the passengers were dressed, and the odor was slightly muted. Normally the disembarkation of Captain John's ship was a minor affair, attended by longshoremen, a few relatives, and perhaps a few folks hoping for the sailors' custom. Not this time. Word preceded its arrival and by the time it docked, half the city waited on High Street or Hanover Quay. The railing on Long Bridge facing Belfast Lough was one long line of spectators.

Crispin had his easel set up on the northeast corner of High Street, looking across the narrow inlet at Hanover Quay. He made a few sketches as the ship came in, then ran down toward the alley leading off High to Waring Street to capture the arriving passengers; mothers in expensive clothing, now ragged-looking, toting babies and holding the hands of small children, men carrying trunks on their shoulders or water-stained leather bags dangling just above the planks, a few dispirited young men carrying almost nothing, and even a few negros—mostly young girls who were carrying exactly nothing. They got off the boat, no doubt to their great relief, thought Crispin, but then they just stood there, having no idea what to do.

It wasn't long, however, before a well-dressed woman and a priest appeared. As the woman approached the crowd, Crispin recognized her as Henry's mother, Ann. He imagined the priest was from St. Ann's Church; the first and largest Roman Catholic church in town. Ann was helped atop a packing crate alongside the dock. She held up both arms, waved, and shouted, "*Attention! Attention! Écoute moi!*" (Listen to me!)

She then went on to tell them that the churches would take care of them. "*Si vous êtes protestant, suivez-moi! Si vous êtes catholique, suivez le Père Vincent!*" (If you are Protestant, follow me. If you are Catholic, follow Father Vincent.) Someone helped her down and she raised her hands, gathering those who would go with her.

The majority moved toward Father Vincent, but a few moved toward her. Others still milled around the end of the gangplank, looking forlorn. Ann approached them and shouted,

"*Si vous ne savez pas où aller, suivez-moi!*" (If you don't know where to go, follow me!)

When the two groups had fully formed, Father Vincent headed down the alley toward Waring Street, and Ann led her group west on High Street, presumably toward the Presbyterian meeting house on Rosemary Lane. It seemed as though the Christians of the town would handle the influx.

But, of course, that couldn't last for long. Crispin stopped documenting after the third ship. The people, the reports, were much the same except for the rising violence reported, as well as the total inadequacy of assistance from France. And by the time the fourth ship had arrived from Saint-Domingue, with reports of more atrocities and greater brutality—as well as with diseases prominent in the West Indies—the city couldn't deal with them any longer. St. Ann's and the Presbyterian meeting house, White Linen Hall and the Poor House, were all overflowing with refugees. Which made it a blessing when winter weather on the Atlantic made the crossing impossible for a number of months. In any case, most of the refugees wanted to get back to France as soon as possible, so several of the ships that might otherwise have wintered in Belfast were engaged to take refugees to France.

By mid-December the refugee ships had returned. Father Vincent railed against the revolutionary French government's insistence that priests take an oath of allegiance to the state or be imprisoned. Rumblings of assistance against the revolution from the monarchs of other European nations were heard. Ann Neilson spoke with the returning crews and translated for Crispin stories about the king's attempt to escape France, pending changes to France's armies with the supposed reason of protecting her borders, and other rumors whose truth could not be verified. Sam and Henry didn't want to hear this and still wanted to go ahead with their publishing plans.

Crispin didn't actually hear a collective sigh of relief when the last refugee left, but he pretended he did in an anonymous article that appeared in *The Northern Star's* first issue on January 1, 1792. And, of course, they didn't all leave on ships. Some just melted into the city's population or found a way to become invisible in the countryside. Revolutions, he thought. This is what can happen. For the first time, in the Saint-Domingue revolution, it looked possible that a slave uprising would work. Crispin wondered what part 'The Rights of Man,' the American Revolution, and the French Revolution might have played in the origin of this slave uprising. He'd never doubted that slaves were people deserving of liberty as much as anyone else. But he hadn't thought about the price of achieving it. Now it was becoming clear. He decided it was time to return to France to find his friends, to see which rumors were true, and to see what the French were really making of their revolution.

CRISPIN MADE certain that Seamus could handle the logistics of *The Northern Star*, said his good-byes to Sam and Henry, packed up, and made his way to the dock. Because tensions between France and England were rising, few merchants were willing to send large ships from Belfast to France. Crispin had to take a merchant vessel to London and a packet to Le Havre. No one wanted the mail to cease operating between the two countries, or the Claret to stop flowing, or any other of the luxuries small enough to ship on the packet to stop being exchanged, so the packet still ran; rain, snow, sleet wind, or whatever, evidently, because it was the wettest, coldest crossing Crispin had yet experienced.

So it was that Crispin arrived in Le Havre on January 20. The weather didn't improve in France, but he found a seat in a coach to Paris the next day, and they slogged through mud and brittle ice for the next three days. He arrived at Gouverneur Morris's home in Paris on the 23rd, just in time to witness sodden citizens crashing through shop windows to steal the few remaining cakes and eclairs, and coming back through broken shop doors with more basic things like bread and flour. He stopped a woman he'd seen stashing a sack of flour under her skirt. And asked her why she needed to steal it.

"*Ne comprenez-vous pas,*" she said. (I don't understand you.) She brushed by him and rushed on her way. He wiped the rain off his face, walked up the steps to Gouverneur's door, and was about to knock when a voice from above him said, "I'll tell you why she needs to steal it." He looked up but could not see the source of the voice. "It's because there's no flour and no bread here. Again!"

Crispin backed down the few stairs and scanned the upper stories once more, but still couldn't tell where the voice was coming from. "Gouverneur?" he said.

But the voice went on. "And what's worse, because of that damned rebellion in Saint-Domingue, there's no sugar and no coffee. Can you imagine it! No coffee!"

"Gouverneur!" shouted Crispin. "It's me, Crispin Graves. Can you let me in before I drown or they they run off with *me?*"

A head stuck further out from a window above Crispin on his right. Crispin could now see the balding top.

"Who did you say you were?"

"Crispin! Lewis and Gilly's friend."

The head pushed out far enough so Crispin could see the

eyes. "The Gilly that left me in order to cook for that damned Marquis who's now bolted off to the north somewhere to fight some imagined Prussian army?"

"I guess so. I haven't seen him since last summer."

"And I'm supposed to let you in?"

"If you don't mind," said Crispin.

"Hmmph."

The head pulled back in and the window slammed shut. In a moment the front door opened a crack. "Monsieur?"

"Oui," said Crispin.

The door was opened a little wider by a French man in some sort of disheveled livery. "*Entrez! Vite!*" (Come in! Quick!)

Crispin shuffled his valise and easel into his left hand, picked up his bag, and made what haste he could into the house. The servant slammed the door and bolted it. Crispin set his things down at the head of the staircase on the right just in front of the door and slipped his coat off. The liveried man took it, holding it away from himself so it dripped only on the floor.

He hadn't moved before Crispin heard the distinctive sound of Gouverneur making his way down the stairs. Clunk, "Ow," footstep. Clunk, "Ow! Merde!" footstep.

"Why don't you live on the ground floor if stairs are so uncomfortable," said Crispin as Gouverneur got to the bottom and extended his hand.

"Can't see anything from the windows down here," said Gouverneur. He looked appraisingly at Crispin. "Did you bring coffee?"

"Where would I get coffee?" said Crispin.

"Worth a try," said Gouverneur turning away to retrace the stairs.

"Actually—"

Gouverneur spun back around, almost twisting off his wooden leg. "Did you?"

Crispin leaned down and opened his soggy bag. "Not very much. But I remembered you liked it. Most that gets to Belfast these days stays there, but I brought you a little." He took a covered earthen jar out of his bag and held it up toward Gouverneur—who nodded at it and then at the liveried man. Crispin handed the jar to him.

"You're coming from Belfast?"

Crispin nodded.

"A story there?"

"Many," said Crispin. "And from some other places as well. And I only need to stay here a day or two, if you don't mind, until I find lodging."

"Oh," said Gouverneur, waving a hand in the air, "stay forever if you wish. Only don't bother me if my door is shut." He turned back toward the stairs. "Pierre! *Faites le café*, (Make coffee!)" he said, and thumped upward. Crispin watched him for a minute, then turned back to Pierre who stood there with Crispin's coat in one hand and the jar of coffee in the other looking at a loss for what to do next.

Gouverneur turned his head back toward Crispin. "Aren't you coming?"

"I'll let you get up first."

"Leave *les baggages* there. Pierre will bring them. He knows where to put them."

He thumped the rest of the way up and Crispin followed.

7

URGENT MESSAGES

"If you should desire to go out with the women," said Captain Cathcart to Isabella, "you should have both your maid and my two female servants with you. And always, always, cover your face with the veil."

"Except for the veil, that's very little different from Madrid," she replied.

"One difference," said Cathcart. "In Madrid, only your honor was at stake. Here it's your life."

Isabella stared at him.

"They take the place of women very seriously, here. Just assume your safety lies in the fact that you are a foreigner under diplomatic immunity. But that is a very thin layer of protection. It would be better, if you must go out, to go with me, your 'uncle,' or with your fiancé."

"My fiancé?"

"Well, of course. Lewis."

"Who told you he was my fiancé?"

"That's what your father told me to call him."

Isabella's face had turned quite red, the veins in her neck stood out, and her fists were clenched. "He did, did he?"

Cathcart gave her a puzzled look and continued. "Just remember what I told you."

"And just where is my so-called fiancé, now?" she asked in a voice devoid of inflection.

"He's in my study making a clear copy of the information he will be taking to Mr. Jefferson. He should be finished shortly."

"Are you going there?"

Cathcart nodded.

"Perhaps you could tell him I await his *pleasure* here."

Cathcart tossed another puzzled look her way, turned his furrowed brow toward Sophia, shook his head, and left.

WHEN LEWIS ENTERED the sitting room sometime later, Isabella stood and walked toward him as if to welcome him. Lewis's smile grew as she approached. Until she was almost up to him. She looked intently into his eyes and smacked him across the face with her right hand. She raised her left hand as if to smack him with that, but he caught it in mid-air before it struck. Then she raised her right hand again, and he caught that as well.

"You must tell me what that was for," said Lewis, "and I will decide if you are allowed to strike me a second time." Both of her wrists remained locked in his grip even though she struggled to release them.

"So! My fiancé wants to know what was *that* for!" she shouted. "I trusted you! I thought you loved me!"

"But I do!" said Lewis.

"Pah! My father pays you to love me. He has bought you with my dowry."

"What are you talking about?"

"The good Captain says father told him to call me your fiancée."

"I know nothing about that," said Lewis.

"So you never talked with my father about me?"

Lewis sighed. "Well, yes, I did. We talked." He loosened his grip on her wrists but did not let go. "It was his idea. He talked to me about you. Just as we were leaving."

Isabella looked at Sophia in triumph. "So he *did* buy you."

"We did not talk about money, except that I told him I had none."

"And..."

"And... he said it didn't matter. He wanted you to be happy. And if you wanted to...ah...develop our relationship, that would be fine with him."

She let her arms go limp in his hands.

"Why did you not tell me, earlier?"

"For just this reason. I really do love you. But I was afraid if I told you I'd spoken with your father before asking you about it, you would be angry."

"Well, I *was* angry!" she said, with dwindling conviction.

"I got that impression," said Lewis, grinning, though at this point, the anger seemed to have leeched out of her. He also found that they had somehow interlaced fingers on both hands.

Isabella turned her deep eyes away from him, bowed her head, withdrew her hands, and started shaking.

"Are you all right?" Lewis asked. Then he suddenly realized she was laughing. She turned back to him and put her two hands on his cheeks, softly rubbing the one she'd slapped.

"I owe you an apology," she said. "And you have no idea how hard it is for a Spaniard to say that." She turned toward Sophia and made a twirling motion with one hand, whereupon Sophia turned away. Then Isabella turned back. "There. She will not protect you from me now." She took a step closer to him, stood on tiptoes, and kissed him on the mouth. He wrapped his arms around her and...

It was not *too* many minutes later that Lewis was on one knee before her while she gazed at him with tilted head.

"Will you marry me?"

She looked at him intently for a moment, then went to her own knees and kissed him again. "Sí," she said softly. "I would be ...I must use Spanish...*estar entusiasmado, contentisimo encantado* (thrilled, overjoyed). Is that enough?" She looked into his eyes. "I thought I would be a *soltero*, and then you came along." She hugged him harder and then pushed back far enough so she could look at him. "Yes. Yes, I will marry you. Of course I will marry you. You couldn't possibly have thought I would say No, could you?"

Lewis stood and raised Isabella, embracing her once again. "I certainly hoped you wouldn't," he whispered into her hair.

With her head on his shoulder, she said quietly, "I know you've been watching, dear Sophia. Perhaps you could go and tell the Captain he may call me Lewis's fiancée."

"But how soon will you be back?" asked Isabella.

They were outside walking side-by-side in the courtyard, Sophia following at a discreet distance.

Lewis sighed. "Not nearly soon enough for me." He held out his left hand, thumb up. "One week to get back to Lisbon. Hopefully, only one more week before finding a ship to sail back to America." He held up his pointer along with his thumb. Then the rest of his fingers on that hand. "Three to six weeks to get to New York." Three fingers of his right hand went up. "I don't know after that. If we can get out before it gets too cold, maybe another eight weeks to get back?"

"But probably not," said Isabella.

Lewis nodded. "Probably not. I have to find Jefferson, convey the message and wait for a response. I don't think the New York harbor freezes up like Philadelphia, but no one will try the crossing after late October. Then it isn't likely we'll cross before March. That might be to Brest or Lisbon or who knows where, and then I'll have to find a ship coming here."

Isabella took his left hand in both of hers as they walked, and leaned against him.

"I don't know if I can survive that long." She looked up toward him and he looked back at her. "Is this what our life will be like? Me always waiting somewhere for you?"

"When we're married," said Lewis, "I'll take you with me everywhere. It won't be the settled life of a Doña on her estate."

Looking up at him, she squeezed his hand. "Thank God."

"Really?"

"I couldn't have endured such a life," she said. "There is too much world out there I want to see."

"Me, too," said Lewis. "And the prospect is infinitely more satisfying knowing I'll see it with you."

About a week later, civilian Lewis Elliot boarded *Avance* for the trip to Lisbon.

Captain Cathcart gave Lewis a book in Arabic. He didn't tell Lewis what it was about, but he did say to show it to no one, and that he wanted it back within a year.

"And I also want a response from Jefferson—and from Washington, and from whomever seems to be running things in the newfangled government. I needed an answer several years ago. I must have one soon or there will be no men left to ransom. Nor will the Bashaw stop his predations without an answer. Either in the form of cash or in the form of cannon-balls. *I need an answer!*"

Lewis, leaning on the taffrail of *Avance*, looked up from his musings to see what must be Malta, off the larboard side. He thought of the story of St. Paul, who'd beached on the other side of the island. He didn't know who claimed possession of the island now—the Knights of St. John, Spain, France, the Barbers—but it was a fresh reminder of the impermanence of rulers and empires and powers. And here he was, on a mission attempting to sustain commerce, which would bring in capital, which might, just might, enable this new 'power,' the United States, to remain a power for a little while. How long had Rome endured? Maybe six-hundred years? And Spain? And England? And France? And what were they fighting for, really?

He turned all the way around to look back onto the deck. There was little for the sailors to do in the fresh breeze other than an occasional correction, so most of the men were before the mast, talking, throwing dice, playing cards...until the Lieutenant came on deck and they all made as if they were extremely busy with something. *Anything.*

To be happy. To be content with life. That's all most of them wanted. Enough money so they didn't have to worry about where the next meal was coming from. Enough freedom so they could let off steam or do whatever they wanted now and then. A roof over their head when needed. Warm clothes. What did *he* want?

Well, he hadn't known it, but now he did. He wanted Isabella. He wanted a life with her in which she could be safe, they could have a family, maybe eventually settle down with a house and friends. How was that going to happen?

He sighed and headed for the hatch. He needed to study the Arabic book, to sound out the words, remember or figure out what they meant, gather the meaning from within their strange way of thinking and saying things. He wanted to have something to say to Cathcart when he returned the book. He wanted to understand what it meant that some languages were written left to right and others right to left. Why did the French, Spanish and English say 'twenty-one' and the Germans and Dutch say 'one and twenty?' Why did they put the verb at the end instead of the beginning? What difference did this make to the way they saw the world?

And what difference did their religion make? A religion that said all men who don't believe as you do are your enemies and are to be plundered and enslaved versus a religion that said you are to love all men as yourself, even— maybe especially— your enemies. And how can a people who believe either of those deal with a people who believe the opposite?

He climbed down the ladder and went to his small state-room where the tiny porthole allowed barely enough light to read by. Besides, he thought, if you don't do what the religion you espouse says you ought to do, if you're consumed with avarice and the lust for power, what does it matter what religion you profess? Money and power are your religion. Then you take those principles from the religion you say you believe, the ones you think support your position, and use them to rationalize whatever you want to do.

He thought about Isabella's conversion to Anglicanism. That had taken character, hadn't it? Maybe, initially, it was done just to annoy her father. But that wasn't why she was sticking to it. What did it mean to her? And what did it mean to him? If he was going to say he believed it, he had to live according to its principles. But what did that mean to him in this new career he was headed into? Could he do both?

He figured out what the Arabic book was. And why Cathcart had told him to let no one see it. As an infidel, *he* wasn't supposed to see the Koran.

"You have to understand how they think if you're going to deal with them," Cathcart had said. But so far, he'd scarcely been able to make heads or tails of it. He suddenly realized that was not because he didn't understand the Arabic. He knew what each and every word meant. But he had not been able to grasp whatever meaning they were intended to convey taken together. He just didn't think like that.

LISBON WAS A MAD DASH. He gathered the papers Col. Humphreys wanted taken to the States in addition to those he had from Captains O'Brien and Cathcart. He got a few lessons in being a diplomat as well as in self-defense. And after doing several days-worth of work in two days, he rushed to the pier and boarded the Spanish merchantman that would take him to New York. Even as far up the Tagus as Lisbon was situated, the growing seasonal unrest of the Atlantic was evident. They would have to move quickly to stay ahead of winter storms. Lewis hoped the sea would be kinder on the return journey than it had been on the trip over.

Which generally proved to be the case. Lewis improved his Spanish talking with the crew, though he learned many words he probably would not use in conversation with Isabella. He enjoyed being a passenger with no responsibilities other than to safeguard his messages and learn to understand not only Arabic, but Arabs.

Captain Santiago often talked with him. Upon learning that Lewis had crossed before, had been to China, was first mate and First Lieutenant on various ships, he asked him to collaborate as they found the best way to avoid November storms and counter-currents. If they stayed far enough north and sighted land near Halifax, they could avoid the Gulf

Stream altogether, and hopefully arrive in New York before nor'easters started kicking up.

Fortunately, the trip and the ship lived up to its name, *Grato* (Pleasant).

They docked in New York late in the afternoon of November 25 at Hunter's Key near the Meat Market. Lewis paid his respects to Captain Santiago and disembarked. Even in the few months he'd been gone, new buildings had sprouted. It took him a moment to get his bearings. Then he nodded, headed south along the key to the Old Slip Market, turned right, then turned left on Dock Street. In two long blocks he was at Broadway.

When he'd left in April, the government had been meeting at Fraunces Tavern. He'd start there. If that didn't work, he supposed he could call at Jay's house at 6 Broadway. His job was to find Jefferson and deliver his missives with all possible haste.

"Eh, 'aven't been 'ere since middle of August, I 'spose," said the garrulous proprietor. "Don'cha know they's moved to Philly and taken 'alf my revenue wif 'em?"

"No, Sir," said Lewis. "I didn't know that."

"Where ya bin? Ever'one knows 'at."

"Well, no one in Lisbon knew that," said Lewis.

"Just got in? On *Grato?*"

Lewis nodded.

"Ah! I was 'spectin' 'er. S'got my Port an' my Madiera, I 'ope."

"I believe so, Sir," said Lewis.

At which point the proprietor turned to a customer and that was all Lewis got out of him. *Jay's house it is*, he thought.

He went out into the gloom, crossed the street and headed down to number six. His heart thudded when he saw no lights in the windows. But he went up to the door and banged the knocker a couple of times anyway. No response.

So, he thought, *it's Hamilton's house.* He turned and walked the other way up Broadway. He didn't quite remember the number. Maybe it was twenty-six. Or was it twenty-eight? The stupes of the two dwellings looked identical except for the numbers. He decided to try twenty-eight. The door was answered by a black man dressed as a butler.

"Hamilton?" asked Lewis. The man pointed next door and closed his door without a word. Lewis raised his eyebrows. Yes, it was that kind of a neighborhood.

Then he raised the knocker on number twenty-six. But before he could let it fall, the door swung open. "Who are you?" said the boy, maybe about eight years old, standing there in an aggressive posture.

"You don't remember me?"

"Who's at the door?" asked a pleasant female voice. Then Eliza Hamilton appeared, looking out with a pleasant expression.

"Why, it's Mr. Elliot!"

Lewis bowed. "Mrs. Hamilton."

"I thought you were off to exotic places," she said. "And, please, call me Eliza. You're a grown man now."

"Yes, m'am," he said. Then Alexander's head popped into the doorway.

"Lewis!" he said. He looked at his son and wife. "Philip? Eliza? Are you going to let him stand there?"

"Oh. Goodness!" said Eliza. "Do come in! Come in!"

She and Philip stood aside as Lewis entered. Hamilton stuck out his hand and Lewis shook it. Philip shut the door.

"What brings you to us?" Hamilton asked, smiling, "Which you should not take to mean that I'm not glad to see you. But it is a strange time to come calling."

"I just got in from Lisbon, Sir," said Lewis.

"Ah, were you with my friend Humphreys?"

"Yes, Sir."

"Have you brought news for me?"

"Perhaps, Sir," said Lewis. "I was instructed not to open the satchel until I arrived."

Hamilton reached for it, but Lewis said, "He asked me to open it myself and give letters to those whose names are on them."

"Oh. Well, open it and let's see." He waved Lewis to a table at the back of the vestibule. Lewis went to it, set his diplomatic satchel down, procured a key from a pocket and opened it. He pulled out the first envelope.

"Who is it for?" asked Hamilton.

"Thomas Jefferson."

"Oh," said Hamilton, his face falling. "What would he want with that fellow?"

Lewis stood before the main door of the building that had been built to be the Pennsylvania State House. But now, dubbed Independence Hall by the Marquis de Lafayette, it served as the seat of the United States government. Vastly different as it was from the colossal edifices of royalty and government in Europe, colonial architecture had its charms. Even during this time of financial crisis, the white wooden doorframe that stretched to more than twice Lewis's height was freshly painted and scrubbed to a clean gloss. The walkway and the few stairs up to the door were clear of last night's snow. The multiple-paned windows even seemed to be clean. It was a good first impression.

Before Lewis could knock on the door, it was opened by a

uniformed man—not armed or dressed like a soldier, but clearly serious just the same.

"Please state your name and business," he said.

Lewis drew credentials out of his courier's valise and handed them to the man, at the same time indicating his business.

"I have dispatches from Europe and Africa for the Secretary of State."

The man tilted his head and raised his eyebrows at that, but he took the papers from Lewis. After putting on his spectacles, looking at the papers, looking over his spectacles at Lewis, and then back at the papers, he said, "Welcome home, Mr. Elliot. You will find Mr. Jefferson's office on the second floor, third door on the right, off the gallery."

He nodded and waved Lewis in.

The staircase was certainly unlike the imposing, oversized, marble one in Don Diego's home, but charming nonetheless. Lewis wanted to take the stairs two at a time, so eager was he finally to find the Secretary of State and fulfill his mission. But he thought better of it. Wouldn't be so good to arrive breathless and unable to talk. He slid his hand along the smooth dark wood railing atop white spindles as he took each step with deliberate care.

The gallery was abuzz with mostly young men rushing hither and yon, ignoring him as they carried precious papers from one place to another. He glanced at them briefly as he made his way to the third door. He knocked.

"Come!" said a voice from inside.

He opened the door, walked in, shut the door, and turned to survey the room. It was larger than he would have expected; a meeting room rather than an office. A slim red-haired man in a green topcoat sat facing the wall to Lewis's right, at the middle of the long side of a rectangular table that was surrounded by at least eight chairs.

The man didn't look up. "I've told you you needn't knock," he said. "It disturbs my concentration. You can place them at the end to my right."

Not certain what to do, Lewis didn't move.

After what seemed like minutes, the man looked up and took Lewis in.

"Who are you?"

"I'm Lewis Elliot, Sir, arrived in New York from Lisbon five days ago."

The man's countenance changed. "Oh," he said. "Sorry. That probably was not quite the greeting you hoped for." He smiled faintly. "You've come from Humphreys?"

"Yes, Sir. And from Captains Cathcart and O'Brien. And I bring greetings from William Short, Joel Barlow, and Count von Fersen."

"That's quite a comprehensive list. And your timing could not be better. I'm just writing a report for the president and the congress on the situation in the Mediterranean, about which my information was sparse and old. I hope your dispatches will improve it."

Lewis nodded.

Jefferson stood. "Come," he said. He turned and strode toward a door behind him which he opened and entered, leaving Lewis to follow.

By the time Lewis entered, Jefferson was seated behind a large mahogany desk.

He held his hand out toward Lewis. "Show me what you have."

Lewis removed the dispatches from his diplomatic pouch and handed them to Jefferson.

Jefferson nodded as he took them and began sorting as he

laid them on his desk. Head down, concentrating on the various envelopes, he said, "You may wait in my antechamber. If Pembroke ever gets back, you may ask him to provide coffee. Please wait for me there as I may have questions for you."

He looked up. "Did you see these men yourself, or are you simply carrying letters Col. Humphreys assembled?"

"I not only saw them all myself, Sir," said Lewis, "but I spent extensive time with all of them."

Jefferson seemed to see Lewis differently as he said that. "All of them? Including my friend Mr. Short?"

"Yes, Sir."

Jefferson grimaced, nodding. "Then request Pembroke to get coffee for yourself and me, both, and knock when he has done so."

Lewis nodded and retreated, closing the door quietly.

THE ELUSIVE PEMBROKE entered the antechamber without knocking or looking, evidently, because after depositing a pile of papers on the right side of Jefferson's table, he raised his head and started violently when he saw Lewis.

"Who-oo are you?" he asked.

Lewis couldn't suppress a grin. "That's the third time today I've been asked that," he said. He reached his hand out to Pembroke. "I'm Lewis Elliot, carrying dispatches from overseas to Mr. Jefferson."

"You almost gave me a heart attack," said Pembroke, offering a limp hand.

"And you must be the indefatigable Pembroke, Jefferson's long-suffering clerk," said Lewis.

Pembroke stood up a little straighter and puffed out his chest. "Yes," he said. "I have that privilege."

Lewis wasn't entirely sure of the best way to convey Jefferson's order. He went out on a limb. "Mr. Jefferson told me to ask if you would kindly provide coffee service for himself and me. I'm certain he'd expect you to get some for yourself as well."

"That would be unusual, but if you think that's what he wanted, I shall certainly get coffee for three."

"His thanks," said Lewis.

Pembroke nodded, wiped his forehead with the back of his hand and started toward the door. Then he turned back.

"Um, how will I get in carrying the tray?"

"I suppose you could leave the door slightly ajar."

"Oh, no. That would never do. Mr. Jefferson cannot countenance the door being slightly ajar."

Lewis nodded. "I can understand that," he said. "You never know who might wander in."

"Absolutely correct," said Pembroke.

"Well then, if you'll just tap the door lightly with your toe when you arrive with the coffee, I'll open it for you."

"Would you?" said Pembroke, a wide smile illuminating his face.

"Delighted to do so," said Lewis.

Pembroke turned his lanky frame and exited.

He arrived back in about fifteen minutes, apparently without incident. Lewis opened the door and Pembroke brought the tray in, setting it on the table.

He turned to Lewis. "So you have a secret meeting with Mr. Jefferson?"

"I don't know how secret it is," said Lewis. "But I have a meeting with him after he finishes reading the dispatches."

Pembroke leaned into him conspiratorially. "Oh, every meeting is secret these days," he said. He looked around the room in which he and Lewis were the only occupants, and lowered his voice. "You never know when a spy from the Secretary of the Treasury might be trying to pry into State Department business."

"A spy from Mr. Hamilton?"

"Ssshhh!" said Pembroke, raising his right forefinger to his lips. "We don't use his name here. We know who he is."

He turned his attention back to the silver service on the tray. "Shall I pour the coffee now?"

Lewis inclined his head toward Jefferson's office door. "He said to knock when you returned with the coffee, so I think we can take it into his office and—"

"Oh, no. I never go into his office."

"Oh," said Lewis, trying to determine the relationship between Pembroke and Jefferson.

"Then perhaps you should pour yours and take it here, and I'll bring the tray into his office."

Lewis decided that even though the silliness about Hamilton might be just because of Pembroke's timidity, he might be wiser not to mention that he had spent the night ensconced at the home of the Secretary of the Treasury before catching the stagecoach from New York.

THE COFFEE WAS LONG GONE by the time Jefferson was through with questions related to the Barbary pirates and the situation in Europe.

"So you say Cathcart wants an answer right away?"

"Yes, Sir."

Jefferson looked down at the papers now spread over the entirety of his desk. "I suppose we can try to get something to him through the usual channels."

Lewis didn't answer immediately as Jefferson's gaze surveyed the dispatches.

"Ah, Sir," said Lewis. "I'd like to bring it myself, if possible."

"Why would you want to make that trip again, just having come home?"

"Well, Sir, there's kind of a special reason."

"And what would that be?"

"That would be that my fiancée is in Tripoli with Captain Cathcart."

"What? Do you intend to marry a *Müslüman kadin?*" (Muslim woman)

"No, Sir. My betrothed is the daughter of Don Diego de Gardoqui y Arriquibar."

Jefferson's head snapped up and his voice went into the upper register. "Diego's daughter?"

Lewis nodded.

"How'd you manage that?"

Lewis smiled. "I think it may have been managed for me, Sir, though I may have helped a little."

Jefferson gave him another appraising glance. "There seems to be a great deal to you, Mr. Elliot," he said. "I don't have time for the story behind all this now, but perhaps you would dine with me and my daughter, Maria, tonight at my home? This is just the sort of story she'd like to hear."

"I thought your daughters were Patsy and Polly."

"Ah, well," said Jefferson, sitting back in his chair and smiling fully for the first time, though the smile soon dissolved into a wistful expression. "Since they fancy themselves full grown, they've put aside those names. Now they're Martha and Mary, or Maria when she's in the mood."

Jefferson jotted something down on a small note card and handed it to Lewis. "That's the address. We eat at eight, sharp, but we do not dress for dinner. What you're wearing now will be suitable."

Jefferson scribbled something on one of the other pieces of paper on his desk and also handed that to Lewis. "I just signed this so the bursar should honor it if he has cash today. Stop by his office in the building to the right as you exit."

Lewis took the paper and saw that Jefferson had written his signature at the bottom. It was confirmation of what seemed to Lewis an immense salary conferred on him by Col. Humphreys.

Jefferson looked back at the papers. "If you would be so kind as to remove the coffee service when you leave..."

Lewis opened the door and took the coffee service to the table where he set it down. Jefferson didn't look up as Lewis returned, pulled the door to, and allowed it to click softly shut.

In the six years since Lewis had lived there, Philadelphia had been built up immensely. For instance, his hotel on Lombard Street hadn't been there when he was apprenticed to Robert Morris in the mid-eighties. Nor had the New Market on Second Street between Pine and Cedar Streets been there. The new building projects, added to the fact that it was now the capital of the United States, multiplied the number and the busyness of its citizens. If commerce was diminished by a lack of ready cash, Lewis certainly couldn't tell by the number of men and women strolling along, carrying parcels and bags of recently purchased goods.

Of course, he was now walking on High Street (formerly Market Street), still the site of the largest market in Philadelphia—with a correspondingly large number of high-end stores on either side of the divided street. That's where people went to shop. Earlier, Lewis had gone there himself after opening an account at Mr. Morris's bank around the corner on Chestnut and Third.

The shop where he had gotten his first "grown-up" clothes as an apprentice to Mr. Morris seemed to be thriving. He entered and found the very same clerk who had served him almost eight years ago. Normally, he would have had to wait a week or more for his custom-made clothing, but they'd had a cancelled order for clothing that just happened to fit him. So, he had new clothes to wear to the Jefferson's, even though Jefferson had said he needn't dress for dinner. He was tired of those old clothes, anyway.

High Street was also where Jefferson had leased a house. Lewis looked at the note he'd been given—No. 274, right on the northeast corner of Third Street. He pulled his newly purchased watch from the watch pocket of the newly purchased trousers, which were the first he had owned that had such a pocket, Lewis reflected. If he was going to be a diplomat, he had to know the time. 7:34. He still had at least twenty minutes to kill.

It occurred to him that he ought to bring something as a thank-you gift. It was unlikely he could give Jefferson anything he didn't have, and he certainly wouldn't attempt to bring wine to someone who had lived in Paris for six years. Maybe he should get something for Polly...ah, Mary...ah, Maria? She probably didn't need anything, either, but finding some little trinket to please her would undoubtedly please her father as well. How old was she now? Fifteen? Sixteen?

He found a shop that specialized in decorative items for the home, went inside, and was immediately drawn to a wall upon which hung multiple flowers pressed between two pieces of glass, held together with lead, like stained-glass windows. He found one small enough to purchase and took it to the counter.

As he was paying, he asked the clerk if he knew what kind of flower it was. The clerk pulled back the paper in which he was wrapping it and glanced at it.

"Looks like lily of the valley to me," he said. "Comes out in the spring. Spreads everywhere."

"Is that good or bad?"

"Depends on whether you're the gardener," said the clerk, laughing. But he offered no more information. Lewis thanked him and left.

At five minutes to eight, Lewis thought it would be appropriate to knock. After all, if dinner was at eight, he ought to be there in enough time to hang up his coat beforehand. A well-dressed black man opened the door, invited Lewis in, and took his hat and coat.

"You may wait in the library," he said, pointing down the hall before him toward the first door on the left.

Almost as he stepped into the room, Jefferson's younger daughter fairly bounced down the hall from the other direction and collided with him.

"Oh, sorry!" she said, a bright smile coming to her perfect face. "Hi! I'm Polly."

"Hi yourself. I'm Lewis. And I thought you were Mary."

She giggled and said, "Oh, I am when my stuffy sister, currently great with child, is around. The nuns at the convent school called me 'Ma-*rye*-ah' which is also what they say in Virginia even though they say 'Ma-*ree*-ah' here in Pennsylvania, and..."

"Whoa," said Lewis, laughing. "You lost me in the convent school. Were you going to become a nun?"

"No, that was Patsy, but she changed her mind, I think because of Papa and maybe Mr. Short who she was thinking of marrying only she didn't because he didn't want to move to Virginia but she..."

"Polly, dear," said a voice from behind her. "Are you boring Mr. Elliot to tears?"

She twirled to face him. "Why, no, Papa. He is such a very good listener..."

"Perhaps that is because you didn't provide him the slightest chance to engage in the conversation."

Polly looked as if she'd been stung. She turned back to Lewis, her eyes watering up. "Mr. Lewis," she said earnestly, "was I boring you to tears?"

"Why, No, Ma-*rye*-ah," said Lewis. "You were most enchanting."

Over her head, Lewis saw Jefferson shaking his head and grinning. Polly turned back to him.

"See," she said holding her arms out to both sides. "I wasn't boring him. He said I was enchanting."

"Well, I know he has made a friend for life," said Jefferson, "whether or not he was bored to tears. Come. Let us dine."

"Ah, Sir" said Lewis, "I do happen to have a little parcel for my friend for life, as a small token of my thanks for your kind invitation."

Jefferson nodded and Lewis pulled out the wrapped flower, handing it to Polly.

"For me?" she asked.

Lewis nodded.

As Polly unwrapped it and it became evident what it was, her face registered great surprise.

"Thank you so much," she said. "No one has ever given me anything like this."

Jefferson grinned. "He doesn't know our customs, dear," he said as he turned to walk in the direction from which Polly had come. She let him get a few steps away, placed her left arm under Lewis's right elbow, and followed.

"Come," she said. "We shall at least be great friends even though I'm a girl. You will come to see me, before Papa and I leave for Monticello? I thought it might be more fun than Eppington here, but nobody comes to visit, and Papa is always working."

Jefferson led them to a large dining room where three places were set at one end of a massive table Lewis thought could seat twenty or more. Jefferson moved to the end, Polly moved to his near side, and Lewis held out the chair for her.

"Why thank you, sir," she said, sitting.

Lewis walked behind Jefferson to the chair on his left. Jefferson nodded and the two took their seats. In a moment two black men, dressed as the man at the door had been, and a black woman, attired like a seamstress or some 'commoner' white woman might have been, appeared with dishes of carrots, potatoes, a dark stew, and a bottle of French wine. The food was set on the table between Jefferson and Lewis, served to Lewis first, then Jefferson, and then Polly. As the food was being served, wine was poured for all of them.

"Polly is barely able to contain herself waiting to hear about your Isabella," said Jefferson after they had each had a few bites. "Perhaps you could humor her."

Lewis smiled and set his fork down. "There is nothing I'd rather speak about," he said. He opened his mouth to say more, but immediately held himself in check as Polly's questions burst from her.

"Is she beautiful? Does she have deep brown eyes, not like my watery blue ones? Long black hair? Gorgeous gowns?" She stopped, breathless.

"Yes," said Lewis, grinning.

"Yes, what?" said Polly.

"Yes, to all of that," said Lewis, "and oh so much more."

"Did you kiss her?"

"Polly," said Jefferson, looking at Polly with mild annoyance. "That is not a question to ask a gentleman."

Lewis grinned and mouthed Yes silently while shaking his head No.

"Oh, you are so fortunate, Mr. Lewis," she said. "I have never been kissed."

"And well you should not have been at your tender age," said her father.

"That's just *Lewis*," said Lewis. "Not Mr. Lewis or Mr. Elliot. I'm not that much older than you."

At this point a strange look passed over Polly's face.

"He's engaged," said Jefferson. "He will be marrying Señorita Isabella."

Polly looked at her father and heaved a sigh. "Well, I hope someone will kiss me and marry me someday," she said. She turned back to Lewis. "Mr. Just Lewis, if you were not engaged to Señorita Isabella, would you consider marrying me?"

Lewis's jaw dropped as he was rescued by Jefferson. "Mr. Elliot and I have matters to discuss," he said. "Perhaps there will still be some time for all of us to converse after that."

"Oh, Papa," she said. "Have I said something wrong again? I know I'm not my sister and I lack her finesse. But he did give me lily of the valley."

"He didn't know the association of marriage and lily of the valley in our Virginia customs, dear."

Lewis suddenly realized what the mysterious custom was and rose to the occasion. "I should certainly give the matter great consideration," said Lewis, "were I not, as your father noted, already spoken for."

Lewis felt that the look Polly gave him for that statement

was worth whatever displeasure it might have caused her father.

Dinner continued with chatter about the Philadelphia weather, the difference between Philly and Paris, and sundry other non-threatening matters. After the pudding, Jefferson pushed his chair back. "Come," he said, motioning to Lewis and, heading out the door.

They made their way back to the library. Over his shoulder Jefferson said, "You'll have her eating out of your hand if you're not careful." But he turned and smiled at Lewis. "Well done. You'll make a fine diplomat."

He waved toward a chair. Lewis sat and Jefferson sat in a chair across a short table from him. One of his men came in and poured a small glass of port for each.

After they had sipped and Lewis had commented on the quality of the port, Jefferson looked him in the eyes. "Would you like to work for me?"

Lewis set his glass on the table before him. "I have learned, Sir, that being a diplomat may involve a level of deception and intrigue that is inimical to my personality. Were I to work for you, would you expect that of me?"

"It is just because I do not expect that of you that I would like you to work for me."

Lewis nodded. "Thank you, Sir. Yes, I would like to work for you. As you know, however, I'm currently engaged by Col. Humphreys."

"Do not concern yourself," said Jefferson. "That's the same as working for me. If you like, and do not mind the travel, you may become liaison between me and my people in Europe, including Col. Humphreys."

"Would you mind if Isabella travelled with me?"

"Not at all. In fact, that would aid in the secrecy with which I would expect you to conduct yourself."

He took another appraising look at Lewis. "Would you be willing to carry large sums of money?"

"I believe so, Sir, given the proper training."

Jefferson nodded. "That will be done. And one more thing."

Lewis gave Jefferson his undivided attention.

"I would like you to speak with the president about the situation in the Mediterranean, about the reports you have brought me and about what you have seen yourself. Can you do that?"

"Yes, Sir. With pleasure."

"Excellent. I don't know when it will be. Perhaps it will be after we return from the Christmas holiday—"

The door fell open to Polly's reddening face. "Sorry, Papa," she said. "I was just wondering when you would come out to visit some more."

Jefferson shook his head. "I'm certain you will love your children as much as I love mine," said Jefferson to Lewis, "even though there may be times when you would like to..."

"Oh no you wouldn't, Papa," said Polly gleefully. "You always only love us."

Lewis watched Jefferson's response, realizing that Polly's words were entirely true.

Jefferson stood and waved Lewis toward the door as Polly led them to the sitting room.

Lewis looked with some dismay at the scones and coffee set on a low table before their chairs. There was only so much conversation he could take. But he held in his feelings and sat in the chair to which Polly directed him.

"This looks lovely," he said, thinking, but not saying, "but it's been a long day and I can't stay long."

After Polly had extracted as many details about Isabella and his relationship with her as she could, she blurted out,

"They have to get married at Monticello, Father! Of course you see that."

Lewis expected Jefferson to demur or make some vague, non-committal, response, but he picked it up.

"I should like that," he said, "and not just to humor my daughter. Don Diego is a very important man, and this would provide a welcome opportunity to interact with him and his friends, perhaps even to bring us closer together as two nations."

Lewis caught the meaning immediately. Nothing escaped politics. No matter how much Jefferson claimed to dislike royalty, he knew that some of their tactics worked—like bringing two royal families from different countries together through marriage. This tactic was several millenia old, Lewis realized, and he had fallen right into it. Or maybe not. He had fallen for Isabella, and her father had fallen into it. And now Jefferson. But Lewis liked the Spanish. He was grateful for the part they had played in the American Revolution. He decided he would willingly pursue what might be a side-benefit of his marriage. And he realized, too, what a world of problems being married in America might prevent for Isabella and Don Diego.

He looked Jefferson in the eyes and realized that Jefferson knew he had figured it out. "I should be honored if you would be willing to host Isabella and me for our vows," he said.

Jefferson nodded, thereby acknowledging Lewis's perspicacity, Lewis perceived, but also affirming his own willingness to have the event at Monticello.

"However," he said, "At the moment Monticello looks more like a brick kiln than a home. I should need some time..." He looked over at Lewis. "When do you expect to be married?"

Lewis steepled his hands to his lips and breathed out. He closed his eyes for a moment and then lowered his hands and spoke. "I should hope by late summer, '92, the Atlantic Ocean and Don Diego being willing."

"We shall count on it then," said Jefferson, rising from his chair.

Polly was trying not to act like a delighted five-year-old, with minimal success. Finally, she grabbed her father's right arm with both hands. "Oh, thank you, thank you!" she said. Then she released him. "I shall write to Patsy immediately!" She rushed from the room.

Jefferson's lips contracted slightly, then became a grin. "She's impetuous, yes," he said, "but it's not a bad idea."

As Lewis made his way to the hotel, he shook his head. Somehow George Washington came to mind—his unalterable conviction that The Divine had made possible both the American Revolution and the Republic.

I could never have imagined how things would turn out, he thought. *What would mother and father think of me now, if they knew, or Aunt Virginia and Uncle James?* He lifted his eyes up toward the brittle December stars. "Thank you, Lord of heaven and earth," he said aloud. "You seem still to be at work on this continent."

IT WAS a bit of *deja vu* for Lewis the next morning as he raised his hand to knock on the door of the Robert Morris house on Market Street at the corner of Sixth, where President George Washington had been living for several months since he had moved in in December of 1790. High Street had been called Market Street eight years ago when he, Gilly, and Crispin had been sent to Philadelphia to begin the apprenticeships that would be foundational to their lives. Robert Morris, to whom they had been sent, had lived on Front Street at the time, but within a couple of years the Market Street house had become his residence and the place where Lewis's apprenticeship had concluded.

Suddenly, Lewis withheld his knock as a young lady exited the house next door. Well, yes, in the years since he had seen her, she had changed somewhat, but he recognized her easily.

"Hetty?" he called.

As she looked around to see where the voice was coming from, a younger young woman charged out, craned her head to see over the garden wall separating the two properties, and pointed right at Lewis.

"Is that you, Lewy?" she shouted. Not waiting for an answer, she ran out her gate and in through the gate of the president's home to give Lewis a great hug.

"Where have you been?" she cried. "We missed you!"

Following as quickly as decorum would allow, Hetty rushed toward Lewis, only to halt a couple of feet in front of him. "Lewis!" she said.

Lewis carefully moved Maria to his right side and held out his left arm for Hetty. She hesitated only a moment before stepping into his embrace.

"How I had hoped you would not forget me," she said, resting her head on his lapel. She looked up at him. "But it doesn't matter now, since father has pledged me to James Marshall."

Lewis was thunderstruck. Oh, he *had* forgotten her. Isabella had quite taken her out of his mind. He and Hetty had not actually had an understanding—she was only thirteen at the time, after all—but perhaps they had an understanding that one day they might have an understanding. He couldn't say this, of course. So he said, "Do you like him?"

"Oh, he is very nice," she said. "And, yes. Quite likable. But he is not you."

"Well since she's going to marry James," said Maria, "could you marry me?"

The door opened suddenly, saving Lewis. He glanced at the head poking out. "Pembroke?"

"Yes," he said, "and I heard that last. How many proposals of marriage are you going to get here in Philadelphia?"

"You heard about Polly?"

"It's all she ever talks about," he said, "except of course your…"

Lewis gave his 'kill' glare to Pembroke, kissed each of the Morris girls on the tops of their heads, and said, "May I call on you later today? I have a meeting to attend right now."

"With the president and Mr. Jefferson," said Pembroke, giving Lewis a look that asked if this was better. Lewis winked at him.

"Perhaps you could come for tea?" said Maria.

"I should very much like that," he said as Pembroke ushered him inside.

As soon as the door was shut, Lewis leaned against it and sighed.

"Do you know everyone in Philadelphia?" asked Pembroke, amazement poking through his raspy voice.

Lewis laughed slightly. "No. Just a few."

Jefferson trotted from the upstairs hallway down the stairs to Lewis's right and swiveled at the bottom, heading down the hall toward the back of the house.

"Ten minutes, Mr. Elliot," he said, voice fading as he turned left to the necessary room.

"I'll take your coat," said Pembroke.

Lewis shed it off his shoulders and handed it to Pembroke as another person made his way down the stairs.

"Mr. Elliot!" said a large voice. "I'm so glad I could see you today!"

"He's coming for tea at your house this afternoon," said Pembroke.

Lewis and Robert Morris both turned a look on him.

"I...I'll just be going," he said, grasping the coat as if it was a shield.

"How did that transpire?" asked Morris.

"Hetty and Maria came out just as I was about to knock on this door," said Lewis. "We had quite a reunion—that Pembroke happened to witness."

Morris strode over to Lewis, extending his hand. "That will be grand," he said. "But why not make it dinner? We have much to catch up on."

"Like when did you become the president's next door neighbor?"

Morris laughed. "Like that. And like how did you become a courier for Jefferson? I knew you would go far, but I wasn't thinking of 'far' quite so literally."

Lewis grinned and shook his head. "Nor I," he said.

Then Jefferson, returning from the back of the house, caught his eye. "I guess I'd better go," he said.

"Yes. I won't be in this meeting, but I look forward to seeing you tonight." Morris nodded and headed out to the street.

SEVERAL MEN in addition to the president were assembled when Lewis and Jefferson walked in, Jefferson's hand awkwardly on the shoulder of the taller Lewis.

"Some of you know my new courier, Lewis Elliot," said Jefferson.

"Ah," said Washington. "Lieutenant Elliot, if I remember correctly."

Hamilton grinned. "However briefly," he said, "and by the grace of General Schuyler."

Lewis wondered why Hamilton had found it necessary to slight him thus, but he didn't have much time to think about it.

Jefferson grimaced, coming to his support. "And later lieutenant in the French navy by his own merits."

Which Lewis knew to be not entirely true. It had been more a case of being at the right place at the right time. But what interested him was the not-so-congenial back and forth between Hamilton and Jefferson, which Washington watched like a spectator might have done as he and Gilly kicked their ball back and forth all those years ago.

"General Henry Knox," said Hamilton, nodding at the man to Washington's right, "is Secretary of War."

Knox nodded toward Lewis. "Welcome to the field of battle," he said.

"Mr. Vice-President Adams is also here today to listen to your report," said Jefferson.

Adams nodded. "I'm a plain man from New England," he said, "and would welcome plain words about the trouble we're facing in the Mediterranean—since it so often concerns seamen from my part of the country."

Jefferson gestured to the second chair to the left of President Washington, who sat at the head of the oval table. Lewis rounded the table behind the president and took his seat.

"The reports you brought from Captains O'Brien and Cathcart gave us a good understanding of the difficulties they face," Jefferson said to Lewis and the table at large. "Perhaps you could share some personal observations from your time in Algiers and Tripoli."

Without telling him exactly what to say, Jefferson had prepped Lewis on this question. Still, it was with some trepidation that Lewis began speaking to this august assemblage—many of the most important people of the government of the United States.

"The cities are alike," said Lewis, "in that they have small, narrow and apparently shallow harbors. Both harbors have some protection from the sea in the form of peninsulas that extend around them on one side. But more important, they both have uncountable numbers of small craft, evidently rowed by slaves, that have the ability to move swiftly and accurately toward ships inside and outside the harbors. I spent time with some of the corsairs that provide the strike forces of those boats. They are large, tough, humorless men, armed with multiple swords, knives, and the occasional pistol. Their practice is to approach ships, even as they are being fired upon, board them, and overwhelm the crews."

"It was such tactics that overwhelmed the *Maria* of Boston, I'm told," said Adams.

Lewis nodded. "That's what Captain O'Brien said."

"What about the cities themselves?" asked Jefferson.

"I didn't go ashore at Algiers," said Lewis. "But my impression from Captain Cathcart is that it is little different form Tripoli except for being far more mountainous."

"What impressed you particularly?" asked Jefferson.

Without hesitation, Lewis replied, "The slave market."

"Why?" asked General Knox.

"Because the slaves were white," said Lewis, "or more properly, they were red. Badly burned by the sun, bearing the welts of whips and even dried blood, many could scarcely stumble to the raised platforms from which they were sold."

"Were there any women?" asked Hamilton.

"Many," said Lewis. "But they were covered from head to foot in black cloth, with only their eyes visible." He looked around the table. "Of course, I couldn't see what they looked like, but Captain Cathcart told me that many of the villages along the shores of Italy and Spain were abandoned because of fear of Barbary raids for slaves. And, in addition, they traffic slaves from farther north, inland, and from Russia."

"Did you actually see any of those?" asked Hamilton, skepticism dripping through the apparently innocuous question.

"In fact, yes," said Lewis. "Captain Cathcart had been able to buy a couple of women from Austro-Hungary, whom he freed and employed as maids in the complex. My fiancée often went out to the market with them. In that case, it was an advantage that all women wore black, and specifically, in this case, also wore veils over their faces. No one knew who they were, and they were mostly left alone."

"What do you mean, 'mostly?'" asked Knox.

Lewis turned toward him and Hamilton, seated diagonally across from him. "I mean that they were often accosted and taunted by the men of the place since no woman of good family would be out at the market or anywhere else without male accompaniment."

"Well, that is sobering to be sure," said Adams. "But what will we do about our enslaved sailors?"

"I have conferred with Mr. Hamilton," said Washington, "and I believe we've set aside $40,000 to send with Mr. Elliot back to Cathcart and O'Brien."

Jefferson rose suddenly to his feet as if to respond, but Washington silenced him with a wave. He returned to his seat.

"I know it's nowhere near what they demanded, but it's all we can spare. I feel deeply for the pain those men experience, but they are some dozens. Here we must be concerned with the millions of people in our new little republic, and how they fare."

Hamilton looked directly at Lewis and then at Jefferson. "You are certain that Mr. Elliot can carry those funds to Captain Cathcart?"

Jefferson's face reddened. "He is experienced and trained,"

he said stiffly, "and he will have two men with him, in plain clothes, to assist—should there be any trouble."

Washington looked from Lewis to Jefferson to Hamilton. "I recall now, Alex, that Mr. Elliot did some rather remarkable riding to convey messages between us some years ago." He laughed faintly. "Perhaps you didn't know, but he even ate one of your missives so it wouldn't get into the wrong hands."

"Then...then...how——" said Hamilton raising his hands slightly above the table.

"He memorized the letter prior to eating it."

Hamilton looked at Lewis. "No," he said, softly, looking away. "He never told me."

"Thank you, Mr. Elliot," said Washington, looking from Hamilton back to Lewis with a faint smile. "For your report, for the service you have already rendered, and for the service you are about to render."

Lewis nodded. "You are most welcome, Sir."

"Secretary Jefferson," said Washington, "is there anything else we need to know or do before we send Mr. Elliot on his way?"

"If that is all you have," said Jefferson, "it must suffice." He nodded, rose from his seat, and beckoned to Lewis. The two exited.

In the hallway Jefferson asked, "Are you set to depart on the 21st?"

"As set as I can be," said Lewis. "I've procured berths for myself and two others on the *Confiança* out of Lisbon. The captain assured me that everything looks good for a three to four-week crossing."

"Good. You will need to go to Mr. Morris's bank to pick up the currency, probably on the 20th. It will be in French livres, some paper, some metal. Let me know when you are going, and I'll provide an escort."

Lewis nodded. "Would you mind..." he began, then paused.

"What is it?"

"Can you explain to me what happened in there with you and Mr. Hamilton?"

"And with you?" asked Jefferson, grinning.

Lewis nodded.

"In war," said Jefferson, "a general chooses his aides. They do so many things for him, become so close to him and all who interact with him, that they are called his 'family'."

"Yes," said Lewis, more a question than a statement.

"Mr. Hamilton may have considered you one of his 'family' since you worked for him during the war. Now he sees you as part of my 'family.' He probably thinks of that as a betrayal—"

"But..."

"Yes, I know. You haven't changed in your feelings toward him, nor do you think you've betrayed him. He has come to dislike me. I don't, at the moment, particularly dislike him. I think most of his policies are wrong. Yet he has the president's ear and nearly all he wills is carried out. We are at odds, he and I. And if he sees you as part of my family, he is now at odds with you."

Lewis let out a sigh.

"Sorry," said Jefferson. "That's politics."

"*Am* I part of your family?"

Jefferson patted him on the shoulder and smirked.

"Since you signed up with Humphreys." He tilted his head toward the door. "I have to get back, now," he said, "before Hamilton convinces President Washington to adopt some new travesty."

"Yes, Sir," said Lewis to Jefferson's departing back. "Thank you, Sir," he whispered. He was part of a family.

~

ON THE TRIP TO LISBON, Lewis was escorted, he was made to understand, by two reliable distant cousins to the Jeffersons. More family. They would accompany him there, meet Humphreys, and return to Virginia. Humphreys would provide escorts for the trip to Tripoli from Lisbon. The paper money was divided among the three, each of whom carried it in a pouch under his outer clothing. The gold was in a small, heavy, box, each piece wrapped with cloth to prevent them jingling against one another and alerting any would-be thief to their existence. One of the three men was to stay in the cabin at all times, with the locked box chained to him.

It wasn't a convenient arrangement, but it worked.

They encountered no storms such as Lewis had endured on his last voyage to Europe, so March crawled into April and, though it had seemed interminable, it was actually a rather quick crossing.

Lewis had a few days to spend in Lisbon before boarding a craft to the Mediterranean. He had two or three conferences with Humphreys, to which he could hardly pay attention.

When the Rock of Gibraltar reminded Lewis of the billowing skirts of Isabella's dresses and her face rose above it with a beatific smile, he knew he was besotted. They encountered no Barbary ships on their way to Tripoli, and by one sweltering afternoon in early May, 1791, Lewis could make out the massive, round tower on the Lungo Mare Vittorio, the spur of land that sprang out of the sea on Tripoli's western side. He never thought he could love a landscape feature, but he loved this one. Only because it meant he would be with his fiancée, of course, and he was sure he'd forget it as soon as they were away from there. For now, it was a connection to her and he loved it.

As soon as the gangplank was lowered, Lewis rushed ashore and negotiated for one of the uncovered coaches lining the quay. No sooner was that done than he called his two escorts, and they, with the luggage, dashed to the coach, heavy rifles conspicuous on their shoulders.

Nothing moved swiftly in Tripoli, and the slow gait of the two horses frustrated Lewis more than usual. But he said nothing, because he knew it would only precipitate a pause to explain why they were moving at that rate. They finally arrived at Via Puglia, where Lewis jumped down to rattle the knocker on the gate. After a couple of minutes that seemed to last about an hour each, the gate was opened a hand's width and a Tripolitan looked out. Lewis recognized him.

"*Ilnah ha'anna*, Lewis," (It's me, Lewis!) he shouted. The man's face brightened. He opened his side of the gate and moved toward the other side to open that. But before he had it open, he shouted toward the courtyard, "*Luis huna!*" (Lewis is here!). Lewis took that as his cue to run through the open gate. He heard "*Luis huna!*" echoing through the house.

Her entrance was nothing like as graceful as it had been in Madrid, but it was quicker. And that was enough for Lewis.

"Oh, Lew!" Isabella cried, running down the steps and into the courtyard.

"*¡Finalmente estás aquí!*" (You're finally here!). She rushed into his arms before he could respond. "*¡No te vayas nunca más sin mí!*" (Don't ever go away without me again!)

"No, my love," he said, kissing the top of her head, engulfed in the feel and scent of her ambrosial hair. "I couldn't bear it."

8

GETTING TO PHILADELPHIA, 1792

It was amazing that mail still came, given the general state of affairs in Paris. The war with other continental powers started in April, 1792, with Rochambeau invading the Netherlands. In May conscriptions began—which meant that any French male of suitable age might be grabbed off the street and assigned to a French regiment. Gilly stayed off the street. Even though his service in the French armed forces had not been difficult, once had been enough. He had Renée go out to do any required errands. It wasn't particularly safe for Crispin to be out either, since he had no quick way of proving either his English or American citizenship, if either of them would have done any good anyway.

And then the "enrollment" ramped up, as the German mercenaries who had been hired by the French reverted to the Austrian-Prussian coalition. Neither Gilly nor Crispin personally knew any priests, but nevertheless they felt sorry for those they saw being rounded up for deportation late in May. The priests had only to sign an oath to the government, rather than to the church, to be allowed to stay. But most of them wouldn't.

The events of June, including rioting mobs, the invasion of the Tuileries Palace, the humiliation of Louis XVI, the denunciation of Lafayette at the end of the month and his virtual exile to his troops in the north, capped it for Crispin. He had moved in with Gilly and Renée in March and had spent his time surreptitiously drawing whatever he found interesting. It became more and more risky.

"You must leave," he told Gilly and Renée on July 1. "It has become violent and irrational and will only become worse."

Renée looked at Gilly who said, "*Il dit que nous devons partir.*" (He says we must leave.)

"*Il a raison,*" she replied. "*J'ai peur ici.*" (He's right. I'm afraid here.)

"But oowhere weell oowe go?" said Gilly. "'ow will I leeve?"

"I have an—"

Gilly interrupted Crispin. "And do oowe not meet Louis in 'avre, sometime?"

"Yes, but we haven't heard from him and likely will not."

At which opportune moment one of Lafayette's servants entered the kitchen and said in a staccato sort of way, "*Une lettre pour tu,*" tossing it on the preparation table. He turned his back on them quickly and stomped out.

Crispin raised his eyes to Gilly, nodding toward the servant, in an unspoken question about his rudeness.

"They no like me. I no good enough for them," he said.

"Another reason to leave."

"*Et la chef, il s'en va aussi,*" said Renée. "*Pourquoi resterais-tu? Il n'y a rien pour vous ici maintenant.*" (And the chef, he is also leaving. There is nothing for you to stay for now.)

Crispin picked up the letter and glanced at it. "It's from Lewis!" he said. "Addressed to you and me."

"*Ouvrez-le!*" said Gilly. (Open it !)

Crispin needed no translation for that and tore the envelope open, pulled out the letter, and scanned it. "He'll be in Havre with his fiancée—" he looked up at Gilly and they both raised eyebrows.

"*Sa fiancée?*"

"Seems like it," said Crispin, "probably by July 11." He raised his eyes from the letter and looked first at Gilly and then at Renée. "We should be there."

Gilly wavered between a glower and a smile. "*Et tu pense que je devrais partir de là?*"

Crispin nodded. "If you said, 'I think you should leave from there,' you were right."

"*Mais vers où?*" asked Renée. (But to where?)

"To America, of course," said Crispin.

"But 'ow?" asked Gilly.

"I have money," said Crispin. "Let me do this for you."

"But oowhere in America? And 'ow weell oowe leeve oowhen we get there?"

Crispin sighed. "Did you not work with one of the finest chefs in Paris?"

Gilly nodded.

"And did you not want to open your own restaurant?"

"*C'est mon rêve!*" (It's my dream!)

"Look, I haven't learned much French yet. Would you mind doing English?"

"*Mais mon rêve est en français!*" (But my dream is in French!)

Crispin screwed up his face. "If I understand you correctly, my response is that it will have to be in English because I want to help you open a French restaurant in Philadelphia."

Gilly looked thunderstruck. "*Vraiment?*" (Really?)

"Oui!" said Crispin, shaking his head. "I give up. Speak French while you can."

"*D'accord.*" (All right.)

Gilly looked at Renée. "*Tu viendras?*" (Are you coming?)

"*Bien sûr!*" (Of course!)

"*D'accord,*" said Gilly looking back at Crispin. "*Nous irons. Um,* 'ow much monee?" (We're going.)

"Enough," said Crispin. "Do not worry."

"*Il dit ne t'inquiète pas.*" (He says not to worry.)

Renée rushed around the table and hugged Crispin. He held his hands up, away from her, for only a moment before hugging her back.

"And now," he said, "we have to get out of here while it's still possible."

JULY 11 FOUND them in Le Havre on the Tour (tower) François Premier looking west for signs of a ship they hoped would arrive. They had received another letter from Lewis telling them the brigantine, *Eurybia,* out of Lisbon, should arrive on the rising tide of July 11. That turned out to be 2:32 PM. So they waited in the blistering afternoon sun, scanning the Channel for a quick, two-masted ship rounding the Gatteville Point.

When they finally did see what looked like their ship, they made haste to the Brise-lamas where military packets usually docked. Normally, a courier ship like this would have few passengers, and those would be chiefly military. But in this case, quite a number of well-dressed men and women disembarked along with an enormous amount of baggage which sailors immediately began to pack into a waiting wagon drawn by two horses.

Following them, a magnificently clad young woman appeared by the rail, looking at the dock, and then behind her a French officer who took her hand and walked with her down the gangplank. As they reached the bottom, he looked over and smiled at Gilly, Renée, and Crispin, then turned his head to speak with the young woman, turned back and pointed.

"Lewis?" said Crispin. "Can it be?"

"Louis!" shouted Renée, running toward him. Gilly ran after.

It looked as though Renée would rush up and hug him, but she skidded suddenly to a stop and looked at the stunning young woman. *"Puis-je?"* (May I?)

The young woman laughed brilliantly and said, *"Bien sûr!"*

Whereupon Renée fell upon Lewis and hugged him as if she'd never let go.

Gilly approached and took his right hand, shaking it fiercely, and Crispin stood behind them, grinning.

He looked at the young woman and said, "Welcome to France. I'm Crispin, Lewis's friend, and these two are the excitable French brother and sister, Gilly and Renée."

Still smiling, the young woman, curtsied slightly. "I am Isabella. It is a delight to meet the great friends of my Lewis of whom he has told me so much."

Gilly backed off, drawing Renée with him. He turned to Isabella.

"Louis 'elp rescue 'er from Brest and the fever, *mais* she nevair 'ad chance to thank 'im," said Gilly.

Lewis placed an arm around Isabella. "This is my wonderful fiancée, of whom I am not worthy," he said, grinning.

"So true," she said looking serious until she could hide her mirth no longer. She laughed again and said, "He must make a habit of rescuing maidens, because he rescued me as well."

Crispin didn't miss the loving look Lewis gave Isabella.

Lewis became suddenly serious. "We've taken lodgings briefly on Rue Louis XIII. Perhaps you would join us there in, say, two hours?" He looked over all the baggage and the men placing it on the wagon. "That should give us time to...."

At which point Crispin's attention was drawn back to the gangplank down which another young woman, not quite so well dressed, but nearly as beautiful, carried an enormous hat box. Isabella looked over at her and smiled.

"I wouldn't trust anyone but Sophia with that box," she said, neglecting to mention its contents.

A landau pulled around the wagon and stopped in front of them. Lewis helped Isabella into the front bench. When Sophia arrived with the box, Lewis took it from her, placed it carefully on the far side of the seat behind Isabella, and helped Sophia get in.

"We'll see you shortly," he said. "We can talk then." He walked around the landau and got in on the other side, speaking softly to the driver.

Then the whole entourage moved sedately up the quay, turning left at the first street.

It was only a couple of days later that Crispin continued to wave long after they could see him. He'd follow as soon as he could but errands in England awaited him first.

ONCE THE SHIP docked in Philadelphia at the Mervyn wharf between Walnut and Spruce streets, they lost the breeze that had somewhat protected them from the mid-August heat. Gilly, Renée and Lewis stood on the larboard quarterdeck, wiping sweat from their foreheads and staying out of the way of the sailors on the main deck preparing for disembarkment.

"*C'est la plus grande ville des États-Unis?*" (This is the largest city in the United States?) Renée asked as the top of the gangplank was raised to the ship.

Though they had entered a forest of masts, surrounded by docks with crowds of workers scurrying about like ants whose nest has been uncovered, the city itself was not particularly remarkable; church steeples and the spires of government buildings notwithstanding.

"You know," said Gilly, "thees countree is *seulement un bébe'*." (...only a baby.)

"It may be a baby compared to France," said Lewis, "but it's growing quickly."

"Say that in *français*?" asked Gilly, nodding toward Renée.

Lewis shook his head. "I'm sure Renée will learn English more quickly than you did," he said grinning, "and with less resistance."

"*Mais oui*," she said. "I weel!"

As though he had not heard the last interchange, Gilly went on, "But doo not forget that Bretagne eez far older than this 'France' you spik of."

Isabella joined them at the rail. Lewis put his arm around her as Sophia came to stand on his other side. "Speaking of older cultures," he said, "the one they come from is as old as yours."

"Old and set in ways that probably cannot endure," Isabella said, laying her head against Lewis's shoulder. "I don't see my country having a revolution like yours, Gilly." She raised her head and looked at him. "Just falling away into the last century or dividing into little ethnic kingdoms like Italy." She leaned back against Lewis's shoulder. "But not without a lot of bloodshed."

Suddenly they were accosted by a voice from the wharf. "Is that Mr. Lewis? And Mr. Y'vant?"

"That sounds like Mr. B. Morris," said Lewis. "Do you see him?"

"Someone is waving over there," said Sophia, dropping the

pretense that she didn't speak English and pointing to her right. "It looks like a woman."

Lewis shaded his brow and looked that way. "It's Hetty!" he said. "Hetty Morris. And there's Maria, trailing behind her."

"And the voice," said Gilly. Mr. Morris was walking as quickly as his dignity and breath would permit, but still a number of steps behind the young women. Lewis and Gilly waved. Lewis pointed to the gangplank that had just connected with the ship. He turned to Sophia. "Can you prepare señorita's luggage to be transported?" Sophia smiled, knowing the question was merely a courtesy, and nodded slightly. Lewis looked back at Isabella and took her hand.

"*Ven mi tesoro*," (Come, my treasure)," he said. "I would like my friends to meet you."

THEY HAD BARELY SET foot on the wharf when their little greeting party was scattered by the breathless arrival of another well-wisher. Polly Jefferson fairly leapt on Lewis and threw her arms around him.

"Oh, I'm so glad to see you!" she cried. She released him and took a step back. "I know you're going to get married and it's not to me but that's all right because Papa promised he'd find someone suitable. And we said you'd get married at Monticello but you can't because Patsy is about to deliver a grandson to Papa, we hope, and she's going to do it at Monticello and Papa is there with her."

Polly turned her head slightly and caught sight of Isabella.

"But it wouldn't have been big enough anyway so you're going to get married at St. Mary's since it's the biggest church in town and..."

The flow of words suddenly stopped, and her mouth dropped open as she turned her full attention to Isabella.

"You're his fiancée?" she whispered. "You're so beautiful..."

She lapsed into silence again. Isabella curtsied slightly. "I'm Isabella," she said, smiling. "And you are...?"

"Um, I'm Polly Jefferson but now I go by Mary or Maria..." Then she thought to curtsy in return. "Papa says I'm a social catastrophe..."

"Nonsense," said Isabella. "I think you're delightful."

Polly smiled brilliantly. "Thank you so much!" she said. "And I'm here to take you..." she started, but then she seemed to notice Hetty and the Morrises for the first time. "I mean, *we're* here to take you..." She faltered.

Isabella let go of Lewis's hand and threaded her arm, first, through Polly's and then through Hetty's. "I am at your disposal, ladies," she said. "Take me where you will."

So Polly started off back up the wharf, Isabella and Hetty in tow.

Lewis looked at the retreating figures and then at Robert Morris. "That's why I love her," he said.

Robert shook his head. "I hope it won't be inconvenient that we do have some plans for you," he said. "Don Diego arrived a couple of days ago with the news that his daughter was to be married, and it had to be arranged quickly so that the important people would be in town for the occasion."

"Important people, Mr. Morris?" said Lewis.

Robert grinned. "Please call me Robert," he said. "You've earned it. And yes. Do you not realize that this is a very significant event for our two countries?"

Lewis grinned in return. "Here I thought it was about Isabella and me."

"When you marry the daughter of a Don, it is never only about you. Don Diego de Gardoqui y Arriquibar is a very important man. I think nearly everyone of importance in the government will be there."

Lewis shook his head.

"That's why it will be at St. Mary's. Many Americans have never been in a Catholic church, but they would be willing to do so. Catholics will never go into a protestant church. Besides, it has the largest gallery in the city. And the reception will be at Oeller's Hotel for the same reason—it has the largest room in the city."

At that point, Gilly caught Lewis's eye as he and Renée stepped off the gangplank. He was distracted as Maria Morris rushed up to him and hugged him.

"Gilly!" she cried, nuzzling into his shoulder and then backing up and looking at Renée. "And are you also engaged?"

"*Mais, non!*" he said. "This eez my seester, Renée."

Marie curtsied. "*Enchanté!*" she said. She reached out a hand to Renée. "*S'il-te-plait viens avec moi.*" (Please come with me.)

Relief flooded Renée's face as she looked at Gilly for approval. He nodded. She took Maria's hand and they also started up the wharf.

"Mr. Morris," said Gilly looking at Robert. "I 'ave a beeznus proposeetion for you."

"Please call me Robert," said Morris with a slight smile. "It appears as though my apprentices have returned to me as grown men in possession of their fortunes. What is your proposition?"

"I want to start a café."

"You need money?"

"*Non.* I have money. I need eenstruction."

"Well, I definitely have plenty of that. How may I help?"

"First, I should like to buy the two Negroes oowe brought you oowhen we first come to you. Then you should tell me oowhere to set *mon café*. Then..."

Gilly was stopped by being bumped by Marcus,

Gouverneur Morris's clerk who had originally assisted Lewis, Gilly, and Crispin as they entered Robert Morris's service in 1783.

"That's not how we do business in Philadelphia," he said. "It generally involves a dinner or two, lots of wine and cigars, and a less public place."

"Oh," said Gilly, turning to shake Marcus's hand. "Once more you learn me."

"No, I *teach* you. You learn *from* me. But more of that later. Who is this ravishing lady coming down the gangplank followed by a mountain of baggage?"

"*Oui*," said Gilly. "Thees eez the *belle* Sophia, companion to Señorita Isabella."

Sophia stepped off the gangplank and bowed her head toward Marcus.

"*Encantado de conocerte*," said Marcus, bowing in return. (Delighted to meet you.)

"She speak Eenglish," said Gilly.

Sophia turned toward Gilly with a grin, then back to Marcus. "I do," she said. "But I appreciate it when someone greets me in my own language." She stepped out of the way for the baggage carriers who then moved down onto the wharf. Looking to Marcus she said, "Do you happen to know where I am to take my lady's things?"

"Why, yes," said Marcus. "In fact, Mr. Morris has dispatched me for the very purpose of seeing to the comfort of all of your party. If you will come with me?"

He held out his arm and Sophia took it.

"Gilly?" he said. "Would you join us?"

He motioned with his head to the baggage carriers, and they followed him to the chaise farther up the wharf.

Lewis and Robert were left standing on the wharf watching the others.

"What an interesting little group of meetings," said Lewis.

Robert grinned and tipped his head in the direction in which the others had gone. "Shall we?" he said.

And they walked up the wharf together.

Lewis, Gilly and fifteen-year-old Charles Morris had been joined in the Morris's drawing room by James and Lloyd Elliot, Lewis's uncle and cousin from Gloucester, Virginia, some three-hundred miles away. It was nearly two in the afternoon and they were awaiting the women whom they had expected back from their shopping expedition much earlier.

"Imagine my surprise when this huge coach and two creaks into the yard, horses snorting, coachmen in livery—two of them Negroes."

"'Are you gentlemen lost?' I said."

"'No, Sir,' said the driver. 'I don't think so. Are you Captain James Elliot?'"

"'Yes, that's me," I said."

"'Did you not get a letter from Senator Lee?' he says."

"'Ah, yes. I suppose I did,' I said. 'But I thought someone was playing a joke on me.'"

"'It's no joke, Sir. And we have to leave tomorrow to get there in time. Do you know where we can get two more horses? These an' two more 'ill have to do us 'til Fredericksburg.'"

"Well, I sent Lloyd to Courthouse to find two more horses fit to pull a carriage and then went over to Billy Howell's to see if he could watch the place for a few weeks, maybe get some workers—"

"So you hadn't got the crops in yet?" asked Lewis.

He, Gilly and fifteen-year-old Charles Morris had been joined in the Morris's drawing room by James and Lloyd Elliot, Lewis's uncle and cousin from Gloucester, Virginia, some three-hundred miles away. It was nearly noon, and they were awaiting the women whom they had expected back from their shopping expedition much earlier.

"We got the 'baccy in, and the beans and tomatoes and corn," said Lloyd.

"Tomatoes?" said Charles. "I thought they were poisonous."

"Well, we ain't dead yet," said Lloyd, "so I guess not."

"The root vegetables can wait until we get back," said James.

"Did you do radishes this year?" asked Lewis.

"Radishes, onions, potatoes, carrots, beets—course we already ate the greens—"

"Pumpkins?" asked Gilly.

"Yeah, and summer and winter squashes and even them red peppers that ain't hot," said Lloyd.

"So you made it in ten days from southern Virginia?" asked Charles. "You musta bin flying!"

"We..." Lloyd started to say before being interrupted by a clatter at the door. As if the president himself were about to enter the room, the men stood as one.

Mrs. Morris was first in. "Gentlemen," she said. "Please resume your seats. I have the privilege of introducing some beautiful ladies and it might take some time."

They sat and the first to enter was Sophia. Followed immediately by Marcus.

"I'm not one of the beautiful ladies Mrs. Morris referred to," he said, "though..." and he pointed to Sophia, "she is, but not yet dressed in her new attire. I believe Mrs. Morris will make the introductions." He nodded in her direction as he and Sophia went to stand on either side of the door.

"First," said Mrs. Morris, "let me introduce the lovely Mrs. Sears."

Lewis's cousin, Tetty, glided into the room in an amazing peach-colored satin gown, replete with ecru ruffles in various places. Her hair was done up and bedecked with ribbons the same color as the ruffles. Lloyd's mouth dropped open.

"Wow," he said. "I wouldn't have known it was you if Mrs. Morris hadn't said so."

Tetty stuck her tongue out at him, somewhat lessening the dignity of her overall appearance, and then took Marcus's arm to be led to a seat on the divan.

"Next," said Mrs. Morris, "we have the Captain's wife, the stately Mrs. Elliot."

Virginia Elliot entered, looking down to brush something off of her dress. Sophia leaned in to help her and she straightened with a smile.

"Gol!" exclaimed James. "If I wasn't already married to you I'd ask again!"

They all burst into laughter and Virginia turned her head demurely, opening her fan and covering part of her face. Marcus led her over to sit beside Tetty.

"Then my own daughter," said Mrs. Morris, "the kind and gracious Hetty."

Her dress matched Tetty's. And then two more young ladies in similarly matching dresses entered, but Lewis was too distracted to pay much attention. Where was the most important lady?

After everyone was seated Mrs. Morris sighed. "Here in Pennsylvania, we don't normally let the groom see the bride in her wedding dress before the wedding," she said. "But they have different customs in Spain and the bride asked if she might join us. So..." she nodded at Sophia who exited quickly. In a moment she re-entered, holding what seemed to be yards of peach satin, followed by a sight so beautiful Lewis would never forget it....

Two days later, in the late morning of September 20, 1792, many of the guests had already been seated in St.Mary's Roman Catholic Church. Lewis, Lloyd, Gilly, Peter Jay, and Philip Hamilton stood by the daïs looking toward the entrance. There was a bit of a commotion at the door and people rising quickly to their feet as President and Mrs. Washington walked in, Mrs. Washington on Marcus's arm. Marcus led them to the right side of the aisle in the row directly behind Captain and Mrs. Elliot.

As soon as the Washingtons were seated and the rest of the guests had resumed their seats, Sophia led José Ignacio to the front row opposite the Elliots. He nodded slightly to them and slipped in to the middle of the pew. Next came Eliza and Alexander Hamilton, followed closely by Sarah and John Jay and Abigail and John Adams, who were seated in the row behind the president. Mary and Robert Morris sat behind them.

After that, Lewis lost track of who came in, though he did recognize Richard Henry Lee, President pro tempore of the Senate, whose coach had brought his family from Virginia. Lee was seated behind José Ignacio on the left. The entrance of further dignitaries was a blur to Lewis who really cared to see only one person.

And suddenly, there she was, on Don Diego de Gardoqui y Arriquibar's arm—smiling just for Lewis. The organ started playing some march or other, and as Lewis thought Isabella was just about to enter, she was preceded by a little girl—perhaps one of the Hamilton's daughters— scattering rose petals on the white runner overlying the aisle. Lewis could hardly contain his impatience until he looked back up at Isabella, who seemed to know exactly what was going through his mind and smirked through her smile.

Then came the bridesmaids. First, Tetty, of course, since she was the maid of honor, then Hetty and Maria Morris, and last, smiling insanely, Polly Jefferson.

And finally, Isabella. Her every slow, short step to the plodding marriage march was an agony of waiting for Lewis. But she did get there eventually, and took his hand as he turned to face the altar. He let out the breath he hadn't realized he was holding and she squeezed his hand.

Her father gave her away, they knelt and prayed before the altar, and he was allowed to take both of her hands and look her in the eyes as they said their vows. Tetty produced a ring for Lewis, and Lloyd a ring for Isabella.

Lewis did the rest of what he had been told to do through a sort of fog; correctly, he hoped. And then they were outside, down a few steps, into a phaeton carriage, and on the way to the reception at the Oeller Hotel.

IT WAS no surprise to Lewis that most of the people who greeted the bridal party wanted to speak with Don Diego and to meet his daughter. He was surprised, however, at how many of the people he knew, and at how warmly they greeted and congratulated him. Fortunately, though he had been ready to be finished with the greeting long since, it did eventually come to an end as people enthusiastically began to indulge in the enormous feast Don Diego had provided.

Last to come by was Robert Morris. Lewis sighed and shook his head as he took Morris's hand.

"You were not expecting this many people—and these people?"

"No," said Lewis. "It seems to have become a rather political affair."

Morris glanced around the room and nodded. "Don Diego is a very important man," he said. "Every move he makes is a political affair. If his daughter had been married in Spain, the King and Queen would have been there. This is the least we could do." He looked around the room and Lewis followed his gaze to see that the divisions he had experienced in the cabinet had also materialized in this room. Hamilton and his supporters were in one place near George and Martha Washington, who were seated at a table Lewis supposed was always available only to them. Richard Henry Lee and others, like James Monroe, who were not favorable to the administration, were seated as far away from that group as possible. But most people were oblivious to this separation, simply enjoying the others sitting at their tables.

"Pardon me?" said Lewis, snapping his head back to look at Morris.

Morris nodded. "I was saying that, after all, he is the Secretary of the Royal Exchequer of Spain. President Washington and many others in the room have high hopes that he will finally give in and allow the United States free commerce on the Mississippi and lower tariffs in New Orleans."

Lewis nodded and looked around again for Don Diego— who was working the room, greeting his guests and talking affably with everyone in his vicinity. "Do you think this will help us?"

Morris looked over at Lewis with a twinkle in his eye and a wry grin. "You're astute, Lewis," he said. "Having daughters myself, I'm certain he wanted a good match for Isabella. But it is also a good match for him. You will need to take care..." He dropped off and Lewis nodded.

"Yes, I see that," Lewis said after a moment of silence. Then he looked up at Morris and smiled. "So," he said. "Let it begin!"

He turned to Isabella, who was in animated conversation with Mary Morris. Robert glanced at Mary and held out his arm. She pardoned herself and took it as Lewis took Isabella's left hand in both of his.

"*Ven, tesoro,*" he said, nodding toward the room. "You're not going to escape all the duties of a Don's daughter just because we're on this side of the Atlantic. I've discovered that I'm to acquire some, shall we say, diplomatic duties I hadn't anticipated."

He released her hand and she took his arm, looking around to see if anyone was watching them. Quite a few people were, actually.

"Oh, *no me importa,*"(I don't care) she said, and stood on tiptoes to kiss him fiercely on the mouth. Then she pulled away and laughed. "It will give them something to talk about!"

Lewis was awakened by insistent pounding on the front door. He glanced over at Isabella, who had not been awakened, and eased out from under the covers. He assumed that Adelaide would take care of whomever was making that racket at this hour, but he decided to get dressed on the odd chance that it might concern him.

After throwing some water on his face and brushing his hair, he put on the 'day after' suit that Marcus had insisted he buy. He took one last, longing, look at his bride, picked up his shoes, and walked through the bedroom door which he closed with a soft click. He turned toward the stairs just in time to jump against a wall to avoid the rushing Pembroke. Pembroke turned and started to yell, "Mr...Mr. Elliot..."

Lewis hurriedly placed his finger to his lips and pointed back toward the stairs where a clearly agitated Adelaide was striding his way.

"I tried to stop him, sir," she said.

Lewis put his finger to his lips once again and continued down the hall to the stairs, Pembroke fast on his heels. When they reached the bottom of the stairs, he turned to Pembroke. "I thought Mr. Jefferson was out of town," he said.

"He is," said Pembroke. "But I was the only clerk around and President Washington sent me to get you urgently."

"President Washington? What would he want with me?"

"I don't know, sir, he told me where you were and just said to get you. Now. Immediately."

Lewis looked at Adelaide who was more used to such interruptions than he was, but she just held her hands out and rolled her eyes.

"Is he at his home or his office?" asked Lewis.

"His office," said Pembroke. "Please hurry."

Lewis turned to Adelaide. "If you would be so good as to tell Isabella where I have gone," he said, "I would appreciate it."

She nodded. "Of course, sir."

"And you don't need to call me 'sir.' If anything, I should call you 'M'am.'"

That brought about the tiniest smile from Adelaide. "Yes, sir," she said. "But I must."

"Sir?" said Pembroke, hand on the door.

And he rushed off with Lewis following after.

. . .

"Mr. Lewis," said the president, pointing at the chair directly in front of his desk. "Please be seated."

Lewis sat in the leather armchair indicated as Washington sat in his own chair.

"You can imagine my chagrin at having to awaken you so early, and especially on this day of all days. But my need is urgent."

"Sir," said Lewis. "I am honored to help in any way I can."

Washington looked out the window toward the sun rising over the Delaware River. "You may not say that when you hear what I will ask of you. And I am only asking. You do not need to do it if it is inconvenient." He looked back at Lewis. "I have sent men and armies on missions I knew would likely cause some to die. This one is different. It is personal and requires the utmost secrecy."

"Sir, I am certain that however difficult, unpleasant, or dangerous a task it may be, it could never be inconvenient to me to do it for you."

Washington looked at him closely. "I thank you for that, sir, but kindly wait until you hear me out before you make your decision."

Washington turned in his chair and steepled his hands against his chin. Then he spoke. "I believe you have some acquaintance with my good friend the Marquis de Lafayette." He turned back to look at Lewis as if for an answer.

"Very little, sir. At the Yorktown surrender he introduced himself to my father, Captain Thomas Elliot, and thanked him for his service."

"Yes," Washington nodded. "Many of us were thankful for his service. Go on."

"My father introduced him to me and my French friend, Gilly, and an English lad, Crispin, who had helped us. We didn't find out until later that he provided funds so the three of us could continue our education."

"Would you like to repay the favor?"

Lewis, startled, looked directly at Washington. "Of course, sir," he said, "But..."

A wan smile passed the president's lips. "I would be quite content if there were no need, but it is precisely this need that has brought me to the point of such a discourtesy as asking you here at this time of day."

"What can I do, sir?"

"I received a communication last night that caused me great alarm."

He looked up at Lewis. "You may know that Lafayette is like a son to me. And just as would any father seek to relieve his suffering son, so I seek to relieve the suffering of this good man and friend."

Washington looked away again, gazing at a vista only he could see. "It is not easy for a man in my position. In fact, it is most delicate. For these United States cannot afford to go to war with either Austria or France and were it to appear that we were aiding him, that could be the unfortunate result." He turned back to Lewis. "But he is imprisoned in the most atrocious circumstances. I can only think with great dismay of what will happen to him if help is not provided."

He paused, looked down at his hands which were twisting with one another, stilled them, and looked back up. "You have shown yourself to be a resourceful and reliable courier," he said. "And I should like to have you bring something to him."

Lewis settled back in his chair and decided to let Washington tell him what he would on his own timetable.

"Your marriage and particular skills make you especially suited for this mission."

Washington took a breath, pursed his lips, and continued.

"You know that an American citizen cannot take any title of nobility."

He looked at Lewis, who nodded.

"I spoke with your father-in-law this morning—he is an early riser as I am—and he told me that his country has invested citizenship upon you. As an American citizen, you could not take your peerage as Don de Arriquibar. But as a Spanish citizen, you may."

Lewis sat forward and furrowed his brow. "Would I not have to renounce my citizenship in the United States?"

"In this case, you could retain both," said Washington.

Lewis sat back in his chair and said no more.

"Ah," said Washington, "I realize that I have not told you the most important part. You see, our Lafayette was forced to flee for his life by the current government in Paris. If the French get to him, his life is forfeit. For good or ill, the French will not be able to get to him because he is in prison in Belgium. I am told that the conditions are deplorable. And if someone does not supply his needs, they will not be met. I wish to do what I can from my own funds. This cannot be an act of state and Lafayette must not know from whence the funds come. You may inform only three people, men I trust: Mr. Thomas Pinckney in London, Mr. William Short in the Hague, and Mr. Humphreys. And your wife, of course. But under no circumstances is it to be committed to writing. You understand the need for secrecy?"

Lewis nodded slightly.

"Then you shall bring the funds." He smiled again, this time more warmly. "Or, I should say, Don Luis Elías de Arriquibar will bring them. You will go to Lafayette as a Spanish nobleman, son-in-law of the Lord of the Treasury for the Spanish crown. Spain is currently neutral in this affair. The

Austrians, and the King of Prussia, I believe, should allow you to succour him."

"How soon will I need to go, sir?" asked Lewis.

Washington stood, his tall straight frame always intimidating. He turned to the wall on his right and walked over to examine a chart. "On the tide, tomorrow morning," he said. "Which, according to the chart, should be at about 11:30."

Lewis let out an involuntary breath and placed his hands on the arm of the chair. In an instant he regained his composure.

"Ah...Isabella?" he said, standing as well.

"She must accompany you. It will aid in the scenario we are establishing."

Washington made a bit of a grimace and became all seriousness. "I know it is a great deal to ask, but his life may hang in the balance. One of Don Gardoqui's ships is leaving tomorrow for Santa Cruz, Canaria. From thence you will find a ship to London or Rotterdam. London is not mandatory, but should your route take you there you should appraise Mr. Pinckney. You will then go to the Hague and meet with our consul, Mr. Short."

Lewis nodded.

"You know him?"

"Yes, Sir."

"Good. You may speak in English with these two men, but otherwise, I fear, you must speak Spanish, or French—" Washington looked up. "I understand you are fluent in both?"

Lewis nodded.

"Short will help you gain access to the Marquis if possible. If not, you will have to find another way to get the funds to him. I am also sending 2,300 guilders to Madame Lafayette from my personal funds, about which you do not have to be secretive. Short will help you settle that in a way that Madame can access it. After you deliver the, ah, packages, you may go to Humphreys in Lisbon. At that point, you may become Lewis Elliot once more, if you wish, and work for the State Department again."

Lewis, confused, tilted his head and looked at the president.

"Yes, I'm afraid there must be no connection whatsoever between you and the United States government during this mission. However, I will compensate you myself for your trouble."

"There is no need for that, Sir. I have adequate funds. Perhaps you could add whatever financial assistance you were going to provide me to what you are giving the Marquis and his wife?"

Washington nodded. "That would be most welcome," he said.

"I only follow your own example from the war, Sir," said Lewis. The president gave a wan smile and a slight nod.

The sun had risen some time ago, now, and it was fully light. Washington looked out the window. "I'm afraid we must move you along. It would be better for no one to know we had this conversation." He looked back into the room and at Lewis. "And because of the lateness of the season, this may be the last ship to cross this year. You must be on it! Can you do that?"

"Yes, Sir."

"Good." Washington let out a breath as his shoulders slumped and then he slid into his chair. "Mr. Morris will get the funds to you at Señor José Ignacio's residence where you will be fitted out in Spanish noblemen's clothing, and a wig, I imagine, and whatever else they wear. My Martha and Mrs. Morris will help your Isabella and her lady's maid—is it Sophia?—with her preparations. I think Mr. Morris will also dispatch Gouverneur Morris's factotum, Marcus, to attend you.

A Spanish nobleman and his wife would not travel without attendants." He looked past Lewis, distracted. "I believe that is all." Then he looked back at Lewis. "I'm afraid you should be on board before first light so you are not seen leaving." He opened a drawer on the left side of his desk and looked at something. "Ah. That probably means by 6 AM." He looked back at Lewis. "I am certain *you* can do that. Will it terribly discommode your wife?"

Lewis stood and looked directly into Washington's face. "I have no doubt that she will do admirably, Sir. And Sir, thank you for your confidence," he said. "It will be done."

Washington nodded. "You have my undying gratitude, but we must not speak of it again." Lewis bowed slightly. Then the president opened the door and called Pembroke who walked Lewis out of the building, still empty of officials.

"Um," said Pembroke. "Was...was it worth it to be waked so early?"

Lewis gazed at him for a moment and let out a long breath. "Thank you for your part, Mr. Pembroke," he said. "Was it worth it?" He shrugged. "Time will tell."

"Do you want to say anything about..."

Lewis grinned. "But I have no time for telling now," he said.

Then he turned and started back for Morris's house at a pace just short of running.

LEWIS AND ISABELLA were on deck, at the bow, when the *Euskara de Santanda* slipped its berth at about 7:30 the next morning, heading south on the Delaware River with the hope of gliding past Wilmington and anchoring south of Pea Patch Island that evening, and the following day sailing through Delaware Bay and out into the Atlantic. Lewis shared what he had learned from the captain—that it carried timber, flour, whiskey, ginseng, tar, and turpentine, among other things, and would stop at Tenerife, one of Don Gardoqui's depots, to finish filling its hold with cod. That's where he and Isabella would disembark and, hopefully, find a ship to Rotterdam.

Isabella found it amusing that the ship, called a *nao* by the Spanish, was named after the language of the Basque people which she had spoken only in her infancy.

"My father works for the Spanish crown," she said, "but does not let anyone forget that his people are Basque."

"That's like Gilly," said Lewis, "who was conscripted by the French navy and cooks French cuisine, but never lets us forget that he's from Bretagne." He looked out at the fields on the west side of the river and pointed. "That's Pennsylvania," he said. Then he turned and pointed to the east side. "That's New Jersey. And in a few hours we'll see Delaware on the west side. Until a few years ago their people would have said they were from Pennsylvania or New Jersey, or Delaware. Now, I hope, they'll say they're from the United States of America."

They were quiet for a few minutes, just watching the shore go by.

Isabella held Lewis's arm more tightly and snuggled into him. "Can you believe this life we're living?"

"It's amazing," said Marcus, coming to stand beside them.

"What?" said Lewis, turning to him. He stepped back so Isabella could see Marcus. "Our life? The ship? The river? The view or..." and here he couldn't help chuckling a bit "...the turn of events?"

Marcus turned to Isabella then back to Marcus and smiled. "All of the above. You two, of course, but especially me and Sophia being on the same ship sailing to the same place."

"Which might just be your way of approaching an important question, mightn't it?"

Marcus grimaced. "I think maybe I taught you too well."

Lewis grinned. "Perhaps you would like to ask this important question?"

Marcus's face became grave and he looked from Lewis to Isabella and back. "Whom would I ask if I might court Sophia?"

"I suppose, since I am now her legal guardian, it could be me," said Lewis. "But since she is—and has been for many years—Isabella's friend, companion, and lady's maid, you might ask Isabella."

Isabella looked at Lewis, then at Marcus, and said, "Don't you think you should ask *her?*"

Marcus grimaced. "I have not done that yet, since I didn't know if it would even be possible. But working together for these many weeks has brought us close and I believe she would not be averse to the idea."

Lewis placed his arm around Isabella and looked her way, grinning.

She smiled back and then looked at Marcus. "I believe you will find her so inclined," she said.

"Who is so inclined, and to what?" came a melodious voice from behind them.

"Sophia, my dear," said Isabella, reaching a hand out to her. "What marvelous timing. We were just talking about you. We thought Marcus might have something he wanted to ask you."

Marcus's eyes grew large.

With a mischievous little grin, Sophia said, "You wanted to ask me something?"

Marcus 'ummed' a bit, looking down, then lifted his head and said, "Would...ah, would you be willing to have me court you?"

Sophia tilted her head a bit to the right looking puzzled.

"That's not it," Marcus said, falling to one knee. "What I mean is, will you marry me?"

Then Sophia smiled widely. "Ah," she said. *"Si y si,"* (Yes and yes). "Was that what you wanted to ask?"

"Um, don't *you* have to ask someone?"

Sophia turned, smiling, to Isabella who laughed and said, "And you think we had not already decided this?"

Marcus, looking a little confused, rose from the deck.

"Lewis and I will be travelling together, at least until the babies come," she said. "I will need someone to assist me. I would like it to be Sophia. But I cannot ask her to give up her whole life, to serve me past the age of *matrimonio*." She looked over at Lewis.

"Marriageability," he said.

She nodded. "And Lewis will need assistance as well. Is it not a wonderful thing that you have found one another and solved all our problems?"

Marcus beamed. "May I?" he said, holding out both his hands to Sophia. She took them and they pulled one another into a hug.

"Just be careful," said Lewis, "and don't ...."

"Does not the Captain of a ship have the authority to marry?" asked Sophia, turning away from Marcus but keeping one of his hands in hers.

"But he is not a priest," said Lewis.

Sophia turned her head to Lewis and then to Isabella. "I, too, have become an Anglican. If the Captain has a legal right to marry us and we make our vows to one another and to God, will not that suffice?"

"Let me see how the Captain feels about it," said Isabella. "After all, he is one of my uncle's men. But being Catholic, he may not be willing."

WHEN THEY ARRIVED in Tenerife two weeks and a couple of days later, both couples had enjoyed an extended—if somewhat constricted—honeymoon. Santa Cruz was still very warm but the *Mareas del Pino* (lowest tide of the year), a little late this year, delayed their entry. *Euskara* had sat out from the nearly dry harbor for many hours waiting for it to rise again, leaving Lewis and Marcus watching the few ships that had departed earlier vanish to the north.

"I fear that was our ride to Rotterdam," said Lewis. "Don Diego said the connection would be tight."

"So, what do we do?" asked Marcus.

"We go to the *José de Gardoqui e Hijos* office and find out when their next ship is leaving," said Lewis. "Or when we might join another ship going north and eventually get to Rotterdam. Look behind us, there," said Lewis, turning to point at a couple of ships tied up to mooring buoys behind them. "They look like packets and at least one of them might be going in our direction."

They both turned back toward starboard amidships when they felt the slight jar of the boat from the pilot ship. The pilot appeared over the rail, was greeted as he stepped on deck, the mooring line was pulled in, topsails unfurled, and they were underway into the harbor.

At the Gardoqui office, they discovered that, indeed, it was the packet to Rotterdam they had seen leaving. But one of the ships now berthing was a packet from Lisbon that would be returning the next day. From there they could find another packet to almost anywhere they wanted to go.

Lewis returned to his cabin to assist Sophia and Marcus in getting them all packed, especially Isabella, who had not quite accustomed herself to travelling light. At a moment when

Sophia and Marcus had gone up to the main deck, he told her, "I may have to give up my disguise for a short while to see Humphreys in Lisbon. I need to know whatever he knows about what is happening in France and what we may encounter in Holland."

"*¡Vaya!* (Oh!) Could I come with you? I am so tired of being on a ship!"

Lewis let out a breath. "I think this would mean beginning a whole new era of diplomacy," he said, "in which the wife is as much involved as the diplomat." He smiled at her. "But why not? Let's be different. How will we do it? And remember, I am sworn to secrecy to all but Mr. Humphreys and the other two men I told you about."

Isabella fairly glowed, and her eyes sparkled with that impish light that Lewis so loved. "We will be only who we are!" she said, smiling. "I think we can find a way to visit him without telling him who you are at first. We'll see how good your disguise is and then we shall expose you!"

HUMPHREYS PRETENDED NOT to see through the disguise until Lewis mentioned Washington's name, letting his American accent come through.

"Very well done, Lewis," Humphreys said, reverting from French to English. "You almost had me fooled. Of course, much of that was due to the distraction provided by this beautiful woman you've brought along to befuddle friend and foe alike."

"Oh, well," said Lewis, turning his beaming smile toward Isabella, who was smiling coyly behind her hand fan. "It is difficult to fool someone who has known you well."

"But you might have if it hadn't been for the way you said, 'Washington.'"

"I must remember to call him something else," said Lewis.

"In any case, I shall provide letters of introduction to Pinckney and Short that may save you a little time."

"I'd prefer to go straight to the Hague, if possible."

"Probably not possible," said Humphreys. "We rarely have packets going there due to the, shall we say, 'challenge' of passing the French coast unmolested."

On October 22, Thomas Pinckney chose to meet Don Luis Elías de Arriquibar and his wife at his home for afternoon tea rather than at his office. After his butler had let them in and taken their wraps, Pinckney personally led them to his study, conversing in French the while.

Pinckney was tall, slight, balding, of any age between thirty-five and fifty, sharp of eye and nose. His dimpled chin made him look like an elongated version of James Monroe. His gravitas reminded Lewis of Washington, and the graceful manner in which he walked and spoke, of Jefferson. Perhaps he was the best of all of them. The study door was already open, and he stood aside, gesturing for them to enter.

A maid brought in the elaborate tea set, and another followed with cakes and biscuits. The party continued making small talk in French until Pinckney dismissed the servants.

"Close the door, please, Elizabeth," he said in English as the last one was leaving, "and be certain we are not disturbed."

As the door was clicking shut, Pinckney continued the conversation with Lewis and Isabella in French. Then he walked to the door and leaned close to it, listening. He walked back to his chair, sat, and was silent for a few moments, head tilted to one side—after which he straightened his head abruptly.

"Mr. Humphreys told me something of the situation that

brings you here," he said, startling both Lewis and Isabella with English. "But not all. This is the only room in the house without double walls behind which the servants can listen to our conversations and report them to their masters. Still, let us sit closer together and speak softly."

He stood, moved his chair toward them, and seated himself. "He did not tell me the purpose of your visit." He stopped speaking then and looked at Lewis.

"It was not to be written," said Lewis in English.

Pinckney nodded.

"And to be spoken carefully, only to you, Humphreys, and Short. It is about the Marquis."

Pinckney nodded. "Whose name is not to be spoken, I imagine."

Lewis nodded back.

"I knew him well," said Pinckney, "having fought under his leadership at Yorktown." He paused for a moment, apparently thinking of those days. Then he looked directly at Lewis. "But I must tell you something of which the president could not have been aware when he sent you. Do you know anything about September 20?"

Isabella looked at him and smiled. "It was our wedding day," she said.

As Pinckney looked toward her and smiled back, Lewis detected a warmth he had not seen until then.

"Congratulations," he said. "I mean that sincerely, but I did not know. No, the event of September 20 to which I refer had a different kind of significance." He paused, causing Lewis and Isabella to attend to him even more closely.

"You see," he said, "a small battle took place in a little town called Valmy, in Champagne, near the disputed border between France and Prussia. Under most circumstances its outcome would have been considered inconsequential. The

French army merely stopped the advance of the Prussian army, commanded by the Duke of Brunswick. The current government of France, calling itself the National Convention, was euphoric. The Duke of Brunswick, brother to the Elector of Brandenburg, otherwise known as the King of Prussia, was annoyed. But that King, Frederick William II, was enraged. He has chosen to make our Marquis his scapegoat."

"Which means that it will be awkward for anyone to come to his assistance," said Lewis.

Pinckney merely nodded. "If you can gain a hearing with the new Queen Consort of the Netherlands, Wilhelmina, sister to Frederick William and great niece to Frederick the Great, she might be able to help you."

"With all those connections she must be very old," said Isabella.

Pinckney laughed. "You might think so," he said, "but she was only seventeen when she was married last October. I think she would be glad of your company."

"Seventeen?" asked Isabella.

"She's eighteen, now. I imagine it's lonely for a young woman in a foreign court. And as I understand, she will soon give birth." He stopped short and lifted his left hand, first finger pointing upward. "Besides which, the United States owes Holland a great deal of money. Short tells me the king, William I, invites him to the palace regularly to insure he won't forget that. Perhaps he can introduce you."

"That may not be the best foundation for an introduction," said Lewis.

"Ah, but Spaniards closely connected to the crown, as well as the treasury, who are friends with the Americans—that could be a different story. Everyone knows Don Diego. I sincerely doubt King William would turn down an opportunity to meet his son-in-law."

After their little conference, Isabella asked Lewis to accompany her to the home of an artist who had done a small miniature of her when she had studied in England. "I'm afraid I forgot all about it and left it with him without even paying for it. He may not have it still, and he may want more for it. But I think it might be useful in Holland."

The artist, it turned out, had fallen on hard times and was only too happy to rummage through his old paintings until he found the miniature.

"And I can put a small frame on it if you wish," he said, beckoning them to follow him as he entered a dusty storeroom, one wall of which was floor-to-ceiling shelves containing frames. Lewis and Isabella found one they liked and waited while he installed the canvas into it. They paid him and returned to their lodgings.

"That was five times the original price," said Isabella. "But I have an intuition that it may be helpful."

AND SO IT was that a few days after getting to Den Hague via Amsterdam and seeing William Short, Don Luis Elías de Arriquibar and his wife, Señora Isabella de Gardoqui y Arriquibar, stood in Noordeinde Palace at 11 o'clock on the morning of October 29, 1792, before Willem Frederik, Prince of Orange-Nassau, Grand Duke of Luxembourg, aka William I, King of the Netherlands, and his wife, Friederike Luise Wilhelmine of Prussia, Queen consort of the Netherlands.

Formal introductions were made, all in French. Then the ladies and most of the courtiers were dismissed.

King William stood from his throne, gestured to Lewis to follow, and strode to a small door at the side of the great hall. The room they entered was lavishly furnished, the windows draped in deep orange velvet, the heavy upholstered chairs trimmed with dark mahogany, and elegant embossings on all the walls. But Lewis was torn from his observations by a curt question in English.

"Why have you come?"

He turned to stare at King William, heart in his throat. Would this mean the end of his mission? He took a moment to evaluate King William before speaking.

He was tall, erect, young—probably Lewis's own age or younger—not unfriendly looking, but clearly on guard. His clothing was expensive, though not especially regal—merely the typical white britches and stockings under a ruffled white shirt and deep blue velvet jacket with crimson and gold trim. He wore neither wig nor crown.

William spoke first. "I will do you the courtesy of allowing you to call me by my given name, Willem, if you will do the same."

"Lewis," said Lewis in English.

"So you're not married to this Spanish Doña and you are not Don de Arriquibar?"

"I *am* those things. Isabella is my wife, and the title has been conferred upon me."

"You then had to renounce your American citizenship?"

"No, I was made a special case." Lewis straightened and clasped his hands. "If I may ask, how did you know I was American?"

"Mr. Short informed me," he said. "And before you begin to think he is a traitor to you, allow me to tell you that he and I have an agreement. We do not lie to one another."

Willem turned and walked to a window, hands behind him. He gazed out for a moment before turning. "It is not easy in these days. It was probably never easy. But so we have agreed. And so you ought to do also."

"Indeed," said Lewis, "it is very difficult for me to do otherwise."

"So why are you here?"

"We must not lie," said Lewis, "but we must also not betray a secret. I am sworn not to tell anyone except Mr. Short and two others. I assume by your question that he did not tell you."

Willem looked back out the window. "Your country owes my country a great deal of money." He turned, walked to the room's main piece of furniture, a small but heavy table, pulled out an equally heavy chair, and invited Lewis to sit. Then he pulled out another chair, just around a corner from Lewis, and sat. Lewis moved to the designated chair and seated himself.

"But I know you will pay. Eventually. It may not be in time to save us, nor indeed, to save Europe from the bloodbath that awaits us as surely as it will continue in France. I would choose to be friends. Does your secret allow you to tell me whether your mission should concern us here in the Netherlands?"

"It does. And I can tell you that you should have no concern. President Washington..."

"Yes?" said Willem after a moment.

"Perhaps I have already said too much," said Lewis. "I am new to this. But allow me to say that President Washington is more than eager to pay our debts and be at peace with all who would be at peace with us."

"Whose numbers may be diminishing daily."

"Yes."

Willem stood and clapped his hands. Two serving men came in. "*Koffie,*" he said, "*en het gebruikelijke.*" (Coffee and the usual). He looked at Lewis as they retreated. "You're not one of those, how the French say, *vieux jeu,* tea drinkers, I hope?" (old-young, 'stuffy').

Lewis laughed. "The French do sometimes have the best

way of saying things," he said. "No, I am not. If I had my way, *all* tea would be thrown into any available harbor."

"*Goedso!*" (Great!) said Willem with that guttural Niederlandischer pronunciation. "Now perhaps we may become better acquainted."

~

As ISABELLA and the heavily pregnant Queen Consort walked the enormous hallway away from the grand hall, the servants and courtiers were shooed away.

"They will bring us coffee and küchen in my morning room," she said in French. "But I can't bear them hovering about me like drones around their queen."

She glanced up at Isabella and smiled. "Come!" she said, taking Isabella's hand. "It is so seldom I get to have a guest of my own!"

They walked down the hallway as quickly as Wilhelmina could manage, took a few turns, and finally entered a brightly lit room well-bestowed with tulips and other flowers in vases on little tables placed strategically to catch light from the windows.

"It is a glorious day today," said Wilhelmina. "But most often it is raining or cloudy. Berlin was much brighter. This room has the most light. That is why it is my favorite room."

She led Isabella to a long divan with a beautiful, embroidered silk cover and invited her to sit toward one end. Then, holding her belly, she seated herself with a sigh in a matching, upholstered chair, just a hands-breadth or two away from the divan.

"So!" she said. "Now we may talk. Shall we use Spanish?"

Isabella, a little amused by the trek from the grand hall and their current disposition, said in French, "What language would you like to speak? If you don't mind that I ask, what is the language of your heart?"

Wilhelmina turned her fresh, pretty face to Isabella, smiled and said, still in French. "*Allemand,* (German) I suppose. But no one out of Prussia speaks that."

"*Sie werden überrascht sein,*" said Isabella, smiling. (You might be surprised!)

"*Du sprichst Deutsch!*" cried Wilhelmina (You speak German!). She reached for both of Isabella's hands and grasped them, then went on in German leaning into Isabella. "I'm sorry to call you 'du' so soon. May we be 'du'? Will you call me by my name, Wilhelmina?"

"Of course! And you must call me Isabella."

Wilhelmina dropped Isabella's hands quickly as the sound of the door opening signaled the arrival of their refreshments. She turned around and they both watched in silence as the maids poured coffee and set plates before them. When the servants had left and closed the door, Wilhelmina exclaimed, "Oh, I am so happy!"

She pointed at the little cakes on the platter. "Which would you like?"

Isabella sat back on the divan and sighed. "It is so difficult!" But she finally pointed at an *apfel küchen* covered in Bavarian cream. "That one!"

"Let me serve you," said Wilhelmina, taking up the elaborately carved silver fork and placing the *küchen* on Isabella's plate.

Isabella's eyes watered up. Queens did not serve. She nodded in thanks.

"*Bitte,*" said Wilhelmina. "We will have little time to talk, but you must tell me why you have come. You did not come all the way from Spain to share tea with me."

"You are so gracious," said Isabella. She took a mouthful of the *küchen*, closing her eyes. "So good," she said. "I wish my cook could make this." Then she opened her eyes and turned to Wilhelmina.

"I don't wish to presume upon your good will," she said. "But, yes, we are here on a mission. I believe that you are the only one who can do it."

"Me?"

Now Isabella took Wilhelmina's hands. "I didn't know I would love you so well."

Tears ran down Wilhelmina's face. "Nor I you," she said. "I do so wish we could be friends. Consorts don't have friends, you know."

"Nor do Doñas," said Isabella. "Everyone wants something from you."

Wilhelmina glanced over at Isabella with a wistful look. "Tell me what I can do for you," she said. "I will do it with all my heart."

"It is for a friend, actually," said Isabella. "One Marquis. Do you know who I mean?"

Wilhelmina pulled her hands away and sat up straight. "Of course," she said. "I am told he is a horrible man."

"I do not know," said Isabella. "But no human being should have to live like an animal."

Wilhelmina leaned forward once more and took one of Isabella's hands in both of hers. "Yes," she said. "That has troubled me. But my brother hates this man. He blames him for all of Prussia's ills."

"Is it possible for one man to be responsible for that?"

"I don't know. I'm a woman. I'm not supposed to 'bother my head' about such matters."

"Perhaps you could 'bother your head' for a moment. If your brother were captured by the French and held in such a manner, would you want someone to succour him?"

"*Natürlich*," she whispered. (Of course.)

Isabella lifted Wilhelmina's hand and kissed it. "You are the queen——"

"Queen Consort," Wilhelmina interrupted her.

"It doesn't matter. You will be asked to do things. You must decide what you will do."

"I have no money to help him," she said. "Almost nothing belongs to me."

"We have resources to help him. All I ask is that you get them to someone reliable who will use them for the benefit of the Marquis and not for himself."

"I can trust a few of my own servants who have come with me from the Stadtschloss."

Suddenly she sat up and grabbed Isabella's other hand. "I can do something!" she said. "I can actually make something happen!"

"But you must do it quietly," said Isabella, "even secretly."

Wilhelmina released Isabella's hands, jumped to her feet, and began to pace. "I will," she said. "And that will be how I can accomplish something as Consort——" she turned to Isabella, "and eventually as queen."

She stopped pacing, turned to Isabella, and smiled. "History will not know."

"But I will know," said Isabella, rising from the divan. "And those who truly love you will know."

"And you will be my friend?" asked Wilhelmina.

"I already am your friend," said Isabella, going to her and embracing her.

After a moment Wilhelmina disengaged and returned to her seat. "Here," she said, pointing back to Isabella's seat on the divan. "We must eat something, or the servants will wonder."

After a few moments of quiet eating, Wilhelmina turned to

Isabella with a certain shyness and asked, "Do you like being married?"

Isabella closed her eyes and sighed. "Oh," she said, "I love it!" She opened her eyes as Wilhelmina sat back in her chair.

"I do, too," said Wilhelmina. "It was an arranged marriage, but Willem is such a nice man. I'm certain that in private we do not behave as a king and consort ought...." She giggled. "What about you?"

This conversation had continued for some time when Wilhelmina sat up with a jolt. "*Ach je*," she said. (Oh, dear.) "They will come for us soon." She slipped a ring bearing a large topaz off her right fourth finger. "Please," she said. "Please take this so you will not forget me. Come visit me." She sounded desperate. "Please!"

Isabella took the ring and placed it on her own right fourth finger. She leaned over and kissed Wilhelmina. "How could I forget you? But you are a queen. You will see so many people. You may forget me!"

"Never!" said Wilhelmina.

"Because I am traveling, I have very little to give you as a gift. But I hoped we might become friends and I stopped in England to collect something I might give you if we did."

She reached among the folds of her dress and found the pocket in which she had placed the little portrait. She pulled it out and handed it to Wilhelmina.

"Please, won't you take this? Then perhaps you will not forget me either."

Wilhelmina took it as if it were the most precious thing in the world. She studied it for a moment. "You were beautiful." Then she looked up at Isabella. "You *are* beautiful."

A discrete knock at the door caused both women to stand quickly. Wilhelmina took Isabella's hand. "Do not forget me!" she said.

"I will never forget you," said Isabella. "You must come to stay with me in Bilbao."

Wilhelmina looked down at her belly. "I fear it will be a while before I can travel. Perhaps you will visit me again before that?"

And the servants came in to usher them away to their lives.

Kings do not shake hands, but Isabella caught the briefest glance of Lewis and King William shaking hands as she was led to the audience room. She smiled. That could only be a good thing.

ISABELLA AND LEWIS stayed a few more days in the Hague with William Short—during which time Short deposited 2,300 Dutch guilders in an Amsterdam bank for Madame Lafayette—and then found Isabella and Lewis a packet headed back to England.

They were quiet for a while as they stood at the taffrail holding hands, watching Rotterdam recede into the fog.

"You were successful," said Isabella.

Lewis turned to her. "*We* were successful, *Tesora*. It would not have happened without you."

She turned to him with a grin. "*Do* remember that," she said.

Lewis moved closer, placed his arm around her, turned, and walked with her toward the bow. Together they looked ahead, trying to see through the fog.

9

AGONY IN AMERICA

"Do yoo know oowhere Lewee go?' asked Gilly.

"No one knows where Lewis and Isabella have gone," said Robert Morris. "It is customary for newlyweds to tell very few people, or no one, where they will spend their first weeks together."

"'Ee would tell mee," said Gilly, "but 'e jus' disappear two days ago."

"Perhaps," said Mr. Morris. "But even if I knew, I could not tell you." He looked down, shuffled some papers on his desk, and then looked back up. "I assume you wanted something from me."

"As I tell yoo before, I make a café 'ere in Philadelphia," said Gilly.

"And you want me to finance you?"

"*Non*," said Gilly, rather more emphatically than necessary. "Monee I 'ave. But I no know oowhere to buy. Also I want buy Zach and Sadie."

"I'm afraid I've already sold them, but I can tell you to whom and he may be willing to sell them to you."

"*S'il vous plaît*," said Gilly.

"As to where you should buy, I think I have a solution that will please several people." He turned around in his chair to face a large cabinet with multiple cabinet-wide drawers of very shallow height. He opened one of them and lifted several large pieces of paper until he found the one he wanted. Then he drew it out slowly, turned back and placed it on his desk facing Gilly.

Gilly looked at it and shrugged.

"It's a map of the newer parts of the city, west on Market. Or I should say on High Street as they call it now." He pointed to a spot on the map. Gilly examined it and looked up.

"High and Sixth," said Morris. "It's in an area we expect to grow very quickly. Already refugees from the San Domingo rebellion have considerably filled in the area up the hill to the west of there and, unfortunately for them but fortunately for you, we expect many more. It's also both far enough from the government offices while not being too far that certain members of the government might like to meet there if you offered suitable fare——and were open during the hours when they do the real business of government."

"They doo not doo real business' when they meet in thee great 'all?"

"Heavens, no," said Morris, laughing. "Where everyone could hear them? They much prefer small tables in a café where they can whisper together over coffee and *des pâtisseries*."

"My seester learn making *toute sortes de vienoiseries*, I no know 'ow you say, and bread and, *bien sûr, des pâtisseries* with thee chef de Lafayette." (All sorts of croissants and similar, and of course, pastries.)

"I'm sure that will do," said Morris. "Will you do dinner and tea?"

"Huh!" said Gilly. "No *thé* will evair bee seen in my café!"

"That's just as well," said Morris. "We Americans—some of us—have an ambiguous relationship with tea. But I meant the afternoon repast." He picked up the map, turned, and carefully slid it back into its drawer. He turned back.

"*Peut-être,* (perhaps)" said Gilly. "If wee find thee personnel."

Morris nodded, placed his elbows on his desk and leaned his chin on steepled fingers. "You see, an Irish man had contracted to buy the land from me to make a bakery and we agreed on what the building should look like. I went ahead and built the building and his funds dried up. He cannot pay me. I agreed to give him thirty days to raise the funds before I foreclose. His time is almost up. Perhaps he will allow you to buy him out. Or perhaps you can make some other agreement so he can work for you. He does bake very well in the English tradition."

"I weel speak with 'eem," said Gilly. "But you theenk Anglaise 'tradeetion' is good?"

"Not according to French standards, I suppose. But some Americans like it."

"They weel 'ave to bee, 'ow you say, *intruit*."

Morris laughed. "Yes, I think you mean educated."

He opened the desk drawer in front of him, pulled out a small blank piece of paper and wrote on it. Then he rolled the blotter over it and showed it to Gilly. It was a man's name and address. "I will charge you only what Clement has not paid. You will have to work out with him what to do about what he has paid." Morris took the paper back, wrote some more, blotted it, and then handed it to Gilly. "Those are the names of the households to which I sold the boy and his sister. If you wish, I will send a note recommending that they sell them to you."

. . .

Two WEEKS later Renée stood in front of a storefront with two graceful, bowed, paned, windows on either side of a beautifully carved door. Above them, two workmen were completing the bright gold overlay on the last 'e' of the name, 'Café Fraternité.' The building had three stories. The first for impromptu customers, the second for large groups and banquets, the third for living. She turned in response to hearing her name called. Across Sixth Street, rounding the corner from High, Sadie and Zach Sanders preceded Gilly who was waving two sheets of paper in the air.

"*Voir!*" he shouted, exuberance in his voice. '*Certificats de liberté!* 'Freedom papers!"

Zach and Sadie were beaming, but appeared to be a bit overwhelmed.

"*Et* Mr. Morris, 'ee sign the 'affidavit,' 'ee call it. They never be slaves again."

"But oowhat weel they doo?" asked Renée.

At that moment, Renée had to jump out of the way as a heavy freight wagon pulled by four horses rounded the corner from High Street and pulled up in front of the café. Clement emerged through the doorway and set a brick on the wooden porch to hold the door open.

"Who's gonna unload this stuff?" said the driver, jumping down from the box. "I ain't got all day. 'Nother deliv'ry in a couple hour."

"I will," said Clement. "And me," said Zach. In a matter of moments all five were involved in the process of muscling heavy boxes from the wagon to a sack truck, dragging it inside, unloading and returning.

. . .

"THE OVEN IS LOVELY," said Clement.

"*Pour les pains anglais, peut-être*," said Renée in her most sarcastic voice. (For English bread, maybe.)

"Eenglish," said Gilly.

"*Mais...*" (But...)

Gilly interrupted her. "Oowee discuss thees before. Oowee must Eenglish now oowe in America."

"*Mais—*"

Clement threw his baker's hat into the air. "I can't work with her!" he said. "Nothing is good enough for her, she won't speak English, she doesn't want my help. She..."

"*Suffisant!*" yelled Gilly. (Enough!) "Een a month, maybee two, my monee run out. Oowee must make thees work before then."

BY THE TIME Gilly returned from visiting Mrs. Spencer's boarding house in New York, with Polly Potter on his arm, Renée and Clement had sorted out their differences and Zach and Sadie had been installed in two of the four rooms upstairs. Renée had set up an office in the third room and the fourth had been outfitted as a gathering place for business meetings and whatever free time they might have to spend somewhere. Gilly and Polly got rooms in a new boarding house on Sixth Street a little north of High.

By early November, all was in readiness. For someone. For anyone! But there were few takers until Mr. Morris showed up one day, nearly a week after the less than grand opening, with Alexander Hamilton and a few members of their staffs.

The next day a diminutive little man showed up alone. "I want only a perfect croissant with butter, and a bit of dark coffee in the French style," he said. "For two."

Sadie nodded and went back to the kitchen to give the order. In a few moments, another man—a very tall man—appeared and joined the first. Renée came out to serve the men and as she approached with coffee, she heard the tall one say, "If this is as good as he says it is, it will be the only true thing Hamilton ever said."

"Your croissants weel be out in *un moment*," she said, her accent strong.

"I should think Mr. Monroe, here, needs two," said the first man.

"Whereas Madison will barely be able to consume one," said the second man, laughing. "*Mais, merci!*"

As it turned out, however, both men asked for a second croissant, more coffee, a *petite tarte au citron*, and stayed for over an hour.

"I believe Mr. Morris may have had something to do with this as well," said Madison on his way out the door.

"He and Hamilton, two peas in a pod," replied Monroe. "But they were right about this."

The next day, a slim man, somewhat taller than Madison, with red hair and a green jacket, entered, followed by a number of people who appeared to be working for him. In a short while, they were joined by Madison and Monroe.

The red-headed man looked around and said, "It looks more like a tavern in England than a café in France, but I'm taking your word for it that it is good."

Evidently it was. For these men and others with them kept coming—almost every day.

On a cold day near the end of the month, Morris came in and asked to be seated in a dark corner not far from the hearth. The red head and his crew came in around 2 o'clock, as usual, saw someone sitting there, and chose a table on the other side of the large open space. They resumed their habit of huddled conversation. It was more than an hour and a half before they left.

Gilly came out himself to watch them go and then went to see if Mr. Morris required anything more.

"Are they here often," asked Morris, nodding in the direction of the table in which the men had been sitting.

"Almost every day," said Gilly.

"Do you know who they are?"

"Renée 'eard two of them call each other Monroe and Madison. I no know the others."

"That's Thomas Jefferson and his gang," said Morris.

"Thees Jefferson, 'ee was in Paris, non?"

"Yes he was," said Morris, "Before Gouverneur Morris."

"'Ee ees emportant?"

"He is the opposition," said Morris. "But he loves France and all things French. He is greatly enamored of your revolution."

"*Mais*, I am not. It become, 'ow you say, violen'?"

"Yes, violent," said Morris. "Nevertheless, he will make you famous. You will do well here."

"*Merci!*" said Gilly. "*On peut espérer!*" (One may hope.)

After seeing Gilly, Renée, Lewis and Isabella off to Philadelphia on July 12, Crispin had made his way back to England—London, Birmingham, and finally, Liverpool, where his tainted fortune awaited him.

He thought he might be there for a while, so he made his way to Gore's newspaper office to look at the ads in the window. Perhaps he would rent a flat. He couldn't help smirk when he found Gore's paper in the midst of all the others. It was set in Bodoni. He had ordered the full font set from Italy via his solicitor before he left, and it seems it had arrived and been appropriated in his absence. Then he got to studying the ads.

He jumped when he heard a voice right beside him. "I assume I have you to thank for this," said Gore.

Crispin turned to him. "For what?" he said.

"For Bodoni. And I know who you are, Mr. Graves."

Crispin shrugged. "I suppose it's a little something to begin making up for the damage my family has done accumulating wealth."

"Well, whatever it's for, I appreciate it. It's enabled me to add nearly twenty percent more copy, just as easily readable, to each page."

He put his hand on Crispin's shoulder. "And you may see me any time you like," he said. "Just please leave your politics at the door."

"I don't have any politics," said Crispin, looking back at the ads. "But I have a desire to do the right thing." He turned to fix his gaze on Gore. "Do you know anything about the so-called 'Clapham Sect'? Or how I can reach Mr. William Wilberforce?"

"Nothing I would say here," said Gore, "though they are not currently in open conflict with the king. Come with me!"

He strode back inside. Crispin followed and noticed that he had two workers, one setting type and the other inking the larger press.

Gore tipped his head in their direction. "With what I got for selling the Bell fonts, I hired these guys—at least for a while. Things are not so good here, the economy, you know? Everything is going up in price, and some things are difficult or impossible to get."

"So your business will decline?"

"Oh, not mine, no. People are selling their things and

placing ever more ads. No one is buying, however, or at least almost no one, so the ads keep repeating. No, I'll do fine. But these young men may not be able to live on what I can afford to pay them. So they'll scadaddle and find something else if they aren't picked up by a press gang."

"They're still doing that?"

"More than ever. But that's politics, so enough."

He went over to his desk, pulled a pile of papers from one of the slots, and leafed through it.

"Do you have something for me to write on?" he asked.

Crispin pulled out the small notebook and pencil he always kept with him and handed it over. Gore took them and wrote for a short while.

"Closest Clapham office is in Birmingham," he said, still writing. "Wilberforce is in Clapham itself most of the time, I would guess, living at the Henry Thornton house." He looked up at Crispin. "It's not far from London." He looked back at the notebook. "Though this time of year he may be back in Yorkshire." He looked up and handed the notebook and pencil back to Crispin. "He doesn't see well, and he is often ill. I shouldn't be disappointed, if I were you, if he is not able to see you."

Crispin nodded. "No politics?" he said.

Gore grimaced slightly and shrugged. "Not so you'd notice," he said.

"Thank you," said Crispin. "I do not plan to remain in England, so I may not ever see you again. But I have appreciated you."

Gore looked him in the eyes. "You are a remarkable young man," he said, holding out his right hand for Crispin to shake. "I wish you well."

Crispin shook his hand, nodded, turned and left the shop. He headed for his solicitor's office.

·   ·   ·

"How much do you know about shipbuilding?"

Mr. Wright steepled his hands, made his face look contemplative, and spoke expansively. "Well, I've managed the shipyard since your uncle's...ah...passing."

"Have they done anything different from what they were doing when my uncle was alive?"

The steeple vanished and after a moment Wright responded in a flat tone. "Not really, though they are working more quickly as the orders for ships are coming more quickly."

"How difficult would it be to make these ships into packet ships rather than slave ships?"

Wright suddenly placed both hands on the desk and sat up straight in his chair, aghast. "You wouldn't!"

"How difficult?"

Wright settled back into his chair, swiveled, and looked out his window. "I know nothing about shipbuilding," he said. Then he turned back. "But I know about contracts. It would be ruinous not to keep our current contracts. Besides which, no one would pay anywhere near as much for packets. They're barely tenable, financially. Whereas these ships—"

"I don't care about the money," said Crispin. "Could it be done?"

"If you don't want to build these ships, why not just sell the business? I'm certain a buyer could be found."

"Because I want to see fewer slave ships, fewer slaves, and eventually, no slaves," said Crispin.

"You're a dreamer," said Wright, steepling his hands again, "unlike your uncle. Slavery has always existed, and it always will exist. If you don't make the ships, someone else will."

"Let them," said Crispin. "I will not. Please see to terminating whatever contracts we currently have and discover whether the ships under construction can be...re-modeled, I guess, adapted, to become packets. By tomorrow morning I want the creation of the pegs and shackles stopped. I want the molds destroyed. The smithies can make other things. They will not make those things any longer."

Mr. Wright was silent, clenching and unclenching his jaw.

Crispin watched him for a moment. "If you cannot accomplish this, I'm sure I can find someone who will."

"Yes, Sir," said Wright in a clipped little voice. He looked at Crispin as though he had lost his mind, then heaved a sigh. "As you wish."

Crispin nodded and left.

CRISPIN FULLY INTENDED to inspect the shipyard the next day to see whether Wright had complied, but the stage to Birmingham left early that morning and there would not be another for four days. He opted to be on the stage. Birmingham was larger and not so invested in the slave trade. He thought he might find a solicitor there who would be more amenable to his plans.

He returned in the early afternoon a week later, accompanied by an attorney from Birmingham, Mr. Galbraith. As soon as they alighted from the stage, the two of them walked south to the dockyard. When they rounded the corner to the street leading to Graves Shipyard, Crispin saw that nothing had changed. He raised his eyebrows at Galbraith who shrugged and nodded.

The next stop was Wright's office.

"You can't just barge in like this," said the same glaring receptionist.

Crispin and Galbraith barged in anyway, knocking on Wright's door and going in without waiting for a response. Wright looked up from his desk, startled.

"Ah, Mr. Graves. I wrote you a letter but didn't know where to send it."

"I'm here now," said Crispin. "Maybe you would care to read it to me?"

Wright was drumming his fingers against the desk.

"Now?" said Crispin. "Or would you prefer just to tell me what it says." He nodded towards Galbraith and said, "By the way, I'd like you to meet my attorney, Mr. Josiah Galbraith."

"But...but I'm your attorney."

"You were."

"Now look here," said Wright, "I made a contract with your uncle—"

"Whom, you'll notice," said Crispin, "is not here."

"Well, yes," he said, "But I've gotten you the best price you'll ever see for your yard."

"That would be very nice if I were planning to sell it. But at this moment I am not. In any case, it will be your concern no longer. Mr. Galbraith will be attending to my estate henceforth. He is here to see to the transfer of all my papers."

"Um, well..."

"We took the liberty of hiring a couple of lads to remove the paperwork. They are just outside your door arguing with your receptionist as we speak."

The house went to the Claphams. But not before Crispin returned to it briefly. He and Galbraith walked into the back yard. "I'm back, as I said I would be," said Crispin to several fleeing backs. He and Galbraith stood and waited for a few moments. Then Crispin walked down to where the cooking fire had been hastily covered, set up the stakes and crosspiece again, placed the hook and cooking pot on the crosspiece, and looked around on the ground. When he found the spoon, he took out his handkerchief and wiped it off, then put it in the pot and stirred.

"This is too good to waste, fellows," he said. "Come on back and eat."

A head popped out of the bush beside the back door. "Ya meant what ya said, yer Honor, when ya said ya'wn't hurt us?"

"I meant it," said Crispin. "This is Josiah." He pointed at Galbraith. "He is taking charge of the house for an organization that is fighting to end slavery. You can't stay here, but you and others like you can come here—preferably late at night—and we'll help you get to safety." He looked up toward the back stoop and pointed. "You can look under there and, when we can, we will place things there you can use. You are men and brothers. We will do what we can."

Of course, it didn't go down quite as easily as Crispin had hoped, but by the time he had boarded the *Juniper*, out of Liverpool, headed for America, it looked as though his affairs were in order. Much of his family's fortune had been transferred to the Claphams, 'the Saints,' as the populace liked to call them, to be used in their campaign to abolish slavery. The specifications for the ships under construction in his shipyard had been changed and the shipyard itself had been sold to an individual who was willing to sign on the contract that he would not make slave ships.

Crispin took enough money with him to live on for a few months, until he found a job. He also made arrangements to receive a small monthly stipend—which was to be retained in Birmingham—should he need it at a later date. Unless he returned to England at some time in the distant future, he intended for it to revert to the Claphams.

❧

CRISPIN ARRIVED in Philadelphia in mid-October on the last ship of the season from Liverpool. He wasn't quite the impoverished parolee he had been when he had left New York in April, 1791. But he was certainly not as wealthy as he might have been. Now he gazed with interest at the new towers and storefronts before him in Philadelphia by Clifford's Wharf, between Market and Mulberry Streets, bright in the noonday sun.

Well, he thought, *I'm on my own, as usual. I hope I can find Lewis, Gilly, and the others, but I have to make this work myself. Like every other ordinary free man.*

He raised a fisted hand missing two fingers into the air, nodded, then headed below to gather his things.

THE *PENNSYLVANIA PACKET and General Advertiser* had moved to new quarters farther inland on Fifth Street, not far from where Crispin found a room in the gentrifying, formerly unsavory quarter near Mulberry. It was now called *Dunlap's American Daily Advertiser*. Crispin was glad to come in out of the weather—it hadn't been this cold in England or even on the packet coming over. Late November was cold here. He clapped his hands together before removing his hat and scarf.

Mr. Dunlap was shocked to see him, but not so shocked that he didn't try to put him right to work.

"I need sketches of the players," he said, "particularly in those types of conversations where they plot against one another."

"I think you've lost me, Sir," said Crispin. "Is this some sort of sporting competition or drama?"

"Huh!" said Dunlap. "Well put. But no. It's politics. It's war."

"And am I to understand they are the same thing?" he said grinning.

Dunlap looked up from the press he was cleaning. "You have a knack, Mr. Graves." He looked back at the machine and gave a fierce rub to what appeared to be a recalcitrant spot. Crispin noted that the rubbing was out of all proportion to the difficulty of removing it. "They have *become* the same thing. And it *is* a sort of tragedy," he said, looking up again, "because they fight for their point of view, or, more likely, for power, and the real needs of the country are languishing."

"And so you need sketches."

Dunlap tossed the rag he'd been using to a nearby work bench. "Yes. I'd like people to see them in their hauteur and bombast. Then they can decide which side to join."

"There are sides?"

"Oh, yes." Dunlap walked over to a different workbench with a cork board behind it from which several drying engravings were hanging. Crispin followed him. "This is all I have." He held out a couple of engravings that were finals he might print. "Pathetic, huh?"

Crispin had to agree. They showed persons, obviously men but with no details, at a distance, walking together. Perhaps they were talking. Perhaps not.

"I can't print that."

"Why would you need to?"

"Because there's a newspaper war going on. Hamilton and Jefferson trade salvos every day in print. Oh, they don't use their own names. They use high-flown Latin names that have some hidden meaning they think the populace understands, but everyone knows who they are."

"But it's just words?"

"So far. That's why I need illustrations. Your illustrations. You always were excellent at that sort of thing, from the first time I saw you at that party at Morris's."

"You want to elaborate?"

Dunlap let go of the two engravings, one of which fluttered to the bench. He picked it up, crumpled it, and threw it into a trash barrel by the end of the workbench.

"It started with the *Gazette of the United States*, so-called, edited by one John Fenno from New York. This is Hamilton's venue for praising the president and promoting his own policies. Then Jefferson hired this poet from New Jersey, Philip Freneau, to be the editor of a paper for his party's views, the *National Gazette*. They say the nastiest things about Washington, things no one would ever say to his face—or using their real names."

"Like?"

"Oh, for example, the celebration of his sixtieth birthday they called something like the predecessor of other 'monarchial vices,' and his fiscal policies as 'pregnant with every mischief.'"

"Were they?"

"Depends on your point of view."

"I left England to escape politics."

"Out of the frying pan into the fire," said Dunlap. "Do you want to work for me? We'll do both sides."

"You're not just an advertiser?"

"I was. But I can't just let this slip without some sort of corrective. We'll scatter articles and illustrations throughout the advertisements. Who knows? It might even help get people to read more of the ads."

"All right," said Crispin. "But let me get my bearings first. And I'd like to find my friends Gilly and Lewis if they're here in Philadelphia."

"Ah. That Gilly, I think I know. Started a café over on Sixth and High. It's become the hidey-hole for Jefferson and his Democrat-Republicans. Filled with Francophiles," he shrugged, "which makes sense as I hear he has the best French pastries in the city, if not the country."

"His sister worked with Lafayette's kitchen staff. She ought to be good. Where did you say it was?"

"Café Fraternité, Sixth and High. And I'll expect you at work tomorrow morning at six."

"I'll be here," said Crispin, walking out the door.

CRISPIN RETURNED TO HIS ROOM, collected his medium-sized sketchpad and an assortment of pencils, placed them in a valise, and headed out. He couldn't help grinning when he rounded the corner from High to Sixth and saw 'Café Fraternité' emblazoned on the front of the building before him. *This is* just *what I had in mind*, he thought. But he didn't want to see Gilly or Renée quite yet. He hoped they would not be the ones to meet him at the door. He walked to the door and entered.

He was greeted by a woman he thought he had seen before, but could not quite place.

"I'm here for the meeting," he said.

She pointed to the stairs. "You're early," she said. "They start to trickle in at about half eleven."

"That's fine," he said. "I'll make myself comfortable."

"You want coffee? Pâtisserie?"

"Both, *s'il vous plait*."

"Oh, you don't need to sil voos plett me," she said. "I'm from New York."

"Ah," he said, heading up the stairs. *That must be Polly. Gilly collected her from Mrs. Spencer's boarding house? Brave man.*

He placed his coat, scarf and hat on a vacant chair beside a table alongside the window farthest from the stairs. He was in shadow made all the darker by its proximity to light; a place where he was unlikely to be noticed by anyone meeting at the large table in the center but that had enough light to sketch. It would be good beginning his work with Dunlap if he could bring some sketches in the morning.

The room must have been the size of the one below with the addition of the kitchen space. It was not particularly well lit, but well enough with the candles on the table and the one chandelier so he'd be able to make out the features of those who would be meeting. A few upholstered chairs were set about, with tables between them or in front of them, a divan was set against the back wall, a few smaller tables with two or four chairs were closer to the middle, and the center held that table large enough for eight or ten people.

Polly brought a carafe of coffee and an enormous *croissant chocolat.*

"*Uncroyable,*" he said as she set it down. (Unbelievable.)

"I told you I don't do foreign," she said with some asperity. "But I s'pose if you're in with this lot you need to."

"Sorry," said Crispin. "And I'm afraid I have only English coins."

She smiled. "Oh, that ain't no problem. We never turn down hard money here, wherever it come from."

He handed her a pound coin. "Will that do?"

"Oh, that'll do a whole month, yer highness," she said, "meaning no disrespect."

"Well, keep it then," he said. "I'll be back."

Polly took a lit candle from one of the tables, climbed up on a chair by the center table, and lit the candles of the chandelier. Then she flounced off—but not quickly enough so Crispin didn't see her take the coin from her pocket and bite it to see if it was real. Crispin grinned and did a little figuring. According to the act that had been passed in the spring, official United States currency was now the silver dollar, whose value was the same as the Spanish milled dollar he'd known when he'd first been in Pennsylvania. They were worth about a fifth of an

English pound sterling. With coffee at one penny and the croissant at two pennies—he did a quick math problem or two in his head—he should be able to come in every day until sometime in June. He grinned again. *I know where I'll be having breakfast. I wonder what time they open?*

People filtered in in twos and threes and gravitated to those comfortable chairs. Crispin didn't know whether they saw him or not, but they ignored him if they did. He could hear only snatches of conversation, but that was fine. He was only sketching at this point.

The first two were both small men, neither young nor old. They came in holding their hats and scarves, hung their greatcoats on the coat tree, and moved to a set of chairs on both sides of a narrow table. Neither had a wig or fancy clothing, though the wispy blond one had a knot at his neck and a light-colored jacket and the dark, messy-haired one had a dark jacket and a ruffled shirt. He tossed a newspaper on the table and the other picked it up.

The next one in was tall and distinctive looking. When he'd removed his coat, Crispin noted that his black jacket was velvet. His only other distinctive feature was a deep cleft in his chin.

He was followed by Polly and a Negro woman bearing flagons of ale and multiple pastry trays. They set these on the center table and began to distribute plates around the table. They were followed closely by a Negro man carrying multiple carafes like the one in which he had been served coffee. The man set the carafes around the table and, as he was setting the last one down, happened to look in Crispin's direction. He gave a sudden brief cry and Crispin quickly put his finger to his lips. It was Zach. He recognized him easily. The young woman, then, must be Sadie, whom he did not recognize, she had changed so much.

Zach nodded slightly and the three retired as a host of boots was heard on the stairs. The first man to the top had a light-colored, heavy, fur coat and hat which he took off with a sigh. "Pennsylvania gets colder every year," he said. "Would that we could meet from May until September."

A few grunts of agreement met that statement. And after a flurry of coat removals with a few thrown on the divan to avoid toppling the over-burdened coat tree, the entire group moved to the center table. Sadie materialized at that point and began pouring their coffee. She glanced shyly toward the corner at one point, smiling, and Crispin nodded slightly. The group had become so involved in their coffee and pâtisseries that they noticed nothing else.

The man with the fur overcoat wore a deep green velvet jacket that nicely complemented his reddish hair, now starting toward grey. Crispin could only think of his shirt as a blouse; elaborately ruffled as it was, with an opal brooch at its neck. Because this person seemed to be the leader, he sketched him more carefully than the others.

"There's no avoiding having Washington as president for this next term," he said. "No one else could hold the country together. But at least we should have more members sympathetic to the republican cause by next December. Then maybe we can be done with that rascal, Hamilton."

A few 'amens' and grunted assents greeted this remark and then it became difficult to make out anything specific since the conversation devolved into many little conversations around the table. After a suitable time of eating, a single, quiet, conversation resumed, led by the man in the green coat but contributed to by almost everyone at the table. Crispin could make out very little of this, but he used his time to sketch the room, the table with its occupants, even Sadie, Zach, and Polly from memory. He wondered if the party thought Sadie and Zach were slaves and what they would think if they knew they were free.

NEXT MORNING, he had quite a harvest to share with John Dunlap.

"I don't know any of these people," said Crispin, "but here's what they look like." He showed him the participants, one by one.

"That's Freneau," said Dunlap, "the little weasel. And that's Madison. He used to be Washington's friend and I believe he is still his confidant. But he fights against Washington." He pointed to the next one. "That has to be Monroe. Another Virginian."

Crispin turned another page. "Oh, my," said Dunlap. "That's Jefferson and I don't believe I've ever seen a better likeness."

"And the others with him?" asked Crispin. "I couldn't see them well since they all came in at once and sat down, some with their backs to me."

Dunlap looked closely at the next drawing that showed three men. "Looks like Burr and Livingston," he said, "and the last one could be William Giles, a congressman from Virginia." He turned from the pages and looked forthrightly at Crispin. "A little anti-Federalist cabal," he said. Then he looked at the next few pictures.

"Slaves in that tavern? That should make them all feel at home."

"They aren't slaves," said Crispin. "They're freedmen. I paid..." He stopped.

"What?" said Dunlap.

"It's not important," said Crispin. "But I happen to know them."

"A story for another time," said Dunlap, turning back to the presses. "We have work to do."

By MID-AFTERNOON CRISPIN had finished preparing his sketches for print. It would be up to Dunlap what happened to them. He got up from his stool to tell Dunlap, with the idea of then going over to Fraternité and greeting Gilly and company.

"Do you want to do reporting as well?" asked Dunlap after receiving Crispin's news.

"Definitely," he said.

"I could use you to get the thing out, but that would be a waste of your talents. So, next time, don't sketch them. Listen to what they're saying."

"Isn't there a better way to find out what they're saying than spying on them from the shadows?"

"Perhaps. You're welcome to find it."

Crispin stood there for a moment, frowning, thinking about it.

"Well, Go! Get information! Find out what the other side is saying, too."

Crispin turned and grinned. "Do I get paid a salary or by the story?"

"I don't know," said Dunlap, heading to his office at the back of the shop. "Wait there."

He came back in a moment and handed Crispin a bunch of bank notes. "Bank of America," he said. "Hamilton's big triumph."

Crispin gave him a puzzled look.

"I don't know whether it's good or bad, but at least we have something to use as a medium of commerce." He nodded at the bills. "That's your first month's pay."

Crispin glanced at the bills for the first time. "Forty dollars? Will people take it? What will it buy?"

Dunlap shrugged. "You'll find out when you try to spend it," he said. "But it should cover your living expenses for a month, at least, and maybe have something left over if you're careful."

"Right," said Crispin.

"And I expect to see you every day except the Sabbath with illustrations, stories, and even a hand at the presses if we're running behind."

TEA TIME WASN'T until 4 PM, though it wasn't really 'tea' time here, since coffee had mostly taken over. But that meant that Fraternité should be relatively quiet. A good time to visit.

He went in the front door and, seeing no one, shut the door a little more noisily than necessary. Still nothing. Wonderful aromas were emanating from the back of the room under the stairs, so Crispin headed that way. He poked his head into the kitchen and saw a man with a baker's hat, back to him, removing several loaves of bread from a brick oven. Even though he couldn't see the man's face, he knew it wasn't Gilly.

When he opened the back door, the sounds of digging poured into the short hall. Crispin looked out. He saw the privy, chickens clucking about, the head of a cow projecting from a small barn, and a shovelful of dirt flying out from behind the privy.

"Hello!" he shouted.

"Whoooever yoo are," said a voice, "Eef yoo want too talk weeth mee, grab a *pelle* (shovel). I 'ave no time too seet and chatter."

Crispin chuckled to himself, took his overcoat off and set it between the rungs of the small fence that ran down beside the porch stairs. He gathered that '*pelle*' was a shovel. Several picks of various types, along with a couple of shovels, were leaning against the front of the privy. He grabbed one and walked around to the back. There he found the backs of Gilly and Zach, facing him, Zach in a hole about four feet deep, and the Gilly throwing the dirt shoveled up to him into the yard behind him.

"Where do you want me to dig?" said Crispin.

"In thee 'hole, there weeth..." started Gilly, twirling around suddenly. "Creespeen!" he shouted. He tossed his shovel down, ran around the hole, and hugged Crispin. Then he pushed back from him and looked at him. "Steel the same," he said. "You come in my café and not greet me!"

"So Zach told you?"

Zach looked out of the hole and held up the hand not holding the shovel, shrugging.

"I couldn't yesterday," he said. "I was on assignment. But today I'll help you if you wish."

"Eef I weesh? One preevie not enough. Oowee meke two more. You want to 'elp deeg, you welcome."

By three-thirty they stopped in order to prepare for the late-afternoon rush.

"Running café ees no small *travail, tâche?*" (work? job?)

"I think you mean job," said Crispin. "I see that. And you have done wonderfully."

"All thee French come to mee, and thee Americaine whoo love France. It ees beautiful idea."

He looked toward the café and back, nodding toward Zach. "'ee 'elp very much. But I no can pay 'im much. And now we must buy wood for *appentis,* 'ow you say?

"Outhouse. Privy."

"*Oui.* 'Aving café is *tres cher* (very expensive). You come with me? We talk?" He headed up the stairs. "Zach, you clean up 'ere?"

Zach nodded.

"And I help you carry the wood back?" said Crispin.

"*Non.* Oowe get cart."

"And, by the way, do you know where Lewis and Isabella are?"

"Ah," said Gilly. "No one know, except Mr. Morris, and he no say."

"Well, tell me what you do know. And I need to hear all about you and Polly."

Gilly turned and grinned at him, then went in through the back door and yelled to Renée where he was going. Then he headed toward the front door and Crispin followed him out.

CRISPIN REPORTED on the unanimous election of George Washington for a second term as president, and on the second time a bare majority confirmed John Adams in the role of vice president. As Jefferson had believed, those of his philosophy had done better in the elections than their opponents, but they would not be seated until the date stipulated by the constitution, the first Monday of December, 1793. Except for the verbal sniping in the two Gazettes, Philadelphia was mostly quiet through to Washington's inauguration on March 4, 1793. The winter had not been too severe in Philadelphia, a few of the vegetables Gilly had planted had begun to push tiny little leaves through the softening ground, and business was brisk at Fraternité.

Until the news came along later that month that Louis XVI had been beheaded on January 21. Crispin's many conversations with ordinary townsmen and government officials convinced him that a sea change in public attitudes toward the French Revolution and the French might well be in the wind. But not yet. For the moment, the depredations were being played down and the populace seemed ecstatic that the French seemed to be following in the footsteps of the former American colonies.

Then France declared war on England. Actually, word only came to America about this new European difficulty in late March, followed almost immediately by the news that France had also declared war on Spain. Most of the world's warships were owned by those three countries, particularly the first two, so it was clear there would be trouble on the high seas.

Crispin began to help Gilly as a server at Fraternité so he could listen in on what Jefferson and his colleagues were saying. He couldn't draw them in this role, but as a server, being more or less invisible, he was able to hear what they were saying as he tended the fire, arranged chairs and tables, and brought trays laden with food up the stairs or empty dishes down the stairs. But he had to find sources of information other than what he could obtain surreptitiously at Fraternité, sources from the opposing point of view.

So he went back to his first contact in Philadelphia, Robert Morris. When he told Morris who he was and what he was doing, Morris introduced him to people who supported the administration; those who worked for the *Gazette of the United States*, a couple of congressmen, and another senator. It was from Morris, himself, that Crispin learned about the consternation among members of both houses of congress aroused by the president's April declaration of neutrality with respect to the foreign combatants.

But he saw the furthering of tensions for himself when he overheard Jefferson say that two parties had emerged in

America over this foreign war, with an 'ardour' for their causes exceeding that of the Republicans and Federalists—though it was not long before the Republicans had adopted the French cause and pursued it with frenzied malice. Whereas those supporting the English resorted to pursuing the president as though the French Revolution was his fault. The National Gazette wrote an open letter to Washington saying, "Let not the little buzz of the aristocratic few and their contemptible minions," by which Crispin knew they meant Hamilton, in particular, "of speculators, Tories, and British emissaries, be mistaken for the exalted and general voice of the American people."

Congress had adjourned in late March, but that did not prevent an avalanche of opinion from smothering the counsels of the president's cabinet and creating heated public debate. All of which was exacerbated by the arrival in early April of a new French minister to the United States, one Edmond-Charles Genêt, styling himself 'Citizen Genêt.' He was greeted with rapt enthusiasm upon his arrival in Charleston; enough so that Dunlap sent Crispin south to send back news of his activities and his reception.

By the time Crispin caught up with him in late April, Genêt had made his way to Jamestown, contracting along the way to have ships built and crews recruited to prey on British shipping. It was not difficult for Crispin to discover this, as Genêt loudly proclaimed his intentions everywhere a crowd gathered. "Do you want the British out of Florida?" he cried, "the Spanish out of Louisiana? Then come to me. I will commission you and reward you handsomely."

Crispin admired his flawless English, but was less certain of the quality of his actions.

"Join the French navy. Catch British ships heavily laden

with sugar, rum, spices and all the riches of the islands. Get your share of the plunder!"

Crispin knew this could not possibly be in keeping with the Neutrality Act, but it didn't keep crowds from surrounding and applauding him everywhere he went. Crispin traveled in his wake until he arrived in Philadelphia on May 16. Then he quickly dropped his drawings, notes and articles with Dunlap, and went to see what he could discover about Genêt's reception with the president.

Jefferson met Genêt as he entered Philadelphia and took him to greet a crowd at what had become the largest tavern in town, City Tavern, on Walnut and Second Streets. Crispin watched with dismay as the crowd there continued to support him, shouting greetings and toasting him. Then Jefferson, who was Secretary of State, after all, and should be the one accompanying a foreign minister to the United States, took him off to the president's house.

Crispin staked out a spot for his easel and drawing tablet across the street. He was not entirely surprised when Genêt came out of Washington's residence looking a bit downcast. Genêt's spirits revived enormously when the crowd began to shout his name along with "Vive la France!" and other paeans of support.

"Come with me," shouted Genêt. Crispin saw Jefferson's look of concern, but Jefferson followed anyway as Genêt led the crowd down Walnut Street toward the wharfs. He then turned left and continued the march a few blocks to the dock at Arch Street. He stopped and pointed to two merchant ships bearing English flags under French flags.

"Là!" he said. "There, you see? Two English ships that will not profit from your hard work. Our ship, *Embuscade*, has captured them and will distribute their wealth among the people."

Loud cheers followed this exclamation. Hats were thrown into the air and jubilant shouts echoed off the buildings on Front Street. Jefferson spoke to Genêt who seemed to shake him off and to continue preaching the French Revolution. Finally, Jefferson stood in front of him with Monroe alongside, and managed to get him to end his little speech.

Some of the crowd dispersed, but some followed Genêt, Jefferson and Monroe south along Front Street. Crispin followed them long enough to see the three enter a new hotel on Spruce and Front, and then jogged to Dunlap's office. There were so many illustrations and so much news that they would have to set the advertising aside for this next issue. People had to know what was going on.

CRISPIN ATTEMPTED to follow the Genêt case, but most of what was happening was hidden from the eyes of the public. He did, however, watch with interest as Genêt renovated and armed a captured English ship, *Little Sarah*, to become a French privateer, *La Petite Démocrate*, to prey on other English ships—which Crispin, and presumably Genêt, knew was entirely contrary to the wishes and orders of the United States government. The vessel set out to sea on July 10.

This was followed by the publication in multiple newspapers of a set of rules developed by the president and his cabinet that prohibited foreign nationals to arm ships as privateers or bring captured prizes into American ports. Café Fraternité became somewhat of a rallying point for the crowds supporting Genêt and his ambitions.

In early August, crowds became mobs and some thousands of people carrying torches, yelling epithets, praising France, and damning the president, marched from there to the president's house and threatened to drag him out and require him to declare war against England. Crispin did not think it wise to set up his easel and sketch this, though he did make a sketch from memory back at Dunlap's after the crowd dispersed early the next morning.

However, in less than a week after that event, Crispin was able to report that the love of all things French had suffered a serious setback when the news came to Philadelphia via a New York newspaper—corroborated by no less than John Jay and Rufus King—that Genêt threatened to make a direct appeal to the people of the United States over the head of President Washington. It was only a couple of weeks later that the *Gazette of the United States* published news that the entire cabinet had agreed to ask the French to recall Genêt. The rioting petered out, French sailors no longer swaggered about the streets, and calm was on the verge of returning.

Except for one little thing, the alarm raised by the most illustrious doctor in the city, Dr. Benjamin Rush, that yellow fever, a disease that had plagued Philadelphia in the past, had returned.

AT FIRST IT didn't seem like much. In July, Crispin had witnessed a particularly somber and formal funeral. The casket bearers included Secretary of State Jefferson, Secretary of the Treasury Hamilton, Secretary of War Knox, and three Supreme Court justices. The person who had died was the wife of Tobias Lear, President Washington's personal secretary. Washington, himself, attended the funeral, though it had been reported that he did not attend funerals. At the time, no one knew what the twenty-three-year old Polly had died from. When other deaths began multiplying, Crispin made the connection.

On August 20, *Dunlap's American Daily Advertiser*, along with every other newspaper in Philadelphia, received a letter to print from a committee headed by Dr. Rush, suggesting measures to prevent the "progress" of the fever. Their suggestions included avoiding being out in the sun, do not drink too much alcohol, and do not become fatigued. In rooms where infected relatives lay, said the letter, vinegar and camphor "cannot be used too frequently upon handkerchiefs, or in smelling bottles, by persons whose duty calls to visit or attend the sick." This was duly published by Dunlap, along with an illustration from Polly Lear's funeral.

Crispin noticed a few other things that did not appear in the letter. Church bells no longer rang for funerals. Indeed, there were too many funerals for that to be possible. Crews of workmen sloshed water on the wharves and nearby city streets. When Crispin asked one of the workers why they were doing that he shrugged. "Gov'nor's orders is all I knows," he said. Crispin was amazed at the thanks that were shouted to the workers, and the cheering that sometimes occurred as several of them walked down a street, side-by-side, apparently sweeping the disease away. A constant stream of carriages and people on foot could be seen heading both north, out of the city toward Germantown, or west across the Schuylkill River and then, presumably, south toward Wilmington.

But no amount of sweeping could affect the progress of the plague. It wasn't long before gaunt men shouting 'Bring out your dead,' were pulling wagons up and down those same streets—and many others—carrying cadavers whose coverings of canvas seldom stayed in place. But the few former rag-pickers and grounded sailors who were willing to do that couldn't keep up with the volume of dead for long. Bodies— some dead, some living—began to pile up on the streets. The moans of those suffering and dying filled the air along with the stench of the horrible fluids the disease caused its victims to spout; a stench no amount of vinegar or camphor could hide.

Treatments were tried, primarily the bleeding prescribed by Dr. Rush, but they did not work. In fact, some of those few doctors who remained in the city had become ill and died themselves. Hospitals would not accept patients with communicable diseases so there was nowhere for the stricken to go but the streets—where the few pedestrians made a wide berth around them. Crispin heard that Vice-President Adams, working with a group called "Guardians of the Poor," had made the out-buildings of an estate called Bush Hill available as a place to take the ill. In early September he went out to look at it.

He was surprised to see that most of those attending the sick were Negros. He asked one about it. "They say we blacks don' get the fever," he said, "But it ain' true. S'many of us die as them. But we he'p 'em jes' the same."

"Who is *we?*" asked Crispin.

"We is the Free African Society. Mr. Absalom Jones, be our leader."

"I've heard of him," said Lewis. "Would he be around here?"

"Mighthap. I don' know."

Crispin searched until he found some additional attendants, one of whom was not black, spoke with an accent, and seemed to have some authority. "I'm looking for Absalom Jones, Sir. Do you know where I might find him?"

"I am Dr. Deveze," he said.

Oh, a French accent, thought Crispin.

"Perhaps I can help?"

Crispin noted that the man appeared like a doctor only in his bearing and tone of voice. His white jacket was almost as filthy as the clothing and bedding of the patients he attended.

"I'm Crispin Graves, reporting for Mr. Dunlap's paper. I was interested in the fact that the attendants seem to be mostly Negro. Do you believe they are immune to the disease?"

"There are still newspapers in the city?"

"Ours and one or two others," he said. "But we will probably not be able to print for much longer. No paper."

"Besides no eggs, no milk, few *légume*, no..." Dr. Deveze stopped speaking and turned back to his patient. "This one has the hunger. She will recover if she gets food. If not?" He shrugged. "Will you print that? Will you publish this to those farmers who no longer come to the city with their goods?"

"I will print everything I can, Monsieur."

"*Bon!* I believe Mr. Jones is in the barn."

Crispin discovered the barn to be the place where those likely to recover were taken. And wiping their foreheads with moist cloths were Mr. Jones and some other Negros.

"Mr. Jones?" asked Crispin, approaching the only one with grey hair.

"Please, call me Absalom," said Jones, turning to face him, smiling.

"Absalom, then. I'm Crispin Graves. I report—"

"Graves?" asked Absalom.

Crispin nodded.

"I know who you are."

"How would you know?"

"My son happen to court Miss Sadie Sanders. She done tol' us about you." He reached out a hand to be shaken, then pulled it back. "Sorry. Guess we don't do that no mo'." He grimaced. "But we grateful for what you and Gilly done for her and Zach. I wish t'were more like you."

Crispin was silent for a moment. "You might not be so grateful if you knew what my family had been doing for scores of years."

"You ain't your family, then," said Absalom.

"Why are *you* doing this?"

"Dr. Rush an' Mayor Clarkson ask for help. They bin tol' that Black Africans be immune. Maybe we is, maybe we ain't. But we want to help."

"Do you have enough room for those who come?"

"Today, p'raps, but numbers keep increasin.' Soon w'nt be enough room anywheres."

"No room for graves, either," Crispin said softly. "They're just dumping bodies into a great hole now."

"Don' I know, son. Had to hire six more men to pull the carts."

Crispin made a few sketches, one of Absalom in particular, and another of the French doctor, and returned to the city with a heavy heart. Café Fraternité was mostly empty now, as were most taverns and eating places in the city. No food. Fear of catching the disease from someone. Though Jefferson did stop in on his way between his house, west on High Street all the way to the Schuylkill River, and the State House on Chestnut between Fifth and Sixth Streets; occasionally with some of his colleagues or aides. Gilly asked him why he still came to the city when so many had left.

"If the president can do it," he said, "and that damned Secretary of the Treasury, then I can do it. Though Hamilton has taken ill with the pestilence so now he has fled with his family."

Crispin arrived in time to see Jefferson walk away south on Sixth Street. He walked back in to a café devoid of customers. Gilly came out of the kitchen wiping his hands on a towel.

"I have an idea," said Crispin.

. . .

It took very little effort to persuade Gilly to transform the café into a halfway house for patients recovering from the fever. New cases would go to Bush Hill if there was room. If they survived, they could convalesce in the barn for a few days. If the barn became full, some of them could come down to *Fraternité*. Everyone would have to sleep on the floor. Straw aplenty was spread out and blankets were provided by the Mayor's Committee. Chairs and tables were stacked around the edges of the rooms, both upstairs and down, though the upholstered chairs and divans were left available for those well enough to sit. Even though it was good to see more people recovering, *Fraternité* would soon not be able to house any more.

It didn't matter that Gilly wasn't serving customers. He had run out of coffee beans, people had stolen his eggs and then his chickens, and the cow required a round-the-clock guard. The markets had mostly shut down. However, because Clement was a baker, he was able to get flour and continue making the most basic of breads. Working from early morning to late at night every single day, he could provide for the feeding of those staying in the café and sell some to others. Zach and Crispin had to protect him from the lines that formed outside the back door each morning.

Only mutton was left in the larder, a tough nearly rancid chunk at that, some cheeses, and whatever milk the cow decided to produce. They boiled water from the outside well and provided tea in beer mugs to their residents, some of whom were still too weak to hold it up themselves. Sometimes they had nothing to offer at a meal but bread and water, a moist cloth on the forehead of a child suffering an excruciating headache, or an additional blanket for an old woman who still had the chills.

Dunlap and Crispin got the news each day from the Mayor's Committee. They guessed that more than a third of the city's residents had fled, including, by late September, the entire government. Thousands had died and dozens more were dying every day. Even if there had been customers, they all agreed—Gilly, Renée, Sadie, Zach, Polly, Clement, and Crispin—that this was better than just closing down. Even though it would cost them. They had survived the war. They had survived smallpox. They would survive this.

Many of those who remained to help the sick and dying did not survive. Several of the few doctors who had remained in the city died. Men on the Mayor's Committee died. The Negro nurses who had been caring for the sick died. Even members of Dr. Rush's household died, causing people to wonder if his cures could cure at all. And *he* was deathly ill.

To make matters worse, it rained heavily in late September. People had hoped that the coming of rain and cooler weather would end the plague as had happened in the past. But the first two weeks of October were the worst yet. For *Fraternité*, the very worst was that Polly got the fever. And then Crispin. They had to leave and go up to Bush Hill. The others felt it was only a matter of time before they got it.

THEN IT STOPPED. It got really cold on October 16. Crispin was well enough by then to go to the barn, sit up, and read. The only paper still publishing was the *Federal Gazette*. He whooped when he read that the number of new cases had dropped dramatically. On October 25, stores began to reopen and the first ship to dock in months arrived from London.

Finally, on November 13, the all-clear was sounded. The mayor said it was safe to return to the city. Stagecoaches resumed services. Wine, sugar, rum, coffee, tea, cotton, household goods and all the many things that had been used up were off-loaded from ships docking as quickly as the last one was emptied.

The Mayor's Committee gave instructions on how to purify houses, bedding, clothing, and anything the plague had touched. Gilly and company took their advice and purged Café Fraternité as well as they could. But whether the stench would ever go away, they could not tell.

It was over. Crispin came back to Café Fraternité and wrote a summary he hoped Dunlap would publish—if he had survived, if he would ever publish again. He wrote that perhaps one-tenth of the population had died. So many others had left, maybe permanently. Medicine had proven ineffective. Local government had tried hard, but had been only marginally help-ful. Members of the federal government were still hiding out in Germantown, giving citizens yet another reason to distrust them. Both the best and the worst in human nature had been displayed. Yes, the plague was over. But nothing would be the same.

Polly took longer to heal, though she came home. For a few weeks, much of Gilly's time was taken up in looking after her. As some of the old customers returned and new ones came in, Crispin continued to help in the café so Gilly could attend to her. Unfortunately, not all of the old customers returned. Some had died, others no longer went out into the streets.

During the plague, when one had passed a friend on the street, bare acknowledgement of his existence with a nod had replaced hand-shaking. People had not gone to funerals— when there were any—and other normal forms of social cour-tesy and friendly interaction had all but vanished. People were not sure who their friends were any longer. Coolness pervaded the social atmosphere even at *Fraternité*.

Crispin was sitting in *Fraternité* just before Christmas, writing an article reflecting on this unhappy change, when he was interrupted by a young man who appeared to be about his own age and spoke with an English accent. Crispin surprised himself by rising and shaking his outstretched hand.

"William Cobbett," said the young man, dropping his hand. "I'm tired of the whole plague and all its attendant ills. How about you?"

"Surrey?" asked Crispin. "Are you from Surrey?"

Cobbett scrunched up his face. "Am I that obvious? I would have thought my time in New Brunswick and Paris would have moderated that a bit."

Crispin smiled. "If I speak some, can you tell where I'm from? I've come from there recently and may have retrieved some of my former way of talking."

Cobbett tilted his head. "North," he said. "I can't place it, though."

"Philadelphia, New England, Nova Scotia, Ireland, France...I suppose they've all left traces." He gestured to the chair opposite him across the table. Cobbett sat. "I'm Crispin Graves."

"Liverpool!" said Cobbett. "The way you said 'Graves.' Related to the Admiral?"

Crispin grinned. "Hardly," he said. "I probably wouldn't be sitting in a French café if I were." He gazed at Cobbett, taking in both his appearance and expression. "And what brings you to a French café?"

"Truth to tell," said Cobbett, "I'm looking for Frenchmen."

"What on earth for?"

"To teach them English. I spent time in France learning the language, thinking I'd stay there."

"Why would you do that?"

Cobbett took a deep breath. "It seems I offended a number of English officers by pointing out their corruption."

Crispin laughed. "That's all?"

"Not entirely. I also may have written a tract called 'The Soldiers' Friend' in which I exposed the harsh treatment of soldiers, their low pay, the utter disregard officers had for their well-being, indeed for their very lives—"

"Enough," said Crispin, raising his hand. "I understand. I was kidnapped by the army, myself, and served here during the revolution. I was paroled at Yorktown."

Cobbett gave him a strange look. "You must have been very young."

Crispin nodded. "The only thing that saved me was that I learned to play the drum and they needed me."

They were quiet for a moment, sizing one another up. "Do you think I'll find Frenchmen here?" said Cobbett.

"And some women as well," replied Crispin. "I don't know if they'll want to be taught English. Perhaps the refugees from San Domingue." He gazed at him again. "Do you write?"

"Not well. But I'm getting better."

Crispin took a sip of his coffee and set it down, shaking his head. "Cold."

He turned toward the kitchen and yelled, "Sadie?"

She came out in a moment with a fresh carafe.

"Oh, I'm sorry," she said. "I'll get 'nother cup." She dropped the carafe off at the table and went back to the kitchen.

"You have slaves?" asked Cobbett.

"No," said Crispin. "She's a free woman who works here for wages."

She came back with a cup. "You want anythin' to eat?"

Cobbett shook his head and she left.

"But it's difficult for her to stay free since congress passed a law they call 'The Fugitive Slave Law' last February. It makes any dark-skinned person a target for unprincipled men who capture them, claim they're fugitives, take them south and then sell them. She can barely walk the streets on her own."

When Cobbett said nothing, Crispin went on. "How long have you been here?"

"Since April."

"Have you seen the war of words and political cartoons that swirls around us—that took only a short break for the plague?"

"I've watched it with interest. I might want to get into that fray, myself."

"I don't want to. Though one of my sources tells me that Jefferson has resigned from the government as of the end of this year, so it may calm down. I'm thinking of heading west to discover what's happening there."

"With the Indians?"

"The Indians, yes. And with our countrymen who aren't keeping their part of the treaty."

"So, you say, these newly united states aren't keeping their part?"

Crispin looked up sharply. After a pause he said, "No. I was referring to the English. I believe the Americans are keeping most of their parts."

Cobbett was about to make a response when Crispin held up his hand. "This is precisely why I want to go west. I don't want every conversation to devolve into politics." He stood. "You may find plenty of contention and dissent here, as this café is the '*salle du jour*' (the hall of the day) for Francophiles. As for me, I prefer peace and kindness. Good-day, Sir."

Cobbett stood. "Please pardon——"

"Your coffee is paid for," said Crispin. "I'm certain you'll be welcome here. I thank you. You've helped me decide what I must do."

. . .

In January, 1794, Crispin discovered that Dunlap would not be publishing news or illustrations any longer.

"Fella named Claypoole wants to buy me out, but I'm not ready to retire for a year or so. He wants only advertising, so advertising he'll get."

The *Federal Gazette,* which had been so faithful in publishing during the epidemic, printed its last copy at the end of 1793. The *National Gazette,* Freneau's paper that had been such a thorn in Washington's side, had stopped publishing earlier—in Jefferson's absence—at the end of October. *The Gazette of the United States* continued to publish, but was primarily news now that it was not goaded into editorializing by Freneau. Crispin appreciated the break in hostilities. But when he was asked by newcomers—such as the *American Star*—if he would do political cartoons, all the rage now for lampooning your political enemies without precisely saying the offensive things for which they might take out libel suits against you, he wanted no part in it.

"Oowee can no talk you out of eet?" asked Renée.

"No," said Crispin. "I can't live in this environment. I don't know if the west will be better, but at least the primary opponent will be nature, not other people."

As it got a little warmer the port of New York opened, and news came via New York newspapers of the predations on American shipping by both the French and the English. And of the execution of Marie Antoinette by the guillotine in late October. When the Delaware River finally unfroze in April, 1794, news of additional French atrocities arrived with each ship from Europe. Anyone not dedicated inextricably to the French cause stayed away from those who still were.

Fraternité ceased to be the full, raucous place it had been before the plague. Gilly could no longer afford to pay Sadie and Zach. It was fine for Sadie since she married Daniel Jones and went off to live with him and his family. Zach agreed to stay on for room and board. But even that became difficult.

In March, Crispin noted that the United States had reacted, particularly, to British provocations by commissioning the construction of six warships. This was followed by an act establishing the United States Navy. War with England, or maybe with both England and France, seemed imminent. The newspaper wars began heating up again. John Jay was tapped to go to England and make a treaty that would keep the US out of a war. Good luck, he thought.

On that same day Gilly, Polly, Renée and Zach bade him farewell and Godspeed as he boarded a stagecoach to New York City to see if his former employer would hire him to report on what was happening in the west.

10

———

FRONTIERS

ilbao, Spain, was hot in June that year, and still rainy. The resulting humidity did nothing to make Isabella more comfortable as she approached her delivery date.

"*Es hora de que vengas, cariño!*" she said, holding her tummy as she walked the hallway from her dressing room to the breakfast room. (It's time for you to come, dear one!)

"What, *Tesoro?*" said Lewis.

"English, really? At this time in the morning and me with this enormous bulge in the front of me?"

Lewis poked his head out the door of the massive study, just up the hall. "I just wanted to know what you said, love," he said.

"I told the baby it was time to...ooh! Now you stop that!" she said, looking down at her belly. "If you're going to kick, come outside and do it!"

"This is wonderful, *Tesoro,*" said Lewis. "He'll know Spanish and English before he's even born!"

Isabella stuck her tongue out at him. "Next time *you* do this part."

"Not built for it, *Tesoro*. Otherwise, I'd love to do my share."

He went to her and placed his left arm around her waist and took her right elbow with his right hand. She elbowed him in the ribs. "No you wouldn't," she said. "But I know what you *do* love—"

"Isabella, great with child," shouted Sophia in Spanish from farther down the hall. "We await you in the breakfast room."

She shrugged Lewis's arm off and said something in Euskara that Lewis didn't understand but that made Sophia laugh. They continued down the hall.

The conversation reverted to Spanish and Lewis said, "I see you've resurrected that little bit of your native tongue that you had forgotten. Now shall Marcus and I speak Arabic?"

"Marcus doesn't speak Arabic, *Amante*."

"Details," said Lewis.

"Speaking of which," said Sophia, "I received a letter from your father asking when the baby is due so he can be here."

"Why do *you* have a letter from my father?"

"He says you don't respond to his letters."

"And why would I since he's decided to be so stubborn about the American business?"

The light-hearted beginning to the morning was rapidly dissipating. Lewis took Isabella's hand in his, kissed it, and whispered to her. "It will come right in the end, *Tesoro*. He's your father. He's my father, now. Can we let it lie? I'm sure it will come right."

Isabella got that straight line mouth and clenched jaw she couldn't quite control when she was determined about something, or, as Sophia said, when she was being stubborn. Lewis leaned into her, kissed one bulging muscle in her jaw and tickled her face with his mustache. Her mouth slowly morphed into a moue and she suddenly burst out laughing.

"It's not fair for you to make me laugh when I want to be mad."

"But it's fun," said Lewis, smiling.

She looked down the hallway toward Sophia and said, more loudly, "You may tell him the baby is to come early in July and he may come. But he will have to stay with his mother."

Marcus stepped out into the hall from the breakfast room. "Are you people going to negotiate a treaty in the hallway, or may we come to the table for *desayuno*? I'm famished!"

Isabella took Lewis's arm and made better speed toward the breakfast room. "We can't have that," she said.

THE ENTIRE HOUSEHOLD celebrated July 4th by greeting little Diego Roberto Tomás José Nicolas Maria de Arriquibar, otherwise known as Roberto, named Diego after Isabella's father, first, Tomás after Lewis's father, then after Robert Morris, two uncles, and, of course, the mother of Jesus. It was only a day or so later that Don Diego arrived to greet his grandson. Isabella, sitting up in bed, attempted to maintain a stern look as she carefully handed the baby up to him, but she couldn't manage it.

"So you forgive me, my daughter?" he said.

"I should not," she said. "You have acted in a despicable manner with this Wilkinson man. You have used and deceived me and Lewis and made our position extremely difficult."

"I am an agent of the King, my dear. I must do what he says."

"You are a man who should have a conscience."

Little Roberto began to fuss and wave his arms about. Don Diego rocked him carefully. "When I see this little one and remind myself that with him the Almighty has answered my prayer that my family line may continue, I know I am unworthy. I know I have done..." He looked at her. "I have done what my king asked. I have facilitated only what every nation does to promote its interests. But I have done wrong by not telling you and Lewis. We will make it right. Lewis will help."

He handed Roberto back to her and she laid him on her shoulder, patting his back. After a moment she said, "Lewis and I met this James Wilkinson once. He was charming. But I felt unclean after talking with him. He did something to my insides. Will you keep using him?"

"It is not my decision, *querida* (darling), and you should not even know these things. But I will do what I can." He went to the window and stood looking out into the courtyard. "But with all reason lost in France now, with her at war with all of Europe, including us now, I cannot say what will happen."

He looked back at Isabella. "Spain has lost something. Her will? Her soul? The Lords of Britain have taken this over. And the," he grunted, "the '*ciudadanos*' (citizens) of France," he shook his head, "seem bent on destroying everything that has been Europe for centuries. I cannot tell what will happen to us."

Isabelle's eyes fluttered shut as Lewis entered the room and glanced her way. He turned to Don Diego and lifted his head questioningly. Don Diego tilted his head toward the door and they left quietly.

THEY WENT TOGETHER into the study. They had barely sat down when Marcus rushed in.

"A courier who says he needs to see you urgently is here from Humphreys."

"Bring him in, then," said Lewis.

Marcus glanced quickly at Don Diego and back. Lewis smiled briefly and nodded. Marcus left.

"He wondered if you should see the courier with me here," said Don Diego. Not a question.

"He did," said Lewis. He turned in his chair to face Don Diego fully. "This is your house. We are in your country. Our countries are ostensibly allies. It is unlikely I will learn anything in this dispatch that you should not know."

"It is your house now," said Don Diego.

Lewis nodded slightly. "I am grateful. But I still wish to honor you as if it were not."

Marcus came in with a young man in tow who held a canvas courier's pouch. He looked first at Don Diego, then at Lewis, and strode toward Lewis, handing him the pouch.

"Thank you...?"

"Paolo," said the messenger. Then, in halting English, "I work for Mr. David Humphreys. This come from him in... hurry? He say you understand."

"Thank you, Paolo. Marcus, would you mind seeing that this young man is refreshed and has anything he needs? If he needs to stay with us a few days..."

Marcus nodded. "Glad to help. Maybe I'll brush up on my Portuguese."

"Oh," said Paolo, reaching into a pocket for the key and then handing it to Lewis.

Lewis took the key. "*Obrigada. Marcus lhe daré tudo o que você precisa.*" (Marcus will give you anything you need.)

The young man's eyes opened wide and he managed to stammer, "*De nada,*" as he turned to follow Marcus out the door.

Lewis took the key, opened the pouch, and pulled out its contents. Don Diego stood. "I will come back..."

Lewis waved toward the seat. "No need to go," he said. He

read the note in Jay's own hand and eventually came to this sentence: "Mr. Trumbull is my official assistant and my son, Peter, my personal secretary. But if you can get away it would be my pleasure to have your assistance as you are intimately acquainted with my ways of doing and speaking, and you would be a felicitous addition to our delegation."

He looked over at Don Diego. "You may find this of interest, and I think it's something it would be good for you to know and something that my country would want you to know."

Don Diego sat up in his chair with his hands on the table.

"The United States is going to negotiate a treaty with Great Britain. Our friend John Jay is the chief negotiator, and he wants me to join him in London."

"Mmph," said Don Diego. "I don't know whether that news is good or bad for my country. If you have peace with Britain, that may mean you have war with us."

"Not if you and I negotiate a treaty," said Lewis with a smile.

Don Diego didn't smile back. Instead, face grim, he rested his chin on his hands and looked at the table. Then he raised his head, composed himself, and looked back at Lewis.

"When you complete your work in London, come back to me here. I will see what I can do in the meantime."

"OH, HE IS CRUEL," said Isabella when Lewis shared the news. "He had to call on you at just the time when I cannot come with you."

"There will be other times, *Tesoro*," said Lewis quietly.

"And if I must have no more babies in order to be certain that I come with you, that is what I will do."

"Oh, no, no, no," said Lewis, smiling. "We will find a way to bring the babies." He looked lovingly at Isabella and Roberto, then tilted his head. "But it may become complex when Sophia has babies as well. We shall have to set up households in the capitols of all major countries."

"Very humorous, Mr. Don Luis de Arriquibar," she said. "But I am serious. I do *not* want to be left behind to recite poetry and knit baby clothes while you go off on adventures."

"Perhaps, if this conference stretches on, you and Robby could come. Marcus and Sophia could bring you and we could spend time with Mr. Pinckney and some of your friends from school. Would you like that?"

"*Claro!*" (Of course!) she answered loudly, startling Roberto and causing him to wave his little arms about. She kissed his forehead and whispered to him, and he settled back down. "How long is 'stretches on'?"

"It should take a week to get there," he said, "and of course, back." He looked up at the ceiling as if counting something there. "And they don't work every day." He looked back down at her. "Some days the British, I'm sure, will need to talk to their superiors about this or that little thing. Then we'll all agree and someone in the government won't like it so all we've done so far will be scratched."

"So, I will give you four weeks in London without me, and even if you do not write to say it is 'stretched,' I will come."

IN EARLY AUGUST, Lewis assisted Jay in producing a first draft of the potential treaty. He had been there two weeks. Though the negotiating sessions were amicable, it was clear that the king himself was involved in creating Britain's responses, often in minute detail.

Lewis wrote to Isabella telling her she might as well come.

She was there the next morning.

"I hadn't even sent the letter I wrote, and yet you are *here?*"

"I missed you," said Isabella.

There was no argument for that.

"And *Pai* (father) said to get you back by late September since you will have another treaty to negotiate."

"So I heard from Mr. Pinckney," said Lewis. "At a monastery?"

"It's a large and wonderful place, San Lorenzo," she said. "Robby will love crawling around in the garden. And we'll be able to live in *Pai*'s house in Madrid."

Lewis smirked as he breathed out his nose. "So you *do* mean to come with me everywhere."

Isabella smiled coquettishly. "Can you resist me?"

Lewis shook his head. "You know I can't."

It had seemed as though negotiations were going well, as the British had submitted two draft treaties for consideration——one on military and legal affairs, and one on commercial affairs——at the end of August. But even a cursory reading made it clear that this was their first salvo in a series of negotiations that might drag on for a long time. Lewis helped draft revisions of these proposals and an alternate proposal of their own.

Thomas Pinckney left for Spain in late August to work on a treaty with the Spanish. Given the length of time during which negotiations had taken place for the earlier failed treaty in which Lewis had been involved——with Don Diego at the other side of the table——he assumed that these negotiations would move very slowly as well. But in the time it took for Pinckney to get there and send a letter back, much progress had been made. Pinckney's letter told Lewis, in no uncertain terms, to get himself back to Spain or he could miss the signing. Which Lewis knew was hyperbole. But he needed to get back all the same.

Jay reluctantly let him go.

Lewis was amazed that so important a treaty had been entrusted to such an apparently low-ranking official, Señor Manuel de Godoy. He seemed to be only about Lewis's own age. Lewis couldn't tell his place in the Spanish hierarchy, exactly, but his title was equivalent to Assistant Secretary of State. He was pleasant enough and seemed knowledgeable.

When Lewis had a chance to look at the draft treaty the Spanish proposed, he was even more amazed. His first instinct was to say, sign it right here and now. But Pinckney was a more seasoned negotiator, and in his counter-proposal he asked for a bit more of the Louisiana territory from the Spanish, arguing that it had initially belonged to the British and was therefore now, by rights, United States territory. And he demanded full navigation rights to the Mississippi River.

By the end of the year negotiations had moved very little from the initial proposals, but they were going in the right direction. Lewis glanced over at his father-in-law who was glancing back at him with a sort of smile on his face. Lewis shook his head, ever so slightly. This would be a far more successful treaty than the one with Britain, even though the treaty Jay was making would, most likely, secure the northern border of the United States. This one secured the western and southern borders.

Of course, there was nothing to keep ambitious American homesteaders from traveling farther than those borders which, in any case, only existed on paper in national archives. But hopefully neither of these two great powers would wage war against the United States from within these borders or even from the other side. Now all that inhibited the growth of the United States within these borders were the current inhabitants; the Choctaw, Chickasaw, Cherokee, Kickapoo, Miami,

Shawnee, Shoshone and a host of other tribes whose names he didn't know.

On New Year's Eve, 1794, Lewis lay in bed with Isabella snuggled up against him. "It's not done yet," he said quietly.

"*Qué, amor?*" (What, love?) she replied sleepily.

"The end of all wars," he said. "But we may have prevented two, at least."

"*Vá dormir, querido.*" (Go to sleep, dear.) She lifted up onto one elbow. "You have solved enough of the world's problems for one year." She lay back down and tucked into him. "Now, sleep. Next year is on the way."

NOT BEING the capitol any longer, New York had lost several of its newspapers. But not having had the Yellow Fever epidemic, it had not lost them all, nor had it lost people. Crispin found the publisher of the paper he had worked for years ago, one Stephan Loudon, and made him a proposition.

"How would you like someone to go out west and find out what's actually happening?"

Loudon looked up slowly and a grin started on his face. "Well, now..." He looked Crispin over. "I...ah...was about to say 'young man,' but I guess you ain't no young man no more."

"No," said Crispin, standing completely still.

Loudon looked a little discomfited, but continued. "Seems as the *Packet*, well, let's jus' say it up an' went away. But we's about to start the *Herald*. An' somethin' like your gravures would sure help sell 'em."

"How would I get them to you?"

"Guess I'd have ta send someone with you, least after Ft. Henry. Got a runner there and one in Pittsburgh."

He looked back at Crispin. "Guess you'll want some money."

Crispin nodded. "A man has to eat," he said. "And his horse has to eat as well."

"You want a horse?"

"There's a lot of country out there. How far do you think I'd get on foot?"

"I don' know. Don' think I can afford you."

"Did I let you down last time?"

Loudon made a grumbling noise in the back of his throat. "Be here at 8 o'clock Monday mornin'. If I can get you sommat, I will. If not, well. Ain' no other paper worth workin' for, so I guess yer outta luck."

Crispin left the building—which could not be called an office. But maybe they'd make improvements if they were really going to have a paper. When he got back to his room, he took out a sketchbook and drew the 'office,' as it were, from memory. Maybe a 'before and after' series would help them at some point.

"You can take the stage to Brunswick. There's another to Durham where you'll cross the Delaware if it ain' too high and the ice got melted. I got a man at Durham who'll get you a horse. Mayn't be the best, mind you, but it's got four legs to your two."

Crispin gazed at Loudon with the tiniest bit of skepticism.

"Aw'right. I sent him a letter las' night and hope it'll get there afore you. I'll give you another one to show 'im in case it don't."

"I'll need lots of sketchbooks and notebooks, pencils, grease paper sacks and a sturdy knapsack. If you're to get any drawings back in good order, they'll have to be kept dry and not folded."

Loudon nodded. "Got money for that. Can you find your own game to eat?"

"I can find my own game to draw, not to eat."

"The west ain't Massachusetts, you know. No inn on every corner." Loudon laughed. "No corners!"

"Then I'll have to find a way that others have gone west by and may still be going."

"Camp follower's your best bet. Goes after the army to, ah, 'service' them."

"People like to have likenesses of themselves. I can do that. It's how I paid for my first real art supplies."

"You do that, then, 'cause I cain't be your mamma."

Crispin consulted New York legislators who had been in the meetings with General St.Clair when Washington had confirmed his expedition against the Indians. He was told that his best starting point to discover what was happening *now* would be Fort Washington on the Ohio River. He could get passage on a flatboat from Pittsburgh and float down to the fort. Then he'd have to go on foot or horseback north to Fort Recovery. After that, it was anybody's guess as to where he should go and how he should get there.

IT WAS HOT, even this early in the day. Biting bugs were out in their numbers. Crispin estimated that it was mid-June. He'd lost track of the days. He'd left his skin-and-bones horse at Fort Washington. He had no more food, and his canteen was almost empty. He had no maps. No compass. Just this trail that never seemed to end, that they'd told him would lead past Fort

Recovery to where he might find General St. Clair, otherwise known as Mad Anthony, and his troops.

He'd managed to hold on to his knapsack carrying the paper, the grease paper sacks, and the pencils. And his easel. It would have made it so much easier just to drop the easel. Not that it was so very heavy, but that it was clumsy. When he walked off the path a few yards into the woods, which was most of the time now, it kept catching on bushes or low-hanging branches. But he was glad he had it. So much that he wanted to do couldn't be done without it.

Now he moved farther into the woods to avoid what seemed to be a raiding party on the trail in front of him, coming his way quickly. He found a little copse, hunched down and watched. He'd not learned all the distinctions among the tribes, but he thought they might be Seneca or Shawnee. They were whooping it up, mostly, though a few were at the end of the party, being helped by fellow braves as if they were injured. He was a long stone's throw from the main trail, so he gasped as they turned and seemed to be coming his way. How could they know he was there? He held his breath. But they went by without seeing him.

He had an idea. He'd spoken to a friendly Delaware Indian in New York City who helped him understand at least something about Indian culture. He decided on a course of action which, he knew, could cost him his life, but it could also enable him to do what he wanted to do: draw illustrations of Indians, soldiers, ways of life, the outward appearance of different philosophies of life. He realized he wasn't so worried about his own life any longer. He could have died in the war. He could have died in the snow. He could have died on the ocean. He could have died of the fever. But he didn't. He could die now of an Indian arrow or war club. If he died, so be it. He wanted to tell this story of the frontier. Safety was no longer his greatest concern.

So he followed the war party. In a matter of a mile or so, the trail ended at an opening. An entire Indian village lay only a musket shot away, complete with two longhouses, multiple buildings which Crispin took to be dwellings, made of courses of thin tree trunks, and several outbuildings. It didn't have the corn and squash fields Crispin expected to see this time of year. Was it new? Temporary?

It didn't matter. *This is it,* thought Crispin. *I'm going to do it.* He untied his easel from his backpack and opened it up while still concealed in the woods. He looked through the trees to both sides of the trail end until he saw a fallen trunk large enough, and high enough from the ground to sit on. He would have to come out of hiding and walk a few yards in the open to sit on it and get set up. But he gathered from the gleeful sounds coming from the village that its inhabitants would not be occupied in spying out their periphery for a while.

So he set up. He retrieved his precious large tablet from the knapsack, set it on the easel, chose the pencils he would use, and began to sketch. Since no people were walking about, he could only leave space where he would put them. He'd roughed in the plain, the hills beyond, a few clouds, and the edge of the woods surrounding the village when he became aware of human voices nearby.

Crispin's mouth went dry and his heart beat faster, but he didn't look up. He didn't look away from his drawing. He just continued. When he felt the ground shake from people apparently running in his direction, he only looked away from his tablet enough so he could catch them in his peripheral vision and begin to fill them into the places he'd allotted.

As they got nearer, or maybe right up to him, he didn't know, he heard anger in their voices. Questions, maybe. He didn't look up. They began to speak more softly. He imagined that they might be pointing. And then a woman's voice joined the chorus. He still did not look up. But he could see her on the right, out of the corner of his eye, and begin to sketch her into the picture, deftly capturing the tufted ends of her dress and sleeves, the beads around her neck, hanging to her waist, the intricate purse on her right side.

There was more yelling, but Crispin saw her hold up her hand and it ceased. She came around behind him and watched what he was doing. A warrior came around the other side, and soon other warriors and maidens, and then children surrounded him. He finished what he thought was an adequate draft, set his pencil between his teeth, and carefully tore the page from the tablet. He held it up, turned to the left and right, offering it to whomever would take it. A child started to grab for it but was swiftly reprimanded by the woman. Then she nodded and accepted it.

Still without a word or excess movement, Crispin took the pencil from his mouth and pointed to one of the braves. He began to sketch a quick outline. From the facial expressions he could see, Crispin concluded they were interested. He turned back to the brave he was sketching, held his two hands out in front of him, palm to palm about the distance apart of his shoulders, then slanted them a little the same way, and moved the right hand farther out in front of him than the left. The brave looked confused, but another put hands on his shoulders, and turned him slightly. Crispin nodded and continued to sketch. Snatches of conversation mixed with grunts and laughter greeted his every stroke until the brave being sketched, apparently, could take it no longer and came over to see the drawing.

Crispin tore it off carefully and handed it to him. He turned to see the smile on the brave's face. Then several braves came up at once, jostling one another, gesturing to the tablet and to themselves. But Crispin pointed to the woman whom he'd partially drawn earlier and waved her forward. She seemed a little bashful now, and she came forward with head bowed. He gestured with his hands in the way he wanted her to stand and turn and then held his hands up palm out. Once she was before him, he saw that she wasn't as old as he had thought, probably just in her teens, but she was certainly as beautiful as any woman he'd ever seen. Maybe that was why they'd all quieted when she told them to. He let that sift into his mind and began to draw.

NOT HAVING differences in the days of the week, indeed, not having weeks, Crispin soon lost track of how many days he stayed at the village, enjoying their hospitality and sketching one after another. He soon realized that he would not have enough large sheets to do them all. It was only a day, however, before the chief wanted a sketch of himself. After using one of the large sheets for the chief's portrait, Crispin used only sheets from smaller tablets for the rest of the drawings. This occasioned some grumbling, but that calmed down when Crispin started teaching the children how to draw using the burnt ends of sticks on the skins of animals.

He'd once thought of trying to find a wife among the natives and settling down with them. Maybe this was a good beginning. He'd have a fight on his hands, probably, if he wanted *Ah-wen-eyu,* as he had learned the young woman was called, to be that wife. But maybe that's how things were done here. He watched her and he watched the braves around her. Yes, there was interest there, but they all seemed—if not afraid of her, at least in awe of her.

Early one morning, when he left his lodge to get water, he

saw the last of the braves disappear into the trail through the woods. By now the mornings were cool, and this one happened to be rainy. Just the same, he rushed back into the lodge, grabbed his knapsack and easel, without tying it to the knapsack, and rushed out the door. He was met by *Ah-wen-eyu* who waved her hands frantically for him to stop. He pointed in the direction the warriors had gone, then at himself, then back. She shook her head violently and placed her hands out to stop him. He ran by her anyway. When he was a short distance from her he turned back and said the equivalent of "I'm sorry;" what he had gathered they said for the same purpose in this culture, "Mistake."

He ran to the trailhead and plunged into the forest. As he ran, it occurred to him that the mistake was thinking he could ever be one of them, that he would ever understand their ways and be fully accepted. And given the likely reason for what had to be a war party heading out, he knew he couldn't take part in their struggles; at least not in that way. Perhaps he could help them in some other way, but he would not be a fighter against the white man.

The party had a head start and seemed to be traveling quickly. Crispin was glad he'd been toughened up by his time in the west, but he couldn't keep running like this. By the time he made himself stop to catch his breath and rest, it must have been hours. And then he heard shooting. His first impulse was to turn and run back down the trail. But then he stopped. *What did I come here for? Wasn't it to find out what was happening?* he thought. He'd dropped his easel a short way back, so he pulled out a small tablet and a couple of pencils, slid into the wood, and made his way through brambles and pine needles toward the source of the noise.

The way was made tougher by fallen trees. Must have been quite a wind, he thought. Or maybe a tornado, to knock all these trees down. And suddenly he threw himself down to the ground after a bullet slammed into a tree trunk behind him. Had it been aimed at him? He heard firing from all around him, screams of men who were hit, and even distant artillery fire. He curled into himself, only just remembering to keep his tablet dry. This was too much like the siege of Yorktown, which he'd been on the wrong side of. He started to shake uncontrollably.

He must have blacked out, because the next thing he was aware of was the sound of men nearby, speaking English.

"All right, men, back out carefully now. Look for any of ours who are still living. If you find any of theirs who have weapons, take them. Take living ones alive as prisoners."

There was much shuffling through nearby bushes, the sound of fallen tree trunks being moved, men groaning, the clinking of metal against metal and, some way off, horses snorting. He waited until the sounds died down and crawled from his hiding place. The sun was heading down. He didn't want to lose his way, he wanted to find his easel, and he wanted to get back to the village to find out what had happened.

He found the trail, and not far along, just off the trail, his easel. To his great dismay, he also found quivers and broken bows, smashed war clubs, shattered headdresses, and then a body. The body of the first brave he had drawn. With a sickening ache in his belly, he knew for certain now, that they wouldn't want him back at the village. He might, in some way, be blamed for what had happened. He had received only kindness from them, and he had tried to be kind in turn. Would they now think he had betrayed them? Or would they simply hate him for not being one of them; for being one of those white men who were taking their land?

A moment of sadness crept over him, he said a bitter, internal good-bye to *Ah-wen-eyu*, turned around, and started up the trail away from the village. He soon realized it would be too dark to do anything but get lost, so, in the last of the light, he left the path, found a couple of the fallen trees to lean against, took off his knapsack, and sat on the wet ground. He drifted into sleep by the light of a waning moon and the hoot of a hunting owl.

~

THE WEATHER CONTINUED to cool as Crispin headed back east, partly on foot alone, and partly on a barge on the Ohio River in the company of some of General Anthony's soldiers. He left the barge at Maysville where the soldiers were planning to stop for a while, and headed overland, east, hoping to run into Pittsburgh or at least the Monongahela River.

He heard the river before he saw it. At least, a river. But he thought it must be near civilization because the morning sun had a shroud of smoke around it. He got to the top of what he expected to be only a bluff and halted suddenly. It was nearly a straight drop down into the rapidly-flowing, muddy water of what he was pretty sure was the Monongahela River, perhaps two or three-hundred feet below. He dropped to his belly and crawled to the edge. From there he could see for miles to the east. Though the country was hilly, the hills were not so steep and numerous as they were on the west side. It looked peaceful.

It would be difficult to justify calling those few buildings a city. It was a collection of mostly wooden structures; mills, a boatyard, pottery barns, and log cabins—dwellings, probably— with a few brick houses on the southern and eastern peripheries. The city extended north only as far as the swampy-looking point that marked the junction of the Monongahela and Allegheny Rivers where they formed the Ohio. But south, to his right, smoke poured lazily from foundry chimneys and charcoal bakers on iron plantations spaced every few miles down the Monongahela.

Docks and wharfs proliferated along the east side of the river by the iron plantations, but in front of the city as well. Unfortunately, as he'd heard, it wasn't easy to get the rolled iron to markets in the east, or, for that matter, to move any of the things produced here to any markets anywhere. If Americans could navigate the Mississippi, they could get their wares to New Orleans and thence, by ship, to the east coast. As long a trip as that was, it was easier than taking wagonloads of iron or corn over the mountains between here and Philadelphia. But the Spanish controlled the Port of New Orleans as well as the entire Mississippi, and they weren't having it.

Across the Allegheny, to the north, the land seemed mostly flat and cultivated, rather than being the rolling woodlands near his location. Smoke drifted along east of the cluster of buildings just beneath him, so he assumed that there were more iron plantations eastward. Areas clearcut of trees were just at the edge of visibility. Probably they'd been cut for the charcoal furnaces, but this had the advantage of enabling farmers to grow the corn and rye for which the Forks of the Ohio was known.

He had to lean out over the edge a bit in order to see whatever might be on his side of the river. The cliff gradually abated southward to a shore that was more like that of a lake than a river. After scanning for a while he detected a small craft in the middle of the river, crossing east to west, looking as though it might be headed for that spot. That's where I have to get to, he thought. The ferry.

Some of General Anthony's soldiers were from this area and they had told him what to look for. They'd also told him the human and natural things to look *out* for, which was why he was on foot on this side of the Ohio rather than on a flatboat on the river itself. They'd told him the name of the official to whom he should bring the news of their victory, people to stay away from, and people who might help him. A few had asked him to greet their families and tell them they were all right.

Crispin took stock of his current situation. First, he had almost no paper left. He'd managed to save many of his better drawings but had been tempted to tear off small pieces of paper to make more. He couldn't, of course, make drawings on both sides of the paper since that would kill the engraving process. Second, he had no currency of any kind. He didn't suppose they had much here, in any case, but he would need some medium of exchange in order to get food, replace clothing, find a place to stay. He really needed that place to stay so he could rest, but even more, he needed a few days of eating very well.

When he'd been with the Senecas, they'd taught him what leaves and plants and roots he could find in the forest to eat, as well as how to fish and catch frogs. But it was a long, tiresome journey from that place which had now acquired the name of Fallen Timbers, after the blown-over trees at the site of the battle he had witnessed there. He hoped for a rest here, some peace and quiet, a way to send his drawings to Loudon, a store from which to obtain paper. And *yes*, he said to himself. *Did I say peace and quiet?*

THE FERRY MAN allowed him on the ferry even though he had nothing with which to pay.

"Most folks jes' gives me a li'l whiskey," he said, "but see'in as how yer jes' in from the wilds, I don' s'pose yer has any."

"I don't," said Crispin. "But you can't live on whiskey. How does that work out?"

"Well I jes' takes a li'l taste, y'know, jes' to see if's all right. Then I takes it in these li'l flasks—" he took one from a pocket on his jacket and held it up, "an' I gives it to summ'un for summat."

"You have no coins, then, or paper money?"

He spat over the side.

"Tha's what yer cin git fer yer paper money." He shook his head. "Virginie pounds, Pennsylvanie dollars, even them short Bobs we used to git. Useless!"

Crispin raised his eyebrows. "I've been to many places and never—"

"Ain' one o' them damned English, is yer?" He shook his head. "Or them damned Frenchies. An' I can see you ain' no Indian even though you dress like 'em."

"No. I'm American."

"An' maybe that ain' so great anymore, neither."

They were almost to the eastern shore and Crispin caught sight of what looked like a tavern or inn. "Can I get something to eat there?" he said, pointing.

"Sign o' the Green Tree?" the ferry man asked. "Best food in town if'n yer has summat to pay with. Kinda dear for the likes o' me."

"What did you mean..." Crispin stopped in mid-sentence. He decided he didn't want to know what the ferry man meant that maybe it wasn't so great to be American anymore. "Um, if I get any whiskey, I'll come back and give you some. Thanks for the lift."

"I'd be obliged," the man said.

Crispin jumped off and headed for the tavern. It was too late for breakfast, if they had any, and too early for dinner. He hoped they might have something. Maybe they'd take a drawing as payment, or maybe he could work for food. He'd served tables and done just about everything else that needed doing except the actual cooking at *Fraternité*. So he'd offer his services if that would get him a meal.

"Turns out we's short-handed today," said the man who came out from the back, blowing flour off his shirt. "If yer can really serve tables and like, yer can stay a day or two."

He looked Crispin up and down. "Yer look sturdy enough, a little peaked, is all. I'll give yer breakfast if yer stays through dinner an' the meetin' we's havin' later."

"That would be great," said Crispin, tossing his knapsack and easel on a bench by the fireplace. Even though it was cool, no fire had been lit. "Want me to get this going?"

"Nah," said the man. "Not now. Later when the Mingo Creek boys comes in, if it's cold."

Crispin followed him into the kitchen hoping to get that meal as soon as possible.

The Tavern filled up as the day progressed, and long after dinner had been served more men came in. Finally, after sunset, a few men came in dressed like bankers or officials rather than workers. Crispin heard snatches of their conversation as he served them.

"'Fraid Presley's not going to change his mind."

"Which could get him killed."

"I know, Hugh," said the other. "What can we do? Bradford's got everyone stirred up and those as disagree with him are afraid to say anything."

"But both of those negotiators Washington sent said they'd have to recommend for military force if he didn't back down."

"Yeates and Ross did, but that attorney general..."

"William Bradford," said Hugh.

"...didn't."

"Right. But none of David's boys bothered to answer Pastor Parkinson's question as to whether it was right or wrong, what was done..."

"Burning down Neville's house? Or the other houses and the tarring and feathering..."

"McFarlane's funeral, though, that was when the match was lit..."

Crispin couldn't stay any longer. But he had the unpleasant conviction that this was not going to be the oasis of peace and quiet he'd hoped for.

It brought to mind the last time he hung about in taverns listening to the locals talk. That was in Massachusetts in '88 when what they now called 'Shays' Rebellion' was being fomented. This was real news. Loudon would want both pictures and stories for this.

Crispin cleared off tables after the last customers had left. The owner came out of the kitchen, wiping his brow with an enormous handkerchief. "You done well," he said. "Because of the harvestin' an all..."

Crispin looked at the man, showing some confusion.

"Well the corn an' rye is in, but there's pumpkin an' squash an some apples still on trees an', o' course, they got to do some things with the corn..."

Whiskey, thought Crispin. He nodded. The man nodded back. "Anyway, yer can stay an' work for a while if yer'd like."

"I'd like," said Crispin.

"Got a couple beds upstairs. Yer can use one."

Crispin nodded again.

"Is there anywhere I can get some paper?" he asked.

"Paper? What for?"

"For drawing," said Crispin. "I usually draw pictures to earn my living."

The man grimaced. "We got a schoolhouse and maybe one store that gets supplies for it. An' we need paper for our ledgers. Maybe they'll have summat."

"When do you want me to start in the morning?"

"I begin bakin' long before the first rooster thinks 'bout gettin' up. Yer could light my fire," he said, laughing. "But no need. We don' keep travelers no more, so folks don't start comin' in 'til nigh on eleven. I won' need yer before then."

EARLY THE NEXT MORNING, Crispin walked the mile or so to Pittsburgh on a rutted road wide enough for three carts passing each other at the same time. Dust filled his eyes and tiny biting flies attacked him. Down here, as well, since the wind was now coming from the south, he had to contend with smoke. It wouldn't be his favorite walk, he thought.

He found a general store near what he took to be the schoolhouse. The proprietress was busy behind a counter when he arrived, so he backed into a corner from which he could see her, took out his last tablet with any free pages, and sketched her, the counter, and the shelves on either side. When he was finished and she looked like she was free, he approached the counter.

"May I help you?" she asked.

He smiled and offered her the sketch. With a puzzled look, she took it and glanced at it. Then she stared at it, at Crispin, and back to the sketch.

"You did this?"

He only smiled. It seemed obvious enough that he didn't need to respond. Besides, he'd learned the value of silence from his time with *Ah-wen-eyu.*

Looking up, she asked, "What do you want?" Not unpleasantly, but with a degree of skepticism.

"I need paper," he said. "And more pencils."

She nodded. "And I'm guessing you have no money to pay for them."

"No whiskey, either," he said with a smile.

Finally she gave in and smiled back. "I've never been paid with a portrait, before," she said. Then she dropped the smile. "*And I never will be again.*" She gave him a hard look. "But this time, well, this time it might buy you some paper." She smiled again, set the drawing on the counter, and turned away.

Crispin tried not to stare as she walked away from him and went through a door at the back of the store, but even from the back, with her graceful way of walking and that little flick of her hair, she was worth staring at. A short time later she came back, her arms laden with paper tablets of various sizes.

"We were supposed to get a schoolmaster who could teach the children to draw." She dropped the whole bundle on the counter and said with no inflection, "This one couldn't draw flies..." She looked up to see if Crispin had gotten the joke.

He smiled and nodded. "I can do both," he said.

She sniffed the air. "Ah, yes," she said. "I see. Well, I don't precisely *see*, but..."

"I've been in the wilderness since..." he stopped, looked off into the distance, frowned, and looked back at her.

"What day is it today?"

"It's Thursday."

"No, I mean, what's the date?"

She gave him a peculiar look. "It's October second."

"October, already?" he said, raising his voice. "No wonder it's cold."

"So how long were you out there?" she asked.

"Since the end of May, I guess."

"And those are the same clothes you started with?"

He looked down at his tattered leather trousers and jacket. He really did look like a frontiersman. And a dirt poor one at that—which he supposed was true. He looked back up.

"I didn't have a camp following."

She laughed. It was a pleasant sound. Like bubbles popping up through the water of a stream. He looked at her more closely. Even nice. Behind the gruff exterior she probably had to retain at this post, she was really cute.

He held out his hand. "I'm Crispin."

She shook it. "I'm Susan," she said. "Susan Anderson. It's nice to meet someone with a sense of humor." She pointed at the paper she'd brought out. "Look through this and see if there's something you can use." She pointed at him, her finger starting to point at about his shoulder and moving down toward his feet. "In the meantime, I'm going to see what we can do about those things I imagine you call clothes." She headed off to the back again.

"I don't call them," he said loudly to her retreating form. "They have no ears."

"No nose, either," she replied without turning back. "Obviously."

"WHAT DID you do with my old clothes?" Crispin asked, looking up at Susan on the stepladder.

"I thought about washing them," she replied.

Crispin nodded, waiting for her to finish. When she went back to stocking shelves instead, he asked, "But what did you *do?*"

She turned a mournful face on him. "What we do to all undesirable things around here," she said. "I tarred and feathered them." She backed down the ladder, pulled a couple of jars from a wooden crate, climbed back up the ladder and reached up to set them on the shelf. As she did, she lost one and it dropped.

Crispin caught it in the air. He held it up and looked at it. "Marmalade?"

She just gazed at him in shock. He held it up to her and she took it, brushing his fingers with hers as she did so.

Crispin ignored that and scrunched up his face momentarily. "Well, I suppose tar might help them stay together a little longer. But feathers?"

"You are obtuse," she said. "But thank you for catching that. It would have been a mess." She put it in place, climbed back down the ladder and faced Crispin.

"I burned them. I have no idea how you will ever pay me for all this, but I couldn't help myself."

He reached out and took her hands in his. She didn't flinch. "I'm working at the Green Tree," he said. "Maybe I can come in and pay you a little bit each week."

She didn't let go of his hands. "If Donald Bradford and his gang don't burn down the city and the Federal army on the way here doesn't shoot us all, I'd like that."

The bell on the door announced a customer and Crispin let her hands slide slowly from his.

"That's what we'll...ah, I'll do then," he said. "See you tomorrow?"

"I'll be here," she said, a little grumpily, looking down.

"Ah," said Crispin after a moment, pointing at her. "You're hiding a grin!"

She looked up and said through clenched teeth, "Am not!" Then she burst into laughter. The customer, a middle-aged lady, gave her a concerned look.

"Now don't do that to me again," she whispered. "Or they'll be talking about me all over town."

She walked away from him toward the customer with a couple of exaggerated sways.

"May I help you?" she said sweetly.

Crispin picked up his packages, grinned, and headed out. Maybe this *will* become my favorite walk, he thought.

~

At about 7 AM, on the same day Crispin was looking over the Monongahela River from the cliff on its western shore, back in Philadelphia Zach rushed into the kitchen at *Fraternité* and dragged Gilly, followed by Renée, Polly, and Clement, out the front door of the café. He pointed at the name written over the windows. Someone had blacked out the last six letters of *Fraternité* and substituted several others instead.

"R-I-C-I-D-E," read Polly. "What's that?"

"The whole word reads, 'fratricide,'" said Clement. "It means killing your brother."

Word had arrived from France just days ago that Robespierre and all of his Jacobin allies had been guillotined in France——just the most recent round of killing off the officials that had killed off the last officials of whatever the government happened to be calling itself in this iteration. News continued to trickle in from Saint-Domingue, as well, including the expulsion of the Spanish from Hispaniola, and the effective exodus of the French military from the island due to their enormous loss of soldiers and officers to yellow fever. The onslaught of rebellious Black slaves against the French, and of reprisals by surviving French landowners against almost any person with dark skin, continued to be reported in hideous detail. Emotions were high in Philadelphia, particularly between people of different national origins and colors, and tempers were short.

"Oowhat do it mean?" asked Renée.

"It means that people are tired of all the killing in France and the French colonies." said Clement. "It means they are turning against the French in America."

"It means oowee must change name," said Gilly. "I 'ave been theenkeeng of thees. Oowee weel become Café Internationale. I weel prepare some deesh I learn in China. Oowee weel 'ave deesh from many deeferent countrees."

"How can you do that?" asked Polly. "You don't have the ingredients."

"Ah, but I doo," said Gilly. "I 'ave been growing them een my garden. And next year oowee weel 'ave beeger garden. I talk weeth Mr. Morris. 'Ee let us use empty land be'ind café."

"My bread will burn if I don't get back," said Clement. "Do what you will. I hope we'll have patrons who will eat it."

"Ooh!" said Renée. "*Ma feuilletée!*" she charged back in on Clement's heels.

Polly looked up at the vandalized sign. "Is this bad for us?" she asked.

Gilly moved to stand behind her and placed his arms around her. "I 'ope not," he said. They stood there that way for a few moments, looking up at the sign, and then he said, "Ma chérie, oowould you like to get married?"

She turned around in his arms leaned back and looked at him. "Why do you ask this now, and not when you came to get me in New York?"

"*Je'n sais pas,*" he said. (I don't know.)

She leaned back into him.

"I no know oowhy I not ask you then. But now is serious time. Oowee need family. Oowee need steeck together. Maybee you need leetle ones?"

He held her out from himself. "Oowee 'ere to stay, now, even eef deeficult. Ees nowhere better for us to bee, even eef times...ah, *s'avarier*. Get bad? I oowant to know that yoo stay weeth mee."

He pulled her back to himself.

"I'll stay with you, you big lout," she said.

He held her shoulders and pushed her far enough away so he could see her eyes. "Oowhat ees 'lout'?"

"Eet ees yooo," she said laughing. "And yes, I will marry you. I thought you'd never ask! And yes, I 'oowant leetle ones.'" She reached up and held his face with both hands. "And maybe you could do something about that accent of yours."

"Oowhat ees 'accent'?" he said.

She pushed away and rolled her eyes.

Gilly grinned. "I know oowhat ees accent," he said, laughing. "Is thees better?"

"Only slightly," she said. "*Et* now oowee had better get eenside and work 'ard for thee customers come een a few meenute."

"You mek fun!" Gilly said, grinning. "*N'est pas gentil!*" (It's not nice!)

She pushed him aside and jumped up the two steps to the door slapping his hand away as he chased her in.

BACK IN PITTSBURGH IN MID-OCTOBER, word had it that Washington and Hamilton were in Bedford, in the gap between two runs of peaks in the Allegheny Mountains. It would be only a matter of days before Hamilton, at least, arrived with what was reported to be at least 12,000 militia troops.

"We can't muster mor'n a couple hundred," said someone in a dark corner at the Sign O' the Green Tree. Another man stood and headed for the bar. "You got any more o' Amos's whiskey?"

"He hasn't been by for a few days," said Crispin. "His stock's all gone."

"Well, whose ya got?"

Crispin looked at the row of jugs under the bar. "None with names on them," he said.

The man shook his head.

"Hurry up, Bradford," said another voice from the corner.

"They's hidin' their whiskey," he said back. "'Fraid of the federals that's comin'."

"An' you better be, too," said a third voice. "If'n I was you, I'd hightail it outta here afore they catches you an' hangs you on the spot."

"Oh, shut yer gab, Evan," said Bradford.

"He's right," said the first one.

Bradford turned to the corner. "So. You guys can get yer own whiskey. I'm tired of this squabblin'."

He turned to Crispin and said, "Nevermind." He tilted his head quickly in the direction of the corner. "They'll pay my bill." Then he turned and stomped out.

After a few minutes, the three in the corner stood and one of them, the one Bradford had called Evan, came to the bar."

"Yeah," he said. "Guess I can't pay you in whiskey."

Crispin looked up and grinned. "What was that all about?"

"You don't know?"

"Inform me."

The other two walked out the door and Evan invited Crispin to sit at the table they'd just vacated. Crispin looked around. Only one other customer, and he appeared to have fallen asleep on his arm at his table on the other side of the room. Crispin nodded and followed him.

Evan poured out a long tale of woe and grievances against the new national government, about unfair taxation, the difficulty of making money, of keeping your homestead, of getting anything to market—whether because of the distance to Philadelphia or because the Spanish wouldn't let Americans on the Mississippi....

"It sounds a lot like something I covered a few years ago," said Crispin, "something they called Shays' Rebellion—when it wasn't a rebellion, and it wasn't even led by Shays. He and the others just wanted justice and not to be made even poorer by those who were already rich."

Evan nodded. "But then it got pretty nasty," he said. "That Bradford's a mean piece o' work. Don't care none how bad he hurts someone." He looked up. "That hot tar burns!" he said. "And all over yer body, naked like?" He shook his head. "But then burnin' barns, and finally burning down houses and threatenin' to burn down P'burg? That was a mite too far."

"Shays was accused of threatening to burn down Boston," said Crispin, "but he never did make that threat. Are you saying that Bradford did?"

"Yeah, he made the threat. Heard him myself. And he woulda done it, too, han't been a few guys around him held him back."

"And why?"

"Jus' frustration, I s'pose. Couldn' make a livin', couldn' get many fellas to join him 'cept a few others as mean as him, the eelected officials in Philly wouldn't do nothin' and the feds ignored us."

"So what happens now?"

"I reckon we just backs down and a few folks disappears."

"If they're bringing that whole big army here, don't you think they'll want to catch some of the, ah, men involved?"

"Oh, they'll do that," said Evan. "But it won't be the right ones and they won't end up doing nothin' to 'em, is my bet. But we'll have to pay the tax if'n we can't get away from the tax man. And that'll make life tougher than it already is."

CRISPIN MANAGED to find a position on a hill above the pass from Bedford from which he could see and sketch the vanguard of the federal army. After the last troops were through he followed the army from a discreet distance until they got to a T-junction where the Bedford road ran into the Pittsburgh road. He turned south as they did, keeping out of sight as much as possible. Though he heard a few shots and saw a column of smoke rising further south, he couldn't tell what had happened.

He moved into some trees when he heard soldiers returning. At intervals, bedraggled farmers walked between armed captors, heading towards Pittsburg, their breath streaming behind them in the cold November wind. Crispin began sketching and slid further into the woods so he wouldn't be caught himself.

Later that evening, a grim Crispin escorted Susan home from the store in silence. She opened the door.

"Would you like to come in?"

"Will it not make them talk about you all over town?"

She smiled. "Let them," she said.

He went in. The door opened on a smallish room containing more furniture than was really comfortable. Susan watched him look around.

"Before my husband was killed, we had a larger house," she said. "I hoped maybe to have a larger house again someday, so I didn't sell off our things."

Crispin breathed out and nodded.

"So what happened?" Susan asked.

He pulled his sketchbook from under his coat and opened it. Carefully he pulled off page after page and set them on the lone table in the center of the room. Susan lit a thin stick from the coals of the fire, brought it over to the table, and lit the candles in the crude chandelier above it. Then she examined the drawings.

"They're very good, you know."

Crispin nodded.

"And very terrible."

He nodded again, standing still with his arms hanging

beside him. She looked at him, then went to him and placed her arms around him.

"I'm sorry," she said.

He wrapped his arms around her as well. They stood like that for what seemed to Crispin like a very long time and no time. "Will there be peace anywhere?" he asked, finally.

She leaned against his chest and said softly, "Perhaps we have to make our own."

Crispin breathed out heavily. His mind whirled. *I've been alone for far too long,* he thought. *My family abandoned me... No, that's not fair. They died... But my uncle betrayed me. Well, he did, but that worked out in some ways. And I was able to begin to undo some of the damage the family had done... I have no friends. Again, to be fair, I left my friends—nobody's fault, we all had our lives to live... I tried living with the Indians. Seemed interesting. But now clearly impossible. I can never be one of them... And now I've found this person. This amazing, beautiful, funny, pleasant person. And I think I don't ever want to be without her.* The whirling stopped and he made a split-second decision.

He dropped to one knee. Taking both Susan's hands in his he said, "Will you marry me?" He looked up at her and couldn't quite see her expression in the dim, flickering light. "Maybe we could get that larger house?" He paused. "Maybe we could make our own peace?"

She took her hands out of his, placed them around his face, and gently lifted. He stood.

"Yes," she said, looking deep into his eyes. "I will gladly marry you. I don't care about the house. But I care fiercely about you, and I don't want to be without you."

He closed his eyes and drew her to himself. "May I kiss you?" he said.

"I wish you would," she said, lifting her face toward his.

11

———

AFTERMATHS AND EFFECTS

"Have you finished the copies?" Thomas Pinckney asked Lewis.

It was November 1, 1795. Just four days earlier, after tough negotiations in which Spain mostly acquiesced to the demands of the United States, Spain and the United States had concluded the treaty that Americans had wanted for over a decade; the same terms John Jay had unsuccessfully attempted to get all those years ago when Lewis first worked with him.

"I've completed the two English copies for us and am just concluding our Spanish copy. Señor Godoy has initialed all the significant points in both languages, so I think we are ready to hand it to Mr. Washington and the senate."

"Good. You will accompany me back to London and from there I think you may safely sail to Philadelphia with the documents."

From the monastery window where he was standing, Pinckney wandered over to where Lewis sat at an expansive table, large documents spread out in a semi-circle before him, and looked over his shoulder. "You have the handwriting of an artist," he said. "Another reason, I suppose, that Mr. Jay desires to have you with his delegation."

"Thank you," said Lewis, looking up. "I enjoy making it beautiful." He looked back down at the document he was working on. "If I make only one mistake, I have to start over. That is why I asked my wife to visit her grandmother with our children." He looked up at Pinckney. "Very little peace and quiet with..."

Pinckney nodded. "No need to say more," he said. He moved to one side and leaned on the table to see the final English draft. He nodded as he read.

Lewis made a final flourish on the Spanish copy, tossed a small amount of sand over it, set the quill in the ink pot, stood, and stretched.

"Tiring work?" asked Pinckney.

"Not as tiring as the negotiations," said Lewis, stifling a yawn. "But one does get cramped from sitting in that position for long periods."

"Isabella's grandmother?" said Pinckney. "She must be quite old."

"Until recently," said Lewis, looking at him with a straight face, "no one knew that Cain and Abel had an older sister."

Pinckney chuckled. "Irascible?"

"She wouldn't talk to Isabella after she converted to Anglicanism. But now, it seems, she wants her there all the time."

"Yes. Grandchildren—and great-grandchildren, I suppose—cover a multitude of sins. That's the difficult side of this business; not being with them." He patted Lewis on the shoulder. "Well, I hope your travels won't keep you from them for too long."

"Can't be less than a year, give or take a month," said Lewis. "But you mean from the grandmother, don't you? Because Isabella, Roberto and Alzane will be coming with me."

"I admire that in you," said Pinckney, "but I don't know how long you'll be able to keep it up."

"We wouldn't be able to do it at all with my State Department salary, but…" he shrugged.

"You are blessed. Or perhaps very shrewd?"

Lewis smiled. "I was far more smitten than shrewd," he said. "But Don Diego—now he was shrewd!"

"BUT *ABUELA* (GRANDMA), Louis must go, therefore Roberto, Alzana and I must go. You know how much trouble these men can get into if we women are not there to take care of them!"

Isabella, Roberto and Alzana were visiting her father's mother in Santoña. While the children slept, Isabella and *Abuela* were in the sunroom looking through tall windows at the sweeping beach of Laredo, south across the inlet, upon which the sun was shining brightly.

"But I am only just getting to know my *bisnietos* (Great grandchildren). How can you take them from me?"

"What if I bring you back another little *bisnieta?*"

"You are…?"

Isabella shrugged. "I said, 'What if?'" she said. 'How can I know?"

"You had better!" said *Abuela.* "I will wait for you. My children will think me cruel for not dying so they can take possession of all I own, but I will wait for you!"

Isabella got up, knelt beside her grandmother's chair, and placed her arm around her shoulders. "Your children have no need of your things," she said. "It is *you* they need. I hope you will stay alive for many more years so your *bisnietos* can enjoy you!"

"Humph," said the old lady. But she couldn't quite suppress a smile.

IT WAS late November before they got to London. There could be no thought of sailing to Philadelphia for the several months it took winter to pass through. The Jays had not been able to sail back, either, until the spring, after concluding their treaty the previous year.

A mild winter permitted a ship to leave in late January and make a near record crossing, to arrive in Philadelphia on February 19. Lewis took the documents to the current Secretary of State, one Timothy Pickering. After various parties had read it, Lewis was called into Pickering's office to be interviewed about the process. John Jay, and several cabinet members whom Lewis had not met were there.

"This is brilliant," said Pickering. "How did you do it?"

"Mr. Pinckney was the brilliant one," said Lewis. "He stated his requirements slowly and carefully and never backed down."

"And I imagine you supported him with your own careful translations," said Jay.

"It was Señor Rendòn who taught me Spanish," said Lewis, smiling. "I just did my best."

A knock on the door was answered by a clerk. The door opened to President Washington. Everyone stood immediately.

"Please be seated, gentlemen," said Washington. When everyone was seated, he looked at Lewis. "Ah. Mr. Elliot. Another successful mission."

Lewis bowed his head. He thought of all the things he should say about what others had done to make it successful,

not the least of whom was his father-in-law, but he was tongue-
tied.

"I just wanted to add my thanks. This treaty may be the
single most important foreign agreement of the decade and for
decades to come. I cannot adequately express my pleasure at
having been able to see it accomplished during my tenure."

He nodded his head to everyone around the table. "Good
day, gentlemen," he said, "Carry on."

THE JAYS INVITED Lewis and family to stay in their home until
they could find appropriate lodging for themselves. Isabella was
overwhelmed at the joyfulness and noisiness in their still
orderly household. Somehow, Roberto and Azana disappeared
into the bowels of the house, and she could hear them giggling
as they played with the Jay's children and grandchildren. She
sat with Lewis as John and Sarah Jay shared what had
happened with his treaty.

The jubilation and celebration of Christmas in London had
been overshadowed in a matter of months by rioting in Philadelphia. Apparently, the ordinary folks of the United States
thought Jay had given away the ship with his treaty. In vain did
he extol the virtues of staying out of war to a people who
wanted revenge and plunder.

Only half-jokingly Jay noted, "I could have ridden from
Philadelphia to Boston at night by the light of burning Jay
effigies."

Lewis shook his head. "I've seen carnage in America and
carnage in France. I've seen sailors who were slaves in Barbary
port cities. I've seen the might of both England and France on
the seas. Is that what they wanted?"

"In any case, they didn't get what they wanted," said Jay.

They sat quietly for a moment.

"When congress ratified the treaty in June, I was so glad to get back to the supreme court," said Jay.

By that point in the conversation, Isabella and Sarah had been long embarked in a *tête-à-tête* in Spanish. Lewis listened with half his attention now and then and heard some sage advice about raising children. He smiled. *Why don't all diplomats bring their families with them?*

CRISPIN OBSERVED that the tensions of many months of federal military presence and of Secretary of the Treasury Alexander Hamilton's continuing antagonistic interrogation of residents, high and low alike, made the Forks of the Ohio a haunted place. People did not feel safe on the streets, fearing that at any instant they might be taken for questioning on little pretext, or no pretext at all. As Crispin had been told would happen, the chief leaders of the rebellion, David Bradford and his compatriots, had long since fled into Spanish territories and were beyond apprehension.

Crispin watched and sketched as the tax men—the Neville Connection, as they were called—came, registered the stills in which the whiskey was made, collected taxes, and retired back into the shadows. At least they registered the stills they could find. The big, visible, commercial stills that got kickbacks and a lower rate of taxation to begin with, fared well. Of course they paid their taxes. Whiskey was a favorite national drink, after all. They would make money. Crispin thought some of this should be brought to the attention of the wider public. Loudon, in New York—who hadn't paid him for all the sketches he had sent, in any case—was not the channel. Crispin ended that connection.

It turned out that his friend, John Dunlap, was an officer in the militia that came to Pittsburgh to quell the uprising. Crispin found him, one day in January, 1795, in the Sign of the Green Tree. During their conversation he learned that the *General Advertiser* in Philadelphia had stopped publication the previous November. Within a few months, Dunlap had sent Crispin its font set and presses, and he set up shop in Pittsburgh.

But he had to be careful what he printed. Little farmers, hoping to make an extra dollar, did not do so well as their big commercial competitors, particularly if they paid the taxes. But most of these folks eluded the tax collectors. Obviously, Crispin did not want to give away any information on these regular folk. On the other hand, he didn't want to annoy the owners of the large firms. On the third hand, there was Hamilton and the army to consider. He decided to do advertising and small bits of local news; not the commentary and political skirmishing he'd seen in Philadelphia. He also didn't want to work all night. Hence, the *Pittsburgh Advertiser and Evening News*. He could collect ads and news, set, publish, and distribute in daylight hours. Mostly.

Which was particularly useful as he began publication in the back room of Anderson's General Store. And as he began his married life with the former Mrs. Susan Anderson.

GILLY HATED KEEPING TRACK. Primarily, of money spent and earned. He kept track of his vegetables and spices, particularly the Chinese ones he had recovered from Mrs. Spencer's garden. He was out there every morning tending lovingly to them. He kept track of his recipes. No one but he was ever to see what he wrote down, if indeed he wrote anything down. He kept track of his cooking utensils and implements. Each had a place and was always returned to its place after every use, carefully washed and dried. He kept track of his flour. His sugar. His coffee. His chocolate. His potatoes. But he hated keeping track of his money.

"Arrrgh!" he shouted one morning, tossing the ledger on the floor where it smacked down in front of the just arrived Polly. Baby Renée started screaming.

"Now look what you've done!" said Polly, rocking the baby as she calmed down. Then she looked up and said in a much softer voice, "What is it that has you so agitated?"

"Eet ees thees bouks! Thees monee! I cannot do." He stood, walked over to the ledger and retrieved it from the floor. "I was not beelt to doo bouks!"

"Or to speak English without a French accent, I fear," she replied. "Would you like me to give it a try?"

"But ees man's job. I am supposed to doo."

"Does that really matter? Aren't we doing this together?"

Gilly turned to look at her closely. He realized his fists were clenched and released them. He took a couple of deep breaths. Then he walked over to Polly and placed his arms gently around both her and Renée. "*Ma petite aime et ma femme. Je vous aimez.*" (My little love and my wife. I love you.) He kissed Polly on the forehead. "Eef you want, you can doo. Eet would be great 'elp."

"Thank you," she said. "If it will mean that you are less grumpy, it will be a pleasure."

"What ees 'grumpy?'"

"Eet ees yoo oowhen yoo doo thee bouks!" she said laughing.

"*Pas bon?*" he said, looking at her with a worried expression.

"No. Not good," she said.

Which is how Polly began to do the books and found that

she had a great affinity for numbers. After a week working on them, she came to him and said, "We are not doing well."

He looked up at her in alarm.

"But we are not doing poorly, either."

He wiped his forehead as if in relief.

"If we keep on as we're doing, we should be able to buy that back lot from Mr. Morris, and maybe the lot next door. Chinese night is doing especially well."

Gilly beamed and raised a fist to the air. "I knew I could use that...uh, those...uh, *legumes* some day, and thee way they couk theengs."

"Yes. Well keep it up. And maybe we'll need a second Chinese day every week—"

"*Oui.* I 'ave been theenking, but maybee weeth a leetle deeference..."

"Just remember. Not too *cher* and not too much in each dish. We want people to love the food. But remember, they are not the Emperor of China."

"*Oui, ma Chérie,*" said Gilly, having no intention of paying attention to her.

"Don't 'Wee ma cherree,' me," she said laughing. "I know you'll do just as you please—"

"But eet must satisfy mee, *ma Chérie.*"

She sighed. "I know, *mon Chéri.* But remember that everything you spend has to come from somewhere."

Then it was his turn to sigh. "Oowhy must thee monee come before thee taste?"

"Not *before,* Monsieur le Chef, but beside."

To no one's surprise, debate on the second treaty Lewis had worked on, what became Pinckney's Treaty, lasted only a week. At family devotions in the Jay household on the morning of March 8, 1796, Jay thanked God for the endorsement of the treaty.

After family members had gone their various ways and only Lewis and Isabella remained with Jay, he said, "Would you like to take the good news to New Orleans?"

Lewis sat back, exhaled, and turned to him. "How difficult a trip is that?"

But then he glanced over at Isabella whose eyes were shining above her full smile.

"Are you sure, *Tesora?*"

"Didn't we agree that you wouldn't have adventures without me?"

"Yes, my love. But..."

"It will be wonderful for the children."

"*Abuela?*"

"Perhaps we will find a way to give her what I promised?"

Lewis gave her a puzzled look. Opened his mouth as if to ask what that was. Then, with a start, closed it.

The serious Mr. Jay rose with a twinkle in his eye. "I'll give you two some time to talk it over," he said. Then he left the room and closed the door.

Don Diego was more than solicitous. He placed a ship at Lewis and Isabella's disposal. It docked in Philadelphia in late June, was provisioned and made ready by mid-July. After their stop at Charleston on July 19, to fill the rest of the cargo space, they made haste to get around the tip of Florida while the calm before hurricane season lasted. Isabella and Sophia had their hands full with teething and seasick babies, but Lewis and Marcus enjoyed identifying the islands and obstructions they passed.

"It would be shorter and quicker if we could sail along the coast," said Marcus.

"More dangerous than the Tortugas Rocks and Banks and the sand bars around the Great Salt Keys?" asked Lewis.

"Oh," said Marcus. "Is that why we're sailing so far south?"

Lewis laughed. "I have no idea. I just wanted you to think I knew where we were going. These days I trust such matters to the people who do them all the time. And I try to do my own job."

"Which is hard enough," said Marcus.

Lewis nodded and tipped his head toward the hatch amidships. "And keeping them safe. I don't know that I'll be able to take them to my next assignment."

"Which is to where?" asked Marcus.

Lewis looked around. No one was in their vicinity except the few sailors not playing games before the mast. "It's Tripoli. I'm to bring a treaty and some...shall we say, resources, to the Pasha of Tripoli. We'll probably use a Spanish-flagged ship for that, as well. Things seem calm down there right now, but you never know when a pasha or a renegade will decide they want slaves or ransom, or ships, or any of the multitude of things they demand of us. I hope Washington and Adams can quickly launch those six ships congress authorized, oh, I guess over two years ago now. Until they do, there'll be no safety for American merchants in the Mediterranean or even in the Atlantic off North Africa."

"They just do anything they want?"

"Anything they can," said Lewis. "While congress diddles over how much the ships cost, how much the crews should be paid..."

He shook his head and turned away, looking over the rail. "Government is so slow!"

"Well," said Marcus, placing both hands on the rail and

swaying gracefully with the ship's movements, "you're getting something done now."

Lewis nodded. "Yes, and it bodes well for the future if we can stay out of the wars the Europeans insist upon having with one another."

THERE WASN'T much to New Orleans, though its current governor, Francisco Luis Héctor de Carondelet y Bosoist, 5th Baron of Carondelet, had done much to improve it. His reception of Lewis and Isabella was cool. The treaty represented the defeat of his years of effort at keeping the Americans at bay. His initial, very formal, interactions with Lewis and Isabella, were in Spanish. But when he spoke to some of his servants in French, Lewis asked if he'd rather speak French. This seemed to warm him a bit. And when Lewis offered for him to announce and initiate the treaty himself, he seemed to relax.

"It mustn't look as though you Americans are imposing this on Spain," he said. "Far better for it to be seen as a gracious gift from His Majesty."

"It shall appear however you like, My Lord," said Lewis. "You are the commander here."

Francisco bowed his head slightly, "So I am," he said, "not counting a population on the verge of an uprising, irate Indians from multiple tribes always threatening to raid, American and French smugglers..." He waved his hand toward the river. "I have been in this part of the world for too long."

For the first time, he looked at Isabella, as if to acknowledge her unorthodox presence. He bowed slightly, again. "Doña Isabella de Arriquibar, how is it that *you* are willing to be away from our beloved homeland?"

"I do love it, My Lord," she said. "But I love my husband

and my family more. Perhaps, like you, we will settle in our homeland one day."

He nodded. "Today I am posting, and tomorrow I will have the priests announce the reading of the treaty, which I have set for Wednesday. We will celebrate with a dinner, and I believe you may return after that to avoid bad weather on your voyage."

The Baron seemed a little discomfited at the celebration produced by the reading of the treaty on August 3, 1796, but he handled it like a seasoned professional in the service of his king. He bade the party a cordial farewell, and they were back in the Gulf of Mexico by the end of the week.

Unfortunately, they didn't avoid bad weather. But Lewis, writing under a swinging whale oil lamp at the tiny desk in their cabin, whispered to Isabella between a bout of queasiness and the cries of a teething baby, "I forgot to tell you that I mentioned to Gilly when we were likely to be back. He told me Crispin is in Pittsburgh, but he'd ask him to come to Philadelphia in September. Maybe we'll be able to see him."

"And the three of you will be together again," she said, "meeting in the little spot of civilization between the wars in Europe and the wars on the frontier."

"Hopefully, no more wars on the frontier. The Indians aren't happy, but most of them are abiding by the terms of the Greenville Treaty."

Isabella leaned up on her elbow. "Do you suppose we are too much like our parents? Or at least that I am too much like my father?"

"The world is changing, *Tesora.* I think we will need to become like ourselves, because no one has lived in a world like this before."

She lay back down. "I'm glad I'm in it with you, *amante.*"

Lewis got up, blew out the lamp, and came to the side of

the bed. He gently touched the back of his fingers to Isabella's cheek. "So am I, *Tesora*. So am I."

CRISPIN AND SUSAN were the first to arrive. They were met at the door by Sadie, who rushed to Crispin with a little scream and hugged him for all she was worth.

He said, "Meet Susan, my wife." She looked at him for a moment, apparently trying to tell whether she should hug Susan, but before getting a response she embraced her anyway. Susan reciprocated as well as her bulging tummy allowed. Sadie smiled, backed up, and said, "I get the others." She ran back to the kitchen.

Susan took a seat rather clumsily. "Whoof."

Crispin took one of her hands and said, "What is it, dear?"

"I've handled twenty-pound bags of flour, I've wrestled huge barrels of pickles. I've even heaved fifty-pound bags of potatoes." She squeezed his hand. "None of them were as difficult as this little mutt inside me."

"I don't believe he's a mutt, dear," said Crispin. "We know his lineage."

"Ow!" she said. "Well, mutt or not, I'm sure he's a he and he's a kicker."

Polly and Gilly's sister, Renée, ran in, both holding their arms out to Susan. She stood and was encircled by them.

Polly pushed back and said, "Oh, I hope that was all right. Maybe you don't do that in Pittsburgh?"

Renée leaned in and gave her two air kisses, one on either side of her face. "And you no do that, either," she said, laughing. "But oowee do oowhere I come from. You are most oowelcome."

"I would be happy to do that in Pittsburgh," said Susan,

"were you two there!" Polly pointed to the chair behind her. "Can you manage?"

Susan nodded and sat down again.

"And are you just going to ignore me?" asked Crispin.

Whereupon, they took their hugs and air kisses to him.

The door opened again and a small pram appeared, followed by a woman in a long, deep-blue velvet coat holding a baby, and finally by a gentleman in an equally dark coat and a black top hat. The gentleman had his back to them as he shut the door, but when he turned, Renée gasped.

"*Louis!*" she said, running to him and hugging him and knocking his hat off in the process. Then she turned to Isabella, laughing, and hugged her—carefully, though so as not to wake the baby.

"Alzane," whispered Isabella, tilting her head slightly toward her right shoulder where the baby was lying. "She just went to sleep."

Following right behind Lewis and family, Marcus and Sophia entered just as Gilly came out of the back, running. He opened his mouth to shout but Polly quickly put her finger to her lips. He closed his mouth, went over to Lewis and shook his hand vigorously. Then he went to Crispin and shook his hand. "Eet ees so good to see you brother," he said quietly. "Oowee deed not know eef wee ever see you again oowhen you leave."

"I'm also glad to see you again," said Crispin. "And Lewis and Isabella and...?"

A sound in the pram caused Lewis to rock it slightly, but when that didn't work, he reached in and brought forth Roberto. Roberto leaned against him momentarily, but then sat up in his arms, rubbed his eyes, and said, "*Quièn?*"

"These are my friends," said Lewis. "And here we speak English."

"He's only a little over two years old," said Isabella, "and already he has to speak two languages."

"Three if you include *Abuela*'s Euskara," said Lewis.

"True," said Isabella. "But she doesn't expect him to speak back."

"Oh, I had a grandmama like that," said Polly. "You just gave her a word or two and she could go on for twenty minutes."

They all laughed. Then Renée spoke. "You 'ave not meet Susan, yet." She turned to her. "Eef you can get up, maybe oowee can greet you, 'ow you say, properly?"

"And you have not met Sophia, the person at my right hand for most of my life," said Isabella. Sophia did a little curtsy and Renée and Polly went over to hug her, and most everyone followed.

"And there's Marcus," said Lewis. "Our first teacher in Philadelphia!" Gilly and Crispin came to him and shook his hand.

RENÉE SHUT and locked the front door, having put the 'Closed' sign up, as Gilly, Zach, Sadie, and Polly marched in from the kitchen carrying laden trays. Several rectangular tables had been dragged to the center of the room and pushed together. More people had arrived, and they were carrying chairs to the table from other parts of the room. There was Daniel Jones, Sadie's husband, son of Absalom Jones. Renée had married a French immigrant, Charles-André Gwenaël. He and Lewis were chatting in French in one corner while Isabella was commiserating with Susan in another. After the trays had been set on the table and silver laid, Gilly clapped his hands.

"*S'il vous plait!*" he said. "Please! Come to thee table."

There was the usual confusion as people decided where to

sit, but eventually it was Lewis, Isabella and Roberto on one side, Roberto squirming in his chair, Alzane in the pram beside him. Gilly, Polly—holding baby Renée—Charles-André and Renée, sat opposite them. Zach and his wife, Sable, Sadie and Daniel sat on the third side, and Sophia, Marcus, Crispin and Susan on the last; Susan turned to the side with her feet up on a stool.

Gilly stood and smiled. "My *belle femme* want," he looked at her, "*wants* me to speak better English. Oowhat...I mean *what* better place to start?" He looked around at smiling faces. "I try." Then he cleared his throat. "We were three friends," he said. "Sometimes friends who want to murder each other—"

"No, we never did," shouted Lewis.

"Hear!" shouted Crispin.

"Well, maybe I want to murder you because of *anglais*. But we do not. We stay together. We help each other. Then we go different ways, but we always come back together. Now look!" He waved his hands around the table.

"'Ere, today, we are seventeen persons." He looked at Susan. "*Pardon, eigh*teen persons."

"We didn't know oowhat, oh, sorry, *what* we would do. Where we would go. 'ow we would leeve. Eef we would survive. But we deed! And now we are newspaper man," he pointed at Crispin, "diplomat," he pointed at Lewis, "and restauranteur. Zach and Sadie were runaway slave and today, they be free. They do good for people, they help others be free." He looked around at the group, glowing. "And we have wife or husband, all, and many baby. I theenk we no could do this in my country today." He paused.

"Nor in mine," said Isabella.

"We are mostly free in my country," said Crispin. "But we have this permanent division of classes, the so-called noblemen who aren't very noble, and the workers. And we have corruption. I have not been there for years. Perhaps things have changed."

"I think we have a class system of a sort here, too," said Lewis, "and corruption. But we have hope of better things. We may finally have a government that will work, though it may be too early yet to tell."

Isabella spoke up. "In England, I became an Anglican. Being Anglican was all mixed up with being English, just as being Roman Catholic is mixed up with being Spanish," she turned to Gilly, "or French. But there is a God. I didn't become Anglican because it was English, but because it helped me to see that God is a God who cares about human beings. From what Lewis has told me, your President Washington believes He was involved in making your freedom possible. Perhaps we need to thank Him? Lewis?"

Lewis stood. "As usual, my wife is right."

"As *usual?*" she said, looking offended as the others laughed.

Lewis grinned. "As always," he said. "Perhaps we could stand."

"Almighty Father," he said, "we mortals down here do sorely need your help. We believe you have given it to us, over and over, and we have not noticed. Today we want to notice. Today we want to thank you for each person around this table, for the ways you have had us take to get here. Please help us not to take you for granted. Please help us look to you for the right, for the good things we should do and the bad things we should avoid. And as we enjoy your bounty now, let us not forget the men and women and children who have no such bounty to enjoy, and do what we can to help them as You have helped us. We pray this in the name of the Father, and of the Son, and of the Holy Ghost. Amen."

He looked around the table as people opened their eyes and

raised their heads. He smiled and sat. Nothing's changed, he thought, but everything's different.

"No, PLEASE," said Isabella," you must stay at our house while you are here."

"But Lewis said you must go right away," said Susan.

"We must, but Marcus and Sophia will be staying there." She raised her hand to Susan's ear and whispered, "She's in the same way as you, it's just not visible yet." Then she put her hand down and took a step back. "They will be keeping our house for us for whenever we come. And it will also be a temporary residence for our friend, José Ignacio de Viar, the new Minister from Spain, until he finds a home for himself. You will come, won't you?"

"How can we refuse?" said Susan. "But we also must leave as soon as everything is ready, so I won't have this baby on the way home."

THE WHOLE GROUP was on hand on as the *Euskara de Santanda* was pulled away from the dock by the tug, headed toward Bilbao, Spain. They waved until it was well underway.

"Weel we ever see them again?" asked Renée.

"It has a way of happening," said Crispin, "against all expectations." They started wandering back to the café.

"And when must you leave?" Polly asked Susan.

"We hope to join a caravan headed to Carlisle that leaves in a day or two, and get back within ten days."

AFTER THEY LEFT CARLISLE, the trip to Pittsburgh through the tiny village of Bedford was more difficult than the one to

Carlisle had been. But there was evidence that many more caravans and settlers would be coming that way in the near future, as inns were being built along the way and more commerce was evident in the towns. As they came down from the mountains and into the Monongahela River valley, smoke from more chimneys made it clear that life was returning to normal.

"Ow!" said Susan. "Another kick. Maybe the hardest of all. I think he wants to come out very soon."

They passed a couple of Indians walking along the road.

"They're a defeated people now," said Crispin when they'd gone by them. "Do you suppose there's any way we could help them?"

"Well, they did trade with my husband until the wars heated up."

"What did they have to sell?"

"Moccasins, blankets, some leggings and shawls. All things that people liked and needed. I haven't been able to stock them for a while. Maybe now?"

"They're American, too," said Crispin. "If America is to move into a time of prosperity, they should as well."

He stopped the wagon and pulled to the side until the Indians caught up.

"Do you speak English," he asked.

"Yes," said one. "We come from the house of the great father of the white people. We must speak English to make a treaty with them. We are Shoshone."

Crispin nodded and jumped down from the wagon. He held his hand up in salute. "My wife and I have the store, Anderson's General Store, in Pittsburgh. Maybe you know it? We wonder if you and your people might have goods you would like to sell there."

"Let us talk this over with our people," said one. "We know your store. Mr. Anderson has died?"

"Sadly, yes," said Crispin.

"He was always fair with us."

"And we will be also. And with any other of your people who wish to trade with us. We will not give you alcohol or trinkets, but real American money that you may use anywhere."

"We will find you," said the one who was talking.

Crispin nodded and jumped back into the wagon.

"I KNOW I'M GOING HOME," said Susan. "But it feels so very different. I feel like Mary going to Bethlehem, not knowing what will happen, whether she'll stay for a short time or long. Knowing only that if I don't have this baby very soon, I will burst!"

"And since I definitely do not want to be your midwife, I will move with all possible haste that will not bump us unduly and motivate young Jesus, here, to a quicker exit."

Susan smiled. "I am blessed to have you, Joseph, dear."

"At least we don't need an inn or a stable," said Crispin. "In fact, we have everything we need. At times I wondered if I would ever settle down, ever have a family, ever find out what I was supposed to do in this world." He turned to her. "You helped make it all happen. I am blessed to have you."

"Ooo," said Susan, putting a hand on her belly. "I think he's telling me to hurry even more."

Crispin snapped the whip above the horses and accelerated them into a trot.

Within an hour they arrived at their front door. Crispin helped her down, tied the horses to a post near the door, and ran the block to the midwife's home.

"Come quickly, Liza!" he said. "There's no time to lose!"

In a matter of minutes that seemed like hours to Crispin, a woman old enough to be his mother stepped out of the house. She walked decorously behind him as he started to run home.

"Hurry, Liza!" he said. "She could be finished by now!"

"You first-timers always think the birth will be immediate," said the woman. "But babies like to take their time. Now just you walk normally so you won't get all out of breath and faint on me."

They got home. Susan was, indeed, making noises that did not sound good to Crispin.

"You get me a bowl of hot water and some towels," said Liza, "and then you go tend to those horses out front. You have plenty of time."

It took some time to get the fire started, to heat the water, to find the towels (*Now where does she keep the blessed things?*) and to bring them to Liza. He knocked on the door to the bedroom. Liza opened the door wide enough to retrieve the things and said, "Go. The horses."

He went out and untied the stomping horses, leading them and the wagon out to the barn. He opened the large door and led them and the heavily loaded wagon inside.

What was I thinking, leaving them out there with all our supplies and purchases on the wagon? He shook his head. *You were thinking about Susan and the baby.*

And without having to think about it, he freed the horses from the wagon, removed their tack, filled their water troughs and pitched hay into their stalls.

She said I had time, he thought. He ran back to the house anyway.

He arrived breathless and skittered up to the bedroom door. He held up his hand to knock, but held it when he heard no noises from Susan, but only the women talking. He turned his head and moved his ear toward the door to hear better and was startled by the door opening before him.

"You still have a while to wait, young man. Why don't you go rub down those horses?"

Crispin slumped. He turned around, headed out the door, and around to the barn.

When he came back some time later, he heard groaning and grunting noises from the bedroom. He rushed to the door so quickly that he bumped into it before he could stop. It wasn't but a second later that Liza opened the door wide enough to glare at him.

"Go sit down. You'll be a papa soon enough without hovering here."

Crispin wandered to the main room and sat at the table drumming his fingers. As it became dark, he knocked on the bedroom door and handed Liza a burning taper. She thanked him and shut the door.

He went back to the table, lit the chandelier, and blew out his taper. Then he sat and started drumming again.

He cringed at the sound of a sudden, loud cry from Susan. But it waned. In a moment, it was replaced by another cry. This one sounded like the affronted shout of a very small person. Crispin ran to the door and knocked.

Liza opened the door very slightly. "It's a boy," she said. "Mother and baby are both fine. Now *go sit down!* I'll call you when you can come and hold him."

Crispin backed away from the door and let out the breath he found he'd been holding. *Yes, it is a very different life,* he thought. *I never could have guessed.*

He turned and went to the front door, opened it and went out into the cool evening. A young man walked by with a bundle of newspapers under his arm.

"Care for a Philadelphia paper, sir?" asked the lad. "The campaign between Adams and Jefferson is heating up!"

"No, thanks."

The lad walked on.

"I have news of my own," whispered Crispin.

The world is the same as it's always been, he thought, *but everything's different.* He turned and went back into the house, hardly able to wait for the first chance to hold his new son.

AUTHOR'S NOTE

A great many events that influenced the developing United States between 1790 and 1797 did not occur in the United States. As became the norm in the late eighteenth and early nineteenth century, Great Britain and France were facing off against one another with Spain, Portugal, The Netherlands, Austria-Hungary, Prussia, and Russia jumping in on one side or the other from time to time. Revolutions or planning for revolutions took place in France, Ireland, Poland, Belgium and SanDomingue (the name for what we call Haiti and the Dominican Republic today), among other places, spewing refugees across the entire western hemisphere.

The 'great powers' jostled one another for possession of large swaths of North, Central, and South America—none of which should have actually belonged to any of them, having been long inhabited by indigenous peoples. They thought if someone from their country ever set foot there, it should belong to them. Because great riches, easily obtained, came from these lands, they fought or enslaved the inhabitants and they fought one another for them, and their fights on land spilled over onto the seas.

And speaking of seas, the southern and eastern coasts of the Mediterranean Sea, the so-called Barbary Coast, were packed with semi-cooperating Muslim empires whose ships preyed upon any vessel they could find that was not protected by multiple cannons, a treaty, or a large navy (which was the only reason for which they would make a treaty, actually).

Into this fray, the citizens of thirteen colonies just learning how to cooperate with one another threw their resources and hopes. Lewis, Gilly, and Crispin were right there with them. In their story, they interact with many individuals who attempted to use diplomacy to temper the worst of the international tensions as they effected the United States. Some of them were successful, but their success was not universally applauded—which created more tensions and animosity back in the United States. "We the people" were no less voluble or belligerent in the 1790s than today's political antagonists. In fact, they may have set the precedents for some of what we see around us today.

Good men and women and bad men and women, the greedy and the generous, the volatile and the calm, confronted one another both at their polling places and in the streets. Some used rhetoric, some used physical force. Everyone had an opinion. Everyone thought their opinion was right. Strangely similar to today, also. But the point is, they made it through. And so did Lewis, Gilly, and Crispin. And so can we.

I do recommend that we keep up the vigorous dialogue—focusing on ideas rather than persons. I do not recommend that we use violence or laws that subvert the constitution to do that. The fact that our forebearers were just as rowdy and sometimes just as downright nasty as we can be should not only give us hope, but should also give us the determination to keep on, as they did, in order to continue to work on this 'more perfect union' that was the purpose of setting up a government in the first place.

I suggest you do some of your own research to see how they accomplished this task. There's a select bibliography at the end of the book that will give you some starting places. My Young America blog posts will provide background information about daily life and many non-political issues that don't make it to the history books. Have fun. Grow! Become a useful citizen as did all three of our characters. And read the next book, *Fire as Their Element*, to see how the next phase of their lives turned out. I'd love to hear your questions and thoughts at my website, http://gordon-saunders-writer.com.

And you can be my friend forever if you write a review for someplace like Amazon, Apple, Barnes & Noble, Goodreads or Bookbub.

APPENDICES

The Liberty of the Whole Earth:
Characters in order of appearance

New Characters Introduced in each Chapter
(***Bold-Italicized*** characters are fictional)

Chapter 1
Lewis Elliot
Gilly Y'vant
Crispin Graves
JJ Green
Captain James

Chapter 2
Colonel David Humphreys

Chapter 3

Hans Axel, Count von Fersen
Monsieur Montreuse
John Freeth

Chapter 4
Renée Y'vant (Gilly's sister)
Captain Jean-Pierre Belmont
William Short
Captain Richard O'Brien
       Two Algerian corsairs
Joel Barlow
José Ignacio
José de Jaudenes
Isabella de Gardoqui
Don Diego de Gardoqui y Arriquibar

Chapter 5
Captain James Cathcart
William Carmichael
Sophia de Gardoqui

Chapter 6
Publisher Gore
Mr. Wright
Seamus O'Connor
Samuel Neilson
Henry McCracken
Gouverneur Morris

Chapter 7
Philip Hamilton
Mrs. Eliza Hamilton

Sec. of the Treasury, Alexander Hamilton
Secretary of State, Thomas Jefferson
Joshua Pembroke
Polly (Maria) Jefferson
Hetty Morris
Maria Morris
Robert Morris
President George Washington
General Henry Knox
Vice-president John Adams

Chapter 8
Marcus Thomas
Captain James Elliot
Charles Morris
Lloyd Elliot
Mrs. Mary Morris
Mrs. Tetty Elliot Sears
Mrs. Virginia Elliot
Peter Jay
Mrs. Martha Washington
Mrs. Sarah Jay
Supreme Court Justice, John Jay
Mrs. Abigail Adams
Adelaide
US Consul to Britain, Thomas Pinckney
King William I of the Netherlands
Queen Consort of the Netherlands, Wilhelmine of Prussia

Chapter 9
Zach Sanders
Sadie Sanders

Clement Hegerty
Polly Potter
Publisher John Dunlap
Edmond-Charles (Citizen) Genêt
Dr. Jean Deveze
Absalom Jones
William Cobbett

Chapter 10

Señor Manuel de Godoy
Ahweneyu
Mrs. Susan Anderson
David Bradford

Chapter 11

Abuela
Secretary of State, Timothy Pickering
Señor Francisco Luis Héctor de Carondelet
Charles-André Gwenaël
Two Shoshone Indians
Liza the midwife

Character Descriptions

Main Characters

Crispin Graves   Born in 1763, Liverpool, artist, engraver, reporter, former drummer in the British army, on parole.

Gilly (Gilbert) Y'vant   Born 02/17/1766, Brest, Brittany, France, former cook's helper 'boy' on French warship ship *Courageous*

Lewis Elliot   Born in 03/30/1767, Virginian, speaks French & Spanish, Columbia grad, clerk for Hamilton, Jay, R. M. Later becomes **Don Luis Elías de Arriquiba**r.

Fictional Supporting Characters

Captain Emerson James   Captain of Enterprise when she sails from New York

Charles-André Gwenaël   Husband to Renée Y'vant, emigré from France during revolutionary excesses.

Doña Isabella de Gardoqui y Arriquibar   Daughter of Don Diego

Jean Montreuse   Editor/publisher of *Amis du Peuple* in Paris

Polly Potter   maid and cook's helper in Mrs. Spencer's boarding house in New York City

Renée Y'vant Gwenaël   Gilly's sister, born in 1770, rescued by Gilly & Lewis

Sadie Sanders   8 years old in 1783, Escaped slave, befriended by L-C-G, freed by G. to work at his restaurant

Marcus Thomas Factotum and clerk to Gouverneur Morris

Sophia de Arriquibar Lady's maid to Isabella

Susan Anderson Widow who owns/runs a store in Pittsburgh

Zachary Sanders 15 in 1783, Escaped slave, befriended by L-C-G, freed by G & C.

Seamus O'Connor Clerk and assistant to Samuel Neilson, Irish Nationalist and newspaper publisher

Democrat-Republicans

James Madison (1751-1836) Writer of constitution, colleague and supporter of Jefferson, D-R party

James Monroe (1758-1831) United States Minister to France, (Aug. 15, 1794 - Dec. 9, 1796), leader of D-R party in the Senate

Mary or Maria 'Polly' Jefferson Eppes (1778-1804) Younger daughter of Thomas Jefferson

Martha 'Patsy' Jefferson Randolph (1772-1836) Thomas Jefferson's older daughter

Thomas Jefferson (1743-1826) Envoy to France, returns in 1790, Secretary of State, VP under Adams

Thomas Mann Randolph, Jr. (1768-1828)
Husband of Patsy Jefferson

Federalists

Alexander Hamilton (1755-1804) Secretary of the
Treasury, leading Federalist
> **Wife: Eliza Children: Philip**

George Washington (1732-1799) President, attempts
to maintain peace among cabinet members, leads army against
Whiskey Rebellion
> **Wife: Martha**

John Adams (1735-1826) Vice-President under
Washington, 2nd President, Federalist, opposed by Jefferson,
his VP
> **Wife: Abigail**

John Jay (1745-1829) First Chief Justice of the United
States, treaty negotiator, Acting united States Secretary of
State, Minister to Spain (1779-1782)
> **Wife: Sarah Children: Peter**

Robert Morris (1734-1806) Businessman, financier,
fallen on hard times, mentor benefactor to all three main
characters
> **Wife: Mary Children: Hetty, Maria, Charles**

Timothy Pickering (1745-1829) Secretary of State after Jefferson for both Washington and Adams, until 1800.

American Diplomats to Foreign Countries

Col. David Humphreys (1752-1818) American Minister to Portugal (May 13, 1791-July 25, 1797) and Spain (Sept. 10, 1797 - Dec. 28, 1801)

Gouverneur Morris (1752-1816) Dissolute envoy to France, known to other characters from their time with Robert Morris. Also envoy to Great Britain

James Leander Cathcart (1767-1843) Captive of Algiers from merchant ship, *Maria*, Boston

Joel Barlow (1754-1812) American Consul to Algiers (1795-1797), negotiator for U.S. to Barbary states

John Jay (1745-1829) Peace ambassador to England and Spain, Secretary of State, First Supreme Court Judge, creator of unpopular treaties

Richard O'Brien (1758-1824) Captain of the *Dauphine*, in captivity for many years, Barbary Emissary

Thomas Pinckney (1750-1828) 2nd United States Minister to Great Britain (August 9, 1792 – July 27, 1796), negotiator of treaty with Spain (San Lorenzo)

Tobias Lear (1762-1816) Secretary to George Washington, Peace Envoy to Tripoli

William Carmichael (1739-1795) Chargé d'Affaires in Spain (Feb. 20, 1783 - Sept. 5, 1794)

William Short (1759-1849) Jefferson's private secretary, Minister to the Netherlands, Minister to Spain (Sept. 7, 1794 - Nov. 1, 1795)

Gen. James Wilkinson (1757-1825) Acclaimed villain by all, secret Spanish agent in 1790s, failed soldier and politician.

Foreign National Political Figures

Don Diego de Gardoqui y Arriquibar (1735-1798) Representative of Spain replacing Señor Rendòn, proponent of the first Roman Catholic church in New York, Lord of the Spanish Treasury (Secretary of the Royal Exchequer of Spain)

Edmund Charles Genêt (1763-1834) French Envoy to the U.S., April 8, 1793 - January 1794

Francisco Luis Héctor de Carondelet y Bosoist, 5th Baron of Carondelet, (1748–1807) Governor of Spanish Louisiana when Pinckney Treaty came into effect

Gilbert du Motier, Marquis de Lafayette (1757-1834) Chief of Police in Paris, French & American patriot, Revolution turns on him

Hans Axel, Count von Fersen (1755-1810)
Swedish consul to France, 1788–1793

Henry McCracken (1767-1803)   Irish nationalist
leader, executed in Belfast by British

José Ignacio de Viar y Mendiguren (1745-1818)
Aide to Don Diego, later Spanish representative to the United
States

José de Jaudenes y Nebot (1764-1813) Aide to Don
Diego, later Spanish representative to the United States

Samuel Neilson (1761-1803)   A leader of Irish
nationalists, publisher of Northern Star newspaper, founder of
The Society of United Irishmen

Historical Supporting Individuals

David Bradford (1762-1808)   Prominent lawyer in
Pittsburgh, leader of the Whiskey Rebellion

Dr. Jean Deveze (1753-1826?)   French doctor
providing alternative yellow fever treatment in Philadelphia
in 1793

John Dunlap (1747-1812) Printer of Declaration of
Independence, Constitution, publisher of local papers in Philadelphia

John Freeth (1731-1808) Proprietor of Freeth's Coffee House, Birmingham, England

John Gore (Dates unknown) Publisher of Gore's Liverpool Advertiser

Stephan Loudon (Dates unknown) Publisher of *The New York Packett*, (1785-1792), unreliable publisher of several further failed newspapers

William Cobbett (1763-1835) Controversial pamphleteer, journalist, teacher

BIBLIOGRAPHY

Select Bibliography for *The Liberty of the Whole Earth*

Anderson, Laurie Halse. *Fever 1793*. New York: Simon & Schuster Books for Young Readers, 2000.

Berkin, Carol. *A Sovereign People: The Crises of the 1790s and the Birth of American Nationalism*. New York: Basis Books, 2017.

Brown, Richard D. *Knowledge is Power: The Diffusion of Information in Early America, 1700-1865*. Oxford: University Press, 1989.

Calloway, Colin G. *The Victory with No Name: The Native American Defeat of the First American Army*. Oxford: University Press, 2015.

Chávez, Thomas E. *Spain and the Independence of the United States, An Intrinsic Gift*. Albuquerque: University of New Mexico Press, 2002.

Chernow, Ron. *Alexander Hamilton*. New York: Penguin, 2004.

Feldman, Noah. *The Three Lives of James Madison: Genius, Partisan, President*. New York: Farrar, Strous & Giroux, 2017.

Ferling, John. *Apostles of Revolution: Jefferson, Paine, Monroe, and the Struggle against the Old Order in America and Europe*. New York: Bloomsbury, 2018.

__________. *A Leap in the Dark: The Struggle to Create the American Republic*. Oxford: University Press, 2003.

Gardiner, Robert with Bosscher, Philip, ed. *The Heyday of Sail: The Merchant Sailing Ship 1650-1830*. Edison, NJ: Chartwell Books, 1992.

Hibbert, Christopher. *The Days of the French Revolution*. New York: William Morrow, 1980.

Hobsbawm, E.J. *The Age of Revolution: 1789-1848.* New York: New American Library, 1962.

Hogeland, William. *Autumn of the Black Snake: The Creation of the U.S. Army and the Invasion That Opened the West.* New York: Farrar, Straus and Giroux, 2017.

________. *Founding Finance: How Debt, Speculation, Foreclosures, Protests, and Crackdowns Made Us a Nation.* Austin: University of Texas Press, 2012.

________. *The Whiskey Rebellion: George Washington, Alexander Hamilton, and the Frontier rebels Who Challenged America's Newfound Sovereignty.* New York: Simon & Schuster, 2006.

Lane, John E., M.D. Jean Deveze (1753-1826 ?) : Notes on the Yellow Fever Epidemic at Philadelphia in 1793. https://www.ncbi.nlm.nih.gov/pmc/articles/PMC7939912/pdf/annmedhist147404-0024.pdf, accessed on Sept. 22, 2022.

Larkin, Jack. *The Reshaping of Everyday Life: 1790-1840.* Perennial Library, 1989.

Morgan, Robert J. *100 Bible Verses That Made America: Defining Moments That Shaped Our Enduring Foundation of Faith.* (W Publishing Group [Thomas Nelson]), 2020.

Nash, Gary B. *The Unknown American Revolution: The Unruly Birth of Democracy and the Struggle to Create America.* New York: VikingPenguin, 2005.

Richards, Leonard L. *Shays's Rebellion: The American Revolution's Final Battle.* Philadelphia: University of Pennsylvania Press, 2002.

Smith, Admiral W.H. *The Sailor's Word: A Complete Dictionary of Nautical Terms from the Napoleonic and Victorian Navies.* Tucson, AZ: Fireship Press, 2007.

Taylor, Alan. *American Republics: A Continental History of the United States, 1783-1850.* New York: W.W.Norton, 2021.

________. *American Revolutions: A Continental history, 1750-1804.* New York: W.W.Norton & Co., 2016.

Trees, Andrew S. *The Founding Fathers & the Politics of Character*. Princeton: Princeton University Press, 2004.

345

Gordon Saunders at Gullfoss (Golden Falls), Iceland,
2019

Dr. Saunders was born and raised near Boston, Massachusetts, and steeped in the history of that city—so crucial to the founding of the United States. Subsequently, he had the opportunity to live in four different European countries and travel extensively, both in Europe, and throughout the globe. Coming back to America after living in Europe for twenty-five years, he noticed an appalling lack of knowledge of our history, particularly in young people. He wrote the Young America series as a way of informing young people about our history and also promoting thought about the issues that caused dissension in those early days and are with us still.

You can connect with Dr. Saunders at:
gordon-saunders-writer.com

He would love to hear your thoughts about the content of this book.

At his website, you'll also see information about a fantasy series he wrote, The Verduran Pentology, in which a significant number of settings are in the United States during the first half of the nineteenth century (especially in the third book of the series, *The Boatwright*).

Reading the fantasy series will show you even more about life in the United States at this time – for European immigrants as well as for men and women of color, both natives and immigrants.

If you enjoyed this book, you would be doing the author a great favor by writing a review for Amazon, Kobo, Apple, Barnes & Noble or your favorite book vendor.